LIGHT HUNTER

HAYLIE HANSON

THE LUMINAUT
TRILOGY

LIGHT HUNTER

BOOK TWO

HAYLIE HANSON

Cover Designer: Emilie Haney
Interior Art: Kristen Hildebrand
Editors: Katie Phillips & Amy Williams
Interior Formatter: Michelle M. Bruhn

To my Mando Girls, my writing crew,

my friends who stood by me when this book made me

kick and scream, shed tears, and throw my laptop at the wall:

Your "Team Nate" shirts are in the mail.

CHAPTER 1
CALLIE

HURTLING LIKE A CHAOTIC electron made of bronze, glass, and gears through an unstable, space-wormhole-gateway majorly sucks. Zero out of ten, do not recommend.

Like, imagine the suckiest thing ever. Got a mental picture? Awesome. Now multiply that suckiness by a billion. That's Diving through gateways.

No color, sound, or matter exists—except for yours truly and a couple mechs—in whatever you'd call this space between worlds in the multiverse. Just Light, and the feeling of being suspended in a vacuum while falling, face first, into a bottomless hole of nothing, with no end in sight. My stomach drops into my toes—I think it's in my big toe, to be exact, but I'm weirdly not aware of my body. Just my mind, Diver's mind, and Nemo's mind. My tiny robot is beyond pissed about the state of my backpack, whizzing through the air like a pinball in slow motion.

Serves you right for being such a pill, Nemo. You'll live.

Actually, maybe he won't. I might not, either. My first Dive as a Luminaut will be disappointingly short if I can't figure out how to exit this gateway. Preferably somewhere with civilization and a Starbucks, or the equivalent, because my nerves are shot and I need a latte.

"Diver, how do we get out of this... whatever?" I grip the straps in the Luminaut pilot's chair tight, bracing for something, *anything* to stop the stationary-plunging sensation.

Luminaut is Luminaut.

"Okay, but that's not what I asked. At all." Could you try being a bit more unhelpful, Diver? Because I just love it when you give me non-answers. It's my favorite.

Luminaut knows what to do.

Except I don't, but it's fine. I'm fine. This is fine.

Come on, gateway, end already... cease and desist. Do not pass go, do not collect two hundred dollars. Halt, who goes there? Stop in the name of Light, or something.

"...the Light Collective knows we're here..."

Wait a sec, what's happening? Who's talking to me inside my head? It isn't Diver, that's for sure—this is somebody else.

A flash of a dreamlike vision appears around the brilliant Light inside the gateway, like being immersed inside a movie still or a three-dimensional photograph. The weight of time presses between my shoulders, stealing my breath as though I've aged thousands of years in an instant.

"They won't think to look for us at the Tageveld Beacons," the disembodied voice speaks again. *"They're too remote..."*

"The Collective will never stop searching," another voice joins in.

Beacons? Collective? What beacons? A collective of what? And, once again, this all begs the very important question of *whose voices am I hearing?*

I blink, and a hazy visual emerges from the Light surrounding me, three women and a man beside the biggest bearlike dog I've ever seen in my life. They stand on the edge of a cliff surrounded by gigantic trees, swirling fog, and huddled groups of hundreds of people. Behind them, two imposing mechs keep watch—World Divers, just like mine—and beyond that, four lighthouse-ish things burning bright with Light in their spherical tops, shining out across a churning, gray sea of clouds.

"Diver, what am I seeing? Why?"

WHHHHEEEEEE-WHHHHIIIIIRRRR!!!!

My backpack and Nemo make another pass by my head. I miss getting knocked out by a hair, which is good, because exiting this never-ending gateway that's decided to show me in-flight movies is my top priority at the moment—not dealing with the side-effects of a concussion.

Luminaut, we are afraid.

Yep, got the fear part, Diver. I'm equally afraid this is the end of the gateway, and we've crash-landed in the midst of a strange Light vacuum where we're neither dead or alive, but doomed to watch other people's stories play out for eternity in a multiversal time loop.

It would be such a Callie move to get stuck in the middle of a gateway on my first Dive. I can practically hear Dr. Ormandi cackling with "I told you so" laughter.

A blip like a poorly edited film reel splits the vision, one with half a scene cut short and missing. All I can make out is a flash of Light and two figures meeting in midair before a woman's scream rips through every atom holding me together. Her primal anguish tears my guts, making me nauseated, before another flash of Light overtakes my senses. And then, the vision goes black as quick as it came.

"Okay, that was awful." Let's mark subconscious-Light-vision on my list of things I never want to experience again.

What I'd really like to experience is the other side of this flipping gateway. Like, now, please.

As if my prayer and plea have been answered by the deity devoted to helping clueless, teenage Luminauts not kill themselves, the gateway disappears in an enormous burst of

Light, and a dark gray sky filled with swirling clouds materializes before my eyes. A forest landscape like an ocean of pines stretches as far as I can see across the horizon below.

By "below", I mean about a thousand feet below. And Diver and I, falling toward it. Not the semi-suspended falling sensation I felt in the gateway: a couple hundred tons of metal in rapid descent, plummeting toward the trees like a big, bronze bowling ball. That kind of falling.

"Diver!" I scream, and all my spare clothes, my backpack, and the stuff I stole (borrowed? needed? meh) from Dr. Ormandi's basement come flying toward me from behind. I squeeze myself into the pilot's chair so my skull doesn't get crushed, covering my head like they taught us in earthquake drills at school. Who knew that would actually come in handy? "Turn upright!"

What is upright, Luminaut?

For a multiverse-hopping mech, Diver has a terrible sense of direction. "Feet toward trees, head toward clouds. Now!"

Yes, Luminaut.

From my backpack, I hear Nemo's muffled whir-shrieks. Sorry, buddy. You can shred a few extra notebooks later, pending that this world has notebooks.

With a deafening crash, Diver hits the forest canopy feet first, crunching through branches, tree limbs, boughs, and foliage until, at last, we come to a jarring halt, suspended in between two trunks hundreds of feet in the air.

"Wow, that was terrible." I take a cautious look around before closing my eyes to the dizzying feeling brought on by the sight of the ground, and how far I am from it. "Now we're stuck in a tree. Diver, any clue how we can—"

SNAP-CRACK

One of the branches holding Diver in place breaks under his weight, and we plunge further, bumping between the two trees until we're stopped, yet again, by a thatch of boughs.

"That was worse." The leather straps of my seat dig into the tender skin around my neck, cutting under my arms and sides. "Let's try this again. Diver, can you—"

POP-CRUNCH-CRASH

More falling, more banging, more gravity ruining my day, jostling me and the contents of the Crow's Nest roughly until one final, horrific crash brings us to rest on the forest floor.

"Ow." I really hope this didn't break my collar bone or ribs or anything. "At least we can't go any further down."

Probably shouldn't speak too soon, in case the ground under us caves in.

After a tense moment, silent save for the pitter-patter of pine needles, twigs, and cones raining down on Diver's domed head, I let loose a breath and look around. Diver landed on his side, if the horizontal orientation of the surrounding tree trunks is any indication. "Can you stand up, buddy? Or did the fall wreck all those joints I fixed?"

We can try, Luminaut.

Diver pulls himself into a standing position, testing the knee I spent the better part of first semester repairing. He can put weight on it, which is positive. Now to check the status of... everything else.

I take Earth's Light Core out of Diver's Prism, the mechanism that opened our gateway to wherever we landed. The moment I unzip my backpack to hide it, Nemo leaps at my face, whirring his neck-motor rabidly.

"Ah!" I back away from him, and he plops to the floor. After stowing the Light Core, I right his dead-bug position. He rushes me instantly, whir-screeching as his claw-hands lay into my ankles and shins.

"Look," I tell my mech, moving about the Crow's Nest to

organize the rest of my things, "attack me all you want, but I had to get us out of Verona Beach. I'm sorry if Diving disturbed your comfort, oh delicate flower. But at least we aren't piles of Shadowmancer ash right now."

Which is more than I can say for the Verona Beach High School gym that Nate's Darkness destroyed. Or Dr. Ormandi's house, which Nate set on fire. Gosh, I can't believe I made out with that guy. If I ever see his scheming Shadowmancer face again, I'm going to Light blast his smirking lips off, right before I put a hole in his chest where he ought to have a heart. I shudder to think what he's been up to in the short time it took me to Dive away from California.

Or, maybe, it took years. I have no clue if time works the same in gateways. The strange visions I saw could have been time passing rapidly before my eyes. Maybe I'm, like, a thousand years old now. Maybe everyone I know is dead.

Or, maybe, I'm jumping to conclusions. Let's go with that. Assuming it's the present, there are exactly three things I need to do before I can have an existential crisis:

1. Find the hidden Light Core in this forest—wherever this forest *is*.

2. Dive away from said forest to hunt down Light Cores on the other worlds, then find Mariasol's friend Serai Eradah on Ensolorada and ask her how to make a magic bridge out of them, which will reunite the multiverse and destroy Darkness. Or whatever Dr. Ormandi said. I assume that's how it all works, right?

3. Go home to my family and friends before Mom and Dad extend my grounded status indefinitely.

"First things first," I tell myself. "Find the Light Core in the forest." If "forest" is what you can call this place. More like "a giant world of things that shouldn't be as big as they are."

Trees seven hundred feet tall tower over Diver's head, and in the midst of their cloud-height canopy is a Diver-shaped hole still dripping pine needles and cones the size of watermelons onto mounds of tree branch carnage strewn across the forest floor. Not exactly a discreet entrance, but at least I survived. A vast expanse of equally huge trees stretch as far as I can see in every direction, and the air swirls with thick mist that resembles fog but is too fast, too rapidly moving. Watching it makes me lightheaded, like the mist wants to hypnotize me into a mindless stupor and swallow me whole. I look away, blinking to clear my head.

Hmm... gigantic forest. Swirling fog-mist. Seems an awful lot like the landscape I saw in the Light vision just a moment ago, minus the lighthouse-things blazing Light across a gray sea.

"Diver," I say, looking through his domed windows toward the forest below my perch. "Did you see the vision in the gateway, too? Do you know what it means, and if it took place in the same world as this forest?"

He's reluctant to answer. His trepidation fills me, tightening inside my chest. *We have many memories, Luminaut.*

"Memories..." Mariasol said something in her journals about Diver's past Luminauts giving him their memories. "Was what I saw in the gateway one of your memories?"

Luminaut is in danger. It is not safe here.

"You're doing that thing again where you avoid answering the very specific question I asked," I remind Diver. "Is this the same world I saw in the Light vision? I mean, your memory?"

Diver hesitates, but at last, his quiet voice sparks inside my mind. *Yes, Luminaut.*

Awesome! Now we're getting somewhere! "Those light-houses — they had Light in them. Are they still around? Could it be a good place to hunt for a Light Core?"

"*Zrrr-zmmmm!*"

Urgent and painful poking at my ankle followed by a tiny growl as Nemo, who's forgotten he's supposed to hate me, demands I tear him a piece of notebook paper — my English notes.

"No way, I need those for finals next week," I tell my little friend. "I'm not about to flunk junior year, got it?"

Nemo grumbles a bit before wheeling off, rooting through my backpack until he finds a wadded-up volleyball schedule. The grumbling intensifies, accompanied by shredding sounds, and soon, confetti flies through the air.

Five minutes this side of the multiverse and Nemo's already making a mess. Typical.

"I think we should find those lighthouses with the Light in them, and look for clues there," I tell Diver. "I'm going to scout a town where I can get basic supplies for our Light Core hunt, then we'll bail." Because the one thing I didn't pack when I Dove away from California was snacks. And water bottles. Be better next time, Callie. Plan ahead and stuff.

Diver thinks my mini-mart run is a terrible idea. As soon as the words leave my lips, his anxiety strikes deep. *Luminaut must not leave.*

"It'll be fine, I promise." I shove growly Nemo and his bedraggled volleyball schedule into my backpack, then pull on my winter coat and beanie over my hoodie. "I'm not going far. Just trying to scout a road out. I'll be gone a half hour, tops."

Luminaut must come back.

"Of course! I'd never abandon you in the middle of nowhere." I give the Prism a fond pat.

Please, do not go, Luminaut. Stay here.

"Remember the part where I'm human, not a hunk of sentient metal? I'm not going to survive without Hot Pockets and Gatorade." My stomach growls to emphasize my previous statement. "Thirty minutes, buddy."

Shouldering my pack with Nemo, Mariasol's journals, and the Light Core safe inside, I open the hatch door of the Crow's Nest and step onto Diver's shoulder, taking a look around. I'm about fifty feet above the ground up here, but even at this height, I can get a sense of my bearings. Breathable air, positive. No sense of Nate and his Darkness, even more positive. Air so icy it cuts through my winter coat, not positive. But two out of three isn't bad, right?

Luminaut must stay with us.

"It's okay, buddy," I assure Diver.

My mech ignores me. *Luminaut must not go.*

Really, I never pegged Diver for a worrywart. "I'm just getting travel essentials. Promise. Now, put me down on the ground."

As Luminaut wishes, is Diver's reply, and I decipher his "I don't trust your plans further than I can spit" tone clear as day. But he sets me on the ground, regardless.

Shouldering my backpack, I assess the situation in the clearing. Off to my right, a small path leading out has been cut into the gargantuan trees and house-sized underbrush. Paths typically mean people were around to make them, and people mean civilizations with supplies, information, and Starbucks. I can't sense anyone nearby; there's no scent of campfires or the sound of distant voices. But I'm sure if I follow this path, I'll run into someone eventually. I just have to keep my Light keyed into the surroundings, letting it call out to the inner Light of any fellow humans who might be hiking or camping nearby. Ones carrying espresso in thermoses.

"Look, Diver, I already found a path!" Honestly, this Light Core hunting thing is way easier than Dr. Ormandi made it out to be. "See you soon!"

The ferns, branches, and rocks are a lot bigger down here than they appeared fifty feet up in Diver's Crow's Nest. Mossy earth springs like a sponge beneath my feet, blanketed with leaves the size of elephant ears and boulders as big as buses. Roots of the gargantuan trees rise from the earth, waves on the rich, umber-colored sea, before they crest into the depths of the soil. Everything smells of rotten leaves and pungent decay, and I wrinkle my nose as a layer of silvery-gray fog swirls around my face, as shimmery and silky as gauze. It curls around my ankles and legs, inspecting me, before deciding I'm harmless, moving on to Diver's clearing in its spectral exploration.

"Creepy fog." But honestly, this whole forest is creepy, with the lifelike mist and the strange, oversized everything. I really hope the monster-movie flex this world gives off isn't a bad omen.

Ducking under a low-hanging bough encrusted with dark, damp, purple-red lichen, dripping liquid that looks remarkably similar to blood, I get a sinking feeling that Diver warned me not to go hiking alone for a very good reason.

Snap.

And there's the reason right now.

My heartbeat hammers with dread as I come face to face with a creature as big as a rhino, and looking like a cougar mated with a dragon on steroids. Instead of fur, it's covered in brown, black, and green scales, and its eyes are the deepest shade of red.

And, judging by the dried trails of viscera snaking down its protruding saber-fangs, I'd say this thing is *definitely* carnivorous.

"N-nice kitty," I stammer, my voice barely a squeak.

Dragon-cat slithers toward me, its eyes narrowing in on the fluttering pulse in my neck. A low rumble escapes its massive chest, and it licks its lips. Kitty wants a snack, and that snack is me.

"Go away!" I shout, louder and more urgently. "Shoo!"

Probably shouldn't have yelled at the monster, because dragon-cat squares its shoulders, leaning into its haunches before it growls menacingly. Not only am I a snack, I opened my mouth and made myself a threat.

I need a plan of escape, stat. A distraction. A… relatively small rock! Yes!

With a kick powerful enough to angle my surfboard into an oncoming wave (assuming I was surfing, which I would *so* rather do at the moment), I send the rock flying into the gigantic fern fronds off to my left. Dragon-cat's head whirls, and it leaps after the rock with a screech.

Before the dragon-cat has a chance to figure out the noise was nothing but a pebble, I bolt.

Breaths heave, ragged and shallow, and I push and stumble my way through the forest, desperate for a cave or a tree hollow to hide in. A fearsome yowl behind me, and I turn, spying dragon-cat hot on my tail.

Thinking fast, I call Light into my hands to make an orb. The power sticks in my chest when I run, like something stubborn and syrupy-slow caught around the edges of my heart. It takes all my concentration to pull the Light through my arms and form an abysmal orb. I cock back and launch it into the trees to my right. Dragon-cat leaps after the orb, and in hindsight I should have gone with Light orbs instead of rocks from the start, yet I can't slow down. My legs pump like pistons beneath me, fear rising from the pit of my gut toward my throat as strangled cries escape my lips. Dragon-cat is on my heels again, and gaining fast.

I emerge from the underbrush into a small clearing with no visible outlet. Just an impenetrable wall of trees in every direction, and a dragon-cat staring me in the face.

Why can't girls just take walks through the woods without almost dying? This is such a stereotypically bad plot device it's almost funny, except I'm not amused.

Dragon-cat circles me, the red in its eyes gleaming hungrily, and Light blazes in my hands, ready to defend myself. The orb I form looks like a coil of live-wires and lightning sparks, barely controlled before bursting, but it'll do. With all my strength, I launch it at the dragon-cat's face.

"*Yoooooaaaaahhh!*" Dragon-cat shrieks, pawing at its eyes. One of them is mangled, a newly-formed scar like a blackened gash running from ear to nostril, but I can't stop to consider how my Light powers could have caused such a grievous injury. Surviving is priority one.

Spinning, I scan the clearing for an escape, but I can't see any way out besides the way I came in. Dragon-cat leaps, absolutely hellbent on killing me, and I duck away just in time, launching even more Light at its face. A miss, and the monster takes another swipe. I call for more Light, but between dodging dragon-cat's blows and trying to evade its claws, I can't concentrate on my powers. The world's most pitiful orb is all I can conjure, and when I throw it at dragon-cat, it lands short.

Crap, dude.

Dragon-cat slinks toward me, moving in for the kill. With trees at my back and no exit in sight, my brain buzzes with terror, ears muffled to any sound besides the pounding of my pulse. The Light inside me surges just as fast as dragon-cat can pounce, building to a breaking point, and all I can think, feel, or sense is horror that I'm going to die here in the middle of this forest, eaten alive by a predator I can't name on a world I've never known.

As if my fear is a trigger keeping some internal reserve of Light in check, my power suddenly explodes, drowns me, overwhelms every sensation, every feeling. Light blazes, and not just in my hands, but across every inch of skin, taking over, unbidden, until, at last, Light bursts through the clearing, shooting from me like an atomic bomb of pure energy. I can't decide whose scream is louder: mine, or dragon-cat's.

As quick as it blasted the clearing, my Light retreats inside, settling under my heart. Dragon-cat is gone—no sign of the monster remains. Black marks scorch every trunk around me, and low-hanging branches cling to each other like shriveled toothpicks. I trace the shapes made by my Light, scarring the deep bark.

Did my power really do this?

"Raaaaooooooowwwww!"

Another petrifying creature launches itself into the clearing, snarling around bared teeth: a bear-dog fiercer than two dragon-cats put together, like a wolf and a grizzly bear had a baby—but, like, a giant wolf and a giant bear, because this forest is nothing if not consistent in its giantness. The bear-dog approaches, its shrewd eyes settling on the Light flaring in my hands.

Can forest monsters *please* stop attacking me every two seconds? Because that would be awesome. Vegetarianism is underrated, bear-dog. You should try it.

Hold on a minute—bear-dog? This is the same creature I saw in Diver's memory, except that one was tame, docile-looking. If I didn't know better, I'd think this one was aggressively protecting something.

"Ay! Hjaltenzi!"

Or, someone.

A young, distinctly male voice behind my shoulder rings sharp with warning. Light zips away from my hands, and a pointy thing pokes between my shoulder blades.

Whoever's behind me, he's armed. Fantastic.

The boy lets out a string of angry-sounding words I can't comprehend, but nonetheless sense I should obey—pronto. I concentrate on what he's trying to say, not just the actual words, my Light reaching out to connect with this person's inner Light until understanding dawns on me at last.

"I repeat, do not move, or I'll shoot you." You got it, guy who lurks around clearings armed to the teeth. No sudden moves. The pointy-thing presses me again, almost piercing my coat. "Now, turn around."

Slowly, I turn, coming face to face with the business end of a crossbow and its intimidating wielder. A boy about my age, no less than six and a half feet tall, and so aggressively angular I could cut glass on his cheekbones. He sticks the crossbow into my puffer jacket and backs me into a tree, his blue-gray eyes like two solid chunks of ice in his equally cold face. A strange, almost liquid-like quality makes them appear ever-flowing behind the veneer of glacial chill.

Extremely hostile locals. Noted.

Crossbow-guy brings the tip of an arrow to rest in the hollow of my throat, and the bear-dog lumbers protectively to his side, the growl on its lips only slightly less dangerous.

"Tell me how you came to be lost in the forest and learned the magic of skyfire — sorceress."

CHAPTER 2
NATE

SCREW YOU, CALLIE JAMES, you lying, scheming, two-faced Luminaut punk.

"Oh, please, Nate! Even *you* aren't that heartless!" I'm doing a spot-on impersonation of her voice right now. "I need precisely two hours to get my Light Core from my quote-unquote 'friend's house,' and after that, it's yours. I'll even shake hands because I'd never break my promise, I swear on my precious family's life! Don't hurt them, boo hoo hoo!"

That was really good, wasn't it? If you stick around long enough, I'll do an impersonation of a Shadowmancer about to go backside up in a pile of his own ashes.

Except, that one won't be an impression.

There, there, dry your eyes. If you're going to weep for anything, weep for the multiverse, and all the people whose lives she's about to destroy with her special brand of Luminaut chaos.

Am I really so stupid that I thought I could trust Callie to keep a promise? What was I thinking, believing the word of a creature of Light? All Light does—all it's ever done—is betray. I should have known she'd take off and leave me standing here in the shallows, painting a morose picture in the pale blue light of the full December moon. Picasso this is not, unless by "Picasso," you mean pathetic.

It's a very Blue Period look.

If going back on her word wasn't bad enough, she had to rub salt in the wound, calling *me* the villain. Nice joke, but guess what? It's not funny. I'm not the bad guy here: I warned her about the danger she was in, had conversations ad nauseam about how catastrophic her powers are, and reminded her it's always been her choice to be safe from Light forever. Light destroys everything it touches — don't I know firsthand? My own mother *died* because of Light. Think I didn't mention that? You bet I did. Did it do any good? Ha!

"Gasp! Nate, you monster!" Like she knows who the real monster is. But apparently *I'm* the worst person in the multiverse because I vandalized (okay, destroyed) some property, and made a couple petty remarks about how maybe I'd kill her family and my dad.

Doesn't she get sarcasm? Hyperbole? Figures of speech? Nada.

Are you ready for the kicker? This is rich. The crowning glory of her scheme: she and her love-sick buddy she's kept friendzoned since second grade used a fake-out decoy — stupid glow sticks! — to trick me.

Glow sticks! Tied up with packing tape! And I fell for it!

What happened next, you say? Since you're so riveted, practically on the edge of your seat with suspense, I'll tell you: she Dove through her gateway to Darkness-knows-where after flipping me a giant, metaphorical middle finger. I saw that look on her face through Diver's dome. She regrets nothing, and hates me more than she's ever hated anyone or anything.

The only recourse I've got — other than weaving a tapestry of every obscenity I know into the air above the waves, which I already did — is to use what little time I have to figure out how I'm going to answer for my failure the second I go beyond the Veil. I had one job, and I blew it.

No — *she* blew it. So long, dreams of destroying Light Cores and preventing multiverse-wide mass murder. It was fun while it lasted.

How could this have happened? Everything I wanted was mine for the taking. But I stood there like a slack-jawed dweeb, watching the Light inside Diver disappear down the hole she opened in the ocean.

If I knew where she'd gone, I'd follow her and —

Why is something crawling around near my foot? Can't this sea animal see I'm trying to figure out my next line of defense? Verona Beach can't throw me one freaking bone, can it?

"A sand crab." Marine biology, who gave you the audacity to interrupt my thoughts at a time like this? The creature skitters about my shoes, looking for a place to burrow into the swash zone. "Tide's turning. You don't have long left."

Get out of here, tiny crustacean, before the multiverse is destroyed by a Luminaut with a vendetta. Save yourself, before it's too late.

What enrages me the most is how little she cares about the consequences. How small all of that destruction and death will feel compared with fulfilling her massive, Lightbound "destiny."

It makes me so mad, I could just...

My Darkness stirs to life, shadowy tentacles of power twisting around my fingers and arms, begging me to ash something to alleviate the cyclone of emotions tearing through my chest. Tendrils extend from my fingertips, reaching for the sand crab, caressing the shell on its back with subtle menace. Tiny bits of ash flake into the silt, and the crab burrows faster, seeking refuge from the Darkness trying to rip it apart.

Before the Darkness wraps itself around the creature entirely, the crab burrows deep into the sand, escaping its doom just in time. Darkness retreats, and I ease into a restless state of semi-calm.

"Did I tell you to get out of here?" And be grateful for your exoskeleton. I kick the tiny mound of sand the crab dug with my toe. Not all of us are going to get as lucky as Ms. Sand Crab. Not all of us can escape pain and punishment.

In case you were wondering, "all of us" is me.

If I had any evidence of Callie's deception to show in my defense, I would, but she's long gone. Her friend, Will, left more than an hour ago, dragging his surfboard up Millionaire Hill, and her family's probably running around the high school in a panic looking for her. I wasn't going to hurt them, despite what I said — remember the jokey-ha-ha thing? I get that it's not what most people joke about, but the fact Callie believed me was highly amusing.

It's a lot less amusing now.

Waves roll in, playing tag with the shore before retreating into the vastness of the open sea, no trace of the power with which they'd smashed violently against the cliffs and shaken the pier. No more gigantic hole in the middle, splitting the fabric of space and reality. No more Coast Guard chopper, buzzing around like an unwanted party guest. No more mechs and Light and Luminauts. Lingering sirens blaring along the highway to investigate the high school gym I took down mingled with the noxious smell of smoke from Dad's house are the only evidence it was real. The beach is completely deserted. Just me, standing on a strip of sand and surf I used to know in the haze of foggy memory, a few hundred yards from the place I was Turned.

Last human memory, meet last Shadowmancer memory. Hello, irony, it's nice to see you again. Did you miss me? I didn't miss you.

"Little one..."

A spiderlike voice pierces my thoughts. *She's* calling me. And *she* doesn't like to be kept waiting.

This melancholy little interlude was short, wasn't it? Thanks again, Callie. I definitely wanted to negotiate my entire existence tonight. Enjoy that Light Core you technically stole from me. And while you're at it, go suck eggs.

"Little one, come."

Yeah, I hear you. And I know I need to play the game of pleading my case and begging for mercy if I have any hope of saving my undead skin from total annihilation. I turn to go, then stop, halfway between moonlight and Shadow. Something in the deep wants to stay here a moment longer — a vague whisper of an unnamed thing I could never grasp, no matter how far I reached.

"Little one, I'm waiting...."

Time's up.

I slip away from the human world into the small space between time and Shadow that we Shadowmancers call the Veil, taking one last look at Verona Beach before I make my way through the Shadow Plain. Gliding on an invisible breeze across the depths of Shadow and gloom, as opaque as ink spilled over the moonless midnight sky, I approach the prison of the Queen Beyond the Stars.

She's my boss, the Queen Beyond the Stars. The Prime Shadowmancer, Former Luminaut and Opposition Leader, Destroyer of the Lightbridge, Defeater of the Light Collective, Ender of Light's Reign of Terror. The one whose Darkness saved me from Light, who showed me the truth and found me in the storm.

She's also terrifying, especially when she's pissed. A little extra hype and reverence to grease the wheels never hurts, right?

"Little one." Queen rises from her prison, her spider-silk

white hair floating around her form. She's a relatively tiny person, with over-large black and red eyes set in a round face and a build like a porcelain doll, but don't mistake her for being fragile or weak. She's as ancient as the stars (get the name now?), the most powerful Darkness-wielder to ever exist, and could wipe me out of existence faster than I can form a half-hearted apology.

"Why do you think I've called you back home?" Queen swirls around me, her Darkness coiling tight around my frame, and she floats just above my head as if to remind me of her authority with her physical placement relative to mine. The red in her eyes glows with murderous rage. "Do you think, perhaps, I'm displeased? Has my little one done something to make his Queen punish him?"

It's a bunch of rhetorical questions. She likes to monologue before she ashes somebody. When I was Turned, there were six of us. Now, there's just me, which means I've seen this five times — the Spanish Inquisition act (nobody expects it!), followed by some speech about betraying the cause against Light, and then, poof, ash pile.

And if I don't play the game just right, I'll be pile of ash number six.

"Perhaps it's because my little one no longer needs my guidance and wisdom. Perhaps he believes he knows better than his Queen how things ought to be done." She curls her lips into an expression that might be considered a grin, except for the steely gleam of her razor teeth, shining like the tip of a dagger. I remain still as a statue, eyes averted in proper reverence, waiting for what I know is coming. "Do you have anything to say for yourself?"

This is the next part of the act — giving me a chance to defend myself. A little light groveling and begging for mercy are typically involved. I've never been on the receiving end of Queen's wrath, until now. Especially because I came back to the Shadow Plain with nothing to show for my charades in the human world except a whole lot of not-murdered people, and no Light Core for her to destroy. But that doesn't mean I'm in the dark about how all this is going to go down.

In the dark, get it?

Probably not the best time for puns.

"I followed orders, my Queen." It's mostly true, but I'm gonna leave out the *mostly.* "I did everything I was told."

Present myself as a self-deprecating, charming, and flirty ghost, there to help Callie figure out her cute little mech problem: check. Get close to her and earn her trust: check. Learn her insecurities, doubts, and longings, and play those to my advantage: check. Finally, when the time is right, reveal the power of my Darkness, and show her what I'm willing to do to destroy her Light Core, so she has no choice but to hand it over: check.

"You did *everything*?" Queen's unnervingly soft voice contains just a hint of a derisive laugh. "Then why does the Luminaut's family still live? Why does the old Seer live, for that matter?"

Ah, yes, the murdering. Should have known she'd bring up the two orders I didn't follow.

"I was a weak and trusting Shadowmancer." I know what she wants to hear, and she wants me to swallow my pride and fess up. "I believed the Luminaut would keep her promise to give me the Light Core after I threatened what she cared about. Instead, she betrayed us."

"Betrayed *us*?" Queen doesn't hold back her laugh this time. "No. She betrayed *you*. And in doing so, you betrayed yourself." A rush of something like winter wind as she comes face to face, her eyes boring into me. I suppress a tremor at the sight of them. I know mine look the same, but that doesn't mean Queen's don't fill me with a special kind of horror. "For all your understanding of the evils of Light, you chose to give in to your own fear and weakness. The Luminaut will be your downfall."

Can I put my downfall on hold for another two seconds? I square my shoulders, attempting to portray a level of grit and determination that shows strength, but not the kind that threatens Queen's authority. It's a fine line to walk.

"I did everything else my Queen commanded, but those two things I didn't think were of ultimate necessity." Maybe I can still salvage this. "I set the Seer's house on fire." Let's see if she takes the bait. I dare to raise my eyes onto Queen's increasingly homicidal gaze. "He might be dead."

Except, Dad's *not* dead. But maybe Queen doesn't—

"Do you really think I'm that gullible?" A snarl appears on Queen's thin lips. "I know your human father is a Seer with Fire Manipulation. All you did was mildly inconvenience him."

Hmm, tough crowd. I'm usually so great with strategy and making my own playbook; I can calculate the odds of almost any outcome at the drop of a hat. But when it came down to the wire, I disobeyed a direct command, and it's looking increasingly likely that gamble is a bet I just lost.

"First you disobey me, and now you attempt to deceive me." Queen floats over me until she's behind my shoulders. "You don't get to decide what is necessary when it comes to your orders. Because of your failure, the Luminaut has a Light Core—one you swore to bring to me for destruction."

About that oath... Sorry it didn't work out. Can I take a mulligan?

"Her Light brings nothing but pain and suffering to everything it touches," Queen goes on, circling back around. "I fought against Luminauts. I was once one myself. I alone challenged the Light Collective, was brave enough to stand up to their oppression and lies when others were afraid. And because I was triumphant in ending their cruelty, I was stripped of my power and imprisoned. If anyone knows the way the Luminaut thinks, it's me. But you seem to have forgotten what she is, and what she's capable of doing."

"I didn't forget, my Queen." Callie trying to Light blast my head off my shoulders in the gym left no doubt of her capacity for violence. Lucky for me, she aims like a Stormtrooper, and hit the trophy case instead of my head. But next time, she won't miss.

Queen takes my chin in her frigid hands, cold even against my undead skin, and her fingernails dig into my flesh. It's repulsive, her hands on my face. It feels like maggots worming through a corpse, a clear reminder she can make me less than a corpse, if she wants. Nausea mixed with fierce indignation ignites in my stomach, but I gag it down. I'm on thin ice as it is.

"The consequences of your actions will be far more grave than the lives of half a dozen humans you refused to eliminate for our cause," Queen says. "Any destruction she causes with her Light will be on your hands."

I squeeze my eyes shut, truth hitting me like a gut-punch before the final KO. My screw-ups are the reason Callie is going to shatter the lives of billions, raining Lightbound terror on the multiverse as she tears people apart and levels their existence in her hunt for more Light Cores—all because I told myself murder was something I never signed up for.

I won't let it end like this, reduced to a pitiful failure begging for mercy under Queen's thumb before she inevitably turns me to ash. I have to try again.

"I want another chance, my Queen." Stay strong. No vulnerability. Maintain proper compliance to her will, while carefully presenting my argument. "I've never been anything but loyal in the fight against Light. I made a mistake, but I won't fail again. I swear it."

"You think I should take your word?" Queen finally releases my chin, retreating a safer distance away. "It's true you were faithful once. But how do I know you won't betray me again, and turn your back on my cause?"

"I would never turn my back on Darkness," I answer, "not when I know how devastating the Light is."

All I need is a small crack in the dam, and I can blow it wide open.

Queen considers my promise, suspended in silence, wrapped in Shadow. "Your ability to take your human form and infiltrate places I cannot make you a powerful asset," she says at last. "But I sense you've been weakened by emotion. There's a reason I warned you against using your human form when it was avoidable. And yet, I think, perhaps, you enjoy it."

"I don't enjoy humanity." Careful, Nate—it can't sound like I'm arguing, because that'll go over like a lead balloon. "I know human emotions are weaknesses that betray the cause."

Even you aren't that heartless... It's what Callie and Dad think of me, and of course I'm heartless. Hearts do nothing but break and die, and destroying Light Cores is more important than any "heart" I could ever have. I'd rather be heartless than recklessly use Light to devastate every person in the multiverse like Callie, all so she can find more Light Cores and prove something to herself about how important she is, and worthy of her destiny, and super-de-duper *speeecial.*

"I cannot tolerate deficiencies of character in my servants," Queen reminds me. "Not if I'm going to emerge triumphant. If the Luminaut is allowed to succeed in her hunt, there will be no hope of purifying the worlds of Light's suffering. They'll be lost forever. Is that a consequence you want to bear?"

"I promise I'm not deficient." Give me an inch, a millimeter of hope I've got another shot. "If my Queen gives me one more chance, I'll succeed."

"Perhaps." She glides about, her white hair trailing after her, moving as if we're underwater. The Shadow Plain is weird. Time doesn't exist here, neither does gravity or anything else that makes the human world feel... normal. Even now, I haven't gotten used to the sensation of being stuck, floating, unable to breathe or sense my own pulse, like I'm right on the edge of drowning but can't quite let go and slip away.

"Perhaps my servant needs a true test of loyalty," Queen says. "A task that will prove your resolve to end Light once and for all."

Yes, give me a test. I'm great with tests. Pass 'em all the time.

"You've had a taste of the purity and peace Darkness can bring to those who are suffering under Light's cruelty," Queen goes on. "It's time you witnessed its ultimate truth firsthand." She comes to a standstill, eyeing me with a look I've come to know well: a glint of blood-red intensity in her eyes, the corners of her mouth inching upwards. It's the top of the first inning, and a new game is about to start. "Since you failed at extricating the Light Core from the Luminaut's hands, you must find one entirely on your own to prove you are willing to do what is necessary for the cause. Go to Ictari. Hunt down the Light Core hidden there, and bring it to me for destruction. That is your task."

That's—uh, not what I was expecting.

Me? Find a Light Core? Just me? On my own?

"My Queen—I'm a Shadowmancer. I thought only a Luminaut could find a Light Core." I've gotten pretty good at keeping my reactions in check around Queen, but there's no way my face doesn't betray my confusion.

"Only a Luminaut can activate the power inside the Light Core," Queen corrects me. She tilts her chin to the side as she observes my expression, and her precarious, pre-ashing grimace returns. "Is my little one unhappy with his task? Even after I gave him such a generous opportunity? Perhaps I was mistaken in thinking he wanted a second chance..."

"No, my Queen." I've never spit out three words so fast in my undead-life. "I'll find the Light Core on Ictari. Does my Queen know a specific location where I should begin my hunt? You were able to tell me the Light Core on Earth was in Verona Beach."

Queen's intel was how I was able to find Callie so quickly when Queen sent me to take her Light Core. I only scouted her at the Veil for a day or two before appearing to her the first time in her room. Maybe Queen knows some useful tidbits about Ictari's Light Core, too.

"I am unaware of where the Light Collective hid it after they imprisoned me," she replies. "However, I can tell you this: Ictari was my home world, when I was still lost to Light. Ictarans live in one of two places—in the mountain caves, where my people dwelled, or in vast caverns underneath the Ice Fields. Use your human form to your advantage, and ascertain the Light Core's location by interacting with the populace. Ictarans are honorable people to the last. If you can extract a promise from one of them, they would rather die than break it. And that includes divulging their world's secrets to strangers."

Sounds easy enough. Cross the Veil into Ictari, find an unwitting minion, and manipulate a promise from said minion to lead me to the Light Core. If Callie randomly found a Light Core, surfing in a thunderstorm like a dingbat, I should be able to use my wits to my advantage and find another.

"Yes, my Queen."

"It will be my little one's ultimate test," Queen tells me. "If you can do what is necessary, no matter the cost, it will show me once and for all that you are worthy of being a servant to the Queen Beyond the Stars."

"I won't fail you." Another thought strikes me. "Does my Queen want me to hunt down the Luminaut after I find Ictari's Light Core?"

"Don't fear, little one. I will keep a close eye on the Luminaut," Queen says with a wicked smirk.

"But I thought my Queen was unable to see beyond the Veil?"

Curiosity kills the cat — or, in this case, the Shadowmancer. As soon as the question manifests as words, dangling in the air, Queen turns deadly. Her Darkness coils around me, every inch of skin burning with indescribable pain, a thousand daggers tearing my body apart as the Shadows worm into me, scorching through my muscles until it wraps tight around the bone, turning me to ash from the inside out.

"It isn't your place to ask questions," Queen hisses through her teeth. "You are my servant. You are nothing. You have no authority in the Shadows save what I've given you."

I almost have it... I can almost reach.

Something inside stirs, fighting the Darkness threatening to tear me apart, pushing back with all its might — the sensation of a powerful force I used to know, but have long since forgotten. In my agony, I barely notice Queen's eyes flick, a dawning recognition filled with both horror and eager glee.

"Let the pain you brought upon yourself be a reminder that I saved you, and gave you the truth. If you choose, I can be your destruction as well." As quick as it began, it's over. Queen's Darkness retreats into its mistress faster than I can register the relief that it left me intact. Her eyes betray no hint of disrupted emotion, and the force that fought to save me goes dormant, buried so deep I'm not sure I didn't imagine it.

"Y-yes." I can barely speak over the rawness of my misery, lingering like a burning coal festering away at my hollow insides, unextinguishable. My rage that she turned the tables and attacked is matched only by the fury that I didn't see it coming.

Nate — 0. Queen — 1.

Queen comes to me before I can wince or withdraw. "Do not rest in the Shadows. The Light is gaining power, and our time to act against it is drawing near. We must move quickly. Not a moment can be spared." She pats my cheek, more of a slap than anything kind. "Now go. Do as I've commanded."

I follow orders, but only because I don't want to remain in her presence a second longer than I have to. Without another word, I fly through the Shadow Plain toward the Veil, and I swear to Darkness and Shadow I will get this Light Core. I will *not* fail a second time. Not when Callie is hunting her own Light Core, and getting stronger by the hour.

Ictari, here I come.

CHAPTER 3
TORAN

SKYFIRE.

Ancient magic, older than Mist itself. It is said that sorcerers from the Lands Beyond brought skyfire to Tremurheim; beings who fell from the clouds inside burning vessels of ore and steel, so powerful—and power-hungry—they inflicted mass genocide upon anyone who disagreed with their methods of keeping "peace" amongst the Clans.

Skyfire hasn't been seen for so many Seasons it's become a legend we're forbidden to speak of. Even I, who's researched everything about magic I could sneak my hands on, doubted it was real—until today.

Standing before me is a girl with skyfire. Everything I have read, poured over, analyzed, and studied in secret for fear of discovery is here, in the flesh.

And she's wearing a stupid hat with something that resembles a fluffy nargush egg on top.

"Okay, I know what you saw—think you saw—was probably suspicious, but there's a logical explanation for all of this, which you'll totally believe." The girl's wide brown eyes dart toward the arrow at her neck. An audible gulp bobs in her throat before she flashes a smile, one that quivers at the edge. "Not gonna lie, the crossbow thing is pretty aggro, but I'd be pissed, too, if I thought somebody threatened my dog. Listen, I wasn't going to—"

"My *what*?" The arrow inches closer, pressing into her skin.

"Your dog." The girl points to Kiera beyond my shoulder, carefully watching the movement of my finger near the trigger. "I promise I'd never kill a dog. That's some next-level heinousness. Now, can you put the crossbow down, please?"

"Kiera isn't a dog, whatever that is, she's a Guide's bjorir." I remove my arrow from her neck and jab it into her ridiculous coat made of many small pillows. Wooly stuffing shows through a tear. "This is your last chance: tell me how you got lost, and where you learned to use skyfire."

"Fine, here's the deal." A hint of annoyance enters her words. "I'm trying to find a town so I can hit the mini-mart and get snacks and water bottles, because I've got a long trip ahead of me and I need sustenance. You know, food?" When I nod, she goes on. "Anyway, I was hiking along, minding my own business, when this dragon-cat monster attacked me, and then, you and your bear-dog showed up, and you ripped a hole in my coat with your crossbow. Jerk."

"My name is not 'jerk.'" I pause, considering the implications involved in admitting my name to a sorceress. The decision bounces back and forth a moment before I admit, "I'm Toran Rykjiersen, Guide of Gravenskov."

The girl blinks very hard. "Holy Norse nomenclature, Batman."

"Batman is not even close," I correct her. "I'm Toran." Accent and strange manner of dress aside, it's more than obvious she's foreign. I lean in and say it slower and louder, so she understands. "*Tor-an*."

"Wow, rude." A smirk appears on her face, one more than a little mean. "I'm Callie James. Is that easy enough? Or should I get in your face and yell, too?"

"That's a strange name." My perfectly reasonable observation only seems to make her more irritated. "Now, tell me: how did you learn to use skyfire?"

"Listen, Blunty McBluntface." Callie tries to slip away from my crossbow to no avail. "I don't have to answer, especially since you won't stow your bow, even though it's pretty clear I'm a non-threat at this point."

"My name is—"

"Toran Rick-*yeer*-son, yes, got it." Callie blows air slowly through her lips and shrugs. "Look, sorry, but I don't know what skyfire is. Can't help you. Now, *please* get the weaponry out of my face."

"It isn't in your face, it's in my hand. And I saw you use skyfire to defend yourself from an attacking dramora." I narrow my gaze. "Are you suggesting I'm mistaken?"

Her eyes get large, and her face pales a bit. She no longer seems irked, but terrified her magic has been discovered—because even the suspicion of magic means I'm obligated to report her to the Gravenskov Village Council for immediate execution.

"Oh, I, um, I was just, uh…" Her fingers twitch, possibly from nerves, or possibly because she intends to use her skyfire against me. It originated in her hands when the dramora leapt, then spread until she was consumed by it. I prepare the trigger just in case. "What did you call it? Skyfire? Yeah, uh… it's just a thing I do."

"Just a thing?" She answers as if magic is safe, benign.

As if The Incident didn't put my entire family in jeopardy, particularly Heike.

"Look, Toran, I think we got off on the wrong foot." Callie eases away from the tree, glancing cautiously between my face and my weapon. "You're from around here, right? Local? Can you tell me where I could get some food, water, and camping supplies? Then I promise I'll get out of your hair for good."

"You're not in my hair, don't be an idiot." Out of my hair? I look at Kiera and shake my head. My bjorir meets my eyes and snorts as if to say we should abandon the sorceress and let the dramora have her.

I'm inclined to agree.

"Okay, super literal." Callie does the hard blinking again, like she's equal parts surprised and confused. I'm not the one who was talking about being in another person's hair, so if anyone has cause to be confused, it's me. "Anyway," she goes on, "can you take me to your town, or whatever, so I can get what I need?"

I stiffen. "The Village Council didn't receive any petitions for foreign clemency," I inform Callie. "You wouldn't be welcome in my village."

Her presence at the gate would cause trouble with the Volorad, and the last thing I need are the Village Council's personal guards causing more trouble for me and my sister than she's already in.

"Come on, do me a favor," Callie persists. "It's the least you can do after threatening me and poking holes in my jacket." When I remain unmoved, she sighs. "Okay, then how about we do a deal? You help me, I'll help you. Why are you in the woods? You've got some serious hiking gear going on. Are you, like, a tree Viking trying to hunt down some reindeer, or foraging for food? Something I could help you find, and then you'll help me get my supplies?"

I'm about to tell her the only "help" a sorceress with skyfire could offer is helping me get into heaps of trouble, but then, I remember that she's foreign, and lost, and those two things mean that somehow, she had the means to get lost in the forest in the first place.

Could she have crashed here inside a flaming vessel, like skyfire sorcerers of old traversed across the clouds? Or just her own two feet? Either way, she presents an opportunity, if I can work a deal with her in my favor: an opportunity for Heike and me to be safe in the wake of The Incident, away from vengeful Village Councils who would steal our hope and our future for a simple misunderstanding.

I just hope we aren't too late.

"If all you want is some food and basic gear, you won't cause trouble," I say. "Keep your skyfire hidden. Magic is illegal in Tremurheim, upon pain of death."

"'Upon pain of death?'" She repeats, then laughs. "Does everybody around here talk like some old-school fantasy novel, or just you?" Another laugh, and she swishes her hand through the air, as though ineffectually batting away the Mist accumulating around her ugly hat. "Don't worry, no magic. I just want to buy my stuff and get going."

"And repay me for holding up my end of the deal." I cast a measured look in her direction. "Do I have your word you'll follow through?"

"Yeah, sure." Callie adjusts her colorful knapsack into place. "So, what are you hunting?"

"I'm not hunting anything, I'm a Guide." She must be more foreign than I thought, if she doesn't know what a Guide is. "We make maps, chart paths, take travelers from village to village, and monitor Mist activity and forest predation."

"Did you say maps?" Callie's eyebrow arch. "Any chance you could lend me one when I'm done with my supply run? Because there's this very specific place I need to find."

"What place?" Wherever it is, she'll need a Guide to take her there, whether I lend her a map or not.

And I certainly will not.

Before Callie can answer, a clicking hiss above our heads sets Kiera on edge, and I glance toward the treetops. Skuddima float far above our heads, their sightless eyes and gaping mouths wide and blackened as they call back and forth to each other. Gray, spectral bodies only slightly more opaque than Mist trail behind their faces, curling around the branches. More clicks as they send out signals for the hunt, gathering in a tight-knit pack before flying off to stalk their prey.

"Are those things g-ghosts?" Callie stammers, horrified by the sight of the skuddima. Kiera emits her own clicks and growls to confuse them, but the diversion won't work for long.

"They're skuddima—Mist spirits," I reply. "Come. Let's depart." We can continue our discussion of maps and places she needs to go once we've left the dangers of the forest behind.

"Will they fly down and eat our faces?" Callie doesn't take a step, even though Kiera and I have already crossed the clearing.

"Yes, if they hear you talking," I caution.

"No talking, got it." She makes a strange gesture in which both of her thumbs point upwards from her fists.

Lands Beyond, she's odd. I jerk my chin, and this time, she follows.

The difficult work of climbing boulders, clearing away fern fronds, and ducking through the underbrush growing over the forest paths, all while watching out for predators and staying away from Mist pockets, is made much more difficult by the fact Callie was not paying attention when I told her to stop talking. Or, she's blatantly ignoring instructions, which seems equally likely.

"That's a pretty cool trick your dog—erm, bjorir—knows for keeping the ghost-things away," Callie trails after me, talking. "So, how do you know so much about skyfire?"

My shoulders tense, creeping toward my ears. "That's none of your business."

"Well, *I'm* not the one who brought it up in the first place," Callie argues. "Where I'm from, they're called Light powers. Why did you call it skyfire?"

"Because that's what it's called." I hope my reply will encourage her to finally shut up. "In ancient times, sorcerers from the Lands Beyond used it to cause chaos and destruction, and in consequence, all magic is illegal in Tremurheim."

There, now she can't have any reason to possibly keep—

"News flash, Toran, Light powers are good, not chaotic or destructive, so obviously skyfire and Light powers are two entirely different things." Never mind, she's still talking. "Is this place called Tremurheim?"

"Yes." End of talking.

"Sounds dour, and severe. Explains a lot about you."

"Hmph." Cease speaking.

"But that still doesn't tell me how you know so much about skyfire," Callie adds, because she has decided that her endless queries are far more important than making sure the pack of skuddima didn't follow us. Or perhaps she'll alert a rogue dramora to our presence, or, on the off chance we wander under a nargush nest, they'll swoop down and snatch us up for supper.

Kiera butts her muzzle into my shoulder and grumbles. Yes, letting the predators have her would have been easier.

"Hey, Crabby Butthead, aka Toran, you didn't answer my question," Callie pipes up. "You pinned me with your crossbow and demanded I tell you about my 'skyfire,' but you won't do me the courtesy of explaining how you know so much about it?"

Glaring over my shoulder, I snap a reply. "I read."

I will not be mentioning *what* I read, or *why* I read it.

"Yeah, the snobby, bookish hipster vibe is coming off strong, trust me. You're super popular in school, I'm sure." A brief pause, just long enough to give me hope she has finally run out of nonsense words. But, alas. "Assuming you're still in school. How old are you, anyway?"

Old enough to keep my mouth shut in a forest of predators that hide in the Mist, and use the surroundings to their advantage. This part of the forest is infested with skuddima, who hunt mostly by sound from treetop Mist accumulation, and Callie is more than making sounds—with all her incessant chatter, she's practically begging for an attack. I scan the treetops above us. Thankfully, they're clear.

"I'm going to guess... Eighteen? Nineteen?" Callie makes her own prediction when I refuse to answer.

"Seventeen," I say over my shoulder.

"Huh, me, too. I pegged you as older. Must be all the smugness seeping from your pores," she says. "Well, technically, I'll be seventeen in a week. I left home right before my birthday. Hey, since you make maps, how big is Tremurheim, exactly? Are we talking gigantic oceans of doom to cross, or a pretty small, self-contained nightmare country? Because I'd kinda like to be home for my birthday. I overheard my mom and dad talking about getting me a new phone, and—"

"Why did you leave your home?" I slow my walking so I can watch her reaction to my question. "Is it because your skyfire was discovered?"

Callie stops speaking the exact moment I want her to continue. Her mouth snaps shut and her face stills momentarily, before morphing into a grimace of rage, sadness, and all-consuming grief.

"No, it wasn't because of that," she admits at last. "My Light powers helped me escape from—let's just say, a really messy situation."

She used her skyfire openly? Now I'm the one doing the hard

blink. "Nobody arrested you, or tried to execute you?"

"No." Her response is terse. "I was in a jam, threats were being made, I had to leave, that's it. Can we drop the topic?"

"What kind of threats?" She continued to ask questions long after I told her to stop, I will do the same.

"It was just—I thought I could trust someone, but I was wrong." The sorrow on her face intensifies, and she doesn't say another word, even as the trees and Mist thin and the outskirts of Gravenskov peek through the spaces between trunks.

At least she's no longer making us an easy target for predators, but her response makes me leery, especially since she could be the single spark of hope in resolving The Incident before it gets out of hand. I understand not trusting people, because people are cruel and only seek their own ends, but if I'm going to use Callie's desire to go to a "very specific place" to my advantage, I have to believe she won't lead me into even worse danger. Those "threats" she mentioned, and the people making them, could still be imminent.

Then again, what other choice do Heike and I have?

"Whoa, is this where you live? Talk about a horror show." Callie remembers she has a tongue as she takes in Gravenskov from our vantage point just outside the tree line. "Why is the top of the wall sharpened into jagged spikes?" She catches sight of something that makes her appear ill. "Is that an animal caught up in the spikes? Its wings are all torn, and it's dripping entrails. That's literally disgusting. Isn't anybody going to clean that up?"

"Carcasses deter nargush, the dead animal in question," I reply. "They won't eat their own." Wherever Callie is from—and, hopefully, where she's trying to go—has no nargush. Or Mist, dramora, and skuddima. Perhaps there are no Village Councils or Volorad, either: all monsters of the human variety.

"Does every animal in Tremurheim strongly resemble a

dragon, or just the ones that eat you?" Callie's wide-eyed, addled look is back, the one that makes me think I'm equally addled to consider trusting her help.

"I don't know what a dragon is. Stop asking questions about animals." Forest spare me, the *questions*. "I'm going to check a different entrance, one with less—"

"Geez, don't bite my head off, I'm just curious," Callie interrupts. She interrupts frequently, each statement more idiotic than the last.

"I didn't bite your head off, that's horrific." Even Kiera growls at the assumption. With a few pats to her flank, I signal her off toward the gate to the kennel at the Guide Hall. She gives Callie a withering look of disdain before shuffling off.

"It's just an expression. Calm thine self." Callie adjusts her knapsack. "Aren't we going to get my supplies?" She starts down the path leading through the karpeah pastures, but I catch her by the elbow, pulling her back. A few of the lumbering animals bay when she shrieks, their udders shaking back and forth.

"What are you doing?" I tighten my grip as she struggles against it. "Don't you see the Volorad patrolling near the gate? Give them a reason to execute you, and they will. Nobody in Gravenskov likes foreigners, especially Volorad."

"Let go of me." Callie twists herself free at last, fixing me with a nasty-looking scowl. "I think you left a mark on my arm."

"That isn't any of my concern." I glance at the green-clad Volorad, marching back and forth across the entry gate. Walking up with Callie on my heels is begging for trouble, and my family has been in more than enough trouble of late. "We're taking another route in. Hide here, in the trees, while I make sure it's clear."

"So the giant, thou-shalt-not-pass gate of surly pike-people isn't the only way in?" Callie gets a look on her face like she might be scheming, or, at least, open to the idea of it, which isn't at all a comfort. "You definitely didn't mention secret entrances."

"I wasn't obliged to." Enough talk on that account. Knowing her, she'd try to find it herself and wind up blurting my name when the Volorad inevitably caught her. I motion for her to follow, leading her to a hiding spot behind a few scraggly trees. "Stay here until I come for you."

"Yeah, like that's gonna happen," Callie mutters. "What happens if one of those skuddima things tries to eat me?"

With any luck, it would eat her tongue first, and all Tremurheim would be spared a headache. "Then may the forest spare you, lest your ancestors greet you in the Lands Beyond."

"Seriously? You're going to just leave me here to get eaten by—hey!" Callie does not like it when I turn and saunter away, making my way through the trees until I'm once again facing the gate and the karpeah fields.

Many of the creatures are out grazing today, and only one keeper seems to be watching them, which is helpful for providing cover, but makes scouting a route to the secret entrance in the village wall a difficult activity. If I can't see a Volorad, they can't see me—which, depending on who spots who first, puts me at either an advantage, or deadly disadvantage. I don't like not knowing that my path is clear, but I don't think we'll have another—

"Toran!"

A slender pair of arms wraps around my neck from behind, pulling me down until my back is almost bent in half.

"I thought I saw you come through the trees!" My attacker gives my throat a strangling squeeze of affection. "I've been waiting for you for hours."

"Forest spare you, Heike. Your greetings could be less painful." I can hardly squeak the words, so I give my sister's forearm a pat instead. When she releases me, I turn, finding her cheerful smile. "Did you say hours? You're supposed to be in courses today." Heike clasps her hands behind her back, and her smile widens. Never a good sign. "Did you skip again? Head-mistress Ula will report this to Papa, and your free-roaming Archive privileges will be over."

"She won't say anything, I forged Papa's signature on my excusal." Forging the signature of the Gravenskov Archivist? Lands Beyond, she's been risky lately. "Anyway, they're just going on about the Aptitude Test, and I already know everything I need to make Guide."

"Forget making Guide. Keep your head down, don't make mischief before the test, and *don't* sneak any more books from the Archive, understand?" I try to peek over her shoulder, but she quicksteps with a sly grin, evading me. "What are you hiding?"

Her gray eyes that are the same color as mine dance with the delight of shared secrets. Whatever she's smuggled out, it's worse than I thought.

"I found the book!" Heike tucks a strand of red-brown hair behind her ear, one that's fallen out of her shoulder-length plaits, and produces a tome from her satchel, grinning with obvious pride. "It's about Obald the Gray, the famous Mist sorcerer. You said he didn't exist, remember? This talks all about his magic; how the Mist obeyed him, and how he carried a sword of ice, just like—"

"Put that away!" I dart a glance over my shoulder at the Volorad whispering behind their hands at the gate, watching Heike and me converse, their eyes on the volume she cradles in her arms. Just beyond earshot is the lone witness to The Incident, the karpeah keeper whose terror I see in my mind every time I close my eyes. Lands Beyond, why did it have to be *him* who's shepherding the herd today?

At least, I assume he's beyond earshot, because if not...

"Why should I put it away?" Heike's brow creases. "I thought you'd be happy."

"Happy you took a forbidden book about an equally forbidden sorcerer out of the Archive under the nose of the Volorad? You're asking to be arrested." I watch the karpeah keeper back away through the herd at the sight of me and Heike, as though afraid The Incident will repeat itself.

"I was only trying to help, Toran."

A guilty pang tears through my chest at Heike's crestfallen face. I turn away from the karpeah keeper, speaking softly. "Hide it in your satchel. We can read it later. I'll ask permission to stay at home tonight instead of the Guide Hall."

"Good!" Heike's smile returns brighter than before, warming the chill in my belly—but only a little. "I miss you at home. It's not the same since your selection. But soon I'll make Guide, too, and we can have all sorts of fun again."

Behind my back, Callie snorts a laugh. "Yeah, Toran is *loads* of fun."

Forest spare me. "I told you to stay hidden while I scouted our route in."

Callie's eyes roll around a scoff. "Yeah, like I'm going to sit quietly in the trees and wait for you to ditch me. Nice try, Toran." She nods toward Heike with her chin. "Who's this? Friend of yours?"

As soon as Heike notices Callie, her eyes go wide, sparkling with the anticipation of meeting a new person—specifically, a foreigner she can pepper with endless questions about the world beyond Gravenskov's imposing walls.

"Hello, I'm Heike Rykjiersen." My sister steps beyond my shoulder, coming to stand before Callie. "Toran is my brother. He didn't tell me he was Guiding a foreign traveler today. What village are you from?"

"Oh, I'm —"

"That's Callie James. She's lost," I explain Callie's unannoun-ced presence. "She needs supplies, and will be on her way shortly."

After she keeps her end of the deal we made, which I won't forget.

"Thanks for talking over me, *Tor-an*," Callie says my name like she's chiding. She has no reason to scold — especially after I was merciful enough not to kill her on sight for using skyfire. She turns to Heike and smiles. "Your name is Hi-kah, did I get that right? Toran is really into properly saying names."

"That doesn't surprise me," Heike replies. A frown turns my lips. "Were you really lost in the forest? Toran says the skuddima have been unusually active of late. Did he save your life?"

"No, actually, he threatened me with a crossbow." Callie glares, and I glare back.

"That doesn't surprise me, either," Heike says, laughing.

My frown deepens, especially after I notice the karpeah keeper from The Incident has left his post and is speaking to the Volorad at the main gate. His hands gesticulate wildly toward us, eyes darting between my sister and the guards with their massive pikes — pikes meant to impale the heart of an offending suspect. No trial before the Council, who have given the Volorad free rein, just a swift, excruciating execution at Morning Drums. Those are the Council's rules, and they are enforced with no mercy.

The Volorad speaking to the karpeah keeper focus their stares on Heike, brandishing pikes.

"We don't have time for introductions," I interrupt whatever conversation Heike was attempting to start with Callie. "Heike, you need to get out of sight. Callie, go hide in the forest until I come for you."

"Um, how about no. Since you admitted you're indifferent to

me getting eaten alive by monsters." Callie hefts her knapsack, which makes a strange, grinding kind of squeal noise. She turns over her shoulder and hisses something I can't make out before grinning nervously. "Sorry, just, uh, ignore that. So, how are we getting through the gate with all the armed guards?"

"Toran and I found a secret way into Gravenskov." Heike turns to Callie conspiratorially. "One less… guarded."

Because our "secret way" isn't guarded at all, hence the imminent need. My stomach drops when the Volorad move for us, determined looks on their faces.

"Heike, stay close to the karpeah," I caution, taking off through the pasture, skirting around the massive legs of the steadily grazing creatures. I glance every way I can, limbs shaking. "Keep your eyes on me."

Heike's face clouds with concern. "Why are you acting like something's wrong?"

"Yeah, why *are* you acting like something's wrong?" Callie pipes up, crossing her arms. I don't answer, keeping watch for the approaching Volorad over my shoulder. They're nowhere in sight—not yet. Heike falls in step with me, moving at a slight jog to keep up with my long strides while Callie lags behind.

"You're still worried about what happened two days ago?" she murmurs so quietly Callie can't hear.

"Yes." I'm more than worried, I'm terrified we've sealed our doom.

"Nobody saw what happened," Heike assures me.

"A karpeah keeper saw." Another cautionary look around. "He was speaking with the Volorad at the gate a moment ago. He saw you with the book about Obald the Gray."

"You don't know that he was speaking about us, or that he saw anything suspicious," Heike replies. She places a hand on my arm, squeezing tight. "Everything will be fine."

"You won't be fine." I give her a look as serious as a pyre. "The karpeah keeper saw *you* that morning, not me. Mark me, Heike, he'll cause trouble. And you know what trouble means."

My sister falls quiet. Because trouble means certain death.

"Look, we're almost there." Heike points out the nondescript spot on the village wall we call our unofficial gate, shining like a beacon of safety.

"Hey, guys?" Callie's voice behind me. "I think I stepped in poop."

"Dramora spawn," I grouch.

Heike giggles at my side. "I like her, she's funny. Where is she from?"

"I don't know, nor do I—"

"Stop right there."

The infinitesimal spark of hope ignited by my plan for escape is snuffed entirely by the sight of five green-cloaked figures with pikes emerging from the outskirts of the karpeah herd, trailed by the hateful keeper who witnessed The Incident. Pikes point at my sister and me, and we stop dead in our tracks before they impale us. The dread that pierces my heart is sharper than any weapon the Volorad guards carry, and I know the words on their lips before they utter a syllable.

"Heike Rykjiersen." One Volorad steps forward as two more grab my sister by the arms. "You are under arrest for the crime of sorcery."

CHAPTER 4
CALLIE

I DOVE INTO TREMURHEIM all of, like, three minutes ago, probably, and already I've been attacked by a man-eating monster, accosted by a cranky-pants jerk with aggressive crossbow pointing habits, and stepped in a gigantic pile of moose-cow dung, smearing it all over my favorite boots. Not the knock-off pair Mom bought me last Christmas because "they look just the same, and were half-price!" No, I had to serve beef Wellington and *coq au vin* at countless weddings with Mom while scuzzy drunk guys asked if I was eighteen and made lewd hand gestures (you know the ones), all so I could save enough money for these sweet boots. Now the prize for all my hard work and harassment is coated in poo.

My first Dive totally sucks.

As if this field of poo wasn't a huge, stinky pile of actual crap to deal with, the crabby, uniformed people with pikes just showed up. *Volorad*, Toran calls them. I duck quickly around the leg of a moose-cow before the Volorad and the leering shepherd accompanying them can spot me, hiding myself behind the creature's enormous flank. With absolutely zero warning, the mean-greenies grab Heike and point their weapons at her heart.

Well, this sure escalated quickly.

"Heike Rykjiersen," a woman with a deep, bellowing voice calls out. "You are under arrest for the crime of sorcery."

Really? Sorcery? Last I checked, Heike didn't do anything magical just now—unless there's something critical that I'm missing.

"Don't do this," Toran pleads, his words cracking with desperation, and it's the first time I've heard any emotion in his voice that wasn't aloof snobbishness.

I peek through the moose-cow's legs, watching the scene unfold. Heike's panic-stricken face goes stark white as she takes in the sight of the pikes, the bindings applied to her wrists. "What's going on? Toran!"

"Let her go, she's innocent!" Toran rushes forward, his eyes like a wild animal that's been cornered, but two fang-like pikes appear inches from his nose, stopping him cold.

"Innocent?" The Volorad in charge strips Heike of her satchel, retrieving a book hidden inside—the one I heard Toran say was forbidden. "We have a credible witness. This is all we need to see."

All they need to see is a book to prove she's a magic sorceress? Majorly sketch. Somebody is *definitely* not admitting the whole story.

"*Whir-whir-whiiiirrzzzzz!*" Nemo punches at my backpack zipper, opening it just enough to stick his head out. He spins around, eyes blinking rapidly.

"Dude, chill," I hiss at my mech. "Don't make noise, or you'll rat us out." But Nemo isn't paying attention to me. He's far too interested in the moose-cow's swishing tail, and batting it with his little claw-hand. The moose-cow makes a groaning moo-ish noise and shifts its weight, putting me in the direct path of a mound of poo, should one happen to spew forth. "Knock it off." I give Nemo a sharp jab with my finger when he swipes the tail again. "This thing could be loaded."

"Whatever you think you saw, or heard, I promise it isn't true," Toran begs, but from my vantage point, the woman doing the talking isn't impressed, much less moved.

"You think I'm going to take the word of a Rykjiersen? Your family is all the same. Troublemakers and rabble-rousers to the last. And now we know why." The Volorad tosses the book onto the grass at Heike's feet. "You will be executed by four pikes through the heart tomorrow at Morning Drums. Forest spare you."

Executed? Yikes on several bikes. She can't mean that. All Heike did was steal a book!

"Toran!" Heike screams for her brother as the Volorad lead her away, sobbing and struggling in vain, through the Gravenskov gate, the shepherd guy following close behind. Toran tries to run after them, but one of the Volorad whirls around, pointing a pike at his gut.

"Where do you think you're going, Guide?" the man snaps. "Just try and stop them. All I have to do is report you to the Council for insubordination, and you'll be joining your sorceress sister faster than you can–"

"*Mmmmoooooooooogh!*" Nemo finally snags the moose-cow's tail, and all it takes is one pull of my mech's hand for the creature to let out a giant moan and a literal deluge of poop. Nauseating, hot, rancid-grass-and-rotten-berries scented poop, which splatters across the pasture like a modern art painting gone disgustingly wrong. I swallow a dry-heave and shove Nemo inside my backpack.

"Nice going, stupid mech." I zip him up as the moose-cow steps away and reveals my hiding spot to Toran and the extremely suspicious Volorad.

"Who are you?" The pike leaves Toran's stomach and jabs into mine instead. It's disappointing enough my boots are completely destroyed, and now my puffer jacket is full of holes. This world has a grudge against my clothes.

"I'm, uh, a traveler." I grin. The Volorad doesn't buy it. "Just a traveler that Toran is escorting, over the river and through the woods. To grandma's house we go."

Toran scowls like he'd happily hand me over to the pike-wielding dude trying to spear my coat, and shed zero tears. Neither person speaks, and the air around me stills, silent, until the moose-cow drops yet another load of poo inches from my feet. Wonderful.

"I was admiring the local wildlife—I mean, uh, the farm animals—while you were doing the whole arresting teenage girls thing." Another awkward grin, and I give the moose-cow's leg a pat. "Some digestive system this thing has, huh? I mean, it works *so well.*"

"Where is your petition for clemency?" Volorad guy sticks out his hand, demanding to see evidence I'm here for legit reasons. Toran's look of rage intensifies along with my panic.

"Travel papers, you mean? Um, yes, I have those." What am I going to pass off as travel papers? With shaking fingers, I unzip my backpack a bit, digging around for a piece of paper Nemo hasn't shredded. My mech gives me a quizzical look, blinking. I shake my head, praying his pinball-machine inner Light will be able to sense my fear. At last, I find an old letter Vice Principal Mackie sent to all VBHS parents about iPad and laptop check-outs—one I forgot to actually give my parents. It's a bit wrinkled, but it still looks official. "Here is my petition."

The Volorad takes the paper from my hands and frowns so hard I think he might be in a competition with Toran for this world's best sourpuss face. "I can't read this."

"Well, duh, I'm foreign."

A tense moment of uncertainty lingers between the three of us as the Volorad tries to decipher the letter and Toran simmers with anger, like he's planning all the ways he can gut me like a fish and which will be most painful. At last, the Volorad growls and throws the letter at Toran's face.

"Get her to the Guide Hall, and let them sort it with the Council." Spinning on his heel, the Volorad stalks away, maneuvering around grazing moose-cows toward the gate.

"Close call." I glance at Toran, whose cold eyes follow the Volorad's back until his green cloak disappears around the other side of the village wall. "What just happened, exactly?"

"They've arrested Heike for sorcery, and will execute her tomorrow at dawn." Toran snaps out of his watchful pose and grabs me by the arm, maneuvering me through the moose-cow pasture.

"Hey—stop! What are you doing?" I try to free myself, wriggling around in his grasp, but Toran only pulls harder.

"I'm taking you to get ration packs," he says, "and then you're going to follow through with your end of our deal: helping me break my sister out of prison, and escape Gravenskov. For good."

"No way, dude. I'm not getting involved." I try to peel his fingers off my forearm as he drags me toward a crack between two tree trunks in the Gravenskov wall. Bracing myself against the sides of the crack, I halt his relentless momentum. "I already got you out of one jam back there. You do what you have to do to save your sister, but this isn't my problem."

Toran yanks on my arm, tugging me through the crack. The side of my head whacks one of the trunks, a painful smart radiating across my skull. "It's just become your problem," he snaps.

Not my only problem, either.

Piles of garbage, and the disgusting scent of excrement mixed with moldy vegetables, fruit, and meat hit my nose like a sledgehammer on the other side of Toran and Heike's "secret" entrance. I can see why it's so secret—it's tucked away in the midst of a dump/sewer combo. Before I can figure out if I want to cover my nose or gag, Toran starts dragging me straight through the mess.

"Oh, my gosh, can you stop?" I grab onto the corner of a derelict shack just beyond the other side of the crack, holding on tight. "My current problem has nothing to do with your sister and everything to do with you, trying to pull my arm out of socket."

"And my current problem has nothing to do with your arm." Yank goes the limb in question when Toran attempts to pry me from the shack. He's pretty strong for not being particularly muscular.

"I don't know you. I don't know your sister." Another tug. "I just followed you here to get food and supplies for my journey." Hard pull. This time, I let go of the building I'm clinging to and aim a swift kick at his shins—one that strikes true. Toran yowls and releases me, rubbing his leg. "Try those shenanigans again, and I'll have that green guy come back and arrest you for kidnapping me."

"Go ahead, call for the Volorad," Toran counters. He leers over me, his eyes twin icebergs lodged in his face. "I'll tell them you're a skyfire sorceress, and you'll die tomorrow morning with my sister."

"So, you're blackmailing me now?" I can't believe this—oh, wait, yes I can. "Has your plan always involved stabbing me in the back, or did you come up with it on the fly?"

"I'll do whatever I have to do to save Heike." Toran shrugs nonchalantly. "If that involves turning you in so I have access to the prison where they're keeping her, so be it."

Just try it, Toran. I'll show you skyfire, alright. And maybe use some Persuasion—but only as a last resort. Toran seems like a last-resort type.

"That stabby Volorad guy told you to take me to the Guide Hall," I remind him instead. "Do you think he's going to be happy you dragged me to the village dump instead of following orders? If you'd stop with the ultimatums for a sec, I have a few questions."

Toran's mouth recedes into a tight line, but at least he doesn't grab me and try to haul me off again. "Ask them, and be quick about it."

"Why did they arrest your sister? Because she stole a book about some old-school sorcerer?" We remain secluded behind the shack, wading in knee-deep garbage, but Toran keeps looking around, as though he's terrified more of those guards are going to poof into our hiding spot out of thin air.

"She didn't steal anything, our father is the village Archivist. He lets us borrow books whenever we want, even from the forbidden section," Toran answers with an impatient huff. "I already told you, magic is strictly forbidden in Tremurheim."

"Upon pain of death—I remember." The over-the-top, melodramatic way he said it remains the only laugh I've had all day. "That doesn't tell me why she was arrested. Being caught with a banned book isn't the same as actually practicing magic."

I've suspected since the Volorad showed up and took Heike that Toran isn't fessing up to something, a secret he doesn't want to divulge. The way he averts his eyes, shifting his gaze toward his toes, confirms it—because for real, he's the most direct person I've ever encountered.

"It's none of your—"

"Business? You made it my business, because according to you, your sister drama is now my problem." I lean against the shack, watching him for any hint of reaction. "The Volorad who arrested Heike said there were witnesses. Witnesses to what?"

Toran's hackles rise, and he does the lip-curling sneer that seems to be his only expression besides scowling. "I don't have to tell you anything."

"Then I don't have to help jailbreak your little sister." I turn, stepping with care around mounds of stinky grossness until I'm about halfway through the crack we used to enter the village. "Forest spare you, or whatever you guys say around here. I'll get my supplies on my own."

"Wait."

I back out of the crack, watching him expectantly. "Yes?"

Toran hangs his head with a sigh, a hint of vulnerability peeking through the stony chill that surrounds him. "There was an incident about two days ago, early in the morning. Heike and I were both outside the wall near the forest, and a karpeah keeper thought he saw her using magic." A pause, like he's debating how much truth to admit. "However, he was mistaken. She's innocent."

"But why would somebody *think* she used magic, unless there's a reason to suspect it in the first place?" Could the reason Toran knows so much about "skyfire" Light powers be because Heike is a Luminaut? The book she stole was about a man named Obald who could turn Mist into ice swords. Sounds a lot like she's researching Seers, too. Another Luminaut to help shoulder the weight of my task would be awesome, but a Seer to find a gateway off this monster-movie world would be even better.

Toran's edginess reminds me of a badger on the defensive. "It was a misunderstanding."

Wow, dude, are you always this evasive? I'm going to need more intel than the non-answer you so reluctantly divulged. "Arresting her seems like a pretty hardcore reaction for a simple misunderstanding."

Toran doesn't like me pressing the matter, because when he speaks, his teeth grind together around a scowl. "It was believed—how it looked—could be interpreted as Heike controlling Mist."

"She swished some fog around?" That's no big deal. There's got to be more to it than that.

"It's not just fog, as you say. Mist is feared by everyone in Tremurheim." A grave look conveys his seriousness—but this kid is never not serious, so it could be his normal face. "Mist has a mind of its own, and a sinister one at that. It swallows people in folds so thick they're never seen or heard from again, left to wander through pockets of gray until they collapse and die. If a person can control Mist, bend that evil to their will… they'd be a deadly and feared sorcerer." He shifts, the uneasy demeanor fading into his typical aloofness. "Even being suspected of such magic is enough to get you arrested, and being caught with an illegal book sealed my sister's fate."

"And what do you expect me to do about it?" Which remains the question of the hour.

"You said you had to go somewhere specific, didn't you?" Toran cocks his diamond-hard chin. "Somewhere that required a map?"

"Yes…" Where's he going with this?

"The only people in Gravenskov with access to maps are Guides," Toran goes on. "And I'm a Guide. Tell me your destination, and I can access a map."

"What about my food and stuff?" I need essentials slightly more than I need a map, as I might have mentioned.

"Yes, that too." He nods for me to elaborate. "Where are you going, and why?"

"The 'why' wasn't part of answering your questions, but okay, fine." I try to remember the specific word the women used in Diver's memory. "There are these lighthouse things, I think they're called Beacons. They had Light, just like my powers, shining on the top. Finding that Light is what I need to do to complete my journey and go home."

"Beacon's flare? You're hunting for Beacon's flare?" I can't tell if his tone is terrified or incredulous.

"Yeah, sure, Beacon's flare." A Light Core by any other name, right?

"Beacon's flare is purported to have been the most dangerous, unstable power source in all of Tremurheim." Toran gawks like I'm the most irrational person he's ever met. "Why would you want to find it?"

"I have my reasons, that's all you need to know," I retort. "I don't owe anything else to butt-faces like you who blackmail me, threaten me, and call me names. So why don't you tell me what you know about those Beacons, Mr. I-Read-About-Secret-Magic, before I tattle to the Volorad about you, too."

By some miracle, Toran's infuriated glower doesn't kill me on the spot.

"If the Beacons still exist — which is doubtful," he answers like the well-read snob he probably is, "they'd be across the Hem at the edge of the Tageveld."

Whoop-de-whoop. "Can you explain to me what a Hem is, and a Tageveld? Because you just said a whole lot of words that don't mean anything to me."

Tora rolls his eyes, snorting through his nose. Impatient, are we? Maybe don't try to blackmail somebody and not expect to give answers to very pertinent questions.

"The Hem is a barren wasteland of Mist and predators," he elaborates. "It is said to have been created by skyfire during the Clan Wars, and separates the forests of Tremurheim from the Tageveld."

He talks like a seasoned college professor in lecture mode. Dr. Ormandi would love him.

"What's a Tageveld?" I motion for Toran to go on.

"The Tageveld is a sea of Mist that marks the furthest boundary of Tremurheim," he continues lecturing. "The Lands Beyond are rumored to exist across it, but nobody believes the Lands Beyond are real, except as a mythical land of ancestral spirits and death."

The rolling ocean of Mist from Diver's memory—the Tageveld. So far, all of this checks out with the blips I saw in the gateway, and is just the right information I need to find Tremurheim's Light Core. As stringent as Toran's personality is, a bookworm is a useful person to have around when you need answers to obscure history questions. "The Beacons at the Tageveld, yes, that's where I need to go. If we could swing a map to the Tageveld into this trade scenario, that would be—"

"I'm not lending you a map." Self-serious scowl. Grr, says Toran's whole face. "Even if you could read it, which you can't, you need a person who can prevent you from getting lost, and knows how to set up deflections for the Hem's many predators. I'll be coming with you to the Tageveld, and Heike, too."

"No." I shake my head so fast I almost give myself whiplash. "Absolutely not. I can find my way on my own, and my Light powers will protect me from predators."

"You think you can find it on your own?" I half expect Toran to bark a derisive laugh, but I don't think he can emote anything other than severe annoyance. "Perhaps, eventually, but only after running out of food and water, and wandering for Seasons while you starve to death in Mist so thick you won't be able to see anything, not even a hand in front of your face."

Crap, he's halfway right. Even with my Luminaut powers guiding me, it would take forever to find the Beacons on my own in a world I'm unfamiliar with—especially one chock full of Mist and monsters.

"You need someone who knows where they're going," Toran continues, "and how to get there. That person is me. And taking you to the Tageveld gets Heike and I out of Gravenskov, thus holding up your end of our bargain."

"Our bargain never included two additional people—who, by the way, I literally *just met*—joining my traveling party." As useful as Toran might be in helping me navigate this cross-country trek through the Mist expediently, I never signed up to babysit two siblings in the wilderness for who knows how long, especially with Darkness on my tail. There's just too many risks to outweigh the potential benefits. "Our deal was I get to buy food and water in your village, you get some equally benign and easy help from me in return. Sorry, Toran, but I'm out."

All I needed was him to lead me to town for supplies, and now that I'm in town, I'll find a way to get them. I make for the street beyond the shack, checking to make sure the coast is clear. Lucky for me, this part of the village seems abandoned. Probably because of the garbage dump issue. I mean, I wouldn't be wandering around Gravenskov's version of a landfill if Toran hadn't towed me here against my will.

"Would you walk away from an innocent girl? One who needs your help?" Toran's accusation stops me mid-step. I should have known he'd try the sympathy card sooner or later.

"Why do you think I'm the key to helping free your sister?" I fix him with a look as serious as any he has in his own arsenal. "You told me magic is forbidden. Some random guy getting suspicious of Heike landed her in prison, facing an execution with no trial. My Light powers are not going to go over well in a jailbreak. If this fails, Heike isn't the only one meeting a violent end."

I mean, I've got Persuasion to help me out of jams — like people trying to murder me — but Toran is another issue. And as right as he is about needing to get across the Hem in a timely manner, if he gets caught, too, nobody is going to cross anything fast.

"I'm well aware this could go wrong, but if we're going to leave Gravenskov, I'd rather risk using your skyfire to help Heike than not use it and let her die." Toran steps toward me with something like a pleading look — as much as a rigid grump can plead. "Do you have a brother or a sister? Some person in your life you'd do anything to save from a mistake?"

Why did he have to remind me the entire reason I'm here in Tremurheim, wasting valuable time arguing with him in a literal trash heap about saving siblings from dire fates, is because I Dove away from California so I could save my own siblings, parents, and friends from Darkness? Everything I'm doing, no matter how unpleasant and downright dangerous it is, has been to protect them from my mistakes — my trust in the wrong people, and not listening to the right ones when I had the chance.

Ugh, I hate it.

"What about your mom and dad?" I ask. "Heike mentioned your Papa... will they be okay? Or will people try to kill them, too?"

"I've been teaching them forest survival skills," Toran says. "Mama is an Herbalist, she knows how to forage, and Papa already forged new identities and petitions for foreign clemency to several of the surrounding villages. Word of Heike's arrest will have spread by now, and I have no doubt they've fled. There are few secrets in Gravenskov."

His admission begs so many questions. "Sounds like your family was preparing for this scenario. Any particular reason?" Is your sister a Luminaut or Seer, and you're conveniently neglecting to tell me the truth?

If Heike was a Luminaut, she'd have used Persuasion to stop the Volorad from arresting her. As much as I hate that part of my power — how it feels, and what it does to people — there's no way I wouldn't use it to save myself, particularly in the face of execution. No, whatever Toran is hiding (and he's totally hiding something) has got to be a potential Seer thing, especially because the accusations involve controlling an elemental substance like Mist.

Heike a Seer…hmm. That changes things. If I needed a reason to want to help Toran and his mysterious sister, it's the potential to find a Seer — and soon.

"The Incident gave us cause to make plans." Toran's voice grows as cold as an arctic wind. "My family's private concerns aren't any of yours. I care about one answer: are you helping me free Heike, or am I calling Volorad to arrest you, too?"

And we're back to blackmailing. Awesome. This really makes me want to rely on your expertise to get me to the Beacons, Toran. It kinda sucks you're my only option for help, and your sister might be a Seer. Otherwise I'd flip you double birds and tell you to peace out forever. Along with some other choice four-letter words.

"Fine. I'll help you get your sister out of the slammer." *Fine* isn't the four-letter word that starts with an 'f' I want to use in this scenario, but whatever.

"Excellent." Don't jump all around and squeal, Toran, you'll give away our hiding spot — just kidding. He shows almost no emotional reaction to my agreement: only a smug half-grin turning the edge of his mouth. "I knew you'd see things my way."

Where have I heard a line like that before? Can anyone say Shadowmancer monster Nate Ormandi? Some horrible gut feeling I should probably learn to trust tells me Toran's propensity to threaten me and leave me for dead if it's in his favor might turn out to be far worse than Nate's lies and deceit.

I hope my gut is wrong. Because whether I like it or not, Toran Rykjiersen is along for a very lengthy ride.

CHAPTER 5

NATE

ICTARI CAN KISS MY frigid, undead—

"Ah–umph!" Swept off my feet again. What is this, some kind of romance novel? Canyon wind isn't my idea of a love interest.

I've been galavanting about the foothills like I'm taking the hobbits to Isengard for probably an hour (I'm not good with time anymore, even beyond the Veil), and I've gotten knocked off my feet and blasted flat on my back by screeching, below-zero gales ripping through the mountain canyons every four-and-a-half seconds. Again, not great with time, but my assessment is more or less accurate—let's just say, I'm splayed across the snow like Shadowmancer roadkill more often than would be considered "comical." We're bordering on "pitiful."

You think I'm exaggerating? Being dramatic for drama's sake? I assure you, I'm not.

"Not again—*ugh!*" Case in point, another gust sweeps me off my feet and lands me on my knees.

Saying Ictari is a bummer would be the understatement of the century. This world is nothing but ice, snow, and hurricane-force winds blowing across a wide stretch of barren plains until the gales hit the face of a gargantuan mountain range, rising from the frozen earth like the jagged purple teeth of an ancient monster buried in a block of permafrost, until only the gaping jaws remain visible. Darkness makes me immune to most unfortunate human pitfalls, like freezing to death, but that doesn't mean I enjoy being this cold. Even the purple-blue sky on the horizon feels stuck in a frostbitten stupor where the sun can't rise or set past twilight.

I always thought Queen was icy and generally detached because she's the Prime Shadowmancer and abandoned human emotions a long time ago. But if this is the world she's from, I doubt she ever possessed any warm feelings to begin with.

"Oof!" Blown down again. Sensing a pattern? I sure am.

Where are the caverns and caves full of people Queen promised I'd find? I have yet to see one living being existing in this hellscape of ice. No animals, no plants, and definitely no humans.

I glide down the slope of another hill, approaching a rocky outcropping that leads straight into the heart of the forbidding-looking mountains. Wind screams through the open mouth of the canyon before me, as dark as the most remote corner of the Shadow Plain. Reminds me of looking over the edge of a skiff in a mounting storm, trying to decide if I'll survive a dive into the depths to retrieve something I desperately want to find.

Strange comparison. Almost like... a memory of doing that exact thing. Except I couldn't have said memory, because I was knocked out by a rogue wave when my skiff capsized. It's all a little blurry, but that's how Queen explained it.

I'm on a tangent. Thanks, Dad, for that genetic gift that keeps on not giving.

Another peek into the canyon reveals humongous mounds of snow resting precariously at intervals along the walls. If I was a human, there's a snowball's chance in hell (snow pun, ha!) I'd consider setting foot in there, let alone going all the way through it in hopes of finding civilization. Unfortunately, the Veil hasn't been useful as a spying mechanism since my arrival on this gawd-awful ice world, because the gauzy filter of Shadow makes the whiteness of the landscape look fuzzy gray, and indistinguishable from one thing to the next. I tried to use the Veil when I first emerged onto the Ice Fields from the Shadows, and failed at making any forward progress. It's about as frustrating as this canyon wind, blowing me bottoms up.

But Light Cores don't find themselves, and I don't lose twice. It's going to take more than a gigantic, intimidating, possibly avalanche-prone canyon to stop me from winning the game against Callie's Light.

Bring it on, canyon.

Wsssssshhhh.

Hmm, what's this? A suspicious bunch of snow and tiny rocks accumulated at my heel, almost as if it was sent skidding downhill when a person made a misstep.

Person? Interesting.

I take a couple long strides toward the mouth of the canyon, keeping my eyes on my peripheral, ears attuned to what's going on behind me. If I'm being followed by somebody, they're incredibly light-footed. Either a small person, or a skilled one. However, for as light on their feet as they are, they aren't as stealthy as they need to be. I catch a flash of person-shaped white skittering over a snow-capped knoll to my back and left, one somebody less observant would miss.

Back and left. The person probably assumes I'm right-handed and plans to attack from my non-dominant side. Guess what, stalker creep? I'm a leftie. I slow my pace as more rocks and snow fall down a nearby hillside, much closer this time.

"You got a name, person following me?" I call out. "Yeah, I'm onto you."

No response. Not that I thought I'd get one, but it's always a good indicator of whether or not a stalker has more than a couple brain cells.

"Why don't you come out and introduce yourself? Make it a fair fight?" A flash of white cloth flies behind another hill, still on my left. Location spotted. "You think I didn't see you run away and hide back there?"

I course correct, making a beeline for the place I saw the person disappear, and then head off the opposite direction, back around the hill, because only an idiot would stay in the exact spot I just said I saw them hiding. With luck, I'll be able to catch them sneaking away to another location, and have the upper hand.

Whack! Something blunt connects with my shoulders.

"Ow! Son of a—"

Whack whack! Front of legs, then back of legs smacked in rapid succession.

Okay, so my stalker is armed.

I spin around, catching sight of the person at last. They're short—really short—and skinny, wielding a long staff made of what looks like lightweight metal or graphite. A furry hood covers the person's hair, and reflective goggles and a knitted gaiter conceal their face, protecting them from the light reflecting off of the snow.

"Back off!" Darkness stirs in my chest just under my skin, begging me to ash my attacker. Ashing seems like overkill for an armed fist fight, don't you think, Darkness? Swallowing the Shadows squirming up my throat, I square up instead, in case I've actually got to throw punches. "Trust me, you don't want this fight."

Does this stalker take my advice? No. They swing the staff wide toward the left side of my head, assuming again that I'm right-handed.

Bad move, pal.

Quick as a flash, I grab the staff in my left hand, the baseball reflexes I have no use for in the Shadow Plain reactivating. My attacker tries to tug the staff out of my grasp, but I'm a lot taller and stronger. Thinking fast, I kick the person's legs out from under them and tear the staff out of their hands, holding it inches from their face once I've rendered them flat on the ground.

"I told you to back off!" I brandish the staff at its former owner. "Now stay down, or I'll hit you a lot harder than you hit me."

"That was great!" My attacker giggles—you heard that right, *giggles*—and eases themselves up on their elbows. "Keep the staff, you won it fair and square, plus I have another one. What's your name?"

This staff is your one means of self-defense, giggling stalker, and you're just going to ask my name and give it to me? What a moron. If I'm not making a weirded out face, I'll kiss my own— well, you know.

My attacker sits up and takes down their hood before pushing the goggles and gaiter away, revealing their face. It's a kid—an eleven- or twelve-year-old boy. Ashy blond hair, so white it's almost silver, falls in messy curls around a forehead only a shade or two more pigmented than the snow. His over-large, almond-shaped brown eyes stare up at me, showing no trace of fear. He looks a little like I'd imagine Queen might, if she could take human form: round-faced and on the small side, but deceptively strong.

"I'm Elion," the boy says. "But you can call me El. You're tall! I don't think I've ever met anyone as tall as you. They must feed you well, wherever you're from. Where *are* you from? And you never told me your name, even though I told you mine. That's rude."

He's a talker, isn't he?

"I'm Nate." No harm in introductions. Plus, he's the first human I've seen, which means more might be close by, and that's information I could use. Pays to be strategically polite.

El hops to his feet the second I back away, a broad smile stretching almost to his earlobes. "I'm happy I found you, Nate. Why are you wandering around the foothills without snow gear? You won't last long, dressed like that. I'm surprised you aren't dead already."

Darkness can manipulate clothing to look however I want, but I'm not hip to Ictari fashion, so I went with my black-jeans-and-jacket outfit. Should have picked extreme winter gear, if El's clothes are the norm.

"I'm fine," I say. "Cold doesn't bother me that much."

"You have well-developed frost immunity," El goes on. "How old are you?"

How did we jump from snow gear to frost immunity to my age? "Why?"

"Because your face is very young for somebody with excellent frost immunity, and you're practically a giant," El explains.

Practically a giant? I'm tall, but not giant—just a hair over six-three. "Uh, I… grew. My mom was tall, too."

"The only tall people I know are old," the kid says, "because they're wealthy enough to get tall and old in the first place. Are you rich? What does your family do? You don't look like a miner. Are you hunters? Builders?"

El's got a lot of nosy questions, but maybe blunt and direct is normal in this world. It's been my experience that people who want to know your personals right off the bat are typically more interested in proving you're trustworthy than they are in lying about themselves. Since I don't think the charming-and-flirty-ghost act is going to work on this kid the way it did (kinda) with Callie, I'll play it naive with him to get what I need: answers.

"I'm seventeen. That's too young to have a real job. But my dad's an oceanographer, and my mom was an electrical engineer."

"I don't know what those jobs are," El says. No, really? Shocker. "You're seventeen?" He brings his gloved hands in front of his eyes, brows knit in concentration as he counts off something on his fingers. When he's finished, his smile returns. "That's only six years older than me!"

"Uh, yeah." Not exactly sure how I'm supposed to respond to an eleven-year-old doing first-grade math with his hands. "Hey, can you tell me—"

"You never answered when I asked you where you're from, and what you're doing out here." Out of all the questions this kid has word-vomited my general direction, those are the two he's hyper-focused on?

"I'm from… somewhere else. And I'm looking for something." It's evasive, but El doesn't seem bothered.

"Are you a scout, then?"

"Sure." I'm scouting something. Semantics.

"I'm a scout, too!" El's grin takes a rapid downward turn. "This is Aragusti territory. You aren't allowed to scout here, not without a permit. And you don't want patrols to catch you without a permit, trust me."

What's Aragusti? Sounds official, like maybe it could be the name of one of the caverns or caves Queen mentioned. If I play dumb, he might admit how to get inside. I shift on my feet, feigning contrition.

"Sorry, I didn't realize I was trespassing on the private property of your cave," I tell El.

"Cavern," El blithely corrects. Cavern, excellent. Now to find out where the entrance is.

"Okay, cavern." I wave my hand through the air. "What I'm

saying is, there aren't signs posted, and I didn't see an entrance. But if you tell me what I need to look out for, how to avoid any places where I might cause trouble, I'd appreciate the—"

"I have an idea!" If this kid keeps interrupting me, I'm going to rethink my previous statement about ashing people. "We can do a trade."

"A trade?" Trades are potentially beneficial, if I can work the deal to my advantage. Queen's advice about Ictarans honoring promises even to the point of death sticks out in my mind. I plant the end of the staff into the snow. "Explain what you're thinking."

"I was scouting a herd of snow stag before I got distracted watching you," El says. "The wind covered most of their tracks, but I saw the stragglers go into that canyon. If you help me scout them for Aragusti hunters, I'll help you scout whatever you need. That way, if the patrols catch you, I can show them my permit and say you're assisting me."

Yes, score! I've got an insider connection with somebody that could lead me straight to civilization, and maybe has additional information on this world's Light Core. I'd never put it past a kid with a motor-mouth to spill the beans on local secrets, and "scout" me in the right direction. If I've got to put up with him for a hot minute for the sake of the cause, I will.

"Sounds like a fair trade," I agree, carefully adding, "Are you good for your word? Can I trust your promise?"

"I never break promises." Sure enough, El pulls the most stoic face I imagine an eleven-year-old knows how to muster. "You can trust me no matter what."

A slow smile spreads across my face. This is going exactly how I need it to go. El's a much easier target for my manipulation tactics than Callie: he's practically eating from the palm of my hand, and I'm not even trying. "Then it's a deal. I help you scout, you help me."

El grins, and pulls the hood over his head before adjusting his snow goggles and gaiter back into place. "Let's go!"

He jogs into the mouth of the canyon, and I follow.

One herd of deer can't be that hard to find. In the meantime, since El likes to talk, he and I are going to have a chat about any Light Core-esque objects he might have seen lying around.

Everything's coming up roses for Nate. All I can assume is Queen's waiting and watching, planning to throw a major wrench in Callie's plans and secure our upper hand. I hope it's a big wrench. An embarrassing, painful, ugly wrench that makes her wish she'd never lied and betrayed me.

You wanted to play games, Callie? So far, I'm winning.

CHAPTER 6
CALLIE

"LISTEN, I'VE BEEN THINKING about how we're going to bust your sister out of jail, and I've got a couple ideas."

Toran and I pause behind the relative seclusion of the derelict shack, placing our last sacks of rations near the crack in the Gravenskov wall. We've spent all afternoon slinking through alleyways between his abandoned childhood home and the imposing Guide Hall where he lives now, gathering everything he insists we'll need for an extended camping trip across the Hem: a lot of food, canteens, Mist lanterns, bedrolls and blankets, weapons, maps, and lean-to building kits. Oh, and about two dozen books.

We don't need the books. I think he's torturing me on purpose.

I told him once or twice that lanterns are useless (because Light powers), and so is stuff to make tents (because we're camping in Diver, but I neglected to mention the fifty-foot-tall robot thing—my bad). He snapped at me, told me I'm an imbecile who knows nothing about what we're up against, and to let him, the omnipotent Guide who goes into the forest every day, handle the travel preparations. So I shut up and spent most of the time imagining the look on his face when he learns his ride out of murder-town is my humongous, sentient, multiverse-hopping mech.

I hope he pees his pants.

"I will make a plan once we've assessed the situation at the holding cells." Toran drops his sack and scowls my general direction. "Stay out of my way, and only use your skyfire when and how I tell you to use it."

"You're making plans for my powers without involving me? First of all, not cool, and second, no way." Have I mentioned he's insufferable? I'm so stoked for our adventure together. I'm sure we won't get into any fights at all whatsoever.

"I don't trust you to make a plan." You don't trust me, Toran? I had no idea! "I have no faith in your intelligence, as evidenced by that farce with the Volorad earlier, nor do I feel confident in your ability to control your powers. You almost leveled a whole section of the forest."

Who does he think he is, telling me I don't control my Light powers very well? How would he even know? They're my powers, not his. Anyone want to remind me why I need this jerk's help again?

Oh, that's right, he knows how to get across the Hem to the Beacons a lot faster than I do. Probably should refrain from Light blasting him, then.

"I don't appreciate you making decisions regarding my powers, so don't do it, mmkay? And I've totally made plans before." Technically, I made half a plan with Will's help, but it worked, and Toran doesn't need to know the fine-print details.

"Then I'm surprised you're still living," Toran retorts.

"Hi, Rude Toran, so nice of you to insult me. Oh, wait, you've been doing that all day." I drop my sack next to where he's placed his. On top of my loaded backpack, it's pretty heavy, and a relieved sigh escapes once it's gone. Nemo gives my shoulder blades a poke through the canvas and grumble-growls about getting squished, and I hiss over my shoulder, "Chill. Bad time."

"What was that?" Toran demands, shifting his cold stare onto my backpack. "You have a bad habit of speaking to your shoulder."

"It was nothing. Just a quirk I have." Besides, he'll meet Nemo soon enough. I hope he pees his pants twice. "Anyway, I can't properly make a plan until you tell me where they're keeping Heike, and what we're up against in the first place. Are we talking about a simple, jail-type situation, or an armored fortress?"

"You aren't making the plan. But in answer to your question, the former," Toran says. "However, since a condemned prisoner is under watch, there will be increased Volorad around the perimeter, and inside the building, too."

"You're pretty familiar with how arrests and executions work around here." I lean against the shack, a slightly more relaxed position for my weary shoulders. "Are these things frequent occurrences?"

"Fairly." Toran busies himself arranging our supplies in neat, grab-and-go stacks that we can snatch in a hurry later on. "Between the Mist and the forest predators, many things are outside of the Village Council's control in Gravenskov. What they can control, they control with severe consequences for even minor infractions."

"Sounds heavy-handed," I say. "Have there been about a thousand revolts against the whole bogus system, or do people generally fall in line?"

"Most citizens follow the rules for the sake of safety and village prosperity. It's a mutually beneficial obedience, and it's the way things have been done since the Clan Wars forced Assimilation." His book-nerdery never ceases to make him sound like a young, way-less-likable Dr. Ormandi.

"But you and your family don't follow the rules," I observe.

"Not if Heike's sneaking forbidden magic books out of your dad's Archive. The Volorad called your family a bunch of trouble-makers."

"I never set out to break rules like Papa and Heike. But I've become involved in subterfuge in spite of myself." Toran's frame goes momentarily rigid with something like thinly veiled rage—or panic—before the distant boom of bass drums distracts him. "Those are the Night Drums; the work day is over. Curfew will begin, and Mist will flood the streets. There's a very small window of time in which we can act." He saunters out of the garbage piles toward the abandoned street beyond, calling over his shoulder, "Come, sorceress, we're scouting the holding cell."

Sorceress? He won't even consider one of my plans, and now can't be bothered to use my name? Wow—just, wow.

"If we don't wind up dead along with Heike, it'll be a miracle," I mutter, then follow him into a dank alley toward our destination.

The gray sky overhead darkens rapidly as we slip between buildings, careful to remain out of sight of the bustling villagers all making their way home from work and school. Soon, night will fall, and I'll have lost a whole day of Light Core hunting, making sure Toran's sister doesn't get impaled in the morning—a day I can't afford to lose with Nate and his Darkness on my trail.

What could he be up to? Slipping in and out of the shadows like the fake ghost he pretended to be, keeping tabs on my movements until it's opportune for him to strike? I thought for sure he'd have caught up to me by now, but I also expect he'll switch gears tactically. He's way too smart to make the same mistake twice. And, despite what Toran thinks, I'm not dumb enough to fall for one of Nate's schemes again. Fool me once, shame on me—fool me twice, prepare to get your face Light bombed.

Click-click-click-hisssss.

From the rooftops, the distinct sound of the monsters Toran called skuddima punctuate the gathering Mist. Looking toward the eaves of the buildings, I see them weaving in and out of the Mist, their hollow, void-like eyes and mouths sending a shiver up my spine.

"Toran," I whisper to the rigid angles marching in front of me. "Where's your dog? Erm, bjorir?"

"Kiera is kenneled at the Guide Hall. We aren't bringing her, we can't spare the rations." He turns his gaze toward the skuddima, calling to one another above the rooftops. "Keep quiet and out of sight. They'll stay with the Mist, and it's hanging too high to pose a threat."

Why is the fear in his eyes saying something entirely different than his mouth? Not reassuring, Toran, just FYI.

"There's the holding cell." Toran and I emerge from our shadowy alley into a wide village promenade, ducking behind an abandoned vendor's stall to avoid the Volorad, because wow, are those mean, green guys (and gals, Tremurheim seems fairly egalitarian) everywhere. They patrol the open square, keeping watch over a stone building with no windows and only one door towering over a bunch of other municipal-type buildings. A couple kids carrying books — probably on their way home from school — call out to Heike to use her magic to free herself, but the Volorad bark them on their way.

Toran wasn't kidding when he said news travels fast in this town.

"You neglected to mention there's only one entrance." I shoot Toran a withering look. "How do you expect us to get in when the single door is heavily guarded?"

"Skyfire can blast through anything, even people," Toran replies with chilly indifference — as though suggesting I murder about two dozen Volorad is no big deal.

"You want me to Light bomb all those guards?" I shake my head. "My Light protects people from harm, not causes it." He's getting me confused with Shadowmancers like Nate, and their ash-and-destruction powers.

Toran stares at me like I'm a prize idiot, which is his most favorite look to give me. "You know nothing about your own magic. Skyfire destroyed entire Clans and wiped out thousands upon thousands of trees to create the Hem. It's dangerous and deadly."

There he goes again, talking about my powers like he knows more about them than I do. So obnoxious. "Whatever you say, Bookly McGeeknerd," I retort. "Regardless, I'm not killing anybody."

"I told you, I'm the one making the plan," Toran snaps. "And my name is —"

"Let it go, *Toran*." I make sure to emphasize that I know his name, because he can't take a single joke. "Seriously, murdering everyone who stands in the way of that building was your plan this whole time? What is *wrong* with you?"

"Nothing is wrong with me." Toran scowls, offended. "Eliminating the people who would kill my sister is a perfectly reasonable response."

Holy yikes, dude. "It's not reasonable, and it's a terrible plan."

"It's a very good plan," Toran argues.

"Nope. It sucks."

He sneers down his nose, lips curled in a way that is all at once arrogant and cruel. "You have a better plan, then, sorceress?"

"Mind using my name for once? Since I'm a real person, not just a means to an end." I flick his arm with my fingernail. Hopefully, it stings. "It's Callie, by the way. In case you forgot whilst you were busy being a myopic bossy-pants."

"Alright, then, *Callie*," Toran growls. "How do you suggest using your skyfire to save my sister?"

I scan the situation, which is not great. More and more Mist descends from the sky into the promenade, and where there's Mist, there's skuddima. Toran doesn't have a lantern or his deflection dog—er, bjorir. If we want to be able to see what we're doing during this operation, and finish before the Mist swallows us whole, we're going to have to act fast.

"Which one of those Volorad has the keys?" I ask. "Assuming the door is locked, as well as the cell they've got Heike in."

"It'll be one of those two beside the door." Toran points out a set of guards, a man and a tall woman, standing on each side of the imposing entry, pikes at ready. "Good luck getting the keys away from them, they'll be tucked under their cloaks and strapped to their person."

"Oh, I'm not going after the keys. I've got enthusiastic reinforcements." I swing my backpack around, praying this actually works. Unzipping the top, Nemo hops out, shaking his fist and whirring angrily as he spins circles around me. "Yeah, I know, you're miffed," I tell my mech. "I kept you cooped up way longer than we planned, but—"

"Sorcery!" Toran's foot connects with Nemo, sending him flying across the length of the stall, and my buddy lands with a crunch and a screech. A couple of the Volorad patrolling nearby glance at our stall, their eyes narrowed suspiciously.

"What the crap!" This time, I smack the back of Toran's head. "Are you trying to give away our position?"

"How dare you bring your evil magic out in the open?" Toran stews, rubbing his head and backing as far away from Nemo as he can. "Skyfire is dangerous enough, and—"

"Shut up!" I clap my hand over his mouth. "Those guards are *this close* to coming over here." Taking a peek around the stall, I scan the area for immediate trouble. Luckily, the Volorad seem to have forgotten the noise. "We're good. Close call."

Nemo rights himself, wheeling up to Toran with all the rage and righteous indignation a tiny robot can feel, and pinches Toran just above the ankle. Hard.

"Ouch!" Toran grits his teeth and grabs the wound. He aims a retaliatory kick, but Nemo's caught on, and whizzes away quick as a blink. "It just pinched me!"

"And you deserved it." I signal Nemo to my side, and he obliges, shaking his fist at Toran one more time. "Toran, this is Nemo, my mech. Not evil magic, not sorcery, a mech. Got it?" He's totally gonna pee his pants when he sees Diver. "Nemo, this is Toran. He's awful, but unfortunately, he's joining us."

"Why did you let that *thing* out of your knapsack in the first place?" Toran gives Nemo a glare of pure loathing. If Nemo had a tongue to stick out, he would.

"Because he's going to get the keys." I hope. I've never trusted Nemo with a job this big, but there's a first time for everything, right? I turn to my little buddy. "Okay, Nemo, want to play a game?" Nemo nods so hard at the word "game" his head might wobble off his neck. "Do you see those two people wearing green beside the door?" Nemo peers around the stall and nods again. "One of them has a set of keys. Like I use for my car, remember? If you go find the keys in their pockets and bring them to me, you can keep them forever, but you can't let the other green people catch you. Got it?"

Nemo assesses his odds of winning, and nods a third time, wheeling away across the promenade toward the holding cells with a whir of glee. The Volorad cry out when they see him, leaping and screaming about sorcery, jabbing the air with their pikes, but Nemo is too small and fast. Soon, he's climbing up the leg of the guy beside the door, who dances and shrieks like he's got a live squirrel in his pants.

I guess he does, kinda. Teeny mech, squirrel, same-same.

"Okay, now I'm going to use my Light to distract the rest of them into a couple alleys, and we should be clear to run across the square." I stand, readying a Light orb to toss into the alley in question.

"I would like it to be known this is a horrible plan." Toran's whole look right now is best described as a crabby pout.

"Better than your plan, which is mass murder." I toss one Light orb into an alley to our right, then hop to the other side of the stall, make another orb, and send it flying off to the left. Half the Volorad disappear into one alley, the others into the second, and only two extremely confused guards remain, including the guy by the door trying to shake Nemo out of his clothes. "Okay, let's go!"

I leap out from behind the stall, looking epic and cool in my pompom beanie (it's a great hat), only to come face to face with three Volorad—the ones who heard Toran squealing about Nemo.

"Halt, sorceress!"

Have I mentioned I don't like the non-use of my name? I guess these guards don't know it, and won't learn it, because I shriek and run away after a giant burst of Light flies from my hands.

"I told you this was a horrible plan." Toran's ultra-long legs put him a few paces ahead of me, but I'm a fast sprinter and fall in step with him easily. "We almost got caught because of you."

"No way, it's a great plan. I meant to do that." Actually, I didn't, but whatever. Like I'm going to admit it to Toran. I nod toward the Volorad doing his jig in front of the door. "Look, Nemo just got the keys."

My mech topples from the Volorad's swirling cape with a plop, avoiding being stepped on by the other Volorad trying to calm her companion and also skewer Nemo on the end of her pike. He wheels toward me with the keys, jingling them like a prize.

"Good job, buddy!" I scoop Nemo up onto my shoulder. "I just need them to get the door and the cells open, and they're yours."

Nemo gives the keys a hug. At least somebody is happy. Toran and the Volorad beside the door are not. Because pikes and frowns, and yelling at me.

"You're under arrest, sorceress!" Hi, I'm Callie, not sorceress. "Halt!" Who goes there? It's me, Callie! Not "sorceress!"

The Volorad rush Toran and me, and he doesn't miss the opportunity to turn and complain. "Your plan has gone awry."

"We're fine." I call Light into my hands, and send a couple orbs in a swirly dance around the Volorad, who cover their eyes and cower in fear before darting away in the opposite direction. When we reach the entrance, I face Toran with a smirk. "See? Pretty Lights, not murdery."

Toran glowers, beyond pissed that I'm right. Neener-neener, Toran. He snatches the keys out of Nemo's grasp and shoves one in the lock with so much force I'm worried he'll snap it.

"We could have been killed because of you," he mutters under his breath.

"But we weren't." A pause. "That's not the right key, by the way." Another pause. "Oh, and all the Volorad are coming back."

Sure enough, the guards in question have figured out my Light orbs were a harmless diversion, and are barreling toward us with pikes pointed at our hearts, screaming and going on about a sorceress. I've heard that word a lot today. It's getting a little old. Work on the descriptive language, Tremurheim.

"Dramora spawn," Toran mutters under his breath, and I'm pretty sure that's a swear here, but I'm not going to question it, because at least it's not "sorceress."

The Volorad close in further, and I can make out the terrified-yet-furious whites of their eyes. "Can you hurry up?"

Toran narrows his glare, a drop-dead look on his face. "It's your fault we're being pursued. If you'd used skyfire to kill them like I asked, we'd be—"

"Drop the keys! You are under arrest, Toran Rykjiersen, and the sorceress, too!"

There's that word again. This all seems like a lot of dramatic shouting for no good reason, and I'm just gonna point out not everything is a life-or-death, yell-about-it scenario. A stern talking-to suffices sometimes, okay?

Except this is actually one of those life-or-death, shouty times.

"Do something!" Toran shouts (surprise) and almost drops the keys. "Use your magic!"

"I'm not killing anybody, I already told you that."

"This is your last warning!" A big guy with a beard brandishes his pike inches from Toran's neck. "Drop the keys!"

As much as I can't stand Toran, watching him bleed out would suck because one, gross, and two, blood-spatter might get on my pompom beanie, and it's my favorite hat. This world already wrecked my favorite boots with animal poop, I'm not about to sacrifice my hat to Toran's gushing jugular. I know killing these guards is not going to happen, but one or both of us could die if I don't bust out some major Luminaut flex. So I guess I'm using Persuasion. To save Toran. Blarg.

Before the pike can touch him, I leap in front of Toran, channeling the inner Light of the Volorad. "Stop."

Raising my hand, Light shining bright in my palm, I hold tight to the Light of every guard in the square. All at once, they come to a halt, entrancement masking their faces.

"Drop the pikes." Weapons clatter to the ground. These guys

are a lot easier to control than Sean Pettit and Jase—probably because they've spent their entire adult lives being told what to do.

"Order them to turn to pikes on themselves," Toran snarls, finding the right key for the lock at last.

"Can you stop suggesting murder? I've got a better idea." I turn my attention to the Volorad under my Persuasion spell and grin, calling out, "Go line up in the square and do the chicken dance until Morning Drums."

Blank stares. Single cough. Awkward. From the back of the group, I hear a shout. "What's the chicken dance?"

"Yes, what *is* the chicken dance?" Toran looks up from the lock, uncharacteristic confusion etched across his face.

Oh, right. Nobody in this world goes to California weddings, where everyone gets completely sloshed and dances like a bird.

"It's this." I demonstrate the chicken dance for the Volorad. I'm pretty sure Toran wants to curl up and die. Oh, well. Better than being dead for real.

Once my demonstration is over, the Volorad obediently line up and begin performing, and Toran and I slip inside the jail, locking the door behind us.

"Don't ever do that again." Toran is so disgusted it's dripping off of him like big beads of fury-sweat.

"What, save your ungrateful butt from certain death?" I raise a single eyebrow. "Okay, I'll let you die next time, no big deal."

"Intruders! Halt!"

Awesome, more big, green guards with big, sharp pikes, barreling down a set of stairs in our general direction. Yep, par for the course. Tremurheim is so predictable, isn't it?

"Go on, fight them off, since you don't want me to save you." I shoo Toran toward the Volorad. He balls his fists and tries to throw a punch at the nearest guard, but the pikes make it impossible to hit his target. "Looking strong, Toran."

"Stop being snide and help," he demands.

I lean against the wall and check my nails. Dirty, and the polish is chipped. "You don't want my help."

"Callie, I swear, if you don't—"

"If I don't, what?" I call some Light into my hands, sending fierce orbs flying over our heads toward the Volorad, who turn tail and run up the stairs in a flash.

"Run away! Run away!" They're so afraid of my Light, they lock themselves in a cell halfway up the staircase, trembling like rabbits behind the barred door. Not too bright, these ones.

"How do you like them apples?" I raise my other eyebrow at Toran before waggling them both up and down.

Oh, if looks could kill. Toran doesn't reply, he just spins on his heel after giving me the world's nastiest stink eye, and strides up the stairs. "Heike! Where are you?"

"Toran!" A feeble voice cries out. Toran rushes headlong toward it, and I follow. A few cells up, Heike's hand reaches through the bars, her wide eyes filled with relief and tears. "I'm so glad you came!"

"Of course I came." Toran squeezes Heike's shaking, white fingers. "I would never let anyone hurt you. Ever." Taking the keys from his pocket, he lands on the right one first try, releasing Heike from her cell. She leaps into his arms, holding him tight.

"Thank you, brother," she murmurs, clinging to Toran so tight I'm worried she'll strangle him. But Toran doesn't seem to mind, holding her in a way that reminds me of the way Jase hugged me the night I left California. My heart aches, remembering it—how I knew, in that moment, he cared in spite of everything.

"Come, we must go." Toran sets his sister on her feet. "I've hidden some supplies near our crack in the wall. If we hurry, we'll have enough time to—"

"*You* stashed supplies? What am I, a pack mule? I'm the one who made the plan, and it totally worked, despite your best attempts at blackmailing me along the way." I hold out my palm expectantly. "You owe Nemo those keys."

Nemo swipes his claws in a greedy gimme-gimme, and Toran hands the keys to my mech with an eye roll so impressive I'm shocked they don't drop into the back of his skull permanently.

"Callie! You came, too!" Heike smiles, an expression her brother seems to never have mastered, then approaches Nemo, fascinated. "What's that?"

"That's Nemo, he's my —"

"Introduce the creature later." Toran jumps down several steps. "Hurry, both of you, while the Volorad are distracted. We need to be as far from Gravenskov as possible by morning."

"Hello, Nemo." Heike sneaks a friendly pat of Nemo's head, and he whir-squeals with delight. At least one Rykjiersen sibling won't incur Nemo's mighty wrath.

"What are they doing?" Heike stares at the Volorad doing the chicken dance in a conga line cutting across the promenade the moment we emerge into the forbidding nighttime Mist. The near-sentient fog gathers around them, swallowing the very last dancers, but still, they wiggle their backsides and flap their wings dutifully.

"Some idiotic thing Callie taught them." Toran slams the door behind us.

"They won't stop until Morning Drums," I add.

"I think it looks kind of fun," Heike says, attempting to mimic the arm movements. Toran snorts.

"Fun for infants and imbeciles," he grumbles. "We have to depart. Quickly."

"Oh, fine." Heike casts a glance over her shoulder at the Volorad, giggling hysterically behind her hand whenever they do the butt-shake part.

"Hey, Toran, have I mentioned that I've known your sister for about thirty seconds, and she's already way cooler than you?" We skirt the edges of the large village square, making our escape. The alleys across the way somehow—magically?—appear out of the Mist, despite being completely hidden from view just a moment ago.

"What is *cooler*?" Heike catches my eye. Hers aren't glowing like Dr. Ormandi's always did on the rare occasions he used his Seer powers. Huh. Weird.

"It means you're awesome, and smart," I reply, and grin.

Heike's eyes light up at the compliment—just not in the way I expect them to. "Then I think you're cooler, too, Callie."

This girl knows what's up.

"Stop talking." Toran trails behind, his eyes closed tight as a look of concentration creases his brow. What is he doing? And he thinks *I'm* weird?

"You're going to run into a vendor cart or something," I warn Toran. More and more Mist keeps disappearing from our path despite the thick layer descending on the dancing Volorad, but thinning Mist doesn't mean Toran will notice various obstacles in our path. Seriously, he's griped all day about me slowing him up, he picks *now* to walk around with his eyes shut? "Why are you—"

Click-click-click-hisssss.

Oh, yeah, remember those skuddima I saw earlier, floating in the Mist above the rooftops? Well, the Mist is ground level now, which means they are, too. And they're swishing and swirling right in front of us, a whole pack circling us like wolves about to attack their prey.

Click-click-hissssss.

Crap. How are we going to get out of this one? Because I'm fresh out of plans, and something tells me Persuasion doesn't work on skuddima—not even a little.

CHAPTER 7
NATE

"NATE! LOOK OVER HERE! Do you see those tracks? That could be — oh, wait, those aren't tracks, those are just some rocks. Never mind. Hey, I think those things over there are actually tracks! Or they could be pebbles. Let's go look!"

I can guarantee one thing: they're pebbles.

I know I ashed a high school gymnasium roof, joked around about setting my Darkness loose on innocent bystanders, and walked around in Shadowmancer form looking generally spooky. Our true forms are kinda vampiric, unless you're into that sort of thing. But whatever I did that Callie deemed so "monstrous" — overused cliché, by the way, Callie — it wasn't anything bad enough to deserve getting stuck with Elion, The Distracted Golden Retriever as my scout through an endless canyon, hunting down a herd of non-existent deer.

Did Callie somehow have a hand in this? My current scenario seems like some scheming Luminaut crap designed to throw me off my game and put me behind the Light Core hunting power curve.

"El, if there were any stags in this canyon, you scared them away a long time ago yelling about rocks you think look like tracks." I trudge through the snow to the spot where he's inspecting some scattered pebbles (I was right), almost getting blown off my feet by canyon wind in the process. "Let's call it a day and go back to your cavern. Try again tomorrow."

He can try again tomorrow. *I'm* going to ditch this kid the second I get out of the canyon and into his cavern home. No promise to help me find Ictari's Light Core is worth this much annoyance.

Maybe, I'll whack him with his own staff he stupidly gave me and leave him passed out on the ice. Or, punch him in the throat so he can't talk anymore.

There's an idea...

"But we barely started looking!" El protests. Liar, we've been looking for hours. "We're on the right path, I know it." He knows nothing. "Also, my boss in the hunter's guild said don't come back until I find those stags, not unless I want to eat my own ears for supper."

Cannibalism. Right on. "Are there a lot of people rolling around your cavern without ears?"

"No, that was a joke. Nobody actually eats their own ears." El laughs way too loud for someone insinuating he should devour his own body parts. "But he was serious about the stags. The end of this canyon marks the farthest boundary of Aragusti territory, after that, we're in the mountains. Cavern people aren't allowed to hunt there, so we have to find the herd soon, otherwise nobody in Aragusti will eat meat for a while. Then I really *will* be in trouble." He pauses, cocking his head to one side, and points down a narrow side crevice in the canyon wall. "I think they're through there. I heard stag calls. Let's go!"

"You heard the wind, dingus." I pop my collar to shield my neck and earlobes, and trail after El through the crevice pass. It's one tight squeeze. I'm one hundred percent positive no stag could get through it if I hardly can. Even El, who's short and skinny for his age, pushes and pokes just to get past a narrow set of boulders.

"I'm venturing a guess, but I don't think the herd went through the world's smallest crack," I inform El. He turns and lowers his gaiter onto his neck, his bright grin fading into the twilight.

"No, they didn't, I think they're on the other side," he explains. "We're taking a shortcut."

"As in, you have to be short to cut through here?" I stoop as low as I can, sliding under a giant mass of ice, but it still grazes my hair, leaving icicles clinging to the ends. I'd make a pun about frosted tips if I wasn't so irritated and cold.

"That's funny," El laughs. "I'm used to taking my own shortcuts. I forgot you're a giant."

"I'm not a giant."

"If you say so." He dashes through the crevice into a wider part of the canyon, one large enough for a herd of stag to pass without trouble. "Come on, this way."

I finally squeeze out of the crevice myself, looking up at the jagged canyon while I pick ice shards out of my hair. The sky-height walls reaching for the purple-blue sky of sunset, the rock formations and the jagged edges of cliffs coated in ice — it reminds me of a frozen version of something vaguely familiar, something from Earth that's been lost to fog and Shadow. The blue inside the ice is different from ice on Earth, deeper, darker, more like an ocean trapped in a still life. And the way the twilight gleams off the shards jutting toward the sky, making them sparkle... I feel like I'm standing on the edge of something, looking down into the depths of my fate, my *destiny*, unsure whether I'm ready to take the leap — or if I even want to.

Hold on, there, inner-self, back the thought train up a second. My *destiny*? My destiny is to destroy Light Cores, not whatever interlude into Cliché Land that was.

What's going on with me? Why did the strange sensation of peering into the ocean stop me undead (puns!) in my tracks? It felt realer than a dream, more tangible, like I might have actually lived a moment just like the one that washed over me.

Clichés again. I'll stick to puns.

"Nate!"

Go on, El, yell my name so loudly any deer left in this canyon will bolt away in terror. Great scouting strategy, dweeb. If the yelling doesn't spook them into hiding, the way he keeps jumping around like a jackrabbit on a sugar rush definitely will. Whatever memory or feeling came over me vanishes, as though it was never true to begin with—only Darkness swirls through the hollow of my chest.

"Quit shouting!" I hiss, jogging to catch up with El. "Are you *trying* to scare away your meal ticket?"

"You stopped walking and just stood there with a weird look on your face." El shrugs. "I called your name quietly three times. You forced me to yell. So if I lose the stags, I'm telling my boss it's your fault."

He's sassy *and* talkative. Such a delightful combination.

"Why did they make *you* a scout?" I grouch as we meander along. "We've been wandering around all day and I haven't seen anything that remotely resembles a stag."

"I'm a scout because I'm short for my age, and I can squeeze into small places in the canyons and mines other people can't," El replies. "I used to scout in the mountains. I was born there."

"Then why aren't you scouting the mountains now?" Are all mountain scouts noisy, absent-minded, and incompetent, or is it just El?

"I was scouting some rock rams a few sun-cycles ago, and I accidentally wandered into Aragusti territory." I can't see El's face behind his protective gear, but his shoulders stiffen a fraction of an inch—a reaction I doubt he meant for me to notice. "I tried to run back across the border before the patrols caught me, but cavern people have snow cycles, and they drive faster than I can run. They brought me back to Aragusti and put me in the scout guild."

"So they kidnapped you, and forced you into working for them." Tragic backstory: checks out.

"It's not so bad." El has a very different perspective about kidnapping than most people. "Aragusti is the largest cavern on the Ice Field, and they feed me better than they ever did in the mountains."

"You're food-motivated, aren't you?" El gets more puppylike every passing second. Next thing I know, he'll pee on the carpet— erm, snow.

"Of course I am! Don't you like food? It's practically currency in Aragusti." El glances my way, and I see my reflection in his goggles. There's still ice in my hair.

"I could take it or leave it." Considering Shadowmancers don't need to eat. I pick at the accumulated ice, a downside of having extra-thick, wavy hair in a place like this. More surface area to freeze. "Are you sure you should be talking about food when we're busy scouting?"

"Oh, right. I forgot." He forgot? This kid is either massively immature, massively lacking brain cells, or both. Either way, I'm having second thoughts about this "trade."

Finding a Light Core on my own has got to be easier than putting up with El.

"Look! A frost büni!" El skitters across the snow-covered canyon, leaping for what looks like a mousy snowshoe hare cowering in the lee of an ice-encrusted stone. "Catching one gives you good luck!"

As if luck is going to help this scatter-brained doofus. He can chase down his lucky rodent as long as he likes, but I make my own luck, and I'm finished relying on El to get his job done so we can move on to the important stuff: like my Light Core business.

El's back is turned while he hunts around for the "büni," which hopped away, terrified, a while ago. My Darkness reaches for the Veil, and I slip beyond it in less than the space of a blink. It's time to find these stags.

Okay stags... if I was a herd of deer in a canyon, and a loud, annoying child was running around screaming a couple hundred yards away, where would I sequester myself so I could keep as far away from him as possible?

Thinking like one of these snow stags might be simpler than I thought.

Tracking objects through the Veil is much easier inside the canyon than it was on the Ice Fields or the foothills, mostly because not everything in my field of vision is shades of muted white. With very little traversing through the space between the human world and the Shadows, I spot the stags: they're hiding in a bend in the rock, munching on frozen strips of some kind of blue lichen, using their antlers to peel it off the canyon walls. Relative to our location, they're a short distance in the exact opposite direction we've been headed.

Of course they are, what did I expect? That El could actually do his one job? Yeah, and I've got rainbow unicorns flying out my—forget it. How hard would it be to find this secret cavern without El, or one of the mountain caves to explore on my own? The more time I waste with Mr. Distractible, the more squandered seconds slip by—and I risk Callie gaining the upper hand. If I can't get this kid focused up, he's no use to me.

"Nate?" El's muffled voice, calling for me. Swiftly traversing the Veil to his location, I watch, just for a moment, as he whirls around. "Where are you?"

There's panic in his voice, the kind that betrays fear cutting all the way to his core, and I pinpoint his vulnerability in that moment: he thinks he's alone. Not just alone, because he was alone before he met me. He's *abandoned*. It's the raw need of a person who's been left behind time and time again, one that worries he always will be, because outside of his control, the cruel forces of chaos conspire to keep him that way—a force that doesn't care, and never did.

I know that fear all too well… a surge of pain slams into me as those first days and weeks after Mom died worm their way through my brain. Fear just like El's kept me up all hours, raging into my pillow throughout the moonless night… until the second part of the memory washes over me: the part where Dad came in. Even though he was a poor excuse for a grief counselor, his presence meant I wasn't truly alone.

Forget about me, and my memories. Back to El, and his Big Exploitable Feelings.

Alone… abandoned. The question of the hour is, can I somehow manipulate El's fear in my favor?

How would I have toyed with me when I felt that way? Despite my loneliness, Dad was there—sort of. Emotional repression and forgetting was the Ormandi Operandi, but his physical presence remained constant. Maybe El has a memory that doesn't end with being found.

"I was scouting some rock rams a few sun-cycles ago… accidentally wandered into Aragusti territory." He'd tensed up when he said it, a subconscious reaction that reveals a desire to conceal, shove down, and forget.

Interesting. Let's see if a kid terrified of being left behind is willing to spill the beans on his cavern and its secrets more willingly than one who thinks he's got a new best friend.

Emerging from beyond the Veil, I stride toward El just as he's losing his footing on a good spin. "Hey, dork, while you were busy chasing bunny rabbits, I found the snow stags."

"You did?" El's fear melts away as he bounds toward me. "Where?"

"We're going the wrong way," I inform him. "They're back the opposite direction." I let a pause rest between us. "You thought I ditched you? Ran off with your staff and left you close to mountain territory unarmed?"

He winces, just slightly. Ding-ding-ding, we have a winning button!

"Can you show me where you found the stag?" A stiffness invades El's voice that hasn't been there before. I don't need to see his face to know I temporarily struck a nerve.

"Sure." I nod over my shoulder. "This way."

He follows, staying close on my heels, and no surprise, we find the stags in no time flat.

"They were close, weren't they? I can't believe we were going the wrong direction this whole time!" I can believe it, one hundred percent. At least El's keeping his voice appropriately quiet as we sneak up on the stag herd. They're grazing, and show no signs of noticing us, or scattering. "How'd you know where to look? I didn't see tracks."

"I have a sixth sense for these things." It's called the Veil. "You're welcome, by the way. What do we do now? Backtrack to your cavern to notify the hunter's guild?"

"Hang on." El reaches into the pocket of his snow pants and retrieves a little button, sharp prongs like ice hooks attached to the back. He presses it once, and a flashing light starts to pulse before he attaches it to the icy canyon wall. "There. Now the hunters will know where the herd is. Our job is done."

Our job is *not* done, not until the little dweeb holds up his end of our trade. "So, about getting me out of this canyon and back to your cavern…"

"You're really obsessed with my cavern. You should have worn better gear if you're that cold." El and I sneak away from the stag, resuming normal walking and talking once we're a safer distance away. "If you freeze, you'll have to eat your ears."

The "eat your ears" thing must be a turn of phrase around here.

"I didn't plan on taking the world's longest hiking trip through this ice canyon with you," I counter. "It's not like it's easily navigable, either."

"It is when you've been scouting it for four sun cycles." El lowers his gaiter and lifts his goggles, holding back a laugh. "I'm starting to doubt your scouting abilities."

"Ha ha. You're hilarious. What other jokes do you know?" I should ash him for that lip.

"I know a funny joke about a miner who carried an open flame over a gas vent, but I don't remember if it ends with him catching fire or just blowing up the shaft." El taps his chin. "I also don't remember if it was a gas vent or if he passed gas, but either way, there was gas, and a fire, and maybe he died."

"That's not a joke." Unless you consider getting maimed or dying a joke. I come to a halt, catching his shoulder. "Back to business. I held up my end of the trade and helped you scout your stags. Now, you're going to help me."

"I didn't forget. You just wouldn't shut up about getting out of the canyon." Watch it, El. He hops atop a snowy boulder, settling onto his perch. "Tell me what you need to scout."

How to describe a Light Core in language El would comprehend? I pace around a bit, but I can't think too long or El will get distracted and run off at the first sight of another animal, or an oddly shaped rock.

"I'm looking for an ancient energy source." Depending on how they get energy in this world, it might not be too far-reaching a description. "It would glow bright with light when you looked at it, and would resemble a small rod or shortened staff, but powerful enough to destroy whole cities if it fell into the wrong hands." I watch El for any sign of recognition. "Do you know of anything like that?"

El gives his head a scratch and makes a face. "It sounds kind of like the Cornerstone Key, but I don't think it actually exists."

"Cornerstone Key?"

"Yes, it's an Aragusti legend." Thoughtfulness overtakes El's features. "Our cavern oracles say it's the source of all the vents in the earth that give us warmth and water, and that Aragusti's foundation rests on it. It's supposed to be the most powerful thing in all of Ictari."

"Does it make light?" Sounds like a promising lead, but Light is the clincher.

"Nobody living has ever seen it, but legends say it glows with warmth, just like the sun at the top of its cycle, when the snow melts and we can see the ground," El says. "Some oracles think it might even be a piece of the sun itself given to Aragusti by the gods for safekeeping."

Exactly the kind of information I need. If that legend doesn't scream hidden Light Core, I don't know what else does.

"Cornerstone Key." My chin bobs. "If somebody wanted to find said key, where would they look?"

"Why would anybody want to find it?" El asks. "If a powerful object like that exists, it's probably dangerous."

"Asking questions wasn't a part of our trade," I remind him, my voice dropping low, almost threatening. "Stay focused."

"Focused." I can't be sure with his gaiter covering his neck, but I swear I hear him gulp. "According to the oracles, the

Cornerstone Key is supposed to be at the very bottom of the Cursed Mine." El says those two words, "cursed" and "mine," like they aren't a potential wrench in my plans. The only wrenches I want lobbed are ones thrown at Callie.

"Why is the mine cursed?" Depending on the kind of curse we're talking about, I can possibly salvage my exploration.

"There were lots of cave-ins, and fires and ore wyrm attacks, all sorts of unlucky accidents." El shrugs. "Oracles say the miners dug too deep and got too close to the Cornerstone Key, so the gods cursed the mine with bad luck to keep the Key safe."

I can handle cave-ins, fires, and whatever an ore wyrm is. I'm a Shadowmancer of Darkness, not some puny human. "Is that all? Nothing else? Just miners caught in accidents?"

"Yes. That's all. Nobody but the Oracles actually believes the Cornerstone Key exists. It's more like a…" He trails off, his white eyebrows pinched tight.

"Like a metaphor?" I ask.

"No, it's a thing that you say when you want to describe something, but you don't want to use the actual word for the thing," El elaborates.

"How is that *not* a metaphor?"

"Because I don't know what a metaphor is." No surprise. Bet he doesn't know what an idiom is, either. "The Cornerstone Key is just an excuse for mining accidents," El adds. "The oracles only talk about it when the vents are running cold, or when there's not enough water or food."

"A superstition," I suggest, and El nods.

"That's it," he agrees. "It's a superstition."

"Regardless of what everyone thinks it is or isn't," I wave my hands through the air in a way that feels like Dad, "I've been tasked to find it."

El balks for a moment, completely dumbfounded, then, he

laughs. "You're scouting the Cornerstone Key? Even though it doesn't exist and it's just a story, you still believe in it?" He shakes his head, laughter fading. "You're weird, Nate."

"Sometimes stories are more than what they seem," I caution. "Don't discredit everything you hear that seems too strange to be true." Time to play my hand with El. I take a step toward the canyon mouth, shoving my hands in my pockets, and set my jaw, regarding him with a stony chill. "If you aren't going to hold up your end of the promise, whatever. I've got better things to do than waste my time with somebody who doesn't want to help me, even after I helped him."

Spinning on my heel, I march away. Cold, emotionless, nonchalant. I can't even be bothered to glance back.

Three... two... one...

"Wait!" El leaps off his perch, his feet crunching the snow as he rushes toward me. "A promise is a promise, and I'm not going to break mine."

"Really?" I slow down just a little. "Because if you don't believe this Cornerstone Key exists, then—"

"If it doesn't exist, I can at least help you look for the thing it might actually be. An old gem cache, or a vein of rich metal. I've still kept my promise to you." El pants around shallow breaths as he jogs to keep up with my strides. "And if, by some miracle, it actually exists, then I've definitely kept my promise."

I stop, glancing his way as I feign wariness. "So I can absolutely, without a doubt, no-going-back trust you?"

El juts his pointed chin ferociously, brown eyes glinting. "You can trust me. I don't abandon people, or go back on my word."

Definitely struck a nerve. I'm going to keep this trick in my back pocket to use again later. I allow myself a smile—a triumphant leer disguised as sincerity.

"I knew you wouldn't let me down, El." I rub my arms, which

feel frozen solid, and sway on my feet against a sharp blast of wind. "Lead the way to Aragusti. And fast."

Just like that, I'm back on track.

CHAPTER 8
TORAN

SKUDDIMA.

Tremurheim's top predator, more deadly even than dramora. With stealth, good aim, and a well-placed arrow, one can survive a dramora attack relatively unscathed. But nobody, not even the most skilled Guides or vicious Volorad, can make it out of a skuddima's clutches alive. A whole pack encircling you means nothing but certain death.

It's only a matter of when they'll strike.

Icy suction seeks out a victim to latch onto, and even with my eyes closed, I feel them drawing near. The telltale click-hiss just over my shoulder sends the chill of imminent death down my spine.

Click-click-click-hissss.

An otherworldly sound, like bones scraping against each other in a hollow and ghostly mouth. It makes my skin crawl with threads of ice. Another click-hiss, closer this time, gives me the feeling of a disembodied finger tracing the fine hairs on the back of my neck, and sends a tremor through my insides.

"T-Toran," Heike stammers in a whisper. She moves in close, her pulse hammering so loud and fast I hear it as though it were my own. "What are we going to do?"

"He can start with opening his eyes." A snap of fingers right next to my ear, and if I didn't know opening my eyes would be disastrous for everyone, I would snatch Callie's hand and break every single finger. "Toran, wake up, you silly sleepyhead."

"I'm not asleep," I growl through clenched teeth. "Shut up."

"Are you sure you're not sleepwalking?" Of course I'm sure, ridiculous sorceress. "Because there's half a dozen monsters that are going to eat us."

Callie James can become a skuddima's supper for all I care. I hope they take her, in fact. It would save me yet another headache or embarrassment at her expense. Right after she gets us out of Gravenskov, she and her skyfire can shrivel up and die—the last thing I want to do is owe her a trip to the Beacons. But we have to survive the attack before I can get out of her debt, and if there's as many skuddima in the pack as she claims, we're done for.

"Be quiet." I bat her hand away from my ear. "They hunt by sound."

"Explains why they don't care about the Volorad," Callie whispers.

The Volorad—silently dancing, except for—

Clap-clap-clap-clap.

The Volorad make no sound, except for the clapping part of the dance.

Like a rush of freezing wind, the skuddima whirl away, sensing far easier, more plentiful targets in the entranced Volorad than they do in us.

Exactly the distraction I needed. Perhaps Callie's chicken dance was not so useless.

"They're gone." Heike touches my arm, followed by the light, gentle squeeze of her fingers. "Open your eyes, Toran." But I shake my head.

"Too Misty," I murmur. Another squeeze from Heike, firmer

this time. "I'll be fine, I know my way. We need to run for it."

"I understand."

"Crap, they're going for the Volorad." Why Callie sounds dismayed—panicked, even—I have no idea.

"Good." Mist draws closer, enveloping us in its murky grasp. With the skuddima distracted, it's the perfect time to escape. "Let's be off."

"Those people are sitting ducks," Callie counters. Lands Beyond, what is she talking about now?

"They can't be people and also ducks, whatever a duck is." Does she not realize how stupid she sounds, or does she not care?

"They're not actual ducks, it's—never mind." She sounds annoyed for some reason, as though explaining something to a child.

"If you were halfway intelligent, you'd acknowledge your 'plan' for getting Heike out of prison was inanely childlike, and we're lucky as a fat old bjorir." I pause, trying to sense a gap in the Mist to aid in our retreat. Ah, there. I motion with my hand toward our route. "Head through the Mist that way. It's clear."

"The Volorad are terrified of being eaten alive, but they can't move because of my magic," Callie argues.

"I don't care how they feel, I want my sister and I to escape this village alive." Escaping was the crucial part of our arrangement, but obviously, Callie forgot that detail. Unsurprising. She's the type that would forget to breathe if it wasn't instinctual.

"Leaving a couple dozen people under my Persuasion, unable to move or defend themselves as they chicken-dance their way into a skuddima's gaping mouth-hole was never part of my plan."

I don't like where her argument is headed. "As we've established, your plan was horrible. Now we're doing my plan, which is to leave. Immediately."

Callie doesn't respond. The only sound or sign of reply are her footsteps pounding the stones beneath our feet, growing fainter as she dashes off.

"Where is she going?" I ask Heike, although a sick feeling in my gut tells me I already know the answer. I just don't want to believe she could be that idiotic.

"She's running toward the Volorad." Heike's anxious proclaimation lands like a boulder in my stomach. "You have to help her. She's going to get herself killed."

Daughter of dramora spawn, Callie James is as worthless as she is troublesome.

"Let her die. We can survive in the forest without her help, and find a new village on our own like Mama and Papa." I refuse to open my eyes as I pull Heike forward, using the movement of the Mist to guide my steps. A thick pocket to my left means it's thinner to the right. Sure enough, it parts easily. "Come. She's doomed. We aren't."

Heike refuses to budge. It's a terrible time for my sister's stubborn streak to emerge. "She saved my life, Toran."

"Her assistance was useful," is all the credit I'll give Callie's foolhardy plan, if you can call such nonsense a plan. "But we don't have to sacrifice our lives for her."

"Just open your eyes, and do what I know you can do." Heike grasps my hand, which has gone cold, almost frozen. "It doesn't matter who sees anymore. You have to help save Callie. She'd save you."

And save me she did, when a Volorad's pike was aimed at my neck. She didn't appear happy about it, although I suppose I'm not happy about the prospect of saving her from her foolishness, either. But if I fail—if everything I've worked to conceal and suppress leads to the worst consequence of all...

"I don't want to lose control," I tell my sister.

I hear Callie yelling at the Volorad to stop dancing and save themselves, and in a matter of moments, she will be gone, either impaled on a pike, or sucked dry by skuddima, her body a husk left to wither on the ground. Helping her instead of fleeing means that horrific fate could just as easily befall me — or, Heike.

"You won't, and you know it," Heike says, a promise dwelling deep in her words. "Please, Toran, Callie is going to get hurt."

I don't like it when Heike asks for something in that tone, because we both know that no matter what she asks, I'll comply, even though I might come to regret giving in.

A resigned sigh passes over my lips, the last breath I'll take in hiding. "So be it."

As soon as I open my eyes, the Mist concentrates around me, filling my vision until it burns through my entire mind. The Mist and I become one as easily and quick as a heartbeat, and with a flick of my wrist, it clears a wide margin on either side, obeying the movement of my hands, my unspoken will. Now that I can see the situation before me, I assess what needs to be done. Heike dashes off, taking cover behind a vendor's stall — smart. Callie, on the other hand, stands in the midst of the square, her skyfire flashing through the blanket of Mist. Reflections of shrieking skuddima and roaring Volorad, their pikes silhouetted against the flare, mean Callie has lost control of the situation.

No surprise whatsoever.

Wordlessly, more instinct than command after almost a whole Season of practice, I call the Mist into my hand. It freezes solid the moment it contacts my skin, extending from my fist in a long, pointed pike like the Volorad carry.

It's now or never, I suppose.

"Callie James!" I call for her, parting the thickly gathered Mist with a sweep of my hand. At the sight of me, the Volorad stop and stare, the skuddima turn their attention to a new target, and Callie's face falls with a groan of dismay.

"Ugh, *seriously?*" She tosses her hands, burning with skyfire, into the air, sending the two skuddima who'd been about to attack her flying away, shrieking. "Crabby McScowlsalot is a Seer?"

"Sorcerer!" The Volorad remember they're supposed to be attacking, since Callie broke her spell causing them to dance, and charge me, pikes in hand. The skuddima flying toward me change the direction of their flight, and attack the Volorad instead.

"Sorcery. That's the correct word," I tell Callie. She rolls her eyes, lobbing a ball of skyfire at the skuddima threatening the Volorad.

"No, dummy, you're a Seer. A Water Manipulator, if I had to venture a guess. Let's be real, the ice sword and the neon blue glowing-eye-thingy were a dead giveaway." Her mech — Nemo is its stupid name — clings onto her ugly egg-hat whilst shaking a fist at the skuddima as they soar past. "It's really been *you* this whole time? I thought your sister was the one with powers!"

"You assumed incorrectly. And it's a pike, not a sword." I wield the weapon in question, taking a swipe at a few Volorad who turn tail, crying out as more skuddima beset them. Callie aims a blast at the monsters, letting it fly.

"Well, that sucks. Your sister is awesome, you're terrible." At the sound of her voice, skuddima click-hiss their way toward her, but she deflects them easily. "Hey, did you know Light orbs scare those things off?"

"And did you know sound makes them attack?" I engulf an approaching group of Volorad in a cloud of Mist so thick they'll never be able to muddle their way out. "Stop talking."

"Oh, right, you said that earlier. Guess I wasn't paying attention." She prepares more of her skyfire for defense. "I'm totally the person who dies first in a serial killer movie."

"That makes no sense." She'll be lucky if she doesn't die first, but I have no idea what a movie is, or a serial killer. "Be quiet."

"You be quiet, jerk-face," she counters, letting loose more skyfire onto the skuddima swooping over our heads. "You're talking just as much as me."

"I'm not talking, I'm telling you to shut up." I send a thick cloud of Mist flying toward the Volorad to my left, all of them screaming for my arrest, as Callie keeps the skuddima distracted. With all the noise, the creatures don't know who to attack first.

"Did you hear yourself say the last sentence that just came out of your mouth?" She faces me, blinking hard like she did in the forest. As if she has time to stand there and blink like an addled nargush.

"Of course I did," I answer. "Stop talking and start moving away from this mess."

"Everyone talking all at once seems to confuse them" Callie nods toward the skuddima, darting this way and that with no person to settle upon in the melee of skyfire, Mist, and shouting Volorad. "Maybe we should talk a little more."

"No." I shake my head, controlling the Mist with one hand, pike with the other as I try to ascertain our next move in the midst of the chaotic fray. "The plan you made almost killed us."

"Almost isn't the same as definitely." She grins. "As of this moment, we're alive."

"Barely." I swing my pike at an approaching Volorad, who one moment screams for my execution, and the next screams about not killing him with my ice sword. Why do people keep calling it a sword when it's clearly a pike? "If I didn't know any better, I'd say you were trying to keep me talking on purpose."

"For a dude who likes to tell other people to shut up, you're really bad about doing it yourself." Callie smiles, as though I've finally caught on to some joke she's amused herself with. "Look, the skuddima are flying away, so really, we've only got to worry about the Volorad now."

Glancing around the market promenade, I notice — to my chagrin — she's not wrong. Not that I want to deal with skuddima, particularly, but Callie being right about something means she will taunt me about it. Sure enough, her obnoxious mech points at me and makes a laughing noise. I will crush that creature under my boot the first opportunity I have.

"We need to find Heike, and make for the alleys," I say.

"Got it." Callie holds her glowing hands before a group of Volorad, the flare growing brighter until they are forced to turn the other way. "Where is your sister, by the way?"

From out of the Mist, two arrows zip by, punctuating the air with a sharp *ssszzz* sound. One disappears into the dark of night, hitting nothing, but the other flies too close to an unsuspecting Volorad, grazing the man's arm. He cries out, grabbing the wound, but not before a smattering of blood spills to the stones beneath his feet. Several Volorad encircle him, ushering him away from the scene, looking over their shoulders as their numbers dwindle further. And yet, we're far from safe.

Blood on the ground means skuddima will fly back, and attack.

"Yes! I got him!"

"Lands Beyond, Heike! What are you thinking?" I rush toward my sister across the square. She's holding a Mist lantern and a crossbow in her hands, and smiling in a way that fills me with dread.

"Don't be so dour, Toran," Heike says. "I don't have magic like you and Callie, so I need a crossbow and a lantern."

"Where did you find a weapon?" I grab the bow roughly from her hands, strapping it to my belt at my waist. "You don't even know how to use this."

"Yes, I do, I've been practicing. I hit that Volorad in the shoulder." She grazed him. A mere knick. "Anyway, I took it from the Guide Hall."

"The Guide Hall is locked for the night," I mutter.

"Oh, yes, I know. I snuck in through the kitchen window at the back."

Callie laughs behind my shoulder. "Petty theft for the win." She holds her hand up for Heike, palm toward my sister's face. "High five, you're awesome."

"I, um—" Heike stares at Callie, confused. "What a, uh, lovely hand."

"Never mind." Callie looks around at the few Volorad remaining in the promenade, all of them dashing about in the rapidly accumulating Mist as it gathers in the square. "These green guys with the pikes turned out to be kind of a letdown in terms of villainous opponents, didn't they? I'll call for Diver to meet us, and we can bail."

"Does bail mean leave?" I don't know who or what a Diver is, but nobody will be "bailing" anywhere if skuddima catch up to us. I scan the sky, wary of the monsters I know will descend the moment they catch the scent of blood on the stones.

"Yep, we're totally out of here." Callie closes her eyes with a look of concentration, then nods toward an alley to our left. "He's on his way. Come on, Toran the Cranky Seer."

"It's called 'sorcery', not 'Seer', and you don't get to say 'come,' I am making the plan." I march past her, bumping her shoulder in the process. Unfortunately, Nemo does not go flying into the Mist like I had intended, and both Callie and Nemo grumble and make violent oaths. Dramora spawn. "Our best chance to escape alive is to disappear into the alleys. Come. We depart."

"You know, your plan isn't super great or anything," Callie

says, trailing after me as I create a tunnel through the Mist, one that closes immediately behind us. I can't risk the remaining Volorad pursuing us, despite the danger the Mist presents.

"You have yet to follow my plan, and therefore, can't pass judgment," I argue.

"Yeah, okay, whatever."

"My shoes are sticky." Heike trails just behind Callie, scraping her shoes against the stones as we move through the narrow alley.

"Did you step in poop, too?" Callie flashes my sister a sympathetic look. "I did earlier, and it ruined my favorite boots."

Why does she feel the need to constantly mention excrement? Disgusting.

"No, it's not that." Heike stops, thin lantern light bobbing as she stoops to inspect the source of her tacky soles. "It's... red."

Click-click-click-hissss.

My heart turns to motionless stone, dropping toward my toes at the sound of the skuddima over my shoulder. "It's blood."

The blood from the Volorad's wound—Heike must have stepped in it.

"T-Toran," my sister stammers, backing away from us. My legs turn to frozen statues against the will of my panicking body. "There's a—a—"

Click-click.

I whirl around, coming face-to-face with a gaping mouth, opened to reveal nothing but putrid rot, sucking the air near my face with ferocity. A skeletal, almost featureless white head with a floating, gray-black body, and eyes like unblinking voids. Something truly born of nightmares.

Groooooooaaaannnnnn.

"Toran!" Heike screams. The arrow she fires whizzes past my ear, but passes through the skuddima with no effect.

"Dude, use your powers!" Callie cries.

The sucking intensifies as the skuddima nears my mouth, trying to pry my soul from my body, to enter it and consume me slowly from the inside out. Every part of my insides—heart, lungs, and bone—presses tight to my skin, drawing me further into the creature's sphere until I stumble, my eyes clouding with hypnotic darkness, and I start to lose sight of where the skuddima begins and I end.

"Ahh!"

Heike's shriek cuts the Mist and Darkness, distracting the skuddima at my throat. The specter lifts its head, looking for the source of the noise: two more skuddima beset my sister.

"Heike!" Somehow, my voice still works. I reach for her, trying to break the creature's grasp that roots me to my spot, but she's impossible to reach. One moment more, and we'll both be dead.

Death by skuddima is a horrible way to go.

"Oh, for the love of Pete," Callie grumbles. Her hands glow even brighter, blazing until the skyfire burns away the Mist in the alley. She moves her fingers in a circle and draws a bright ball into being, throwing it at the skuddima latched to Heike before directing it onto my attacker with a flick of her wrist.

Aaaaiiiiiiieeeeee!!! Away the skuddima fly, terrified, toward the rooftops. Air fills my chest, my heart slows to its normal beat, and I am whole and my own once more.

"Who's Pete? Do you really love him?" Heike asks Callie, picking herself up off the ground with the type of enthusiasm and nonchalance you wouldn't expect from somebody who was about to become a skin husk.

Pete can go stick his head in a nargush nest, for all I care.

"No," Callie laughs, "it's—"

"It's useless banter, and we're leaving." Before more

skuddima return, preferably. As we approach the end of the alley, I shoot Callie a glare. "Your skyfire could have blown my head off. Heike's, too."

"Oh, gosh, Toran, you're so humble but really, the gratitude is unnecessary, you're very welcome for saving your life again." She's being sarcastic, she has to be. There is no way I'm about to be gracious to somebody like her.

"I'm not going to thank the person who's done nothing but put mine and my sister's life at risk multiple times, all because you are stupid, careless, and irresponsible." Emerging from the safety of the alley, I part the Mist flooding the street, checking for Volorad, skuddima, or random citizens wandering around after Night Drums. Everything is clear.'

"Careless and irresponsible are the same thing, book geek," Callie retorts with a smirk. "If you're going to insult me, you could at least be clever about it."

"Careless and irresponsible are *not* the same thing." I sneer down my nose. "If you read more, you'd know the difference."

"Don't argue so loudly," Heike says, falling in step with Callie and me on the wide street. She holds her lantern high, peering through the Mist with a wary gaze. "We don't know that the Volorad didn't—"

"Halt, sorcerers! You're under arrest!"

No less than a dozen Volorad pour around the street corner. Half have lantern hooks attached to the end of their pikes, clearing the Mist from the edges of the buildings and crevice-like alleys; the other half brandish their pikes, moving in to strike.

"Hey, the green guards got reinforcements," Callie notes wryly. "Maybe they're better villainous types than I gave them credit for."

Before the Volorad can reach us, I call the Mist toward me and sweep my hand wide, freezing it into a solid wall of icy pikes a hairsbreadth from the noses of the first flank of guards charging our way. They cry out, coming to a stop just before they impale themselves on the deadly diversion.

"Ice wall? Really?" Callie fixes me with a derisive stare. "You didn't think to do that when the skuddima were sucking your face, and your sister's?"

"You try to concentrate your magic when—"

"Stop arguing and run!" Heike takes off at a sprint toward the other end of the street, and Callie and I follow.

"Heike's right, you know," Callie pants around pounding footfalls. "You argue with me too much."

"You're the one who starts the arguments," I—ironically—argue. "If you were more than halfway intelligent, I wouldn't have to—"

"Halt, sorcerers! You're under arrest!"

We skid to an abrupt standstill as more Volorad pour around another street corner to our right, lantern light reflecting in their humorless eyes.

"Same line, wow, it's like they have a script," Callie says.

Absolute nonsense. This is why she starts so many arguments. No concept of when to keep her mouth shut.

"Hey, Crankypants, want to erect another killer ice wall?" Callie suggests, gesturing to the Volorad charging up the street.

"Silence!" I'm running out of ways to say *shut up, be quiet, and stop talking,* all of which she blatantly ignores or doesn't comprehend. I form long spines of Mist along the stone street leading toward the Volorad, a forest of frozen teeth rising from the earth.

"You're pretty good with your Seer powers," Callie remarks as we dash off down yet another alley. "Practice much?"

"More than you."

"Look!" Heike points toward the end of the alley just as Callie is opening her mouth to make some asinine reply. "Our secret escape."

Forest spare me, it's about time we arrived back at the garbage-encrusted alcove hiding our supplies. In a matter of moments, we'll be through the wall and away from Gravenskov forever, where nobody can harm me for having magic ever again. Nobody can accuse my sister of having it in my stead. I'll be free to find somewhere new to start life over, learn even more control and concealment of my magic, and forget every bad thing that happened to my family in this village because of it. Heike and I will be truly safe. Perhaps, one day, we'll even reunite with Mama and Papa—a whole family once more.

"Crap, dude, they found us?"

Callie's pronouncement accompanies the swaying lights and clattering pikes of the Volorad, charging toward our escape route from either side of the street. I gather as much Mist as I can from above, encasing our supplies and exit in a barrier of ice, but our pursuers pick at it with their weapons, sending chunks flying.

"Don't worry, Diver's almost here," Callie assures me. I am assured by absolutely nothing she says.

"You've neglected to mention who or what a Diver is," I point out her obvious omission, focusing my magic on filling in and repairing the gaps made by the Volorad chipping away at my ice blockade, and the skuddima flying through the Mist overhead. "Is this Diver coming quickly?"

"*Very* quick, I hope," Heike adds, casting a leery look at the skuddima. She holds her lantern high, taking the crossbow from my belt in case any Volorad sneak past the ice. We don't have as much time as I'd like, and with all the supplies to gather and get through the crack in the wall... we need nothing short of a miracle to escape unscathed.

Thud. Thud. Thud.

"That'll be him." Callie smiles brightly, as though anticipating the arrival of an old friend. Even the awful mech Nemo claps its horrid claws.

"Him?" Heike scowls.

Thud. Thud. The ground beneath my feet rumbles.

"What's happening?" I look at Callie. "What new magic is this?"

Her smile turns mean, and she says with far too much glee, "Try not to pee your pants when you see him, okay?"

Thud. Thud. CRUNCH.

A boom like I have never heard tears the air, scattering the Mist, as thousands of splinters rain down upon us and the Volorad. The skuddima scatter in horror, and an entire section of the Gravenskov wall rises from the ground, dangling in midair. I turn my neck to see what was once Gravenskov's protective barrier uprooted in the hands of a giant creature made of ore, steel, and glass, one whose domed head glows with two unblinking eyes, zeroing in on me with frightening precision.

The Volorad forget my ice barrier and flee without looking back, their lanterns disappearing into the Misty night until all that's left beside the remains of the village wall are me, Heike, and Callie, standing at the foot of the most horrifying thing I have ever beheld.

"Hey, buddy!" Callie greets the giant creature with a warm hug around its ankle. "Thanks for coming. I hope the hike through the woods wasn't too rough on the knees. We've got to get out of murder-town in a hurry, are you up for hike number two?"

"W-what is that thing?" Heike stares at the beast in awe, approaching it with caution. I would stop her, but I'm too terrified to move, frozen in place like my magic has turned against me, and I've become solid ice.

"This is my World Diver." Callie looks more than a little pleased with herself. "Meet your one-way ticket out of

Gravenskov, Toran."

What in Lands Beyond have I gotten myself into?

CHAPTER 9

NATE

"THERE GOES THE HUNTING PARTY. We're close to Aragusti now."

A pack of things that look like sleds and snowmobiles morphed into a winterized motorcycle speed across the snow a short distance away, having appeared out of thin air, because I can't see anything on the surrounding plains of white that remotely resembles a road, highway, garage, or outpost. A couple of the drivers spot El and raise their arms in greeting, whooping loud. He waves back.

"Sorry, I guess I missed your cavern entrance in all this frozen nothingness." Another visual sweep of the plains reveals they're even flatter and more barren than I'd previously assumed.

El snorts like I'm the idiot in this scenario. "Because it's hidden. Don't you know anything? A visible entrance means mountain scouts can spot Aragusti and launch attacks."

"Pardon me, El the Cavern Expert, but I'm not from around here and I don't know how you snow geniuses do things." This kid and his lip. Belligerent, that's what it is. Belligerent and churlish.

El lowers his gaiter despite the strong wind, and smiles. "We're here."

Uh—where? "There's nothing here, dork."

"Not yet." El crouches, sweeping some snow away from a keypad I would never have noticed. On closer inspection, a tiny antenna with a lightbulb on top rises a fraction of an inch above the snow, blinking intermittently, and the frosty white in the immediate area has sunk ever so slightly beneath the landscape around it.

"I know what to look for now, the little light and the slight indentation of the snow," El says. He taps a code into the keypad, and steps back. "When they brought me here from the mountains, I couldn't remember the code. Hunters had to let me back in. I almost froze to death a few times."

"Thank your lucky little stars." El, forgetting something? Is water wet? It would be more shocking if he actually *remembered* something for a change. "Do you know the code today? Or are you still working through your near-fatal inability to recall numbers?"

"I just—I don't learn numbers and letters very well," El explains with a bit of a wince. "I forget what letter came before the last one I just saw, and when I go back to check I lose track of everything I was trying to learn in the first place. But once something's in my mind, it's there forever. I'm not stupid."

Sharpness pricks my useless heart, a strange emotional reaction to El's admission that gives me temporary pause. If he's dyslexic, or something like that, it's not cool I made fun of him, and kept calling him an idiot behind his back. How often was I made fun of for things outside of my control? A lot, actually. You'd think people would've had an iota of compassion and not teased me about having a dead mom sob story, but you'd be wrong.

"Look, El," I say, "I didn't mean—"

The deafening groan of metal echoes in the frigid air, breaking through the oppressive wind to dampen the screeching gales. A hidden hatch-door opens, revealing a ramp leading down into the earth. It's as wide as a four-lane highway, and the mouth of the opening steams with geothermal heat.

Sulphur—noxious. Of course this place reeks of the quintessential minerals and gasses that make geysers smell like rotten eggs.

"Are you sure this isn't Mordor?" I dry-heave against my will, a human reaction I haven't had since I was Turned.

El cocks his head. "Is that where you're from? Mordor?"

Darkness help me. "No. It's from a book—you know what, never mind."

El smiles like he's teaching Advanced Placement Odors and I'm his naive pupil. "You'll get used to the smell of the vents. It took me a while, but I don't notice them now."

"That's not reassuring," I say. "Haven't you been stuck here for four sun cycles?" Assuming that's a year, or some equally long increment of time.

"Step forward!" From inside the mouth of the entrance, a voice barks orders. "And prepare to present permits!"

El strides down the ramp, removing his thick gloves before whipping a small wallet from his pocket, and I follow. Once my eyes get adjusted to the dim light, I notice two men standing at attention up ahead—probably the patrol members El mentioned in the canyon. Burly guys, short but broad, in gray uniforms. Dotting their exposed hands and neck are glowing, red-orange ovals, like glow worms embedded just under the skin: a body modification El clearly doesn't have.

"Hello, Orio," El greets one of the two men.

"Elion." The person I suppose is Orio steps forward—left-facing, the burlier of the two—and takes El's wallet, looking over the contents with an almost lazy lack of care. "Found the stags, did you?"

"Actually, my new friend, Nate, did," El replies. "He's a scout, too. He doesn't have a permit, he lost it in the snow like a dümfo. But he's with me."

Dümfo? Is that some kind of insult? That little punk, I should—

Actually, that's not a bad bit of strategy on El's part. Smarter to just play along. I pull a grin for the patrol guys, wide and just a bit crooked. "Sorry, the stupid thing blew out of my hands." I shrug, scratching the back of my hair. "What can I say? My bad."

The two patrol guys look between themselves, shaking their heads, and return El's permit. "New and returning scouts need to register at the guild within the hour," Orio says.

"I know." El pockets his wallet. "I'll take care of it."

"Be off, then." Orio waves El and me along.

El skitters down the rest of the ramp, and behind us, the gigantic door lowers back into position, shutting at last with a thud. Along the wall, lights flicker on, a strip of them appearing at our feet to light a path as we travel deeper underground. The snowy plains and unceasing winds disappear, and in their place, sticky heat. It's like going from the arctic to a tropical jungle, except there aren't any plants or animal life: just rocks, steaming vents, and rows and rows of stalactites dripping condensation, a gaping mouth of endless fangs over our heads.

"We'll stop at my place first." El begins shedding his snow gear, revealing a patchy, threadbare jumpsuit that's two sizes too big for him underneath. "I'll pick up my mine scouting supplies, and the extra food packs I'm going to get paid for finding the stags. Then we'll—"

"Didn't that guy just say you had to report to the scout guild?" I remind El. He blows a raspberry.

"I'm not doing that." A sly grin creeps across his face. "I never tell the scout guild anything. None of the scouts do. I just said that so Orio wouldn't report you."

Semi-impressive subversion. Better keep an eye on that.

At the end of the tunnel, heat from thousands of vents slam into me, and below, a giant cavern-town materializes—an entire city taking up every square inch of the hole in the rock and soil. Streets, concrete and metal box-houses, tall buildings, short buildings, wires for electricity, steam powered street cars, and small gardens of vegetation growing under artificial sunlight on the roofs of the homes. Giant flood lights are placed every few blocks, rising toward the roof of the cavern to bathe the city in the strange glow of perpetual midday, the surroundings made artificially bright.

"Watch out for random vents going off," El cautions as the ramp finishes its descent, and gives way to the narrow streets of Aragusti. "If you're standing over one and it erupts, you'll burn your butt."

"Does that make you the *butt* of every joke?" *Butt* of the joke, get it? Ha! I slay me.

El looks inordinately confused that I'd be grinning right now. "Uh, yes. I got blasted a lot when I first came here. It hurts, it isn't funny."

El, just go about your business and give me my puns, okay?

"Elion!" From atop the roof of a square concrete home with a heavy metal door, a woman stands, hands on hips. The orange-red glowing things I noticed on the patrol guards go all the way up her exposed arms. "You better get inside before the other boys eat your payment for those stags."

"They already dropped off my box?" El's face falls, dismayed.

"As soon as the signal came in," the woman says. She turns back to her rooftop garden, the frail vegetable stems composing her crop grazing the hem of her drab jumpsuit-turned-dress.

"You'll be lucky if any is left for you. Caro will fill his greedy stomach before you can eat your ears."

"Thanks, Marini." El grouches some words I'm going to assume are Ictari cussing and barges into an even tinier, more decrepit house next door to the woman's.

Sure enough, an open box sits in the center of a sparse room, furnished only with trunks and double bunks with the world's most derelict stove rusting in the corner. A group of three boys, a little older and bigger than El, are distributing packets of food amongst themselves. More orange-red things, in intricate patterns on their arms, brightly illuminate their faces and the otherwise lightless room, making El's lack of the phenomena even more apparent. They stop and sneer when they spot him seething in the open door.

"Drop it now, Caro, that's mine," El threatens, pointing his index finger at the packets of food.

"First to find the food gets to keep it. Should've got home faster, dümfo," one of the boys — the oldest and largest — laughs derisively. "Are your feet as slow and stupid as your head now? Or is it because you can't see in the dark, and got lost?"

That kid's kind of awful, isn't he? Who are these kleptomaniacs, anyway? El's housemates? Where's the adult in this scenario? They let middle-schoolers live alone without supervision?

"I earned those packs fair and square." El snatches a bag, which resembles camp food, away from one of the boys, a skinny kid closer to the door. "And I'm not stupid."

"You're so stupid you can't even read your own name," the big kid, Caro, taunts. "The box doesn't say 'Elion,' it says 'Caro, Piku, and Niro."

"No, it doesn't say that. It says my name right on the side." El strides through the dim house toward Caro, grabbing the edge of the food bag. The light from the kid's glowing arm-marks bounces off El's livid face. "Give it back, now."

"Make me," Caro retorts, pulling the bag out of El's grasp. "You're too short to take me in a fight, and you know it."

As if physical type has anything to do with it. I was told I was too tall and slim to make a decent catcher, and more than a couple coaches were eating crow by the time Division I scouts had me on the radar. They underestimated me, just like these kids are underestimating El. Well, I know firsthand how hard he swings. Definitely strong enough to bust that kid's ugly face.

What is this, sympathy? Empathy? It's too human, that's all I know, and why it's never a good idea to remain in human form for long. Become too human, and my focus starts to slip—which means I risk losing the game. I press my back against the doorframe, swallowing (metaphorically) the sticky emotions.

"I might be short, but I'm not as weak as you think I am," El snarls, and grabs for the bag again. Caro holds it up and away.

"We don't *think* you're weak, we *know* it," one of the boys across from Caro replies, tugging at the back of El's jumpsuit while Caro dangles food in front of El. "You're a scrawny dümfo outsider. Go away and die in the mountains already."

Okay, that's it. I've had it up to here with these bullies. They're holding El up, and it's wasting my time.

"Hey!" All eyes in the house fall to me as I duck under the door, taking advantage of how intimidating my height is compared to theirs. "Listen up, you little punks, because I'm only going to say this once." My eyes fall to Caro, the lead snot-wipe, and I tower over him menacingly. "Give El his stuff."

Caro tries to look like a tough guy in front of his pals, but the flash of fear in his eyes is unmistakable. "Who do you think you are, wyrm pus?"

I lean in, letting the Darkness rise as far as my eyes. The rest of the bullies and El can only see my back, but Caro's face pales at the sight of the glowing red and black, the Darkness behind my gaze hypnotizing him into a terrified stupor. "I think I'm somebody you don't want to call wyrm pus again."

Caro can't drop El's food packs fast enough. He practically throws them at El's chest before backing as far away from me as the tininess of the house allows—into the farthest corner by the stove, where his uncontrollable shaking rattles the metal sides. Repressing my Darkness, fully in human form, I turn and face the other boys, all of them staring at me with trepidation.

"Anybody else wanna take a shot at me?" I spread my hands, inviting them to try. "Or do you want to make the right decision?"

The other two boys drop El's packets without a word and retreat.

"Thanks, Nate." El pats my shoulder gratefully, and it's the first time a human has touched me with affection since Callie and I—

Stop giving in to emotions, Nate. I'm a Shadowmancer. I use Darkness to sniff out weaknesses and exploit them in the fight against Light, not help human kids out of tough situations with bullies, especially human kids that exist as a means to an end. I don't need to remember kissing a girl, either, and all the things she called me afterward, or how every minute of every hour I've been in human form, all I can see is the hatred burning in her eyes when she Dove. She was a means to an end, too.

I had a momentary lapse, but I won't fail. The game is mine to win.

"I'm ready for mine scouting." El pops a dingy headlamp into place on his forehead, and shoves the last few food packets into a knapsack, his snow gear and the staff he gave me abandoned in a messy heap on one of the bunks. "Come on, let's go."

He strides out the door, and we turn down a wide street, relatively deserted despite its seemingly central location.

"Hey, listen, I know those guys were being total dweebs back there," I say, "but the one kid kind of had a point. Why don't you go back to your home in the mountains?" Another "trade" I could play for in the mines, or another promise I can extract? "The other scouts in this town hate your guts."

"They only hate me because I'm a better scout than any of them ever thought about being, even without spark fins," El replies. "I get all the best jobs. They're jealous dümfos."

"Spark fins?"

"The glowing things under their skin," El explains the strange term. "Mountain people don't have them. It marks me as an outsider with the cavern folk. Usually, I cover my arms and neck so people can't tell, but the vents were really hot this morning before I went out."

"So why don't you get some, and blend in a little better?" I ask. "Or are you an unrepentant rebel?"

"They have to be implanted when both you and the spark fins are babies, otherwise they turn venomous and poison you." A spark fin is a symbiotic parasite. Fascinating. El steps carefully around a steaming vent right in the middle of the pedestrian byway. "Even if I could get spark fins, I don't need them. I'm a good enough scout on my own. I started scouting when I was seven sun-cycles and I haven't stopped since. Not even after —" He catches himself, doing the same shoulder-tense thing he did back in the canyon, the one that betrayed his fear of being abandoned and alone.

"After what?" A pretty benign-sounding press, but a press nonetheless.

"Something bad happened." El immediately shuts down, and further questions on the subject will not be tolerated or answered.

"Anyway, I don't want to go back to scouting the mountains, not when I get paid better here."

"Are all those guys you live with orphans, or just you?" Let's see how he answers this one. Could losing his mom and dad be the 'something bad' he's so reluctant to divulge? Because I can play the dead parent card.

"Piku is," El says. "Caro and Niro both have parents, but they don't want to live with them anymore."

"That's got to be hard, not having a family," I try to tease a reaction.

"Not really. I don't remember having one. And I like scouting, it keeps me out of school." Strike out—El doesn't seem bothered by his lack of parental figures. The 'something bad' must be something else. "Plus, they pay scouts with extra food. I like eating." He pats his knapsack, bulging with food packs.

As he's mentioned once or twice. Or, constantly.

"What about you?" El asks. "You're a scout, but you said you had a mother and a father." Does he remember that? He has a better short term memory than I initially assumed. "Did you run away from them?"

"Sort of." Something like running away. "Remember how I said I don't like personal questions? Stay focused on the mine, and the Cornerstone Key."

"Oh, right. Sorry." El grins. "I promise I'll only think about the imaginary fake thing we're going to find." He gives my arm a light punch, a sort of buddy-buddy move I don't think we're familiar enough to use. "Thanks again for helping me out back there. What did you do to Caro? He was so scared I thought he was going to pee himself."

"I got in his face and told him to suck eggs." And that's all I'm going to say about it.

"What's an egg?"

"Don't worry about eggs. Where are the mines?" If I've learned one thing about El, give him five minutes or change the subject, and he'll completely forget the task at hand.

"We're close." El takes a turn down a side street, and I can't tell anything about what part of town this might be because all the buildings look the same. Another turn, a short walk, and we arrive at the face of the cavern wall. A long row of open mine shafts stretches as far as I can see in either direction.

"Told you," El says with a grin.

"Which one is the Cursed Mine?" I glance to my right. "Is it the one with all the barbed wire and warning signs?"

"No, they're working on adding more support beams and clearing a caved-in section." El veers off, hard and to the left. "The Cursed Mine is down here."

Oh, yes, the ominous, shadowy hole in the earth at the back corner of the cavern, the one that just screams haunted, bottomless pit of despair. "Cursed Mine seems appropriately cursed."

"Don't worry, I don't think there are any ghosts inside." El switches on his headlamp. It still works, despite its outward condition, but does nothing to scatter the oppressive darkness inside the mine.

Trust me, if I say something is oppressively dark, I know what I'm talking about.

"The distinction between thinking something and knowing it is pretty crucial in this scenario." Crucial for him, anyway.

"Ghosts aren't real, it's more likely we'll see lots of ore wyrms and dead bodies." El turns around in the mouth of the cave-like mine, facing me with a teasing smile. "You're not afraid of monsters and ghosts, are you?"

"No." Hard to be afraid of something you kind of, technically, are—if Callie is any expert on the subject of monsters, which I doubt.

"Good." El takes a couple steps into the mine, his headlamp casting a pathetic beam of yellowed light down the craggy shaft before it disappears into the void, swallowed up by such an immense lack of light it's enough to give me the shivers. Even if this place isn't actually cursed and just the scene of a series of unfortunate accidents, it feels sinister and bleak, like the Shadow Plain bled through a crack in space and time, invading the human world.

Not to say the Shadow Plain is sinister and bleak. That's just how a human would perceive it.

"One time, Niro took a couple steps into the Cursed Mine," El goes on talking, as usual. "He says he saw a ghost and it screamed at him to get out, but nobody believed him. Our boss in the miner's guild told him to eat his ears." He takes a blinking button out of his pocket, similar to the one he stuck to the canyon wall to alert the hunters about the stags, and affixes it to the mine floor. "I'm going to mark our path so we don't—ah!"

El shrieks and covers his head, and a flying creature that looks like a miniature gray bat, but with a kitten-like face, lands on his shoulder. I don't usually do "adorable," but this little thing is right up there with Callie's mech, Nemo. The bat-kitten emits a gentle, cooing chirp.

"Careful, El," I deadpan, "it can probably smell fear."

El relaxes when he sees the bat-kitten, and it blinks its shimmering, silver eyes before winging off into the depths of the mine. "Do they have pipilos where you're from?"

"Something similar, they're called bats," I reply. "Are those things lucky, like the rabbits?"

"No, but seeing them means there's enough air in the mine to breathe." El straightens himself and resumes his march through the mine shaft, descending into the dark, placing a glowing button every couple yards. "What you really have to watch out for are cave-ins. There's also rumors that a lot of the old miners set a bunch of traps before they — AH!"

Where El had been, a black hole opening up in the mine's floor appears, and down, down, down he falls, into the deepest part of the earth.

CHAPTER 10
CALLIE

"HEY, TORAN, are you going to reorganize the Crow's Nest in a fit of simmering perma-rage every hour, or only the odd numbered ones?"

Toran pauses his incoherent grumbling to shoot me a crabby scowl. "That depends. How often is the menace going to keep trying to shred my books?"

"Nemo's not a menace," I correct the angry badger in a human skin suit otherwise known as Toran. "He's a precious wonder and everyone loves him."

"I don't love him at all." Say it isn't so, Toran! I couldn't tell you hate my mechs and everything about them in the less than twenty-four hours we've been cooped up together in the Crow's Nest, plodding through the forest toward the infamous Hem of Tremurheim. He aims yet another missed kick at Nemo, who wheels around his ankles, angling for a pinch or a page to sneak. "Don't be shocked if I toss him out that door over there while your back is turned."

"If you toss Nemo, I'll toss you." I meet Toran's eyes, so he knows my threat is serious. "Got it?"

"The only thing worse than that infuriating little headache is the giant monstrosity we're lumbering around in," Toran grouches, because that's his go-to way to express himself. "We'd be faster leaving the World Diver and going on foot, and you know it."

Is the Seer insulting us again, Luminaut?

Yeah, sorry, buddy. Diver's pretty sensitive to Toran's constant barrage of taunts. If the opportunity arises, I make no guarantees my big guy won't "accidentally" crush him underfoot.

And I make no guarantees I'd try to stop him.

A measured pause falls between me and my mech. *Must he be the Seer that Luminaut bonds with? Luminaut can find another Seer.*

Seers are slim pickings, Diver. I only know two, and Dr. Ormandi is a whole multiverse away. *Given the time constraints, and the Darkness on our tail, he's our only option. Unfortunately.*

Diver's gears groan a bit, his version of a robot sigh. *Yes, Luminaut.*

"Listen, if we weren't up here with Diver, we'd be more exposed to monsters and Mist," I say. "Personally, I'll trade going a little bit slower through the trees for protection."

"We have weapons and magic for both of those things," the grouchy grouch grouches grouchily.

"And we also have a mech for travel-related purposes, so we don't have to use the other two things more than necessary." I plop into the Luminaut's chair. "It's not an argument you're going to win. Just drop it."

Toran rolls his eyes and goes back to organizing all of our supplies by category, size, color, and usefulness. It's an awkward silence, but at least he's not berating me or my mechs, or literally everything else about my existence that he takes issue with.

Spoiler alert: Toran could write a novel about all his issues.

In case it wasn't obvious, this trip through the wilderness is going about as well as can be expected. And by "well," I mean the entire situation makes me want to take a screwdriver and jam it through Toran's skull every time he opens his mouth. If that statement doesn't give you a clue about my newfound Seer's rigid, surly, demeaning, eighty-year-old-curmudgeon-in-a-teenager's-body personality, and how well I get along with it, I don't know what will.

Why couldn't Dr. Ormandi have come as my Seer? It would have made everything so much easier. On a mentor scale of Yoda to Obi-Wan, he's bombing hardcore.

"I'm happy to be here in Diver," Heike says, jingling Nemo's keys for him to play with. Nemo whizzes away from the books and joins Heike for a new game. "Callie's Light powers might scare off the predators on foot, but then I couldn't have fun with Nemo."

If Heike weren't along for the ride, Toran and I would have killed each other within the first hour, and Nemo would claw Toran's eyes out at the first sign of weakness.

"You're calling them Light powers now?" Toran stacks his books into piles so neat they would make a librarian weep. "Don't let her confuse you, Heike. It's skyfire."

"Po-tay-to, po-tah-to," I say. "And anyway, the power you call skyfire sounds heinous. Like, killer dangerous. My Light powers are good."

"No, they aren't." Here we go again with the arguing. He'll bust out the book nerdery in less than five seconds. If I had my phone, I could time him. Five, four, three, two— "The entire reason the Hem exists is because of skyfire. I've read many accounts of the Hem's creation, and they all end in skyfire destroying the surrounding forest and killing the entire Mist Clan. They were the only Clan completely eradicated in the war, ones who harnessed the deadliness of the Mist and used it for water, and for protection. The knowledge they could have passed on about the uses of Mist is lost forever—all because of skyfire."

I was off by one second. Crap. I'm usually so accurate.

"Yeah, I get it. Skyfire is bad news, according to you. Except I've only used my Light to help people. So, it's not evil." I pull my knees toward my chest to dull the tug inside, the one that keeps drawing me back to Diver's memory I saw in the gateway — the giant burst of Light, and the woman's blood-curdling scream.

There's no way Toran's tall tales about skyfire and the memory are related. Purely coincidence.

"Not 'according to me,' it's a Tremurheim legend." Toran is never one to bypass the last word in an argument. "Even children know the Hem was created by sorcerers of old using skyfire, leaving nothing but a barren wasteland of Mist and monsters. It's a part of every bedtime story and fairy tale."

"Careful, Toran, you spoke of magic without spitting your words, now the Vredis will come for you," Heike feigns a spooky tone, then laughs. Toran snorts.

"The Vredis isn't real," he mutters.

"What's a Vredis?" I look between the siblings.

"It's the most fearsome monster on the Hem." Heike leaves Nemo with his beloved keys and sits across from me in the Seer's chair. "It was supposed to have been a gigantic bjorir when it was alive, but was mummified by skyfire when the sorcerers attacked. Now it guards the ghosts of the Mist Clan at the Beacons. The story goes, if you speak of magic and don't spit in the direction of the Hem, the Vredis will eat you in your sleep."

"It's a story to scare children," Toran adds. "It keeps them following the rules. Village Councils all over Tremurheim encourage the Vredis story."

"I'm sure that's not traumatizing at all." I don't know how Toran doesn't sense I'm dripping with sarcasm, but his fierce scowl would indicate he didn't pick up on my tone.

"It's extremely traumatizing." Yeah, dude, I got it the first time. "But most people in Tremurheim consider Vredis stories less traumatizing than being swallowed by the Mist, or eaten by forest predators."

"Anything to keep the populace indoctrinated." Heike deepens her voice, imitating Toran to a T. She catches my eye and grins, a shared joke passing between us.

Have I mentioned I'm glad Heike is here? Too bad she wasn't the one with Seer powers, like I assumed. Nothing awesome can ever happen to me. It's written down as a rule somewhere, probably.

"Speaking of the Hem," I say, "where's this supposed map you smuggled out of Gravenskov?"

"You won't be able to read it," Toran dismisses my request.

"Try me." I catch Toran's eye. "There are maps in Verona Beach."

"I don't know what foreign maps look like," Toran replies, "but if your general lack of familiarity with our customs is any indication, they look markedly different from maps of Tremurheim."

"That's a whole lot of words to say you think I'm an idiot."

"I don't *think* you're an idiot, I *know* it."

Big surprise, Toran considers me a certifiable dum-dum. Always be this consistent, okay? I hold out my hand. "Just give me the map."

"Fine. Here." Toran unceremoniously tosses a rolled-up scroll in my general direction. "But don't be dismayed when you need my help."

"As if I'd ask you for help, jerk-face," I mumble under my breath. Toran doesn't hear, but Heike hides a chuckle behind her hand. Unfurling the scroll (because we're still stuck in Bad Fantasy Trope Land), I quickly realize Toran is right. There's no way I can decipher anything on this map. All over the page are swirls of something that might represent Mist, punctuated by symbols like small castles and lines crisscrossing at sharp points like spires or spikes, but this looks more like a medieval tapestry than any map I've ever seen.

"See?" Toran looms over me, radiating smug satisfaction at my confusion. "I was right." He snatches the map from my grasp without waiting for me to offer it. Rude. "The Hem is uninhabited, but many seasons ago, right before Assimilation, remnants of the Tree and Ways Clans attempted to make a path across it with lighted outposts." He points out the small castle symbols, ones with rounded tops of glass similar to the Beacons in Diver's memory. "They were unable to make it all the way to the Beacons themselves," Toran goes on, "and abandoned their building efforts before the outposts were properly manned."

"Too many monsters, too much Mist," Heike cuts in. "It's all very typical Tremurheim."

No joke, Heike.

"The thought was to shine light, like giant lanterns, through the Mist and create a path to the Beacons, in case any surviving members of the Mist Clan tried to make their way back to civilization." Toran traces his finger along said path. "Theoretically, if we follow these outposts, we'll arrive at the Beacons. But nobody knows how far the path extends into the Hem."

"Theoretically?" I lean back into my chair and cross my arms and legs. "You didn't promise to 'theoretically' Guide me to the Beacons in exchange for jailbreaking your sister. You blackmailed me into risking my neck, and using my Light powers in your village, on the condition you'd use your cartography skill and Guiding prowess to take me to the Beacons so I could find my Light Core — er, Beacon's flare."

"You're hunting Beacon's flare?" Heike gives a start, her eyes popping wide in surprise. "Why would you want to find something so dangerous?"

Ugh, the infamous "D" word Nate always used. The last thing I needed to be reminded of in the face of Toran being a snide butthead is Nate and his lies. Just make it stop already.

"Why does everyone keep insisting my powers are dangerous?" I rise to my feet, pacing back and forth to ease my frustration. "Have I killed anybody? No. Did I cause either of you harm? No—and close your mouth right now." I point my finger at Toran before he can argue. "I used my powers to defend myself, and help save Heike. *And* I saved you, too, Toran, because in case you forgot, both the Volorad and skuddima took a shot at you."

"Callie, we aren't saying *you're* dangerous." Heike approaches cautiously, almost like she's afraid I'll hurt her—like I'm exactly the thing she says I'm not. "But Beacon's flare, the Hem, skyfire… all of these things are known to be deadly."

There it is, the other big, bad "D" word Nate liked to throw around. It makes my Light glow hot under my heart, like a burning coal dropped into my chest and I can't dislodge it, or the feeling of sorrowful anger and bleeding heartbreak it makes manifest.

"Have either of you been to the Hem, or the Beacons?" I look between them. Silence. "Yeah, I thought not. All these horrible Hem stories could be made up by your authoritarian Village Council to keep people from rebelling against their iron-fisted rule."

"You don't have to have been to a place to know it's dangerous," Toran argues. "And despite what Heike thinks, I believe you're equally as dangerous as anything on the Hem— until you learn to control your skyfire."

My fists start to shake, and I can hardly contain my agitation. "Light powers."

"Fine, if you insist I call them Light powers, so be it." Toran swishes his hand through the air. "Whatever they are, you have no idea how to properly use them."

"Oh, and *you* do, Seer?" A sneer draws my upper lip.

"I know more than you about controlling magic, and harnessing it to my will." Toran sneers, too, but nastier. Meaner. "You can make flying orbs to frighten skuddima and distract the Volorad, but do you understand what your powers are truly capable of doing? The harm you could cause?"

"You're starting to sound like somebody I know," I warn Toran, narrowing my gaze onto his ice-sculpture face. "Believe me, that's not a good thing."

"Only because that person has far more sense than you ever will."

See what I mean about jamming a screwdriver through the back of his skull? If I could read that stupid map that leads to the Beacons, I'd murder him in his sleep.

"Since you don't believe me about your Light powers being dangerous," Toran opens his mouth again, and I grit my teeth, "tell the World Diver to stop, and I'll demonstrate what I mean."

He wants to prove a point? Well, awesome. I want to prove him wrong about my powers.

"Diver, stop." At the command, my mech ceases forward momentum. "We're having a quick pee break."

Yes, Luminaut.

"It's absolutely disgusting the way you talk about such things," Toran informs me from his spot beside the hatch door.

"It's a necessity, Toran. Aren't you all about necessity?" The moment I open the door, swirling Mist seeps into the Crow's Nest, exploring the space before Toran directs the curious tendrils out. I have to admit, I'm a little jealous of how easily he seems to control his Seer powers.

"I could use a pee break, too," Heike adds, giving Nemo a

friendly pat on the head before joining us at the door.

"Don't start talking like her." Toran glares my way. "She's obscene."

"*She's* also standing right in front of you." Stepping out onto Diver's shoulder, I take a deep breath. It's Misty, and the extra moisture in the air chokes my throat. Smaller breath, in and out. Better. "Okay, Diver, you can put us down."

It's a tight squeeze with three bodies huddled in Diver's palm, but at least the ride to the forest floor is a quick one. I make my way toward an obliging-looking bush as soon as my feet touch the mossy ground. "Keep the Mist from swallowing me up, okay?"

Toran's frown could curdle milk. "Where are you going?"

Get ready for more obscenity, Seer dude, because I'm bursting. "I wasn't lying about the pee break thing."

Heike raises her lantern, scattering the Mist that's gathered around her, and catches up. "I wasn't, either."

Toran is still griping about how gross I am when Heike and I finish up and rejoin him.

"What is it you wanted to show me about my powers?" I crunch through the underbrush toward Toran, his Seer's Eye in a perpetual state of blue glow as he works to keep the Mist away. "It better be fast, because I wasted a solid twelve hours in Gravenskov I didn't have, and I want to be home by Christmas."

"I don't care about Christmas, whatever that is." Does Toran care about anything besides Heike, or himself? Doubtful. "Use your powers to make a mark on that tree over there."

I tilt my head. "What, like, throw an orb at it?"

"Yes. Aim to hit it, if you can."

Don't take shots at my aim, Toran, or I'll use your head as target practice. As I gather a large ball of shimmering Light into my hands, I can't decide who I want to pretend the tree is: Nate, or Toran. I'll just go with both. I launch the orb at the wide base of the trunk where both of them are smirking at me for entirely different reasons, and it lands dead center, a perfect bullseye.

"Good shot, Callie," Heike says with a smile. At least one person thinks I'm cool.

Toran nods, apparently satisfied with my performance. "Now, we go inspect the marks."

"I'm not unfamiliar with the type of marks my Light leaves on things." Heike and I follow him, approaching the tree I hit. "I noticed the same swirling pattern on the trees after the dramora attacked me."

"But do you know what they *are*?" Toran stoops down next to the blackened twirls carved into the wood, like a fresh tattoo just above the roots. "Feel them."

Okay, I'll play along. Won't he be surprised when I tell him they're nothing but benign marks—an oddity my Light leaves behind when it lands on an inanimate object? I press my fingers to the marks, anticipating the look on Toran's face when I tell him he's wrong.

Burning, like a raging inferno under my skin, begins in my fingertips, rocketing through my veins toward my heart until I'm overwhelmed with pain so excruciating it takes my breath away. Nausea creeps into my gut, making me sweat and shake, and it's as though I can feel the tree's torment like it's my own. As quick as I'd touched the mark, I withdraw my hand, shaking it to ease the searing burn.

"Well?" Toran's balled fists rest on his hips. "Tell me what you felt."

"I don't—" I gulp down the bile rising into my throat— "I can't explain what I felt. All I know is my Light powers are good."

"Then why did you feel the tree's pain?"

The tree was in pain. My Light harmed a living thing, and I could feel its anguish.

"Callie, you're pale, are you alright?" Heike touches my shoulder, but I ease away from her grasp. Even the light pressure of her hand feels too heavy against the rawness surging through me, and I can't hide my trembling.

"I'm fine." Total lie. "There's just... some kind of misunderstanding."

"There's no misunderstanding." Gosh, Toran, can you have a little compassion? I'm trying not to be sick. "Skyfire burns away anything it touches. That part of the tree will be dead forever. It will never grow again. The entire Hem is full of trees made black and dead with skyfire. You could have killed this tree. You could have killed every single Volorad. And you could kill me and Heike before we reach the Beacons. You're careless, and somebody is going to get hurt if you don't learn control."

The tree is in pain. I killed a part of it with my Light. It will never grow again where I made the marks. The burn in my hand and heart — that's what the tree felt, too.

But if Light can do this to a tree... Why did Dr. Ormandi tell me Light was good, and benevolent?

The scream of the woman in Diver's memory cuts my mind like a dull knife, rusty and merciless, hacking my understanding of my powers to pieces. I'm willing to admit that Light powers can cause harm, but I refuse to believe Luminauts would ever purposely hurt the people they were meant to protect. One thing doesn't necessarily lead to the other in this scenario, and there are multiple missing pieces to this newly-formed puzzle — ones Toran seems a lot more aware of than I am.

But in order to put the puzzle back together in a way that makes sense, I'm going to have to play along with his demands. This ego crush is going to hurt so bad.

"Okay, I'll admit you can control your powers a lot better than me." I really hate the self-satisfied look on his face when I admit it. "And it's true, I don't have a lot of practice using my Light. Maybe you could train with me when we get to the Hem, and teach me how you got so good at controlling your Water Manipulation. *But only* on the condition this is a cooperative activity, not just you talking down to me like I'm some trash idiot."

"That's unlikely to happen," Heike mutters. Darn it, she's probably right.

"I'll be happy to teach you what I know about controlling magic," Toran says, "because such an arrangement is mutually beneficial for my safety, and Heike's."

"This is not a promise I won't kill you in your sleep." Lest he forget I hate his guts.

"Same to you, sorceress." Seriously, he's so awful. "In return for my services, you will explain to me how you truly came to be here, why you need to find Beacon's flare, and where you're going next. Because I have known from the beginning you are not being honest, or truthful."

"Honest and truthful are the same thing." Can't resist an argument, especially after he called me a liar.

"No, they're—"

"Actually, Toran, they *are* the same thing." Heike is the best, isn't she? I throw my arm around her shoulders and grin. She reaches around, placing her arm on my shoulders too.

"See? Even your sister knows I'm right."

"Leave Heike out of our arguments," Toran threatens.

"I'm stuck in close quarters with you both across the Hem," Heike counters. "I can't help but be involved."

Look at this summer child. So adorable. So naive. "He means he wants you to stop taking my side."

Heike makes an "oh" with her mouth, and smiles. I smile, too, especially because Toran frowns, madder than a hornet that I called out his crap in front of his sister.

"Speaking of the Hem, we're close, and I'd like to make camp on the border by nightfall—if the World Diver can manage it. Which I doubt." Toran spins on his heel, parting the Mist with his hand as he traipses across the pine-needle blanketed ground. "Come. We depart." Heike and I have no choice but to trail behind in his wake.

Why do I have the sinking suspicion that giving Toran an inch means he's going to take a mile? Look at him, walking around all pretentious just because I said he could help me learn to control my Light. Heike better hide my screwdriver.

There's no way Toran is the Seer I'm meant to bond with as a Luminaut. I get the whole concept of opposing personalities forming a functional, working dyad, but this is too extreme even for that. The next time I see Dr. Ormandi, I'm going to rip him to shreds for not coming with me, forcing me to rely on Toran to finish this Light Core hunt and figure out the truth about my powers.

Mentor score F-, *Rick.*

I hope, somehow, across the expanse of the multiverse, he hears me.

CHAPTER 11
NATE

"HELP ME! Help! Nate, help!"

El's headlamp shines up at me from a tiny ledge, little more than a handhold, jutting from the wall of a bottomless cavern. He's barely hanging on by his fingertips, his eyes wide with terror.

"Hang on, I've got to get a rope or something," I call down into the dark.

Panic-stricken, El shakes his head, losing a bit of his grip in the process. "Don't leave me!"

"I'm coming back." Probably.

"I'll fall before you get back." His breath comes out in shallow gasps, and I can see the pulse pounding in his neck even from this distance away. "Give me your hand."

"My arms aren't that long," I argue, but drop onto my belly anyway, my chest and shoulders dangling into the mouth of the cave-in. A pipilo flies up from the depths to perch on the top of my head, trilling a gentle coo before something warm and wet oozes through my hair—something I'm pretty certain is bat poo.

I didn't need a literal (and disgusting) reminder I've gotten myself into some deep crap hanging around with El, okay, bat?

What would Queen demand I do in this situation? Let El fall

to his doom and move right along, that's what she'd say to do. Saving him reaffirms my inability to kill when it's necessary, either by murder or neglect, which is the reason I screwed up so bad in California—the one thing that will keep me from winning the game. This Light Core hunt on Ictari is about finding and destroying Light, not catering to the whims of humans and their emotions.

So why am I dangling on a precipice, reaching for this kid's sweaty palm?

"See, I can't reach you." I stretch a fraction of an inch more, but any further and I'll wind up falling into this back hole of death myself. Not that it matters, because I'm undead, but landing hard at the bottom of an unknown drop would hurt. Can Shadowmancers break bones? I don't want to find out. "You gotta let me get a rope."

"No!" El tightens his grip on the minuscule ledge, using the toe of his boot to try to gain some more ground up the rock face. With one more wobbly attempt at grabbing onto my hand, he stretches his arm as far as his shoulder permits, fingers shuddering with the strain.

"Just a little—"

"NO!"

El's grip slips entirely, and with a horrific tremor, he falls into the dark with a scream that makes my allegedly heartless chest lurch.

Split second decision: use the Veil to get down there (hopefully) first, catch him, and save his life, or walk away and show my commitment to the cause, retaining the upper hand against both Callie's betrayal and Queen's accusations?

The answer is obvious before I even ask it. Why it's obvious, I don't know, but who knows why I've done anything lately? Not me. I mutter that four-letter word that rhymes with spit, and slip beyond the Veil. In less than the blink of an eye, I emerge at the bottom of the cavern.

"Umph—ow!"

El crashes into my face in a heap of bony arms, legs, and knees that feel like dagger blades cutting through my shoulders and sternum. Both of us fall to the ground, splayed out miserably. After laying there for a solid five minutes, I let out a groan of pain, gingerly easing myself around to lean against a protruding boulder.

"I'm one hundred percent sure you broke my clavicle," I say, feeling around the bone in question.

"What's a clavicle?" El's voice comes out hoarse and shaky.

"Forget it." And, shockingly, the bone in question is sound. After testing my knees and ankles under half my weight, I rise to standing height, brushing dust off my backside. "For a short, skinny dork, you weigh a metric ton."

"I don't know what a metric ton is, either." El pulls himself into a sitting position, looking up at the narrow circle of wan light made by the shaft opening above us. His white-blond eyebrows bunch together. "How did you get to the bottom before me? I didn't even see you fall."

"I, uh, landed first because I'm heavier," I conjure a rapid— and false—explanation. "I fell faster than you."

El's frown deepens. "Really? I didn't think it worked like that."

"Well, it does."

Except it doesn't, and he knows it, and I'm dismissing him as stupid just like everyone else, taking advantage of his lack of formal education to play into my lies. Guilt like a hot knife invades my memories, both present and past. Didn't I do this exact thing to Callie not long ago? Manipulating her insecurities and indecisiveness to keep my upper hand?

Geez, man. Spend long enough in human form, and suddenly I'm regrowing a conscience. Like I wanted one of *those* things again.

"It doesn't matter, anyway." El stands, craning his neck to inspect the open shaft about thirty feet above our heads. "How are we going to get back up there?"

"No idea," I say with a shrug. "I've never free-soloed anything, much less a completely vertical mine shaft."

If I wanted, I could be up there at the top of the shaft, waving goodbye to El and all his accident-prone bad luck. One trip beyond the Veil and I'm back on track.

"I have some rope and hooks in my bag," El's voice breaks through the fog of thought.

I blink. Hard. "Then why didn't you give it to me when I said I was going to go find a rope, genius?"

El considers this. "Because I was worried about falling, I guess." Okay, that's fair. "Do you think you could throw the rope high enough to catch the edge?"

"Could I throw it high enough?" Who does El think he's dealing with here, a rodeo wizard? "Yeah, I'll just lasso the very small rock twenty-five feet above our heads with an equally small, if not smaller, rope and hook. Nothing to it."

Hold on—why am I actually considering *staying* down here with this kid? It's enough I saved his life, isn't it? I don't owe him anything else.

Just ditch him, Nate. Ditch him, before he puts me even more at risk of losing whatever slim advantage I might have. Because pretending to be El's older teen buddy who defends him against bullies and saves his scrawny neck was never part of my job description the way charades in human form were in Verona Beach. Get an in, get the Light Core, get out. The end.

"Nate? Did you hear what I said?"

No, I didn't hear what you said, El, I'm too busy with my internal monologue to pay attention to—

A gentle warmth washes over me, a tug deep within, just under the spot I ought to have a heartbeat. Dreamlike sensations manifest in my consciousness: rocking on a skiff, staring into the deep blue at something beautiful just out of my reach. The same kind of call I feel when Queen demands I return beyond the Veil, but softer, sweeter, something halfway hopeful.

It isn't coming from the top of the mine shaft. The need to venture deeper into the earth moves my feet against my will, taking me downward into the dark. Something wants me to find it. The distance between me and that something is great, but with every step, it grows closer.

"Where are you going?" El asks.

"This way." Into the unending cavern, toward a high probability of dangerous things that will hurt, maim, and cause generally unpleasant feelings—so why can't I stop my forward march? What's pulling me toward the other side of the dark?

Light from El's headlamp bobs and sways as he jogs to catch up with me. The sound of his fist slapping blinking trackers to the rock echoes along the wall. "Why? What's this way?"

An emotion I can't name, and a memory that feels like a dream, calling me into the depths of this bottomless hole. "I have a good feeling about scouting this direction."

"Well, I don't." El articulates perfectly what I ought to be thinking. "Do you have some kind of magic scout intuition, or are you crazy? There's nothing down here but ore wyrms and dead pipilos."

The bat-like creature in question wings toward the light of El's lamp, chirp-purring happily. I smirk. "Wrong on at least one count."

"But not the ore wyrms," El argues, placing another tracker.

"The deeper into a mine you go, the more risk of a wyrm attack."

"You can leave, I'm not forcing you to come," I reply.

"Except you're the one who can toss the rope high enough for us to escape this cavern," El counters. "I'm not that tall, or strong."

"Sounds like a you issue." The call toward my unknown destination blossoms like an ache in my stomach. I've felt this somewhere before, I know I have. The muscle memory is more than mere reflex, it's almost... an unconscious, primal need.

"Fine, I guess I'm coming, then." El catches up at last, his headlamp revealing rubble fields as far as the eye can see throughout the cavern. "Forget the monsters, cave-ins, and skeletons down here, it's your hunt for the Cornerstone Key. I just have the supplies and all the food."

"Watch the sarcasm." I give him a chilly look. "You led me to the mine with the Cornerstone Key, nobody's making you come further. Leave, if you want. No skin off my nose."

El's jaw hardens, uncharacteristically stony, and his shoulders tense: the familiar reaction to any indication I might be thinking of ditching him—or forcing him to ditch me. "I promised I'd help you scout the Key. So I'm helping."

Something about this kid makes me think his past trauma might revolve around promises being broken, his belief in something important shattering before his eyes.

Kind of like me.

"Fine," I say, "but don't come crying when you're scared of dead bodies."

El snorts. "I'm not scared of dead bodies."

"Just pipilos, right?"

"Shut up, Nate."

If Queen could see me now, being led by subconscious memory into the vast depths of this mine, bantering with El for no apparent reason—let's not imagine the cornucopia of ways she'd rip me a new one, shall we? That Light Core better be close, because if Queen catches wind of this, she'll demand I return to the Shadow Plain so she can shred me for insubordination, and I have no reasonable excuse to explain why I'm doing what I'm doing.

We've just finished bouldering over a pile of caved-in rocks and rubble (dead-body-free, from what I can see) when El sticks one last tracker into the wall and pipes up. "Hey, can we stop and eat?" El and food, man.

"How about no?" Who has time for human frailties like lunch?

"I'm starving." El states this as though it's common knowledge.

"You aren't starving," I say. "I highly doubt you've dropped below the caloric deficit necessary to constitute starvation."

El frowns. "Huh?"

Thanks, Richard Ormandi, for half my genetics, including the proclivity to give unnecessary scientific explanations to basic questions. "You aren't starving, you're fine."

"But I'm really hungry. I haven't eaten anything since this morning, and all I had was a half pack of food because Caro is a greedy dümfo."

We reach a widened space in the cavern, one with a higher ceiling and several rocky nooks that would be a good spot to take a rest and eat, if I did that kind of thing. I slip into the nearest one, and motion for El to do the same. "Fine, a quick break in here so you can stuff your face, and we're back at it."

Relief relaxes El's features, and he smiles, tossing his knapsack into the nook before rooting through the contents with glee. He pulls out one of the packs he'd shoved in earlier, all wrinkled from being fought over and twisted, and rips open the top, hoovering a smushed piece of something that reeks of fermented fish into his mouth.

"You want some?" El offers me the pack.

"No, I'm good." Especially with a nose-burner like that.

"I haven't seen you eat all day," El says around another mouthful.

"I'm not hungry right now." I don't want to think about what might happen if I put human food in my stomach, much less the stuff El's eating. I'd rather try to figure out what's going on with me: why I'm not completely manipulating El under my thumb and instead keep saving his life, and the origin of the weird sensation pulling me into this cavern.

I feel it even now, stronger when I'm still and quiet.

I've felt this before. Briefly in California, whenever I was with Callie. I felt a pull in my gut toward her, toward *something* about her, but I never stayed long enough to think about what it could mean. Queen was strict about what I could say and do when I "haunted" Callie, and what I was allowed to divulge before she called me back beyond the Veil to report. I always thought the hop-skips that bounced around my stomach when I was fake-flirting were my humanity showing, because not gonna lie, Callie is quick with a joke, smart as a whip, and prettier than I ought to notice for someone who could Light blast me into oblivion. Seriously, witty brunette with freckles and big, brown eyes — let's just say, when I was human, I had a type.

Type aside, it's the same kind of *something* that's worming through me now, and the Luminaut is nowhere in sight. It's something I vaguely remember from before I was Turned, an itch I can't quite scratch.

Something that reminds me of Mom.

Mom…

My emotions shift, focusing inward instead of out for a few brief moments. Every time I think of her, I'm rocketed back to one specific memory, to the day I first started to doubt the goodness of Light. The seed planted by that conversation grew into a tree, gnarled and poisonous.

I let my mind drift back to May of sixth grade, aka, The Second Worst Time. The Worst Time was when Mom died, but this was further back, right after she was diagnosed with cancer and started treatment. I was eleven, almost twelve—same age as El. An eavesdropped conversation between my parents the night before, after Mom got back from her first round of chemo, was driving me up a wall.

"Mom?" I finally venture outside onto the back patio after playing out every scenario regarding her conversation with Dad in my head. I shuffle around a little before sitting on the camp chair across from her. She looks tired, but okay. She hasn't lost her hair yet, and her tawny-brown skin isn't ashen, stretched tight to a skeletal frame. She still looks like Mom: beautiful, serene in a way I could only envy, the silky waves of her dark hair shining in the sun.

"My stars." Her Ensoloradan pet name for me. She reaches across the narrow space separating us and grabs my hand. Hers are warm. Soft. Before long, they'd become cold and frail. "Isn't it a nice day? I don't think your game will be foggy this afternoon."

I didn't want to talk about Little League, or the weather. The only thing I wanted was to address the elephant in the room I wasn't supposed to see—the inevitable that I knew, even then, was coming. I'd stayed up all night writing down plans to slay the tumors growing inside her, pouring over flaws, calculating for possible unknowns in my hypotheses. But when I finally faced Mom and the enormity of her illness, every carefully plotted scheme flew away with the wind, over the cliffs and out to sea.

"Dad said in Ensolorada, they can cure you," I blurt out instead. "For good."

Mom doesn't expect my statement, because her eyes go wide for a moment. *"You heard that conversation?"* Mom asks. I nod. *"Well, yes,"* she admits, *"they can."*

"He said your mom — my grandma — had cancer, too, when you were a kid. He said she's still alive, and old now." I'm starting to make Mom uncomfortable. I also don't care. My need for an answer burns like a hot poker through my skin, inching closer to the bone with every passing moment.

"That's true." Her lips thin a little, a sure sign she's pressing them. She only presses her lips when she's uncertain. *"Why are you asking these questions?"*

"Because I don't think I should do baseball this summer." I pull one of my knobby knees into my chest to keep my heart from leaping out. *"It's a waste of time. We should be out on the water, hunting the Light Core, so we can take Diver to Ensolorada and you can get better."*

Her mouth relaxes, and she closes her eyes like she suddenly needs a nap. *"That's not how it works. The Light Core hasn't called me."*

Pressure pushes against my lungs until I can't breathe, except for short gasps. *"Why? You're a Luminaut."* My throat constricts. *"How can you say the Light hasn't called you?"*

"Maybe we shouldn't talk about this right now," Mom murmurs, giving my hand a squeeze. *"Go get your gear for your game. It's almost time to head out."*

"I don't care if I'm late for warmups, I want you to answer my question." I wrench free from her touch. *"You're going to get sicker before you get better. Stop acting like I can't know things."*

I'll credit my parents this: they wanted my life to remain as normal as possible despite the life-altering threat our family was facing. Mom never failed to drive me to baseball practice, or watch at least part of my games—except at the end, when she couldn't get out of bed, much less sit for nine innings. It was a good intention, if ultimately futile.

The memory plays on, reaching the worst part of all. The part that hurts the most, and still throbs like a fresh wound despite all that's happened since she's been gone.

"Nate. Listen." *Mom's golden-amber eyes fill the intensity of my gaze with their contrasting peace, and I calm enough to breathe again. "I might be a Luminaut, but the Light Core doesn't call to every Lightbound being. It calls to the one meant to find it."*

"Why can't that be you?" *I swallow twice, no, three times, willing my voice not to tremble. "You looked for a long time, and now, you need it. I don't understand how something that's supposed to be good can do something so bad to someone like you."*

"This is more than good and bad, my stars." *Mom leans against the headrest of her lounge chair, long tresses of deepest brown spilling over her athletic shoulders. "We all have to make decisions that are bigger than good or bad, right or wrong. If we go back to Ensolorada, we lose the beauty of this place. You would grow up confined to a man-made oasis under the blazing heat of relentless sun, with only the stars and moon offering a few hours of comfort. Here, you have the cool breeze, and green trees. An ocean surrounded by hills to hike. Blue sky, bluer waters. A skiff that takes us up and down the coastline, wherever we want to sail." She smiles. "It may seem unfair to you now, but I wouldn't trade our life here. Not for an instant."*

She wouldn't, but I'd have given anything for just one day in Ensolorada—one day for them to remove the illness eating her up from the inside out, and make her whole again. All I wanted was a measly little Light Core so I could save my mom, was that too much to ask?

But it was never about what I wanted with Light. Queen taught me that. And in this memory, for the first time, a spark of angry realization flickered through my still-beating heart: the truth that Light was utterly indifferent to everything that mattered to me.

"How do you know the Light never called to you?" *My eyes sting with the tears I'm trying to hold back, but can't. "For sure?"*

"When Light calls, it strikes like lightning," Mom reaches for me, wiping the damp from my cheeks with the pad of her thumb. "It would rise to meet me, to connect with me and my inner Light." A slight shrug of her shoulders. "But it hasn't. And I'm content."

"How can you be content knowing the thing you want most doesn't want you?" It makes no sense. The worst kind of betrayal I can imagine, and she's content?

"I wish I could show you how little the loss of a Light Core means in the face of everything I've gained." Mom sounds like she's speaking to herself, not to me. After a moment's silence, one filled by a salty breeze blowing her hair from her cheeks, she turns to me. "Even if it never calls, we can seek Light in different ways. By different means. Through our own inner Light — through love. When things seem darkest, we can always find love. If there's love, there's Light. Never forget that."

Except Light and love didn't matter, and I never found them, because not quite four years later, everything that was love and Light to me was gone.

The emotional tug in my stomach takes on a sorrowful pulse, like a steady stream of tears flowing down a raw and battered face. I shake my head and rake my sleeve over my eyes, unwilling to decide whether I'm actually crying, or just imagining things.

"Hey, are you almost done shoving food down your pie-hole? I want to get moving." I whip my head toward El only to find him leaning against the rocky wall of the nook, snoring, his fishy-smelling dinner abandoned in his limp hands. "Makes sense you'd fall asleep on me the minute I want to hike out." I take the remains of the food and stuff it back in the pack before latching up his knapsack. "Some thanks for saving your life. I got bat poop in my hair for this, you know?"

Cleaning up messes left behind by sleepy kids remains a one hundred percent Mariasol-move, proof I'm not just Dad's calculating, strategic kid, or Queen's ambitious underling. A thought that, in this particular moment, I find comforting, despite the fact I left the guy who was Mom's son behind a long time ago.

What would Mom say if she knew I Turned to Darkness? Became a Shadowmancer?

I shudder, my arms prickling with icy needles as I'm surrounded by bone-chilling cold. One that has nothing to do with Mom's inevitable disappointment and shame at my choices, and everything to do with Darkness.

"Little one, come to me."

Even in the thin light of El's headlamp, the Veil manifests before my eyes, and the soft, gentle pull under my heart morphs into something inherently sinister at the base of my spine: Queen is calling me into the Shadow Plain.

"Little one." Her voice grows stronger, worming through my mind. *"I need a report on your progress. Immediately."*

CHAPTER 12
CALLIE

GRAY.

All I can see in any direction, no matter where I turn my head, is swirling gray Mist so thick, so tangibly solid, it's like I've fallen into the depths of a gigantic sea of ghosts, abandoned to roam the haunted gray for eternity. Diver stands only twenty feet or so to my left, but I can't decipher even a faint outline of my mech. The only thing I can sense or see, choking my lungs until it's almost impossible to breathe, is gray. It even smells gray here: an indescribable scent of drabness that you can only know if you've experienced it yourself.

The Hem of Tremurheim is basically one great, big slice of "nope" with a side of "thanks, I hate it."

All this gray reminds me of when Mom blanketed every single room with a coat of foggy blah within the first week of moving into our house, covering a spectrum of color coating the walls. Color reminds Mom of her childhood house, painted by Avó Maria to resemble the vibrant streets of Lisbon, her hometown. Mom just wanted things clean and simple.

I wonder what Mom's doing right now—what she thinks happened to me, and if she painted my coral-colored bedroom walls gray, too. I bet she did. She'd probably love the Hem.

Actually, all the moisture in the air would wreck her cooking. Plus no ovens. Or electricity. This is why we can't have nice things in Tremurheim.

"The Hem's really Misty, isn't it?" I don't need to see Toran's face to know he's scowling, because when is he not scowling? But I can make out the faint turn of his mouth into a sour grimace exactly as I predicted.

"I told you it would be, but you obviously weren't paying attention when I—"

"Chill, I'm being sarcastic." Why do I even bother making jokes anymore? Instead, I call a tiny orb into my hands, which helps to burn away some of the gray swallowing us whole. "You want to use your Seer powers and give us a wider clearing to work in?"

"This Mist is different out here," Toran's gruff voice rumbles in my ears. "It's thicker, more volatile. Malevolent. Waiting to strike us down and devour our souls."

"I asked you to clear the Mist, not paint a Debbie Downer mental picture." Yikes, this guy.

"Fine." Toran's blue Seer's Eye cuts through the Mist, and slowly—much more syrupy in its movements than normal—it starts to creep away from us until Diver materializes. Heike holds Nemo on the safety of Diver's foot, and beyond him, blackened skeleton trees pierce the eerie gray, rising like charred toothpicks from the muddy earth.

"Hello, I can see you now!" Heike smiles and waves from her perch. She's so upbeat and cool, how are they even related? "I'll keep watch for the Vredis while you're practicing. I have my crossbow, and Nemo. We can take on monsters even without magic, can't we, Nemo?"

Nemo whirrs his fiercest growl, and Toran groans like he'd like nothing better than to chuck Nemo at the Vredis and bolt the other way. Absolutely no love lost there.

"Don't think about taking on *anything*," Toran warns his sister. "I didn't come this far to have you attacked by what-in-Lands-Beyond lives out here."

Heike purses her lips, and I can see in her faint scowl exactly how she and Toran are related. "I can take care of myself. I practiced crossbow skills with my instructor at the Academy. It's a major requirement of the Aptitude Test for Guide, as you recall."

"I recall you almost got yourself killed, which is why we're out here on the Hem, and you're not taking the Aptitude Test," Toran snaps. Wow, he's terse with Heike today. That's weird; he'd rather bite his tongue off than have an edge with her. "Just sit there, and if you see a predator, tell me."

"And also me. Since I have powers, too." I give Toran an incredulous look. "So, Light made this place, huh? Sorry to burst your bubble, Light burns through Mist. If Light made the Hem, there wouldn't be Mist like this."

"Trees in the forest keep the Mist confined to pockets, or the canopy. None of that exists out here, because sorcerers with skyfire decimated the trees after they slaughtered the Mist Clan. What you see is all that's left." Toran is super grouchy today for no good reason. "You're wasting time. Let's begin, so we can be on our way and find the first outpost before predators attack."

"What predators are you worried about?" I glance around. "There's nothing but Mist out here, and dead trees. Rumors of looming monstrosity have been greatly exaggerated."

"We don't know that," Toran argues, because it's Toran. "People do not survive on the Hem for a reason."

The cause of his extreme grouchiness becomes apparent. "And you don't like that, do you—facing the unknown in an environment outside of your control?"

"Stop talking. Concentrate." Toran draws some Mist into his hand and makes a long, jagged ice sword, which he points at my face. Yep, I hit the nail on the head. "If I have learned one thing, it's that controlling magic requires intense concentration." To show off—I mean, demonstrate what he means—he flicks his wrist, and the ice sword breaks into thousands of tiny shards. "All magic can be used for both offensive and defensive maneuvers, but in order to use it effectively, you have to be calm. Controlled."

"Emotionless?" That was the word Mariasol used in her journals, wasn't it? Mariasol seems like she was a lot more chill than me—and Toran. "That rules you out, you're perpetually crabby."

Heike snorts, holding back a chuckle, while Nemo whir-laughs riotously, pointing his claw finger at Toran. Nemo pretty much has no filter.

"And you're perpetually making jokes, and never take things seriously." Wow, Toran, you're remarkably on point for once; I hate it. He turns and sweeps even more Mist away with his hand, revealing a potential target. "That tree over there is dead, you can't hurt it. Build up as much skyfire as you can, but not so much you lose control, and then launch it at the tree."

"No imaginary predator is going to see it as an invitation to come attack?" I raise an eyebrow.

"Only the Vredis," Heike pipes up, and Toran rolls his eyes.

"If they do, we'll be practicing offensive strategy in real time, won't we?" It's almost like Toran hopes my prediction comes true, just so he can antagonize me about it later.

"Okay, here we go, Light ball versus dead tree." I call Light into my hands, the warm sensation flickering under my heart as it spreads like sunshine throughout my body, down into my toes, along my arms. Familiar brightness surrounds me, comforting me like an old friend—one dripping intangible gold flecked with diamonds and crystalline prisms of every color imaginable. Mist flies away from me as more and more Light builds within.

"That's too much," Toran speaks through the blinding bright. He sounds tinny in my ears, and far away despite how relatively close he stands.

"It's fine. I can control it." When I speak, my voice no longer sounds like my own. It's bigger, more expansive through space, and booming with the echoes of a thousand Luminauts from ages past.

"No, you can't."

"Yes, I can." I face him, and somehow, I've grown taller than he is—which is impossible, because Toran is over six and a half feet tall and I'm five-eight. Even slouching, he would tower over half the basketball players at VBHS. Horror overtakes the icy chill of his eyes, and he stares, jaw gaping, forming yet another frozen sword, one in each hand. His shoulders tense as he prepares to hold his ground.

What—or, who—does he think he's going to attack?

"Callie, what are you doing?" Heike's dim cry comes from far away, across galaxies and endless space, every spare inch occupied by Light. I don't know what she means—I'm not doing anything, except fully existing in my power.

"Come down!" Toran shouts, his ice swords brandished at the ready.

Come down from where?

It takes me a full minute to realize my feet are no longer touching the ground, and I've been suspended by Light in midair. The Light and I are one, defying even gravity as more and more of my power surges through me. The ancient voices of the past, beings of Light who have long since reunited with our power's celestial source, become a part of my soul, overtaking my senses.

Luminaut must stop. This Light is not safe. Diver's warning, as clear as my own inner thoughts, comes to me in the blaze, a premonition I feel in my pounding heart. This is becoming too much, too fast, and if I'm not careful, I'll lose myself to my power entirely.

Panic overtakes the Light, turning it into something unstable, and violent. Cracks appear through the diamonds, building to a break. Light shines not with benevolence, but with merciless brutality, and any part of me that was mine starts to burn away, never to be recovered.

"Control it!" Toran forgets the ice swords, tossing them aside as he rushes to shield Heike, watching the scene unfold with terror. Even Nemo, who has seen me use my Light a hundred times, cowers in fear behind Heike's leg, clinging to somebody other than me for comfort, because I'm anything but soothing. I'm a force to be dreaded, a weapon of pure Light, and any second, I will explode, and annihilate everything in sight.

Please don't do this!

Stop!

The Collective has not authorized the relocation of these refugees. Stand down, or face the consequences.

No!

Voices, the ancient Luminauts of Diver's memory, all of them converging inside the Light, filling me with pain, anguish, grief, and a heart-shattering sense of betrayal, culminating in the woman's scream that's been a source of doubt and horror since I first heard it, played on repeat inside the supernova of Light I've created. Light before me, Light behind, Light in every direction and filling every second of passing time. I'm free-floating, falling away from Tremurheim, from Toran and Heike, from Diver and Nemo. Everything I know or ever knew fades until Light and fear are all that remain.

Do not be afraid ... we are with you.

Another voice reaches out to me, this one soft, gentle, warm, so wonderful and good all my doubt vanishes in an instant.

Who are you? My inner Light calls to the speaker, trying to find her face. It eludes me, but the serenity remains near my heart, filling me until I'm whole.

Fear has no place here. You are safe. Loved. Home.

Home…

I control the Light. It does not control me. I command it, not the other way around. And I command the fear to go away.

As quickly as my feet floated away from the Hem, they return to solid ground, and my Light withdraws inside, coming to rest beneath my heart like an ember glow—the sensation I've known now since the Light Core unlocked my power last summer. Benign, quiet. No unsettling screams, or disembodied voices demanding deadly consequences.

It's almost as if the Light inside me was tainted a long time ago, fractured by the cataclysmic sorrow and fear that bleeds through me every time I use my power for more than orbs and flares. The true power within Light was, at some point in time, shattered and bruised. Wounded by immense grief, just like Diver's memories are wounded.

And it all has something to do with what happened so long ago on Tremurheim: the violence from the memory, and the creation of the Hem. Could it be one and the same?

"What in Lands Beyond were you thinking?"

Oh, Toran, there you are, I had an awesome half second where I forgot you were still here.

"I let my power overtake me to the point where it almost overwhelmed me, but then I regained control. Just like you suggested." I'm a little wobbly on my feet, but the fact I'm standing is kind of a miracle, given how close I almost came to turning into some kind of Light firework. Neither Mariasol or Dr. Ormandi mentioned the Light-levitation part of my power.

How much did my dad tell you? Because there's a lot he likes to leave out…

Go away, Nate's words and gravely, hot-guy voice that always makes me remember the shape of his arms under his t-shirt, and how they encircled my waist just perfectly. I don't need doubt right now — or to be reminded of any other type of feelings I had for Nate. I need Toran to stop berating me.

Which he doesn't. I know, we're all *so* surprised.

"That was not what I suggested you do — Heike and I almost died." Toran is nothing if not overdramatic.

"No, you didn't, I had control of the situation." I sweep my hand across my Light-free form. "See? Puffy jacket, ruined boots, my awesome pom-pom beanie that you hate. Back to normal, and you're alive. Admit you freaked out and got scared. I won't laugh." Well, I won't laugh hard.

Toran looks like he'd rather wrestle a live dramora than admit such a thing.

"I told you to aim your skyfire at that tree, not use it to levitate yourself." That's seriously what Toran is focused on right now? Better than owning the fact he's a scaredy-cat, I guess. I walk away from him, taking Nemo from Heike's arms. My little buddy seems right as rain now that I'm no longer a floating fireball, and he nuzzles my neck before perching on my shoulder.

"When do I listen to you? Pretty much never." I pat Diver's ankle, and my big mech radiates warmth and security now that I'm back to myself.

Luminaut, the Seer was terrified. Diver is pretty happy about it, too.

Bahaha! I was right.

"You should start listening to me," Toran argues. This is exhausting, truly. "What would have happened if we'd been attacked while you were in that state?"

"I guess we'll never know." I shrug my shoulders and flop onto Diver's foot beside Heike. "I have a lot of questions right now, and I'd like to work through the answers, but you being so much yourself is not helping me think."

Questions about why Light contains terror and grief as well as goodness and warmth, the meaning behind the screams of "consequences" that lead to certain death, how it relates to me, my Light Core hunt, the history Dr. Ormandi might have omitted or been ignorant of, and how in the multiverse everything I heard and saw can be fixed—if it's even real to begin with.

Basically, I'm on the verge of what the truth really is, and this Seer only cares about whether or not I hit a tree with my powers like he told me. Part of this arrangement was Toran not treating me like a piece of hot garbage, but he has a pretty shoddy short-term memory.

"You should be answering the questions I'm asking, because they're pertinent to all of our safety." Toran and safety plans—the one true love of his life. I'm sure I'll get their engagement announcement in the mail next week.

"I'm not obligated to do anything you tell me." Is it asking too much for Toran to just drop it? "I thought we had some outposts to find that will lead us to the Beacons. You're the only one who can read the map, as you like to remind me every five minutes. Let's get out of the Mist and move on, so I can process some things in peace."

"You think I'm going to Guide you to the Beacons of the Tageveld after a display like that?" Toran makes another ice sword in his fist. Nice flex, not impressed.

"We had a deal," I remind him, forming a Light orb in my hand to counter his sword, because guess who can flex, too, jerkwad? "And you aren't going to back out of it."

"I don't think you should be making an enemy of Callie, not

after what we just saw her do." Listen to Heike, Toran, she knows what she's talking about. Especially since, you know, I still have a Light ball in my hands, and Toran's forehead is a lot closer than that tree he asked me to hit.

"You think she's *not* an enemy with skyfire like that?" Toran whirls on his sister, his already pale face going paler. "Heike, she was ten feet off the ground and about to explode."

"Okay, here's the deal." I lay out some facts. Toran likes facts. "You don't get to call the shots out here, because you need me. You can't go back to Gravenskov, they'll kill you — because guess what, you decided to throw an ice hissy-fit on some Volorad, and I'm not giving you any supplies to hike back into the forest to find another village. Also, I need you to read that map. Which sucks, but there, I said it. So basically, we're all stuck together until we finish this road trip, whether we like it or not."

Toran plants the tip of his ice sword in the sludgy ground, scowling. "I don't like it."

My hands fly to my heart, and I flutter my eyes as though I'm faint. "Toran, so hurtful! I'm dissolving into a puddle of sadness tears!"

"I don't care." Yeah, he doesn't get a joke. Or sarcasm. Or feelings, generally.

"Let's just go before something terrible happens." Something like the Mist that Toran called "malevolent" invading our bodies and possessing us like creepy zombie puppets. Can Mist do that? I really don't want to ask, because Toran will find some way to turn an answer into an insult, and I'm pretty over his surly attitude and threats to ditch me at the moment.

All I want to do is figure out what my powers are capable of, and what ancient trauma happened out here on the Hem. If it really was created by Luminauts, like Toran says, how did they come to decide destroying millions of acres of forest was necessary to protect the people they were sworn to keep safe?

And, even worse, did they murder the hundreds—maybe thousands—of people he claims?

Wooooaaaannnn

"Okay, what was that?"

Toran, Heike, Nemo, and I look around, each of us scanning a different direction as we peer through the gathering Mist for the source of the noise. I see nothing out of the ordinary, but again, the sound pierces the air.

Woooaaaannn

"Skuddima?" Heike hops off Diver's foot, her crossbow close to her side. Her slim shoulders touch her ears as she spins around, hunting for monsters in the enormous Hem.

"No, skuddima don't make a cry like that," Toran says. His Seer's Eye glows bright as he pushes his hands forward in front of him, and then sweeps them to the side. But the soupy quagmire surrounding us doesn't part. "The Mist has taken on a mind of its own, too."

Luminaut, we are in danger.

A sudden turn of events that doesn't bode well for the three lone humans in the spooky wasteland? The script could write itself.

"This is the part of the horror movie where a monster jumps out, and the whole theater screams." Toran and Heike don't get my reference, if the confused looks on their faces are any indication. Countdown until Toran tells me to shut up in five, four, three, two, one—

"Shut up," he hisses, giving me the I-will-cut-your-tongue-out-of-your-mouth-so-help-me look. Yes, I was totally accurate that time!

Woooaaaaannnn

Whatever is making the strange, almost humanlike cry, it's

getting closer.

Luminaut, we must leave right away. Got it, Diver. Loud and clear.

"Diver's pretty freaked out, so that means we should be, too." I nod toward my mech. "Let's bail."

"I will agree with the slow-moving behemoth for once." Toran turns on his heel, and the space where he once stood is immediately swallowed up by Mist.

"Toran, look, it's a person!" Heike does the exact opposite of what Toran suggested and ventures further into the Mist, holding her lantern high above her head. "It sounds like they need help."

"Heike, come back." Toran's anxiety spikes the second she takes a step, and he tries to move the Mist away from her, with no luck. "Whatever it is, it's not a person."

And yet, wandering through the Mist, a shape materializes, one that looks as human as any of us. It's nothing more than a shadow at the moment, a pale outline blurred by gray all around, but the closer it comes, the more I can see distinctly person-like features, and the more human the cry becomes.

Wooooaaaaaaannnnn

A person… dragging their leg? Whoever it is, they're injured.

"We have to go find them," Heike insists. "It could be a lost Guide from another village."

"No Guide in their senses would *think* about venturing onto the Hem, let alone get close enough to become lost on it." Toran is not having any of this, despite what we're seeing. He shakes his head and grasps Heike by the elbow. "I know how it appears, but it's a trick."

"Or, it could be somebody who needs our help, because they're hurt, lost, and alone." Heike roughly shakes her arm out of Toran's grip, taking a few more steps into the Mist. She starts to disappear even five feet away. "Forest spare you! Come toward my voice!"

The Seer's sister must stop making noise.

"Diver isn't cool with this." Light in my palm burns away some of the Mist as I approach Heike. "He thinks it's a trap." Given Diver is millennia old and has obviously been to Tremurheim before, I'll trust his very reasonable intuition.

"Heike, please." Panic floods Toran's eyes in an uncharacteristic display of helplessness. He takes his sister's arm again, more firmly this time. "I know you want to assist, but it's not safe."

Wooooaaaaannnn

One more pathetic moan, and the person—thing?—stumbles and falls a short distance away, the shape of their broken body crumpling to the ground. Heike ignores any protest, approaching the fallen person with her lantern above her head. Toran uses all his strength to push the Mist away from her, and my Light shines bright

"Please, don't move!" Heike cautions the person. "We're here to help. I'm Heike Rykjiersen of Gravenskov, my brother is Toran, he's a Guide. Callie is our friend. We can get you back to—"

We come to an abrupt halt, staring in shock. Because that's definitely *not* a person.

The thing lying on the ground has the vague shape of a human being, but more closely resembles a scaled, lizard-like version of an eyeless, mouthless zombie. Attached to its "head" is a long, sinewy cord: one that swiftly retracts the lifeless "body" into the Mist.

Well, that can't be good, can it?

WAAAARRRRRRGGGGGG!

The moaning noise becomes a ferocious growl, and before my eyes, a terrifying creature appears out of the Mist. A reptilian monster twenty-five feet tall, its massive head like a crocodile mated with an angler fish. The creature steps into view, giant claws dripping muddy sludge, and the "person" Heike wanted to help is actually the creature's tongue: a fact that becomes obvious when it roars again, revealing hundreds of rows of jagged, sawlike teeth.

Mist gathers in close, controlled by the creature's radar dish gills on its throat that emit thrumming pulse signals with every breath.

"What is that thing?" Heike asks what we're all thinking.

"I don't know," comes Toran's reply. But, just like I predicted earlier, his uncanny ability to turn an answer into an insult manifests even when I'm not the person to ask the question. He turns to me with a vicious sneer. "It would seem your skyfire display attracted predators after all."

Oops.

CHAPTER 13
NATE

"LITTLE ONE, TELL ME: how has your hunt progressed?"

Queen's eyes glow red as they settle onto my face, inspecting me for any sign of weakening cracks or lies she can expose. Her trust in me remains suspect, and the ever-present chill surrounding her feels more poisonous, almost repulsive after so long in my human form. If I could breathe, it would choke the air from my lungs.

This is probably not the best time to mention the magnetic pull toward the back of the mine that's been throwing me off course. Or the part where I saved El's life instead of killing him, or my human emotions and conscience manifesting. Keep it strict, and to the point.

Basically, don't give her a reason to annihilate me. I've played the game to my advantage this long, I don't plan to strike out now.

"The hunt is productive, my Queen." My expression remains neutral as I relate a bare-bones account of my journey through Ictari thus far. "I've learned a local legend regarding a mythical object called the Cornerstone Key. It's supposed to be hidden in the Cursed Mine of Aragusti. I've been making my way through it, but there's a lot of ground to cover."

She nods for me to go on, like she's expecting me to say more. Her hair floats off to the side, revealing more of her face, and she comes closer, eyes digging into me. "And the human companion you've found on this hunt?"

Oh, no. She knows about El.

Gigantic, metaphorical gulp. Whatever I do, I have to play dumb. "My Queen?"

"The humanity in you is stronger than ever," she says, "which means you've been interacting with them for extended periods of time." She pauses, searching me deeper still. "How long have you been up there? Days? Hours? Weeks? Why have you returned to me only half a servant?"

The one odd advantage I have is that we have no concept of time in the Shadow Plain. What feels like moments could be just that: minutes of human time. Then again, hours could be years — decades, even. Between the day I was Turned and the moment Queen let me go topside to spy on Callie, it felt like a couple months. Angry Darkness Summer Camp. But seeing how old Dad became, how sad and withered he looked that night at his house, confirmed it had been a long, long time since the day I went sailing and found —

I found? No. I didn't find anything. Darkness found *me*.

Didn't it?

My mind feels cloudy all of a sudden, like the marine layer that settles over Verona Beach every morning is trying to lift and expose the sun, but the fog remains, wrapped tight to the peaks and valleys of my brain.

Nice one, Nate. Mrs. Kim from AP English would be proud.

"Little one." Cease and desist tangents — when Queen speaks, it's nothing less than a command I answer her question. I know better than to keep her waiting when she's already looking at me so precariously, Darkness tipping the edges of her fingers, ready to strike.

"It's difficult to tell time in the underground cavern, my Queen." No lies right now, she'll see through deceit in a heartbeat. "I can't see the sky to tell if it's day or night. But I know it hasn't been long. I'm hunting as fast as possible, given the constraints. My only desire is to destroy the Light as quickly as possible."

You'd assume Queen would inherently know how serious I am about avenging what Light took from me. But I guess she needs it spelled out from time to time. Talk about giving somebody a complex. If El thinks he has it bad, living with that trio of punks, I've definitely got it worse—what with being constantly belittled, threatened, and reminded over and over who holds power and who doesn't.

"Hmm, yes. I see." Queen considers my words, searching me for one last trace of a lie. She finds nothing in me to attack, because she backs off, her Darkness less menacing. "Very good, little one. It seems you've gotten a promising lead on the Light Core, and a lengthy head start. This is a satisfactory report." She reaches for me, ruffling my hair in a way that reminds me of Mom. "Very good, little one. Very good, indeed."

I want to pull back, rage rising in my guts, because how dare she touch me like Mom used to. She's not my mom—never could be, even if she did save me from the Light that callously abandoned my real one. Queen never does anything unless it's some kind of power play, an attempt to manipulate and keep things under the control of her influence, tied to her will. There's no love with Queen, just vengeance.

Then I remember she just told me she's pleased with my progress, but any hint of dissension will be yet another strike against me—and the rules of this game don't always add up to fair.

"I'm happy you're happy," I say instead.

"It is you who should be pleased," Queen replies, a grin parting her thin lips. "Every step you take brings us closer to victory. Keep true to your path, don't falter. Whatever human you've been manipulating has weakened you, but I still see your Darkness, your resolve against Light. I know when they've outlived their usefulness, you'll do what has to be done."

What has to be done – ashing El, or abandoning him to slowly starve to death in the darkest, deepest part of the mine. Murdering an eleven-year-old kid.

What *has* to be done.

The shudder I've been repressing bubbles to the surface, and my expression slips a fraction of an inch. More than enough for Queen to notice, and the danger of losing my upper hand becomes reality once more.

"Is there a problem?" Queen tilts her head.

"No." I spit it out too fast for her to believe it's true.

"Really?" Queen rises into the Darkness above me, tentacles of Shadow reaching for the skin of my neck, obscuring my face, tangling through my hair. "It seems you're still experiencing the troublesome tendency of caring about useless distractions."

"The only thing I care about is destroying Light." Why does she always question my motives? Everything I did before I Turned, and all I've done since, has been to find Light and destroy it before it caused even more death, like it caused Mom's. Queen knows this better than anyone. Hatred for Light is what made me want to find it in the first place, left me staring into the deep blue, heartbeat hammering in my ears as... as...

As a storm gathered... and then a wave... I think it was a wave...

I remember this. I swear, I do. A rogue wave during a storm took me out, and almost killed me. So when Queen called, I Turned to Darkness to finish my task. I know this story like the back of my hand (I have two moles on my right, and a small scar from a jellyfish sting on my left).

But if that's true, why do I keep seeing visions of gold mixed with blue, like some kind of abstract painting struggling to take shape around the peaceful pull-tug of emotion in my stomach, the one calling me back beyond the Veil to the grounded embrace of the human world?

"If you truly want my cause to succeed, you'll do as I command, and not waste precious time debasing yourself with human company," Queen snaps, the pitchy shrillness of her voice and mounting anger bringing me back to the present. "If I am going to reveal the beauty of Darkness to the Luminaut, and ascertain if she is my worthy opponent, then I must—"

I suck in something almost like a gasp, gagging on the strange combination of Darkness and panic, and I do the one thing I know better than to ever, ever do: interrupt Queen mid-rant. "You're going to appear to Callie in person? How?"

Queen can't go to the Veil. She can't interact with humans. It's impossible—her imprisonment keeps her tethered to the Shadow Plain, unable to hunt Light herself. That's why she calls people to Darkness and creates Shadowmancers who can go beyond the Veil in human form: to keep tabs on the movement of Light. This one very specific thing has been true since the moment I was Turned.

Why are things that have always been true feeling less true all of a sudden?

"Callie?" Queen's Darkness slithers beneath my skin, worming through me as tentacles of Shadow block my sight so I can't predict her next move. "You're using the Luminaut's name?"

Before I can strategize a way out of her grasp, pain like a knife caught fire erupts along my forehead, trailing down my cheek, splitting my skin wide. I grit my teeth to keep from crying out.

"This insubordination is incredibly unfortunate." One excruciating sear, then two. Queen's razor-sharp fingernails, opening my face almost to my skull. "Do I need to remind you, of all Shadowmancers, how dangerous the Light is?" Her Darkness holds me steady while her nails press into my cheekbone, ripping the muscle. "The Luminaut is evil to her core. Light betrayed your human mother to her death. Lest you forget, I have made more sacrifices than you in the battle against Light. Do you think I enjoy being imprisoned? That I didn't know the sacrifice I was making when I took up the cause against Light? My whole existence was erased and rewritten, all for the glory of ending Light."

"Please." I hate begging, but thoughts of tactics and upper hands fly away in the face of this agony, and I'll say anything to make the pain stop. "My Queen..." Even ashing can't be as terrible as this torture, her Darkness slithering around my skull while she shreds my face to pieces.

Please...

Quietly, a spark from the depths of my subconscious begins to burn, fighting back against the Darkness, the terror, the pain, pushing it out until it encompasses me in something warmer, something brighter, something from the past I kept buried inside. A split second, less than a micron of time, passes for me here in timelessness, and in that moment, a flicker of abject horror crosses Queen's features—fear that she's about to lose control of something she thought she'd conquered for good.

As quick as it came, the Darkness leaves. She withdraws her hand, and the pain stops, the spark fading away. Any emotion I imagined in her—other than petrifying cruelty—vanishes. I reach for my cheek, gingerly tracing the open gashes. The sickening sensation of my open flesh under my fingertips makes my hand shake.

"Let this be your last reminder of the price of the cause we fight for," Queen says. "Destroying Light will not come without sacrifice, or pain. Or scars. You must follow all orders if we are to succeed."

I lower my mutilated face, chin dipping into my chest, biting back fury. She won yet another round, any perceived advantage I have dashed, rendered as ugly and fragile as my face. She played me, hurt me, sniffed out my weakness and then tore me to shreds. And I didn't see it coming. *I'm better than this. I know how to play her game.*

Or do I?

What I do know is there's only one acceptable response, as much as I hate to say it: "Yes, my Queen."

"Consider what you've brought upon yourself as a warning. You returned to me half a true servant, and you will leave half a servant as well. And yet, I am merciful. Now, go."

As she backs away, retreating into the Darkness of her prison while I fly toward the Veil, I realize she never answered my question about Callie.

I emerge from the Veil just as El is stirring himself awake. He gives a start, like he didn't realize he'd fallen asleep in the first place, and looks around wildly. "Nate?"

Get it together. Forget that Queen just tore half my face to pieces and threatened to kill me — and implied she'll order me to kill El, when all's said and done. I can't let on she spit me out of the Shadows messed up and battered, inside and out. I straighten my shoulders, willing myself into half-calm. The beam of El's headlamp shines against the non-scarred side of my face.

"I'm right here."

El grins, hopping to his feet and shouldering his knapsack. "Sorry I fell asleep. I guess I'd been awake longer than I realized. Did you get some — eat my ears, what happened to your face? Did you stumble into the queen pipilo's nest, or what?"

What an ironically accurate assumption. But it's not like I could keep two gigantic gashes running almost the whole length of my face a secret from El the way I can hide the Shadowmancer. I have no energy or desire to come up with a lie, but the truth is even less believable. I shrug. "Got up to pee and didn't see a gigantic stalactite in my way." Makes sense enough. "My face had a run in with the sharp bits."

"I run into rocks and stalactites all the time," El argues. "It's why I have to keep repairing my headlamp. I've never gotten marks like that. They look gross, have you seen them? Blackened and dead."

I set my jaw, right on the edge of losing it. "I'm not talking about it. Let's get moving."

"I don't think I brought my salves and bandages, but I can check." El slings his knapsack around, opening the buckle and rooting through the contents. "If it really was a stalactite, they usually drip condensation mixed with vent gasses, and those can be poisonous in mine debris. Let me—"

"I said we're moving." I bare my teeth at him, anger that has nothing to do with El and his insistence on first aid bubbling to a boiling point. "Stop getting distracted every five freaking minutes, and focus. And if you can't do that, get out of here, because you're slowing me down."

El's face falls, something buoyant in his spirit deflating at the harshness of my words. A bit of the trust he might have had in me hardens into stonelike impassibility, and he roughly shifts his knapsack into place on his shoulders.

Why did I say that? Nice going, Nate, way to act like a total dipwad.

"Fine." El's voice tightens. "Let's go."

"El, wait—" Before I can explain myself, he brushes ahead of me, marching further into the mine's cavernous shaft.

"No, you're right, I'm stupid and distractible. Everyone knows it." He hikes ahead, his headlamp's yellowish beam bouncing around the rocks with his steps. "But I'm not useless, I'm a good scout, and we're going to find that fake Cornerstone Key so I can prove you wrong."

El mutters something under his breath, something that sounds remarkably like "dümfo," this world's favorite insult, and he forges on ahead at practically a run. A bend in the cavern takes the light from his headlamp further from my sight, fading along the wall until it disappears entirely.

The pull-tug in my stomach returns in the dark and silence, the spark that I felt in the Shadow Plain growing stronger, brighter, urging me forward in exactly the opposite direction.

"El?" I call, but he can't hear me. He's long gone down another section of the mine. I try again, and louder. "El, you're going the wrong way."

Then again, I got these two tiger stripes on my face because I opened my big, fat mouth when the safety of a human came into question—because caring about them weakens my resolve to destroy Light. Doesn't abandoning El to his stubborn agenda prove I can do what has to be done? That I can allow humans to fall victim to their mortal fates and not intervene, or care? That I can play the game against Light, and win?

I don't need El. I haven't needed him for a long time. I can do this on my own. I can—

Grrrruuuuuugggghhh!

"Ahhh! Nate, help!"

El's panic-stricken shriek combines with the roar of a gigantic monster, the crush of falling rocks and cracking earth, coming from just around the bend in the cavern. Without thinking twice about my previous commitment to ditching him and carrying on alone, I race toward the sound of his voice.

"El! I'm coming!"

"Nate!"

Grrrruuuuuugggghhh!

I turn the corner El disappeared behind and come face to face with an oozing, rock-and-dirt-covered creature the size of a school bus, its gaping mouth filled with rows and rows of shark teeth in an eyeless face. The monster slithers and writhes around the cavern, a prehensile tongue searching for its prey.

Prey that consists of El, and, now, me.

El's eyes latch onto mine, and he utters around raspy breaths two words, the only ones he can enunciate around the roar of the monster, coming in close for the kill: "Ore wyrm!"

CHAPTER 14
CALLIE

HACK HACK HACK.

"Die, beast!"

WWAAAAARRRRRRRRRRR!

Toran's trying to whack the tongue off this monster with his ice sword. And it's not working. Like, at all. Tiny ice shards rain all around as his weapon disintegrates with each blow. But the fierce, eyes-popped, roar-mouth intensity on his face would be seriously funny in combination with this futile attempt at monster slaying if we weren't in danger of being eaten.

"Toran, clear the Mist away instead of going bananas on this thing's tongue." Seriously, he accuses me of concocting bad plans and wasting time? I toss Light flares into the air to signal Diver while the Rykjiersen siblings pretend to fight the final boss in a video game. Heike shoots arrow after arrow into the croc-fish's mouth, but nothing sticks, and Toran's one-sided sword fight is going nowhere fast.

"I can't move this Mist." Toran takes a break in his slashing to glare at me. "The monster is controlling it."

I raise an eyebrow, burning away as much Mist as possible while scanning the gray nothingness for even a vague outline of Diver. "And you're not more powerful than a monster, Seer?"

"I'm not a Seer, I'm a—"

"You're a Seer, Water Manipulation is your specialty, stop being Sir Butthead the Buttface and get rid of this Mist so I can find my mech!"

WAAAAAARRRRRR!

"Toran, I don't think we can kill it." Heike is inherently more logical than her brother, despite what he might believe about himself. She fires off a few more arrows, but all she manages to do is lodge them in the creature's person-decoy tongue. They stick out like a sad little porcupine, and the monster lunges, its snout pushing us further into Mist so thick I can't tell what's before me or behind.

"Right," I agree, "so escaping is the best option." I feel Diver is near, but can't see him in the midst of the soupy plain. "Where are you, buddy? We need to get out of here ASAP."

We are here. Where is Luminaut and the Seer?

Through the gray, a booming footstep rumbles the ground as Diver tries to come to me, but neither of us knows where the other is. "Diver, stop, you might step on us. Let us come to you."

"I can't even see your Diver, let alone the thing that wants to eat us." As much as I hate to agree with Toran, he's not wrong. The gigantic, reptilian thing that had been trying to devour us has vanished into the Mist.

"It's probably controlling the Mist to its advantage, and will come around and attack from a different angle." Heike sounds as book-nerdish as Toran for once. "We read about these types of predators in my self-defense courses for the Guide track at the Academy. They toy with their prey before they attack."

"Surprisingly informative." Toran keeps close to Heike's side, his eyes trained on the subtle movement of the Mist. "I never took any Guide track courses. Now, I regret it."

"You didn't?" Talk about a bewildering statement. "But

you're a Guide, how did you—"

WAAAAAAAHHHHHRRRRRR

Here comes the monster, attacking us from our back left. We barely have time to jump out of the way, missing its snapping jaws by seconds. Unfortunately, nobody coordinated which way we were jumping, and all three of us are separated, unable to see each other even a few feet away. Somehow, Toran will find a way to blame me for this.

"Toran, I can't see you," Heike calls out. She sounds about six feet or so away, but I have no idea where she could be. "Callie, are you alright?"

"Heike, where are you?" Wherever Toran landed, he's completely distraught to be separated from her.

"Hi, I'm here, too." In case they were worried, but probably not.

"Stop talking so loud." Really, Toran? You pretty much shouted for your sister, but okay. "This is your fault anyway, you're the one who levitated yourself with skyfire and alerted the predator to our location."

Didn't I say he'd find a way to blame me? "You're talking just as loud as—ugh, whatever." No use having this argument. "Clear the Mist, so we can get to Diver before that thing strikes again."

"I already told you I can't."

"Did you try?"

"How do you think I *know* I can't move Mist right now? That I guessed?" Toran snorts, and I can just imagine the derisive look on his face. Do I really know Toran that well, or is it because he has exactly three looks, and they're all unpleasant? "I'm not you, I don't attempt whatever idiotic thing comes into my head and hope it works in my favor."

He's right, he's not me. But that does give me an idea...

"So, my old friend, Dr. Ormandi, told me that ancient

Luminauts and Seers worked together to help people and get out of sticky situations like this," I speak into the gray separating us.

"What's a Luminaut?" Toran asks.

"Me. I'm a Luminaut. What you've been calling a skyfire sorcerer. If you'd stop arguing with me about every single thing, I could have explained Luminauts and Seers and all of the multiverse stuff already."

"Multiverse." Toran repeats the word like I've just spouted a fountain of nonsense.

"Yeah, like I said, there's a lot of ground to cover, except you keep telling me to shut up." I wait for him to tell me to shut up again, but he doesn't. "Anyway, we're supposed to be able to use our powers in tandem, because together, we're more powerful than we are individually. Why don't we try to fight off the Mist at the same time, so Diver can find us?"

"Yes, yes, wonderful plan. While we're at it, why don't we invite the predator stalking us to attack immediately?" Toran's voice drips with disdain. "You're suggesting we give away our location in an instant."

"Right, but then, Diver could give the monster a swift butt kicking, and we'd be on our way toward the outposts." How does he not see this is a halfway decent idea?

"You think that piece of lumbering junk could fight off a predator?" Toran barks a hard laugh. "He'd be the last thing to ever—"

"We don't have a lot of options, so I think we should try Callie's plan," Heike interrupts. "I could distract the creature with my lantern and arrows while you both use your powers to find Diver."

"You're not going to make yourself live bait, Heike." Bossy Toran is bossy, and no surprise, he's unwilling to budge on his refusal when it comes to his sister assisting.

"It's not live bait if I—"

"Sounds awesome, Heike, I knew I could count on you." I don't care what Toran thinks, I'm not turning down a legit diversion. "Okay, Toran, on my count, we'll use our powers, and between the two of us, we should be able to burn away some of this Mist. Ready?"

"No."

"I'll take that 'no' to mean 'I'm not ready to be blown away by how awesome this will be,' and not 'I refuse to participate because I'm a stinker.'" I create a small Light orb in my hands, letting it build as I count down. "Four, three, two, one—"

Light flares all around, the single orb I'd built splitting off into dozens of smaller orbs, all of them swirling through the air and burning back the Mist. *Diver,* I channel my mech, *can you see my Light?*

Yes, Luminaut. We are coming.

"Ay, over here!" Heike waves her lantern overhead, visible now that the Mist is clearing, and she fires off a couple arrows. Her outline appears, then her features, and then, the giant gator-fish-lizard (I haven't settled on the best descriptor for this thing). With a roar, the monster charges straight for Heike.

"Toran, are you helping?" I try to find him in the confusion. If he doesn't help out, Diver won't be able to see well enough to reach us before the beastie eats Heike.

"Doesn't it look like I'm helping?" Out of the Mist, Toran's Seer's Eye glows, and a second later, his form and scowling face appears. He pushes the Mist with his open palms, sending it flying away from him. "That thing is distracted by Heike, but the second it sees us, I won't be able to hold the Mist back."

Mist-controlling monsters are gross. Make it easier next time, Tremurheim.

Luminaut, we see you.

Booming footsteps behind my shoulders, and Diver appears, lowering his hand for us to climb onto his palm. He scoops the three of us up to safety just as the gilled gator-fish (gator-fish works best) lunges the exact spot where Heike stood, roaring displeasure that its lunch was snatched. The three of us jog into the Crow's Nest, latching the door firmly behind us.

"See, Toran, I was right," I gloat as soon as we're locked inside. "Our powers are amplified when we use them together."

"No, they aren't, we got incredibly lucky, and the mech had good timing, for once." Oh, Toran, you're never going to pass up an opportunity to backhandedly insult me and Diver, are you?

"Whatever." I plop into the Luminaut's chair. "Get that map, and help me navigate the first outpost on our path."

Toran's scowl could scramble rotten eggs. "Don't bark orders at me."

"Oh, hi, pot, meet kettle," I mutter.

"So nice to see you both getting along," Heike snarks, moving for the domed windows. She chews her bottom lip, watching the landscape. "Uh, Callie? The monster is—"

CRUNCH

Diver lurches to the left, sending our supplies and Nate's old vinyl crate I borrowed indefinitely skidding across the Crow's Nest, thunking against the glass. Leaping from my seat, I rush to see what's going on.

Luminaut, we have a problem.

"Oh, great." Problem is right—and great, it is not.

Gator-fish is an ankle biter. The monster has latched its massive jaws to Diver's lower leg, jerking my mech backward. Mist rolls in rapidly, blocking the gator-fish from view, and I can't see where it's dragging us, but I have a sinking suspicion it's nowhere good. "Diver, can you get rid of that thing?"

We can try, Luminaut.

Diver gives his leg a shake, which sends all of us — and everything in the Crow's Nest — flying around like the contents of a snow globe, if that snow globe was full of things that could give you a concussion. Another shake sends Heike's shoulder into the softest part of my belly, and it's unfortunate she's just about as sharp and angular as her brother, because I might have internal bleeding after this.

"Ow!"

"Sorry!"

"Tell this gigantic menace to stop doing that!" Toran grips the back of the couch, white knuckling the threadbare cushions.

"Have you noticed the monster that tried to eat us is trying to eat Diver now, or were you way too absorbed in your sourpuss, bossy-pants — ah!"

A sharp jolt as gator-fish yanks us again.

Luminaut, we are stuck.

"Try to grab it by the neck and pull it off," I suggest.

"Who are you talking to?" Toran's not used to me speaking to Diver aloud, it's usually an internal activity. Also, his grumpitude is the last thing I need to deal with when I'm guiding Diver through a monster attack.

"Not you," I snap, "just shut up and hang on tight."

"I already told you not to bark orders at —"

Toran doesn't have the opportunity to finish his complaint (small joys, right?) because Diver bends with an absolutely deafening groan of corroded metal and grabs gator-fish by the neck, pulling the monster off of his leg with a horrifying crunch and snap sound that means something, somewhere is probably broken, and I don't have access to a welder or anything similar to fix robotic damage if it's Diver.

Hopefully, the noise came from gator-fish, not my mech. The only thing to do is stumble as quickly as possible to the first outpost and assess the possible damage — right after we get rid of gator-fish.

"Chuck it, buddy!" I call to my mech over the crunching and grinding of gears and decrepit joints.

Yes, Luminaut.

Diver stands upright, the snapping, pissed-off monster still clutched tight in his fist, and squeezes its neck, crushing the gills before he sends it flying like a scaly, reptilian missile into the dense horizon.

Bye-bye, Hem monster. And good riddance.

Almost immediately, Toran's Seer's Eye burns bright, and Mist flees from the landscape for a solid mile-long radius in every direction, revealing a small grove of blackened toothpick trees. One, in particular, stands out as being shaped like a set of twisting antlers on a mound of earth rising higher than the rest of the landscape.

"There!" Toran leaps toward the domed window and points at the trees. He roots through the mess on the floor, retrieving his map, and makes a face that I'd otherwise call a grin if his mouth wasn't so awkwardly downturned. "That's the Horns of the Ways Clan! They bent them into that shape as a sign the first outpost was near. They're based on the ornate designs women of the Ways Clan used to wear in their hair."

"Thanks for the history lesson, I just love learning about ancient topiary," I deadpan.

"Yes, it *is* fascinating." Wow, Toran, I wasn't serious, but cool. You like topiary, which is more than I can say for most things.

"Which direction is the outpost?" Heike joins her brother, peering over his shoulder to look at the map. "It should be northeast of us, shouldn't it?"

"Yes," Toran agrees, rolling up the map like a scroll. He lifts his hand, scattering Mist in the direction we need to travel, and turns to me. "Tell the World Diver to set a course, it should be straight this way."

"Perfect." My smile fades when I hear a telltale sound behind us. A moaning cry piercing the gathering Mist, which quickly obscures our path. "Just one problem."

Luminaut, the creature is back.

Why won't this thing die? Diver crushed its gills and sent it flying, you'd think it would be a goner by now. Monsters out here are annoyingly hard to eliminate.

"Diver, get moving in the northeast direction Toran said to go." I stand and adjust my pompom beanie. "I'm going to go take care of the gator-fish."

"How?" Heike trails after me. "Do you need my help?"

"Heike, stay inside!" Toran, ironically, barks an order.

"If Light frightened off a dramora in the forest, maybe it'll scare this thing, too," I reason, and give Heike's shoulder a squeeze. "I'll let you know if I need your help."

Outside on Diver's shoulder, the Mist moves to engulf me, and the necessity of gills in a giant land-monster like gator-fish becomes apparent. Slowly, Diver lurches forward, testing his leg, which looks okay from this angle. Hot on our heels, the gator-fish drags itself through the sludge, its shape just visible through the Mist. Diver weakened it; it can't move as fast, and only half the gills appear to be working. But it remains dogged in its pursuit of us.

"Okay, let's get this monster off our tail." I create an orb of Light in my palms, small at first, but growing, burning away the Mist until it becomes as large as a beachball, and then bigger still. Light fills me, spreads throughout every inch, and soon I can't tell where the orb ends and I begin.

Okay, this is far enough. What did Toran say about reaching the point I could control the power before it took over? Don't want to overdo it.

Also, I hate that he was right about something. So irritating.

"Take that!" I launch the orb at gator-fish, not aiming to hurt it, just to frighten it off. Light blazes through the Mist, illuminating the gray with fiery gold, until the Light bursts just above gator-fish's head in a thousand tiny twinkles, falling over the monster's scales and into its eyes.

AAARRRRRRHHHHHHHNNNNN!!!

Gator-fish stops in its tracks, clawing at its eyes as though they're burned. The shriek coming from its snapping jaws sounds anguished, and it's in as much pain as the tree Toran asked (ordered) me to hit with my Light in the forest. I want to call out that I'm sorry, that I didn't mean to hurt the thing that was trying to eat me five minutes ago, but the ridiculousness of the sentiment keeps me silent.

Toran burns away the Mist from his perch in the Crow's Nest and Diver limps on in a straight shot toward our destination, but I remain on my mech's shoulder, lost in thought. I might joke around about Light bombing Nate's face, or Toran's scowl, but I never thought I could actually do something like bomb things, or destroy millions of acres of forest, or kill a whole Clan of people. But every passing day, with every living being my Light hurts, it seems like I was mistaken.

Is Light truly good if it can harm? Or am I too inexperienced and too much of a novice to know how to use it the right way? The broken puzzle just lost a few more pieces, and I'm quickly running out of time to put it together.

"Quit gawking around out here!" Toran snaps from the opened hatch door. "The first outpost is up ahead."

I wonder if Toran will ever realize how hypocritical everything that comes out of his mouth sounds. *Don't bark orders, but I'm totally allowed to bark orders:* The First Book of Toran,

Complaints and Grievances, Chapter One, Verse Two. But glancing over my shoulder, I see he's right. Directly in front of us sits an abandoned building, derelict and decayed after centuries of sitting out here in the Mist. Rising from atop the roof, a miniature version of a Beacon, a cylindrical extension with a glass dome at the zenith. It looks just like the picture on Toran's map, one of the infamous outposts that will lead us to the Beacons of the Tageveld.

"Can you scatter the Mist so we can see what we're dealing with?" I ask. Toran wordlessly gets to work, moving his hands around so the Mist floats away, and the finer details of the building are revealed.

Oh, no. Please, let that not be what I think it is.

"What happened here?" Heike appears behind Toran's shoulder, her lantern and crossbow ready. She drinks in the pitiful outpost, venturing further onto Diver's shoulder when he comes to a stop. "Was there a fire?"

My heart drops, my worst fear materializing as what lies scattered around the building comes into clear focus—piles and piles of human-shaped Shadowmancer ash.

"No fire made that," I say, my voice trembling along with my limbs. "A monster did."

CHAPTER 15
NATE

"BACK UP!"

"I'm backing up!"

"*Grrrraaawwwwwww!*" The ore wyrm slithers around, its massive body coating the cavern walls with oozing, steaming pus that renders anything it touches stickier than superglue. If El and I get caught in it, there's no way we're going to be able to move. An easy kill for the wyrm, a disgusting and painful end for us.

I can see why 'wyrm pus' is an insult in Ictari.

"You're not backing up, dingus, you're headed straight for its mouth!"

"*Rrrrrnnnnnnggggghhhh!*" The wyrm comes around again, but not before we get our directions straight in the pale yellow light of El's headlamp and slip into a small crevice off to the left, one with just enough room for El and me to squeeze inside.

"Dingus—is that like dümfo? Because—"

"El! Are you serious?!"

"Sorry!"

"*Gggggggrrrrrnnnnnnn!*" The wyrm roars again, angry to have lost the scent of its prey. It swings its head around, teeth and jaws pulsing with intermittent clicks, as if it's sending out a radar signal to find us.

"What's it doing? I can't see," El hisses.

"Shut up, and don't move!" I hiss back. If the basic biology of carnivorous creatures functions the same here as it does on Earth, animals that can't hunt by sight rely on scent, sound, movement, or all three to find their next meal.

A meal I would very much like not to be us.

What I'd *really* like right now is to figure a way out of our current mess, but we're stuck between an actual rock and a hard place. You'd almost think the wyrm planned it that way. If that's the case, it's a highly efficient strategist, and I oughta take notes. El's back is pressed against a solid rock wall, and mine is pressed to him, shielding him from the wyrm's writhing tongue and sucking jaws, but we're sitting ducks down here. It won't be long until the wyrm finds us.

Hopefully, my lack of a beating heart will come in useful in this scenario. Nothing for the wyrm to hear pounding like thunder under my ribs.

"Nate?" Darkness help me, why is El still talking?

"I told you to be quiet!" Can he not see the ore wyrm's massive, pus-covered body slinking six inches from my face, trying to hunt us down and eat us? Maybe he has a death wish, but I don't.

"Why are you so cold?" El gives a shudder of chill at my back.

"Because I magically turned off all my body heat so I could save your not-being-quiet — ah!"

So much for sarcasm. Maybe I should take my own advice, and shut up more often. The wyrm circles around in the blink of an eye, almost as fast as I come and go with the Veil. Its prehensile tongue and gaping, shark-toothed jaws materialize a hairsbreadth from the tip of my nose.

Another unpleasant fact: this thing has bad breath. If I were still human, it would be enough to gas me out in seconds, rendering me sprawled out and prone. Probably another hunting tactic. This wyrm's an Ictari apex predator.

Of course it makes total sense for El to run face-first into one. He's a homing beacon for trouble.

"Nate, look out!" El cries as the wyrm lunges for our hiding spot. Is he ever going to listen when I tell him to be quiet? It's for his benefit, you know.

"This might hurt." I shove El as far back into the cavern as he'll go, using my whole body and all my strength to keep him from the wyrm, which takes another rock-quaking lunge at our hiding spot. Its tongue isn't quite long enough to reach me—yet. But if it manages to widen the opening of the crevice a few inches more, we're done for.

"Ow!" El elbows me in the kidney. "Whatever my clavicle is, you just broke it!"

"SHUT UP!"

Well, that was a bad idea. For all my admonitions to be quiet, I just yelled, and now, the wyrm has no doubt where we're hiding.

Stupid, Nate. Aren't you supposed to be the strategist in this scenario? The guy with at least three backup plans for any deviation, an infamous five-steps-ahead player when it's down to the clutch? It's how I've always dealt with things I can't predict, much less control: plan for everything.

Then again, strategizing, planning, and running gameplay is hard when you're face-to-face with a stink-breath monster that's trying to devour you whole. I feel like I deserve a bit of slack for this out-of-character moment.

Too bad this ore wyrm won't give it to me

Another slam of the creature's sucking mouth rattles the crevice opening, hard enough to spray my face with rocks, dust, and pebbles.

"Nate! Do something!" El cries as the wyrm lunges again.

All this could be over in a matter of seconds, the ore wyrm reduced to a pile of ashes, if I let the Shadowmancer out. Would Darkness overtake the wyrm—just the wyrm? Or is El in danger of getting ashed inadvertently? With the VBHS gym scenario, I was carefully controlled. Queen taught me how to reign in my emotions to prove a point, not rain down total destruction.

Can I conjure that same emotionless concentration now?

"*Grrrraaaaaawwwwwwnnnn!*" The wyrm surges forward, powerful enough to break through the wall of stone standing between us and its jaws, and if I don't make a choice right freaking now, El and I are seconds away from becoming wyrm food.

Sorry, El. I never wanted you to see this.

"Stay back, as far as you can!"

As soon as the wyrm rears its head for the strike, I let the Shadowmancer take hold, icy Darkness flooding my veins, creeping over my skin, turning me into a being of unrepentant Shadow. My eyes burn red and black, seeking Light to take down and destroy. Darkness immediately seeks out El, whose inner Light burns bright in his horror, but I shove down the raging urge to take him out with a painful cry. This wyrm might not have any Light for my Darkness to feed on, but it's alive, and living things are always better targets for my power than inanimate objects.

"*Raaaaggggggnnnn!*" The wyrm shrieks, oozing even more pus around my feet, trapping me in place. Am I worried about some powerless wyrm? No, I'm the apex here, the Shadowmancer at the top of the food chain. And this wyrm is about to be ash.

Darkness swirls through the cavern, twisting and curling around the wyrm's body. Just as the wyrm realizes it's been trapped, the tentacles of Darkness tighten, pressing into the oozing flesh. Another shriek flies from the wyrm's mouth, this time, one of a terror-stricken animal about to meet a merciless end.

"Bye-bye, wyrm." Eh, work on the line. That was pretty bad.

I hold an open palm in the air, lingering just a moment, before clenching a tight fist. With that singular movement, the wyrm succumbs to the Darkness, evaporating into ashes that fall like blackened snowflakes to the cavern floor. The pus, the teeth, the tongue, the entirety of the wyrm is gone. Ashes remain.

The Shadowmancer smiles, a maniacal laugh of insidious joy pressing against my lips.

But inside, the lingering human, the part of me that's always been and always will be Nate Ormandi, wants to gag and yell and vomit all over himself as I survey the piles of ash in a wyrm-shaped mound near my feet.

I just turned a living creature to ash. Erased the essence of its existence the way Queen murdered her other servants, the way she wanted me to murder Callie's family and Dad. For one brief moment, I was really and truly a Shadowmancer, a creature of Darkness and Shadow that steals life with no remorse.

And I think I could puke, if I had anything in my stomach.

"N-Nate?" El emerges from our crevice hiding spot. My back is to him, and I can't see his face. I don't have to. He's horrified.

I turn, facing him at last, and the look in his eyes at the sight of mine, blazing red and black in a vampiric, demon-like face, are enough to confirm his revulsion. His righteous fear.

"Y-you're—a—a—"

"A monster," the Shadowmancer's venomous purr fills my ears, the only voice El knows made sinister and twisted.

El's expression facing down the truth is just like Callie's that night in the gym. Hatred mixed with heartbreak, the kind of lingering shock that can change a person's DNA. I see it in his eyes just as clearly as I saw it in hers, and the gut-punch of regret stealing my resolve feels the same as it did in the face of her rage and anguish—maybe, actually, worse.

Without a word, El spins on his heel and races away, back through the cavernous shaft toward whatever safety awaits him elsewhere. Because anywhere, even the darkest depths of this cursed mine in the middle of a world made of ice, is safer than remaining in my presence.

"Crap call, man. *Really* crap." I shed my Shadowmancer skin, resuming human form, but it's too late to change anything. El's seen all he needed to see: the Darkness, what it can do, and what I really am.

Well, go on, El. Who needs you? I'm more than capable of finishing this Light Core hunt myself. Get out of here with your bad luck and lack of focus. I'm *glad* you're gone, you hear me? This is exactly what I wanted all along—you just saved me the trouble of ditching you myself.

So why do I feel like my chest got slammed by a Mack truck?

I rest on my haunches, the muscle memory of my catcher's squat coming back to me: weight in my toes, balanced and taut. But instead of a baseball in my hands under the bright warmth of the California sun, there's a palmful of ash slipping through my undead fingers as I sit, alone in the dark.

Queen would be pleased. She'd praise me for finally getting rid of human distractions so I could continue my mission. I'm winning the game—the humiliating subjugation at her hand, and all the sacrifices I agreed to when I was Turned, are finally circling around in my favor. Light will soon be mine for the destroying, my goal within my grasp, and all the easier and quicker with El out of the way.

My strategy unfolded just the way I predicted. El led me straight to the correct mine, spilled the right secrets, and was eating out of the palm of my hand the whole time. I pushed his trigger buttons, figured out his secrets so I could exploit them, and when I'd learned all I could from him, I'd concoct a devious plan to abandon him back in Aragusti. I wasn't about to let my weakness and emotions put my hunt at risk, not like I did with Callie. I'd prove I can make power plays, just like Queen. Manipulate, contort the truth. Twist that knife a little deeper with each new, thinly-veiled threat. Always a step ahead.

I'd find the Light Core, and get what I always wanted.

What I always wanted...

And then, *he* ditched *me.* Turned the tables and left me reeling, shaken out of unearned over-confidence. Just like Callie took off and Dove away with her Light Core, leaving me at a Luminaut's mercy with nothing to show for all the lies, deception, and hurt except my own cocky defeat. Dad tried to stop me from giving in to my worst instincts. He begged me, even. But I made sure it was too late, and left him with no doubt of my capacity for betrayal.

It's what I *always* wanted, right?

Lies. Deceit. Betrayal. The same words played out, over and over. Everything I was blaming on Light—I did it all, too, with Darkness. All I've ever done with this great and terrible power was ensure everyone I cared about since Turning—even if that care was warped by Shadows—thinks I'm a monster.

No. They *know* I'm a monster. A heartless one.

Was it ever really a point of pride? Was I that sickeningly cruel?

Staring at the ash in my hands, I see it now. And I can't look away.

Callie is right to hate. El is right to fear. Dad is right to mourn. I am a Shadowmancer, and I should feel nothing in the face of this realization.

So why is the only thing I care about the fact El ran away from me, horror and disgust etched across his face? I'm not angry about it. I'm just... hurt. Wretched and alone, just like I was that night on the beach, watching the December waves ebb and flow.

"I have to protect myself from heartless monsters like you…"

A shudder ripples over me, remembering the words, and the way Callie looked when she said them. I knew in that moment, without any doubt, I'd broken her heart and lost her forever. It stung then, but now it aches as deep as my bones.

I might have said I was angry at Callie, blamed her for everything that happened in Verona Beach, convinced myself it was all her fault, and she should have just gone along with my plans and let me win the game. But the choice was always hers to make, just like it was mine. This time, with El, I have nobody to blame for my choices but myself.

A tiny, quiet voice inside whispers I've *never* had anyone to blame but me. Not Callie. Not Dad. Not Mom. Not Light. Just me.

The last of the ash slips through my fingers.

Faint scuffling steps approach, and a pale yellow light comes slowly into view. After my mind finally figures out it's not an illusion, El and his headlamp round the corner. He stares at me, at the ashes around my feet, his mouth hardened but determined.

"I'm sorry I ran away," he says.

"Don't be." I watch him, still resting my elbows on the tops of my thighs, trying to decide why he's here, and what he wants. "I'd run away from me, too."

"What *are* you, exactly?" El remains a leery distance away, his eyes narrowing on my human form's face. Nate's face.

"I'm a Shadowmancer," I say. "I don't think there's a word for it on Ictari, but basically, I'm a monster. A dangerous one." More ashes fall from my hands. "You ought to run away again. Being around me could get you seriously hurt. Maybe even killed."

Danger. Injury. Death. It's all coming into horrible focus. I expect when I look up, El will be gone. To my surprise, he remains.

"Would you ever do to me what you did to that ore wyrm?" El asks, his wariness plain.

"No." Without a second thought, I answer, knowing it's more true than anything else has been since before I was Turned. Even if Queen orders me, I'm not going to ash El, just like I was never going to ash Dad, or Callie's family, or hurt her the way Queen wanted me to. She can't ultimately decide how I use my power, and I choose to no longer hurt El — or Callie, or Dad, or anybody else — with Darkness.

This choice has always been mine to make.

"Before I was captured and brought to Aragusti, back when I first started scouting, I was trained by a boy I knew from the mountains, a scout named Ilya." El grips the straps of his knapsack tight. "He was older than me, and we became scouting partners. I trusted him. Even when we got into dangerous situations, he promised he'd never abandon me the way my father had." A pause and he shrugs. "It's why I started scouting at seven sun-cycles. Mam had just died, and Da was long gone. I was starving." If he's sad about it, the sorrow is fleeting, because he regains his composure and goes on. "One day, we scouted too far into Aragusti territory. I knew it was wrong, but Ilya promised we'd find more rams down in the canyon. He said he'd stay with me, even if cavern patrols spotted us on their land. But when the patrols came, Ilya ran ahead and escaped, and left me for dead with Aragusti snowcycles at my back. They might have killed me, but they'd just lost a lot of scouts to a mining accident and needed replacements."

"El, that's not really relevant, but—"

"There's a point, I promise," he interrupts. "I had to tell you that story before I could explain. The reason I came back is because I was about to do to you what Ilya did: break my promise and leave you for dead. I swore a long time ago I'd never do to anyone what he did to me. And so I'm back. And we're going to find that Cornerstone Key."

"I don't know if I want to find it anymore, much less with somebody who could get hurt scouting a mine with a monster." *Monster.* The word feels like poison, closing around my throat and thickening my tongue until my stomach turns.

"Even if you are a monster, you saved my life. Twice." El takes a cautious step toward me, his boots blackened by the ashes of the wyrm. "You defended me to Caro and his dümfo friends. You helped me find the stags in the canyon. Maybe not all monsters are bad. Maybe you're a good one. Or, maybe, you're as evil and dangerous as you say. Either way, we're going to find that Cornerstone Key, even if the only thing we accomplish is proving it exists in the first place."

I can't tell if I want to laugh, or hug him. Instead, I offer one last chance to back out of our deal, free and clear. "That's probably a really stupid decision. I won't hold it against you if you decide to leave. Really, I mean it."

"I might not be known for being very smart," El says. "But I'd rather be called stupid than ever be a person who breaks a promise."

Rising to my full height, I abandon the ashes of my Darkness and clap his shoulder, giving him a quick, almost brotherly squeeze. "Thanks, El." I pause before adding, "I'm glad you came back."

And in all truth, I am.

"Don't get weepy on me, or I'll make you eat your ears." El smiles, shoving me away. "Come on, we have a lot of mine to cover, and that Cornerstone Key isn't going to find itself. I want to know if it's actually real, don't you?"

Do I really want to find the thing Queen is so intent on destroying, the thing she scarred my face for and threatened to end me if I failed? Being her little one has brought nothing but pain, and the tiny voice of defiance getting stronger by the minute—Nate's voice—says I don't have to do anything just because she says so.

And yet, still.

I want to find the source of the pull-tug in my stomach, the spark of faint awareness calling me deeper and deeper into the mine like the suppressed memory of a long-lost dream. And so, for that reason, for my *own* choice, I'll journey on.

"Alright, let's get moving," I say. "And try to stay away from bottomless pits and gigantic wyrms from now on."

CHAPTER 16
CALLIE

"THIS IS EXACTLY why I keep telling you skyfire is dangerous."

Toran sweeps his hand across the devastating scene, taking care to point out the vaguely person-shaped piles of ash surrounding the outpost. Deep trenches, small craters, and easily identifiable tracks encircle the perimeter of the outpost, but none come close to the ashes scattered around the structure: almost as if the Hem's predators knew better than to disturb the final resting place of these doomed people. Or were too terrified to come near.

"These were members of the Tree and Ways Clans," he says. "A living, breathing part of Tremurheim history, erased forever because of your magic."

"My magic didn't do this." As little as I've come to realize I know about Light—what it is, what it's used for, and how to control it—I know without a doubt my power didn't cause this destruction. "This was a monster. A Shadowmancer."

"Such things don't exist," Toran snaps, looking at me with renewed disgust. "The more nonsense you speak, the more idiotic you make yourself sound."

"What's a Shadowmancer?" Heike asks before I can punch Toran in the throat. Does she know how many times she's inadvertently saved her brother's trachea?

"Shadowmancers used to be human, but they've been consumed by Darkness, and exist to destroy Light like mine." I take a few steps toward one of the ashen remains, a Clan member who tried to build an outpost in the ceaseless Mist so that a lost Clan could find its way home — and met a horrific end. A tremor runs through me, and I turn away. "I don't know why a Shadowmancer killed these people, but if they thought the outposts were going to somehow lead them to Tremurheim's Light Core, they'd kill anybody in the way, so they could destroy it themselves."

"What you just said made no sense at all." Toran stares at me with a snarl so severe I'm not sure he won't transform into a wolf and bite me. "I'm going inside to see if there's anything salvageable."

"If a Shadowmancer was here, you won't find anything but ash," I warn him.

"How is it you know so much about Shadowmancers, or whatever it is you claim destroyed this outpost?" Toran stops, his hand on the decrepit door, and the ice in his eyes hardens. "It's almost as if you've met one before."

Met, flirted, made out with, all the same difference.

"A Shadowmancer sounds a little like the old Witch of Arjendenstag." Heike follows Toran inside, and so do I, because there's no use standing around out here with the depressing piles of ash that used to be people. Any distraction will help contain my growing nausea.

"What's the witch thing about?" I glance at Heike, ducking past the bowed threshold.

"Another bedtime story to scare children," Toran answers with a snort. "Heike, let me see that lantern. It's dark as night in here."

"I have Light powers," I remind him.

"I still don't believe you when you say skyfire didn't do this, so the last thing I'm going to do is let even more of it loose in such a small space." He takes the lantern Heike passes him and holds it high, revealing even more piles of ash and little else inside the decayed building. "Dramora spawn," he mutters.

The ancient Shadowmancer who killed these Clanspeople didn't leave anything to chance: no survivors, no quarter, no mercy. I can feel their terror surging through my Light, cries of horror echoing through the eons until the ghosts of their screams embedded in the walls, the floorboards, the rickety steps leading up to the domed glass. I cover my mouth with my hand and close my eyes, swallowing back revulsion. If a Shadowmancer killed every last person in the outpost to keep them from reaching a hidden Light Core, what would a Shadowmancer do to keep me, a Luminaut, from finding it?

It's a stark reminder how lucky my family and I got with Nate. How everything I sacrificed in leaving, and how terribly I miss them, was to prevent them from meeting this same fate.

Then again, he could have gone back on his word. After all, I went back on mine when I made my play for the Light Core. Nate could have ashed them all the second I Dove away from Verona Beach. The sick feeling in my stomach intensifies until I'm queasy, sweating hard under my layers of winter gear as bile rises into my throat. I have to hope they're okay—that Nate was somehow bluffing. The alternative is too world-shattering to consider.

All the more reason to find these missing Light Cores as fast as I can, and take him down.

"If this building is constructed like all other ancient Tremurheim structures from the Clan Era, there should be a couple of storage rooms this way." Toran takes the lantern and wanders off toward the back, carefully stepping around the ashes. I lean against the wall, arms gripped tight to my stomach.

"Callie, are you alright?" Heike's voice softly parts the darkness closing in around us. I make a tiny Light orb, little more than a candle flame, and hold it between us.

"Tell me your witch story," I change the subject, because I'm not alright. Not at all. "I like fairy tales."

"Well, Toran thinks it's ridiculous, of course." Heike leans against the wall beside me. It feels good, the warmth of her arm next to mine, because I've gone cold. "But just because something is a made-up fairy tale doesn't mean it can't be true." She grins across the glowing Light. "The story goes that the Witch started life as a good sorceress, one who could control the earth and make things grow, but she lost her true love and was corrupted by evil magic."

Wow, already an eye roll. "Sounds like every bad magic trope in every fairy tale I've ever heard. Woman falls in love, lover jilts her, woman turns evil." I snort through my nose. "Boring."

Heike chuckles. "Yes, it's a common theme in our fairy tales, too. Silly, isn't it? Anyway, when the Witch was good, she grew bountiful gardens wherever she went, and was kind and generous to all she encountered. But then, her love abandoned her, and a dark shadow consumed her heart. She grew hungry and hateful, and her new powers made her crave human flesh. So she lured people out into the forest to devour them. The only evidence anybody could find of the Witch and her victims were piles of ash. For many Seasons, she hunted wayward villagers, her magic prolonging her life, until people forgot she was ever good to begin with."

Tremurheim's witch fairy tale is dark and forbidding—definitely in keeping with the vibe. It kind of reminds me a little of Hansel and Gretel. "How was the Witch defeated?" Two clever kids shoved her into an oven when her back was turned?

"She wasn't," Heike replies. "This story has a happy ending.

That's why I like it."

"Yeah?" I could do with a happy ending right about now — happier than the ending these poor piles of ash got at the hands of a vengeful Shadowmancer. Where was the Luminaut meant to protect them?

Destroying the forest and creating the Hem, according to Toran.

"A skyfire sorcerer in disguise, one who was good and brave, took a bounty on the Witch offered by the village of Arjendenstag," Heike relates the tale with measured reverence. "The sorcerer faced many perils on the journey, because the Witch was cunning and sly, but at last hunted her down. But instead of slaying her, the sorcerer used skyfire to remove the shadow of evil from the Witch's heart. The Witch became a good sorceress once more, and she made one last garden grow from the ashes of all the people she'd killed. It was the most beautiful garden anyone had ever seen. Then she and the sorcerer who saved her disappeared in a flash of skyfire, and were never seen again. The people of Arjendenstag say the white-flowering trees that bloom near their village are proof the story is true." A pause, and a wry smirk turns the corners of her mouth. "Toran says it's all a nest of nargush droppings."

It doesn't surprise me that Toran would hate a story about an evil person atoning for their crimes, and making something beautiful out of death. But it proves he's at least partly wrong about Light being used only for destruction, if a Luminaut used their Light to save a lost witch, and the villagers she threatened, from her sorrowful revenge. Take that, jerk-face.

"What's your brother's deal, anyway?" I can finally address the elephant in the room now that said elephant has wandered off.

Heike looks perplexed. "His deal?"

"You know, his… Toran-ness."

"Oh, yes, I know what you mean," she laughs. "He can be difficult to get along with sometimes."

"Sometimes? He's done nothing but insult me and tell me my powers are dangerous since the moment I met him. Oh, and that's not mentioning the blackmail."

"That's true. And so you know, I think it's awful how he treats you." Heike rests the small of her back on her clasped hands. Her expression is uncertain, like she's not sure she should tell me something, but is resolved to, anyway. "Toran has always been rigid and kind of bossy, but he never used to be unkind. He took care of me when our parents were working late, because Archivist's days are long and Herbalists have to be available at all hours to patients. I made up the games we played, he made up the rules, and always made sure I was fed and put to bed, and ready for courses the next morning. We were best of friends." She squirms a bit, something dark I can't decipher passing over her features. Then again, it could be nothing but a shadow. "Lately, he's been… mean. Capricious. He still treats me like I'm the little girl he had to take care of, except now, the world isn't fun and fair, it's cruel and terrifying — and I'm *not* a little girl." She blows a puff of air through pursed lips. "Nothing has been the same since his selection."

"What's *selection*?" Heike says it like it's something important, a word that holds a different meaning here.

"I suppose things are done differently in your village," Heike replies with an embarrassed flush. "I shouldn't have assumed it's the same. Anyway, selection happens when a person turns sixteen. The Village Council takes into account a person's Aptitude Exam results and their course of study, and they select them for a position in the village."

"So, they pick your future job," I surmise. "Sounds sketchy.

Why can't you choose for yourself?"

"The needs of the village come first. But most people try to sway the Aptitude Exam results by studying for a certain course track in secret." Heike flashes a sly smile across the Light in my hand. "I was studying for the Guide track."

"Yeah, I remember." So that's why she was sneaking out of the village through the garbage dump all the time.

"Well, Toran didn't study for the Guide track," Heike elaborates. "He wanted to be the next Archivist, and Papa wanted to train him. He easily passed into the Archivist and Record Keeper track."

Toran, holed up in a dusty library with books and absolutely zero contact with other humans? Sounds perfect for him—and explains his earlier comment about not studying Tremurheim's many predators in school. "So why is he a Guide, and not the next Archivist of Gravenskov?"

"When it came time for everyone in his year group to appear before the Village Council to receive their selections, they passed him over for Archivist, and selected him for Guide instead." She shifts her feet, kicking a small pebble away from her toe. "We've never been certain why. Papa thinks it's because he's politically outspoken and has disagreed with the Council on certain things... but it could also be because Papa is still young, and Gravenskov lost several Guides to skuddima the Season before. Either way, Toran was devastated. He'd done everything right, you know? Followed all the rules, received high marks, was respectful and diligent. He felt as though he'd been handed a death sentence for no reason at all."

"Why is being a Guide a death sentence?" I catch her eye. "Because of all the predators and Mist in the forest?"

"Yes, Guides don't often survive past twenty or twenty-one," Heike says. "Some do, but it's rare."

A nerd like Toran suddenly being told he'd not only have to become an expert outdoorsman overnight, but one fated to die young, would be enough of a betrayal to rip his book-loving, live-by-the-rules soul to shreds.

"So why'd you want to be a Guide, if it's so dangerous?" Seems like a bummer job. Heike is so bubbly, and a natural story-teller. Wouldn't she be happier doing something where she could use her people skills?

"I wanted to see what Tremurheim was like outside Gravenskov." Heike rests her head against the wall, a far-off look in her eyes. "I know all about life inside the village, and it's boring. Why stay cooped up forever when you can escape every day? Even for a while? It's why I started sneaking into the forbidden section with Toran to read about sorcery. More interesting than school-work, in my opinion."

We share that opinion, Heike.

"You definitely got your escape wish," I deadpan. "We can't get further from Gravenskov than where we're going."

"That's true." Heike smiles, genuinely excited at the prospect of seeing the furthest corner of Tremurheim. "And in the end, Toran being selected for Guide was a good thing. He started having visions right after he moved into the Guide Hall, and going into the forest for field notes every day allowed him time to learn to control his magic, and more freedom to research it at the Archive than he'd had at the Academy."

"He has visions?" News to me. Keeping secrets, Toran?

"He sees things that aren't there," Heike drops her voice, even though Toran isn't anywhere in sight. "It's the one thing he would never want anybody but me to know. He says they're like windows in the sky, in the trees, in the Mist. He can't explain what it is, so he pretends they aren't there. But when he would sleep at night, he'd be surrounded by water on all sides, just floating there, and the sky over his head would be blue, and so bright he couldn't see anything. He said it was horrible."

Sounds a lot like Toran is already Seeing gateways, and envisioning the gorgeous California sky over the deep, blue-green ocean. And he hates it. No surprise. Like, at all.

But if he saw California, or Verona Beach, or even *me* in his Sight….

"He tries to hide how out of control he feels," Heike goes on, "but after everything that happened with his selection, manifesting magic was one blow too many. At least, that's what I think. Toran doesn't like to talk about it. He doesn't talk about *anything* anymore." She rolls her eyes a bit, betraying her impatience. "All he wants to do is shield me from everything he thinks is bad."

"Sounds like an accurate assumption. And it sucks to feel that way. Believe me, I know." How out of control and overwhelmed was I when I first manifested my Luminaut powers? To say I was in over my head was an understatement. "But it doesn't give him a free pass to treat people like garbage. If he'd explained all of this to me, I could have helped him understand. I have a friend back home who's a Seer, too. He's a Fire Manipulator, and had his powers completely under control and wasn't a jerk to people in the process. I can help Toran, if he'd—"

"If he'd let you," Heike finishes for me. "But he won't. Once he's made up his mind about something, he doesn't change it— like your skyfire being dangerous, or me being too naive and immature to be left alone without his protection. He's stubborn that way."

"No joke." I'm pretty sure Toran was born stubborn and set in his ways. "Thanks for explaining all this, Heike. Good talk."

"I've wanted to talk to you for *so* long," Heike admits, a little over-gushy, but sincere. I smile at the sweet eagerness in her voice. "There are so many things I want to know about your village, why you came to Tremurheim, why you're trying to find Beacon's flare, how you travel in Diver, all of it."

"We've got a long trip ahead of us," I assure her with a laugh. "Plenty of time for explaining everything, I promise."

"Heike, where are you?" Toran and the lantern appear from the back of the outpost, a small, crusty box of something in his hand. A scowl turns his mouth sour when he sees us. "Why didn't you follow me?"

"I didn't think it was necessary for two people to go searching through old storage rooms." Heike glances at me. "Besides, I wanted to stay with Callie."

Toran bristles, and halfway pouts. "You should have stayed with me."

"Chill out. Sometimes girls just want to hang out with other girls." And spill all their brother's Seer secrets in the process. I nod toward the box. "What's that?"

"Lantern oil."

I raise an eyebrow. "Lantern oil that's a couple hundred years old?"

"Do you have any other way to keep my sister's lantern burning so she isn't lost in the Mist?" Toran raises his eyebrow right back.

"Sure do." I take the lantern from him and extinguish the flame inside, filling it instead with the tiny Light orb in my palm. Light glows, bright and steady, and more brilliant than the unstable fire.

"Thank you, Callie!" Heike smiles, admiring her new Light lantern. "It's beautiful, and much better than a—"

"That's not safe." Toran stares at the lantern with abject horror. "It's skyfire." He glares at me next. "Are you trying to harm her?"

"Absolutely not." I want to snark that if I was going to harm anyone with my Light, it would be him over his awesome sister, but by some miracle, I keep my tongue checked.

"You don't know for sure skyfire won't shatter the glass," Toran argues. It's his favorite thing, seriously. I bet he wakes up in the morning and says to himself *"What arguments should I start with Callie today? So many to choose from. I'll pick them all."*

"At least it's not going to explode and blow her hand off, like that stuff might." I nod toward the box he carries, then turn to the rickety stairs in the far corner of the outpost's main room. "Speaking of Lighting things up, aren't we here to reignite the outpost so it can shine our path to the next one?" A small hatch door blocks most of the glass dome from the rest of the outpost. "Anybody want to help me pull this open?"

"Don't touch that, you could cause the whole ceiling to cave in," Toran cautions.

"I'll help!" Heike rushes to join me.

"These steps can't bear the weight of two people, they're old." Toran stands at the foot of the stairs, watching me and Heike climb like he's waiting for both of us to drop out of the bottom and break our necks.

"Calm down, we aren't—"

A shiver runs down my spine, the feeling of fine spider silk grazing my hair over my shoulder, poisonous and sinister. The chilly creep of death shudders along my arms, threatening to pull me just beyond the reach of this world, deep down into a realm I never want to return to again. A realm of shadow and monsters, a nightmare made real in the worst possible way.

Darkness.

"Who's there?" I go stiff with fear, forgetting that Heike is right behind me, and Toran is behind her. I could be all alone in the room, or here with a hundred people—all I can sense is the Darkness crawling over my shoulder. "Nate?"

"Who's Nate?" Heike's voice floats toward my ears from somewhere far away.

I mumble sounds—I can't form words—pushing past her and Toran as I move to inspect the outpost, heart clenched tight in my chest. Darkness, shadows, horror… the evidence is all around, but the source of the dread is nowhere to be seen.

"Nate? Where are you?" No answer. Not even a hint of his laugh, or a flash of his wavy hair around the corner. It's as if this Darkness wants to see me, but not for me to see it. A monstrous cat spying on a mouse before laying the inevitable trap.

Nate never played games like this. Pretended to haunt me, yes. Attacked openly, yes. But hide and seek? He was too brazen for that. A new tactic, maybe? Or something else? I venture further into the dark, careful not to disturb the piles of ashen remains, but nothing, no tentacles or dark fog manifesting as physical fear, can be found.

And then, just like that, all trace of the Darkness is gone as quick as it came.

"What in Lands Beyond is wrong with you?" Toran rounds the corner, Heike on his heels.

"I thought—I was sure there was something back here…"

"You were calling for somebody named Nate," Toran's grimace is angled shadows in the lantern's Light. "Who is that?"

"He's my… it's complicated." Something tells me 'my mortal enemy I had a crush on and kissed because I thought he was a ghost' isn't going to go over well as an explanation, especially with somebody as incredulous as Toran.

"What does 'it's complicated' mean? Were you lovers?" Heike's eyes gleam; she's so into this potential-ex-boyfriend thing it's not even funny.

"Remember that fairy tale you told me? About the Witch? It's a little like that." Except I'm not about to go all spooky and eat people alive. Gross. Regardless, Heike sighs wistfully.

"That's so romantic, Callie, you *have* to tell me about him." Heike Rykjiersen, a fan of romantic tragedy. Who knew?

"Why did you think you heard this 'Nate' person back here?" Toran isn't having it with the 'it's complicated' explanation, which doesn't shock me, but I was hoping he'd be cool for once in his life and drop it. "Somebody from your foreign village would not be hiding in an abandoned outpost on the Hem, unless there's something else about 'Nate' you aren't telling us."

And, of course, Toran is going to automatically assume the latter.

"It turned out to be nothing, I was just paranoid," I dodge his question. "Let's Light this dome and get out of here, before something else can happen. I've got the creeps all of a sudden."

"What creeps?" Toran growls. "You're not being truthful."

"Yeah, you're one to talk," I retort, pushing past him toward the stairs.

"What is that supposed to mean?" Toran follows close on my heels.

"You've been hiding the fact you're Seeing gateways," I answer from the bottom of the stairs. "What else are you Seeing? Had any visions you can't explain? Seers will See the Luminaut they're supposed to bond with at the onset of Sight. And if you tell me you were Seeing me, I will gouge your eyes out, because there is absolutely no way I want you bossing me around the multiverse, telling me I'm an idiot, for the rest of my Luminaut life."

"Who told you about that?" Toran goes prickly as a porcupine, and whirls on his sister. "Was it you?"

"Why can't she know?" Heike frowns. "Callie has a friend with magic like yours, she told me so. She can help you, Toran."

"And you believed her?" Toran shakes his head like Heike

should know better. "She could be lying."

"Why would I lie about it?" I cross my arms over my chest. Toran faces me, undaunted in his suspicion.

"Why wouldn't you lie?"

I know I should stop arguing. Just go Light the dome and be done with this, so we can move on. My time crunch doesn't allow for the endless cycle of cross-examination and rebuttal Toran always pulls, and really, I'd rather be home for Christmas than go toe-to-toe with him once an hour, wasting even more valuable time on Tremurheim when I still have other worlds to go to, and even more Light Cores to find before I can do the whole restore-the-Lightbridge thing. But for some reason, I just can't stop.

"Because sometimes, people *do* tell the truth, Toran," I say. "The whole entire world isn't out to get you. Not everybody you meet is trying to wreck your life just because they're malicious."

"I didn't say they were," Toran sneers. "I said *you* were."

Okay, I'm done. I lean over the step, nearly eye-level with him, and get right in his face. "What is your problem with me, dude? Why are you such a gigantic bully all the time?"

"I don't owe an explanation to somebody who won't explain themselves in return."

"Toran—" Heike tries to get her brother's attention.

"Okay, fine, if you want honest explanations, here's one: Nate is this guy I know, and he's also an undead monster—a Shadow-mancer, the kind of creature that did this." I gesture to the ashes covering the floor. "He's pursuing me across the multiverse, trying to destroy my Light, and I thought I sensed him, but I was wrong. Are you happy?"

"Toran, Callie, you need to see—"

"I knew you were hiding something insidious." Toran growls and backs away, right into Heike's shoulder. "A monster that turns people to ashes is chasing you, and you neglected to tell me?

I refuse to—"

"Toran, stop!" Heike points to something just beyond the outpost's front door: tiny, wispy blue orbs, almost like free-floating Christmas lights, hovering just beyond the door, tinkling with an almost musical sound, beckoning us into the Mist. "They've come."

They? Ominous, and creepy.

"Oh, no." Toran rushes out the door, swearing under his breath. "Dramora spawn, they got it."

"Got what?" I run outside, joining him and Heike, and look out across the Hem. The absence of something I never thought I could lose becomes apparent immediately, and the panicked fear exploding in my stomach numbs me to any other sensation. "Where is Diver?"

My mech is gone. No trace of him, not even his footprints, remain. Just deep gashes in the earth, like something heavy was dragged against its will by something—several somethings—equally heavy.

"It's the Uldru," Heike says with a look of dread. "The walking forest. Those are the spores they leave behind after an abduction." She points out the blue lights, fading with every passing second. "They've made off with Diver."

CHAPTER 17
CALLIE

"WHERE DO YOU THINK you're going?"

Where does it freaking look like I'm going, Toran? I don't pause in my sprint, chasing the glowing blue Uldru spores through the Mist, burning away the omnipresent fog with Light. Over my shoulder, I call out the obvious. "I'm going to get my World Diver, and Nemo, and my Light Core, and also all of our stuff."

Really, this guy thinks *I'm* an idiot?

"You're going to get yourself killed!" Like he cares. "You have no plan, no idea what you're running into. Do you even know what Uldru look like?"

"Do you?" I pause for a moment, keeping an eye on the spores in my peripheral. They're growing dim, and fast, but of course, Toran has decided this is the perfect moment for yet another argument. "I don't have time for this; my mechs and my Light Core just got carried off by a pack of walking trees, and the only way to find them is by following those things." I nod toward the spores, tinkling like bells. "So, pardon me if I don't stop and listen to you berate me for the next five minutes, but I have better things to do."

Once more, I take off, barreling after the spores as quickly as they fade from my sight.

"You're headed for certain death." Have I told you lately you're morbid, Toran?

"If you don't want to help me save your one and only ride, fine, go wait in the ash-encrusted outpost for me to get back." In fact, please do, because I don't need to deal with Toran being the epitome of himself when my only way back home is trapped in the clutches of kidnapping, probably-carnivorous trees. At least Diver is metal, but that doesn't mean they won't tear him limb from limb trying to find a meal.

Did Nate have something to do with this? Is he using his Darkness to control the Uldru? Is that why I felt the chill of shadow run down my spine in the outpost? That would definitely be a new strategy, and one I'd never predict, or see coming. Diver didn't even call to my inner Light that he was in danger, or needed help.

But why not?

"Callie, wait, you're going too fast!" Heike's boots slap the muddy earth under our feet, her lantern swinging wildly in her hand. But I can't slow down, not when the spores are evaporating around me, becoming one with the Misty gray.

Diver, where are you? I reach out for my mech, hoping he's not too far away to sense my inner Light. I can't feel his, which fills me with an impending sense of dread like little else. Even Nate opening up the roof of the VBHS gym with his Darkness was less nerve-wracking than this. *Please, buddy, answer me.*

At first, I get nothing. But then, something small and strangled breaks through the immense quiet. Something closer than I imagined.

Luminaut... help.

Wherever Diver is, he isn't far, and he's absolutely terrified. His inner Light finds mine, and fills me with all the horror he's experiencing at the hands of the things that grabbed him.

I'm coming, don't give up. Keep talking to me so I know where you are. He's so close I can practically taste it, but I can't see him — or any supposed Uldru — in the least. Just Mist, Mist, and even more Mist.

Luminaut, the trees move silently, and obscure themselves with fog. The Seer must act.

I take a pause in my dogged pursuit of the blue spores and face Toran, panting heavily. "Diver says the Uldru are obscuring themselves with Mist. Clear it away."

"This is the second time today you've asked me to willingly expose my sister and myself to predators." Toran stands in the Light of Heike's lantern, the Mist moving away from him like a crowd of admirers parts for the visiting Prince of Awfulness. "I am not going to—"

"Shut up and listen to me." I am sick to death of arguments. I stalk toward Toran, Light burning in my hands like twin balls of rage-flame, spreading over every inch of me until I'm transformed into a living torch of Light. In this instant, Toran's eyes betray a hint of well-placed fear. "I have had it up to here with your threats, and insults, and literally everything else. I can't guarantee I won't murder you at some point, but so help me, Toran, if you don't clear this Mist away so I can find my World Diver and Nemo, I will blow your head off your shoulders right here and now."

Toran's apprehension that I'll actually follow through and kill him shines through his eyes, and cracks the aloof mask obscuring his face. Even Heike looks afraid of facing down a pissed-off, powerful Luminaut. If I wasn't so worried about everything I'm about to lose if Toran doesn't comply, I'd wonder who it is I'm becoming, and why I'm using my Light in exactly the way Nate swore I would — to cause fear, pain, and potentially, destructive harm.

Toran doesn't say a word, just raises his hand—fingers trembling slightly—and the Mist parts, recoiling away from us like a scroll unfurling in reverse. The fading blue spores shine bright without Mist obscuring their path, and yet I don't see the giant Uldru anywhere.

"You know, for as big and dangerous as you implied these trees are, I don't—holy crud what is that!"

My Light flares in surprise as a decaying tree limb the size of a bus sweeps around us. We barely have time to leap out of the way before the entire monster materializes from the retreating Mist, and then another, and another, and another—all of them moving with precise silence, a forest of whispering danger and decay. Toran inadvertently revealed the Uldru's hiding spot, and they are *not* happy. Their fury bleeds from every swipe of their limbs, every flash of bright spores as more and more of the tiny blue creatures flood the air. The Uldru are tall as skyscrapers, with gnarled trunks and roots like octopus tentacles cutting long gashes in the dirt. They appear all around us as if out of thin air; blackened, deadened things, just like the skeleton trees punctuating the flat landscape of the Hem, but living, and much larger, spewing spores and pulsing with goo that looks like a combination of sap and blood.

High above my head, suspended between the branches of two of the Uldru, is Diver.

Luminaut!

"Diver!" I rush toward him, and everything else, including the danger presented by the enormous zombie-trees, fades from my vision. All I can see is Diver, and all I can feel is the horror in his Light. "I'm coming, buddy!"

One of the Uldru try to sweep me off my feet, and I turn, mercilessly blasting the arm-branch with a fierce ball of Light. The

Uldru emits a strange, shriek-like sound, the first I've heard them make, and the twigs and branches making up the marred limb snap together quickly at high volume. The Uldru withdraws, backing away from me. Another counterattacks, sending a wave of spores to blind me, but I'm ready, and Light blasts them away, scattering the spores a thousand different directions into the Mist.

"Let go of my Diver!" I send a flare at one of the Uldru holding Diver, but it's not enough to get the monster to drop my mech. Darting around to avoid being stepped on or swiped, I look around for my companions. "Toran, Heike, help me!"

But Toran has encased himself and Heike in ice, sharp spines sticking out like a sea urchin to deflect any Uldru that might come in close contact. Typical Toran shenanigans. Why does he point-blank refuse to help me with anything? It's not like he's going to get anywhere without Diver to take him. This affects both of us equally.

Okay, fine, it affects me way more than him, but still, would it kill him to assist?

"Toran!" I race toward his ice encasement and tap one of the spines with my finger. Light cracks the ice, sending sparkling shards crashing to the ground. Toran looks at me with a scowl (he's so dependable!). "Before you demand to know what I'm doing," I interrupt him the second his jaw drops in defiance, "I broke your ice shell because I need your help getting Diver away from those trees."

"It's a lost cause; he's not worth saving." Toran helps Heike to her feet, and she brushes ice off her shoulders. "The safest thing to do is hide in the outpost until they pass, and then hike back to the forest. We'll make for another village. You can use your magic to control the villagers regarding the clemency issue, and then we can strategize another plan."

We duck and roll out of the way of an incoming Uldru branch.

Despite their uncanny ability to move across the Hem in near silence, the apparent weakness in the monsters' design is they're too big and too slow moving to make a pinpoint accurate offense. We're easily outmaneuvering them just by being small, quick humans.

"You think I'm going to let these zombie-trees make off with Diver? That's funny." I shoot a blast of Light at an Uldru trying to squish us under its root-foot, and we run away from the crashing limb just in time.

"I'm not joking." Gosh, Toran, really? I had no idea you were serious about ditching my mech, and my other mech, and my Light Core with a bunch of monsters in the middle of nowhere. Thanks so much for clarifying.

"And I'm not, either." I throw some Light toward the Uldru holding Diver's left arm, but the tree won't let go. Stubborn tree.

"How can we help, Callie?" Heike to the rescue.

"I'm working on a strategy." And also I'm avoiding being crushed or swiped, and keeping Toran and Heike from being crushed or swiped. I've got a lot going on.

"You? Strategy?" Toran scoffs. "Those two words don't belong in the same sentence together."

"Okay, maybe not. But I need to get Diver out of this situation, and fast, before they rip him apart and I can't fix him." So stop pointing out useless minutiae, and making fun of me.

"Maybe we could distract the two Uldru holding him long enough for them to drop him, and then we escape," Heike suggests.

"That's a great idea," I agree. "You're pretty fast, you could zig-zag all around their feet while I—"

"We? No. We are not helping." Toran shakes his head. "Heike will do no such thing, and neither will you. We're doing exactly what I said. Hiding, then hiking back. We can find a village to lay low for a while, and if we're lucky, we may not have to leave."

"Toran, we should make this decision together, as a group," Heike says, but no surprise, her brother completely ignores her. We find ourselves leaping away from some Uldru sap instead, heavy blobs of goo dripping around our feet to glue us in place.

"I'm not going to hide out in Tremurheim forever," I remind him. Seriously, Toran, *why* are you choosing this exact moment to have this conversation? Your timing is just... epic fail. I shoot a couple blasts of Light at an Uldru about to pick us up and squeeze us to death in its gnarled branch hands. The Uldru retreats, but another will attack any second, and from what direction, I can't predict. Plus there's still the issue of *literally all of our supplies and my Light Core inside Diver.*

"You aren't going to have a choice this time." Toran calls for some Mist, the foggy gray gathering around his hands as he forms his favorite twin ice swords and engulfs us, obscuring our position from the Uldru. I can no longer see Diver, and my gut drops to my toes. If I can't see my mech, I can't save him, and if I can't save him, I'm lost.

"Come, I'll help lead us out of here," Toran tells Heike and me, and gives me a bossy kind of chin-nod. "We'll use the Mist to make our getaway, and you will use your skyfire from the outpost to scare them off entirely."

"No." I shake my head as soon as he turns to go. "I'm not doing any of that. I'm rescuing Diver."

Time comes to a temporary standstill as Toran and I face each other down, each convinced our plan is right, the other is wrong, and all of our previous arguments and disagreements reach a breaking point at this very moment. Heike looks between us, uncertain who to follow, as we stare into the reality that one of us will have to yield, but neither is willing to budge.

"You're going to get us killed." Toran points an ice sword at my face. "You are reckless and impulsive, and it will be your downfall."

"I'm not going to hurt anyone, especially not you or Heike." I shake my head, backing away. "You can go back to the outpost and hide, but I am not leaving Diver. I have to find the Light Core in the Beacons, or—"

"Or what?" Toran jabs his other sword at my heart. "Or your Shadowmancer enemy will find you? What if he kills my sister? You're knowingly involving us in a selfish scheme that has a very real probability of death, and you never once stopped to think about the consequences."

That's really not fair, but whether or not he knows how his words wound—or cares—is a question his face doesn't answer. Unfeeling cold hardens his features, as impenetrable as the ice in his hands.

Blue spores gather around us, scattering the Mist cloud Toran was using for camouflage, and the Uldru bring the offense. Toran snarls, jabbing an Uldru's incoming branch finger with one weapon while keeping the other on me. A single tap of my Light-filled finger shatters the sword, and shards like diamonds fall to the ground.

"You don't get to go back on your word like this." It's good luck the Uldru are not super fast-moving, because otherwise, we'd be arguing from inside their clutches right now instead of dodging them while we shout at each other. "I did everything in my power to get you and Heike out of Gravenskov, and you promised you'd take me to the Beacons in return."

Remember the conditions of your blackmail, Toran? Then again, his memory has always been selective.

"Callie is right. A promise is a promise." Heike attempts to insert herself, but her protest isn't heeded. All Toran cares about is yelling in my face while he brandishes his ice swords at my vital organs.

"Forget the Beacons! Beacon flare is only a myth, and I'm not going to risk everything dear to me to get you there for no good reason." Toran swings at the Uldru to his left, and connects with a long, spindly branch wrapping itself around his ice sword. He releases the weapon and makes a new one, stabbing until the Uldru retreats.

"And I'm not going to sacrifice everything I set out to protect, or let Diving away from my home be in vain, just so you can run back to the forest with your tail between your legs." My Light gets hotter, as fiery as the anger rising into my throat. The blast I toss at a wayward Uldru slices the limb clean off the giant tree, and the creature sends a million spores to try to engulf me. Light flashes and sends them scattering, and nothing the gigantic trees throw at me seems to be able to deflect my power.

Which gives me an idea. Not a very good one, but it's better than nothing, right?

"You're going to get someone hurt or killed sooner than later," Toran snaps, ice encasing his body like armor. "You never listened when I tried to explain how dangerous your power is."

"You like to think you know everything." Light builds all around, turning me into a human firework, shining through the Mist. Heike shields her eyes, and so does Toran. "Fine. Think what you want. But while I'm using Light, stay out of my way."

I turn away from them, rushing headlong into the branches and creaking tree limbs, losing myself further and further inside the walking forest. My eyes remain on Diver, my Light tuned into his.

My Light can't hurt you, can it, Diver?

A brief pause as Diver attempts to free his leg from the Uldru's grasp to no avail. *No, Luminaut. Light is in us and all around. We cannot be harmed by it.*

Awesome-sauce. Then prepare to get dropped, because I'm about to blast the crap out of these trees.

Light gathers inside, glowing brighter and brighter, and I rise higher and higher into the air, my power carrying me upwards and away from the ground until I'm level with Diver and the Uldru holding him. The monsters back away from me, afraid my Light will hurt them and terrified of the golden, diamond-dripping beams of beauty and fierce protection shooting from my hands.

"Let go of my World Diver." When I speak, my voice is not only mine, but the voices of a thousand past Luminauts, coalescing as one. I raise my hands before me, Light aiming at the Uldru, and suddenly, I'm losing control of it. Fear and anger manifest in my power, and I start to burn with fire—no longer benign and protective, but a force to cause terror and death.

Every part of me that is Callie is incinerated, transforming my soul into a vast sea of raw power and energy. Violence, and the need to commit it, swells like a cresting wave, rumbling and churning into a barrel before it finally breaks around me, the vague sensation registering in my mind that the power is using me, not the other way around.

Light bursts, blowing splintering bits of Uldru every direction. The two zombie-trees holding Diver drop him, writhing and screeching in pain as the others lumber away as fast as possible, each one of them missing pieces of themselves as they retreat into the gathering Mist. None of the Uldru leave spores behind, ensuring without a doubt they won't be pursued, because to the fleeing monsters, I've become worse than them.

Stop. Come back to yourself. Who speaks the words—me, my inner Light, or Diver, I don't know—but with a gasping breath, I suck air into my lungs and expel the Light, gaining enough control over my power to look around. Uldru carnage litters the ground below, pieces of branches and limbs like corpses strewn across a long lost battlefield my Light only knows in broken memories.

I did this... my Light caused this devastation.

I float back to the ground, using every last bit of concentration to recall the flaming tendrils of Light inside, and I know — for sure and certain — this is what Nate meant when he said Light could destroy. I am dangerous. Deadly. I scarred the trees in the forest, blinded the gator-fish, and now, I amputated entire parts of the Uldru. If I wanted, I could kill millions of people with a flick of my wrist, because my power is capable of that kind of violence. I felt it just now, in my uncontrolled rage and fear, when I thought I was going to lose Diver for good.

But... how? Why is this power that's supposed to be good capable of such terrible brutality?

"You filthy dramora spawn!" Toran is at my side in an instant, his eyes so ferocious I don't even recognize them. "You almost killed us all!"

I can't deny what he says. "I'm sorry. I'm so sorry."

"Toran, we're fine." Heike touches his arm, but he rips himself away from her grasp, knocking her Light lantern to the ground. The crystalline crunch of broken glass fills the immense silence hanging in the Misty air.

"Don't you dare defend her, Heike." Toran's pale face goes stark white with fury. "This has gone on for too long. Promise or no, you are not going to put my sister and me in peril any longer, either by fault or association."

"I know what I did was dangerous, and yeah, I could have caused a lot more harm than I did," I admit. Sucks to eat crow, but right now, humility is also true. "But this is why I need help. You told me you'd teach me to control my powers, and — "

"I don't care what I said or did." Toran spits at my feet, his saliva sticking to the toe of my boot. "Even hiking across the Hem, completely exposed, is safer than staying with you one second longer."

"So that's it?" I trail after him as he stalks away. "You're ditching me because I Light blasted the Uldru that were trying to kill us? What I did just proves I need you to stay and teach me more than ever. Because you're not wrong to say one day somebody could get hurt."

"*Could* get hurt?" Toran faces me, completely unmoved in his decision. "*Will* get hurt. See the difference?" When I don't respond, he shakes his head, disgusted. "Find help elsewhere. I refuse to stay."

"You can't do this to me," I cry. "After all I did to help you free Heike, this is unfair, and you know it."

A pitiless shrug is Toran's callous reply. "I can, and I am. And I couldn't care less what happens to you in the meantime."

All the rage at his insults, his constant criticisms, everything I repressed because he promised he'd Guide me to the Beacons and help me understand my Light powers bubbles to the surface in the face of this final betrayal. "Leave, then." My voice shakes, on the verge of furious tears. "But before you go, I want you to know that you're the biggest dirtbag I have ever had the misfortune of meeting, and I never want to see your face again as long as I live. A skuddima can suck your soul out, for all I care. I don't think you ever had one to begin with."

Yeah, I went there. And wow, does it feel good. Cathartic, even. But then, the reality I'm about to be ditched on a barren wasteland with no means to find this world's Light Core sets in, and no Water Manipulating Seer to help me find my way through the Mist, and I wish instantly I could take it all back.

The indifference on Toran's face says it wouldn't matter if I did. He'd still spit on me again, and gladly.

"Come, Heike." He jerks his chin over his shoulder. "We're through with this witch."

Not a sorceress this time — a *witch*. Toran doesn't even believe in witches. He must think I'm something truly horrendous to have called me that. Irredeemable.

"Let's calm down, and make a plan together," Heike tries again to talk sense into her enraged brother. "I don't think — "

"I said we're through." Toran gives his sister a look that says she had better follow him, so help whatever Tremurheim deity they swear to. She looks between me and him, clearly torn. Her eyes dart back and forth as she clutches her broken lantern to her chest, my Light still glowing inside despite the cracks in the glass. But she doesn't move.

"Heike!" Toran grabs his sister's arm and pulls her to his side, his Seer's Eye blazing before Mist swallows them both, obscuring them from sight. Whichever path they take away from me, I can't follow, because the Mist separates me from their movements like a massive barrier, wider than the ocean and as high as the gray sky above.

When the Mist finally clears, I'm all alone with Diver and hundreds of torn, mangled branches littering the ground. No trace of the Rykjiersens exists, the absence so effortless it's as though they never existed in my life at all save for one, singular question lingering around their sudden disappearance:

How am I going to finish my Light Core hunt, get off this world, and, eventually, go back home to Verona Beach without a Seer?

CHAPTER 18
CALLIE

"ARE YOU OKAY, DIVER?"

It's difficult to inspect my mech, because the person I was relying on to scatter the Mist so I could assess for damage has just decided to bail on me at the worst possible time, and Light is minimally effective at getting rid of Mist this oppressively thick. I scramble onto Diver's foot, trying to see his rusty, already-aged joints through the gathering fog. "Did those Uldru beat you up, or are you doing alright?"

The trees ambushed from behind, we could not see or hear them coming. But we are not too bad, Luminaut. We can move.

Whew, that's one relief, at least. Everything else...

A pause settles between me and Diver, awkward and uncomfortable, until my mech points out the glaring lack of two people who were here only a moment ago. *The Seer has gone, and the sister.*

"Yep, Toran bailed on us." It takes a lot of effort not to spit the words, but he's not here to spit on anymore, so what's the use? "He decided it was safer to go off on his own than stay one more second around my Light powers. Good riddance, huh?"

The situation is most unfortunate, Luminaut. Diver never liked Toran much, but he knows lacking a Seer means we're in dire straits, and joking about it isn't going to make us feel any better.

"I know, buddy." A sigh passes over my lips. "Can you take me up to the Crow's Nest? I've got a lot to figure out all of a sudden."

Yes, Luminaut.

I hop into Diver's palm, flying through the damp, sticky veil of Mist engulfing us both like funereal gauze. Strange how much Toran's mere presence filtered it away, even when he didn't lift a finger. Which, let's be honest, was often. Still, it's an unsettling omen how dense it feels all of a sudden, a tangible weight pressing between my shoulders.

Of course Toran had to walk off and leave me surrounded by the one thing he could control, with no way out. It's the biggest "up-yours" he could give—like a Fire Manipulator leaving their Luminaut to burn in a forest-fire inferno, or an Earth Manipulator abandoning someone to the mudslide descending like a sludgy wall of death down a hill. The Water Manipulator ran away, and I'm drowning in a crushing wasteland of unnavigable fog.

Screw you, Toran. You're the human embodiment of period cramps, you hear me?

Of course he can't hear me.

"Nurrr, Callie, Light is so dangerous, and you're going to kill my sister. I'm allergic to jokes and compromise, grouch gripe mooooaaan." I pause my extremely accurate Toran impression to throw open the hatch of the Crow's Nest. Nemo waits anxiously beside the Luminaut chair, watching the horizon, but wheels toward me with flailing arms when he hears me slam the door. "Hey, buddy, are you okay?"

Nemo is, thankfully, more than okay, and begs me to pick him up. I'm happy to oblige, settling him on my shoulder as I take stock of the situation in the Crow's Nest. Mostly, everything looks okay—it's a mess, but when is it not? All of Toran and Heike's things are still here—extra clothes, ration packs, canteens, bedrolls and blankets, Toran's mini-library he insisted on carting out of Gravenskov. By some miracle, the books are still stacked neat as a pin. If I didn't know any better, I'd say the Rykjiersens had gone on a quick walk, and were coming back in a few minutes. At least Toran's books will make decent kindling, in case I want to burn a papier-mâché effigy of his face.

And of course, if he were here, the mere whisper of kindling would ensure some kind of insult or jeer about my Light powers would be his response. *"Your skyfire could set everyone I love ablaze, not just that paper, because you're evil and so are your powers, and I don't think I told you yet, but you're incompetent and I despise your mechs."*

I don't need Toran. In fact, my stress levels are far lower without him. I'll finish this Light Core hunt on my own. Put my mind to it, like Dad always said. He told me I was lazy, a slacker who didn't measure up to her potential—well, guess who was carrying a 3.9 GPA and starting on the volleyball team, all while learning to use superpowers and secretly repairing a gigantic mech before she Dove away from home? This girl. Who's the slacker now, Dad?

When I get home for Christmas, I'll be sure to tell him he can add "saved the multiverse from Darkness tentacles and ash" to my long list of accomplishments—my college résumé is more than padded. He'll be so happy to see me again. Mom will be happy, too. Ryan and Tyler will be annoyed but also secretly happy, Jase will feign apathy before he hugs me anyway, and Livvy will jump into my arms and call me her big sissy. Mom will make my favorite vanilla birthday cake with chocolate buttercream, seventeen candles on top... I can hear them singing, everyone but Tyler off key, my younger brothers sneaking swipes of frosting, Jase pretending he's too cool to care, but mumbling along under his breath.

And I'll be there, because my birthday means it's Christmas Eve...

I have to be there...

Because if I'm not—

If I'm not there.

A sob bursts from my lips, and I know, in my heart, I won't be home for my birthday and Christmas. For all I know, Christmas has long since passed. My family has mourned, and carried on without me. They had my favorite cake in my honor because I wasn't there, and I won't be, and might never be again.

Why did Toran have to leave me in a lurch? How could he do this to my family? He knew I wanted to go home, and I needed him to take me to the Beacons in order to do that. Why did he have to devastate everyone I love with his stubborn ego?

But you wouldn't have made it home, whether he helped you or not. You were meant for bigger things than this small beach town. This was never going to be a weekend excursion into the unknown... You are a Luminaut.

Go away, Dr. Ormandi. I don't need your voice in my head, either. Toran's insults about my uncontrolled powers and carelessness are a hard enough pill to swallow. Nate's inconvenient words about the danger of Light—words I convinced myself were lies—are another. The last thing I want is to be reminded of the enormity of the task my old mentor warned me about, but I refused to heed.

It wasn't like Dr. Ormandi was all that truthful. He can't blame me for not paying attention. He didn't even mention that ancient Luminauts were possibly ruthless, Machiavellian over-lords who maybe murdered whole Clans—if Toran and Nate are to be believed, anyway.

The unknown woman's scream, reverberating through the

flash of Light. It's horrible, hearing her in my head every time the doubt creeps in. Then again, the fact I hear her in the first place means answers about Toran's rightness and my wrongness — or, the other way around — might be closer than I think.

What if the truth has been with me all along?

Thoughts part, coalescing into something as clear as the first rays of sun breaking through the fog hanging over the ocean. The missing piece of the puzzle — I think I just figured it out.

"Diver," I murmur, my voice smaller than I want it to be, "I need to know — is what Toran said true? Did Light powers make the Hem?"

Diver's heavy grief presses like an unshakeable weight, dragging me down further. *We do not want to show you, Luminaut.*

"Please, Diver," I ask once again.

Luminaut will be in pain, as we are in pain. The memory hurts. It will hurt Luminaut.

"I don't care." I shake my head, finding strength in my voice again. "I need the truth. Show me what you know. Your Luminaut commands you."

My mind goes quiet and dark before Diver's flickering spark makes its way through the gloom. *Come, Luminaut, we will show you.*

Faint Light pulses in the Prism, beckoning me close while simultaneously repulsing me with the anguish it contains. Diver can't stand to show me this memory. He's kept it hidden — buried — mere snippets peering through the chaos of the gateway when we Dove, but now that I demand this truth he's so faithfully concealed, he will reveal it, no matter how much it hurts.

And it hurts my mech. His grief throbs through me like a wound freshly opened in scarred, bleeding flesh. I set Nemo on the floor, and reach for the Prism, connecting to the Light inside: Diver's Light. The Light of an untold number of Luminauts who've shared their memories with him, whether good or bad.

The heaviness of the memories steals the breath from my lungs and almost takes me to my knees, rattling me, flooding my heart and mind with thousands of images and emotions. Some are happy, like a blip of Mariasol in the Crow's Nest with Dr. Ormandi, dancing to a Rolling Stones album while he reads a textbook, or playing hide and seek with (absolutely flipping adorable) toddler Nate. Most of them, though, contain immense sadness. Diver's sadness, and heartache. His brokenness bears down, an anvil sinking me into the depths of time, but somehow, I remain steady. The images and voices continue to fly by, traveling back to an era long since past, one humans may not remember except in myth and legend.

The rocketing swiftness of the flying memories comes to a jarring halt, and before me, a short, porcelain-skinned, childlike woman with pale blonde hair stands beside a tall, lithe woman with golden-brown skin and amber eyes similar to Mariasol's. They're keeping watch beside two Divers on what look like cliffs beside an ocean. Except this ocean isn't made up of water. Tidal waves of Mist, gigantic ebbs and flows that never quite reach the cliff face, stretch into infinity. The gargantuan Tremurheim trees are sparse here, thinned out into what resembles a long runway, and on the very edge of the cliff, a set of four lighthouse-like structures: cylindrical buildings with giant glass domes on top, shining bright with Light. I've dropped in on the middle of a conversation, one boiling over with urgency and tension.

"The Light Collective knows we're here," the taller of the two women says. Her amber eyes glow green, vines snaking up her arms and legs, and my subconscious registers she's a Seer, and an Earth Manipulator.

"They won't think to look for us at the Tageveld Beacons," the Seer's Luminaut, the short, blonde woman, reassures her. "They're too remote."

Another Luminaut, this one with long, black hair and almond-

*shaped dark eyes, joins them with her Seer, a man with glowing blue eyes
and the giant bjorir — much bigger than Toran's old bjorir, Kiera. This
one is eight feet tall at the shoulder, sheltering a group of huddled
Clanspeople in the shadow of its girth. The people wear gauzy clothes
that shimmer, reflecting the Mist until they blend into it entirely.
Members of the infamous Mist Clan even wore Mist-like camouflage.*

*"The Collective will never stop searching," the dark-haired
Luminaut warns.*

*Her Seer, the Water Manipulator with the bjorir, nods in agreement.
"Hiding the Mist Clan from the war is a temporary solution to a
permanent problem, and will incur the Collective's wrath."*

*I sense the Earth Seer's name in Diver's Light — Saeli. And she's
terrified by this pronouncement.*

*The small, blonde Luminaut — the name Diver remembers is Elara —
remains dauntless, a defiant sneer on her lips. "Let them try to stop us.
We're ready."*

Saeli is not ready. But she remains silent.

*"We haven't much time," the Water Seer says, his deep voice grave.
He glances at the cylindrical buildings, the Light in their glass spheres
fading as the Mist beyond the cliffs rises higher. He lifts his hand,
keeping the Mist from breaching the edge of the cliffs, and motions for
the people cowering beside his bjorir to follow him. "This way. Quickly."*

A blip in the memory, like a schism left by something altered
or removed, and I'm skipped ahead through time — a few
moments, a few hours, a few days? Most likely hours, from what
I can see: the four Luminauts and Seers wait next to their World
Divers, all of the Mist Clan refugees ready to board. A flash of
Light appears, a bright blaze in the middle of a glimmering,
golden band cutting across the sky: the Lightbridge.

This memory originated before the Lightbridge was
destroyed? Wow, Diver, you're a geriatric. Big old grandpa mech.
His emotions shift, my mech's fear of what comes next striking

like a sledgehammer, pounding through my chest.

"Please, don't act rashly," Saeli murmurs to Elara, so soft I strain to hear.

"I'll do what needs to be done," Elara answers. The look on her face as she watches three Lights descend from the bridge in the sky is resolute, determined — and full of barely-contained rage.

Blip — fast forward. Diver's fear turns to anguish so heavy I falter, losing my footing beneath the weight.

The Lights falling from the sky touch ground, and forms begin to take shape. Three World Divers, all of them illuminated with the power of Light, shine like beacons of imminent destruction, massive footfalls shaking the earth with every step until they come to a halt. From their domed tops, three sets of Luminauts and Seers emerge. They approach the Mist Clan refugees, and even from this distance, there's something terrible about them, something forbidding. Every inch of their bodies, from the tips of their hair to their toes, are filled with Light — but it isn't benevolent or protective.

These people are using Light to make themselves living weapons.

"The Collective has not authorized the relocation of these refugees off their home world," one of the terrifying Luminauts announces to the group. *"Stand down, or face the consequences."*

That's a really overused line, ancient scary Luminaut. Just FYI.

"You would murder us and all these people, simply for helping them flee war and persecution?" Elara's curled lip transforms into a wolfish snarl. Her teeth are sharp, and gleam, daggerlike, in the Light of the Beacons. *"We will do what is right, and you cannot stop us."*

One last blip, and all I can see is Light as the Luminauts — the two trying to help the Mist Clan, and the three Collective meanies — clash together in midair, their Light burning away everything around them until nothing remains except the echoes of human screams. The Hem as I have seen it, barren save for blackened, skeletal trees, is all that remains of their vicious Light battle, the scent of decay and char hanging in the air. Littering the cliffs are the corpses of the Mist Clan, the dark-haired Luminaut and her Seer, the mutilated body of the Water Seer's bjorir, and the shattered, crystal shards of the Beacons' domed tops.

One scream in particular — the blood-curdling scream from the gateway — lingers, and Saeli falls to the ground, hands pressed to the hole in her chest made by a stray blast of Light. Her vibrant vines try to repair the gaping wound, but wither away as life fades from her eyes, red blood pouring over the green around her form.

"No!" Elara descends and runs to her Seer, panic in her wide, brown eyes. "No, please. Saeli, stay with me." She shakes her Seer, Light blazing in her hands. She presses her palms over Saeli's heart. "You can't leave me." Tears well, golden dewdrops shimmering with Light, but they never quite reach her cheeks. "Saeli, sister of my heart. I need you."

"Let this be the consequence of your apostasy, Elara." The heartless Collective Luminauts don't bother to acknowledge the loss of three of their own, or the mass murder of an entire Clan. They simply retreat to their World Divers, the Seers that accompanied them following like mindless puppets, and then, they take to the Lightbridge, leaving Diver's devastated Luminaut shrieking, inconsolable, rocking the body of her dying Seer in the middle of the newly-formed Hem. Mist swirls around them until they're lost in it entirely.

I leap away from Diver's Prism, blinking hard to clear my vision, bright spots mixed with dark ones clouding my eyes. Everything Diver felt, everything his Luminaut and Seer felt, rolls through me with so much turmoil I could throw up. Elara's rage, palpable enough to burn. Saeli's fear and anguish that her Luminaut was losing control. And floating above it all, Diver's hopeless realization that he couldn't stop the death and pain he watched unfold, until a part of his Light shattered entirely in Saeli's scream, and Elara's livid grief.

"Diver." I swallow down the rising sickness. "I know this is true, but... how?"

The Light Collective did many terrible things, Luminaut.

Terrible, murderous things.

One thing is for sure and certain: Toran was right. Light powers — and Luminauts — slaughtered the Mist Clan and created the Hem of Tremurheim. I never wanted to believe him, because he was so wantonly malicious in the way he presented it, but of all the horrible things he said and did, lie to me was not one of them.

And if Toran didn't lie, that means Nate didn't lie, either — not entirely. He told me Light was dangerous, and how much harm I could cause. I always thought if he deceived me about being a ghost and manipulated my trust in order to gain my Light Core, he must have made up everything else. But no. About this, he was truthful.

But that means Dr. Ormandi wasn't. He was either ignorant of Light's horrible history, or he purposely obscured it, spinning a false narrative of benevolent protectors guarding the multiverse, keeping it safe from Darkness, because it's what he needed — wanted — to believe. His version of the story made his wife's death and Nate's turn to Darkness worth the loss. And then, he passed his lies on to me, a naive teenager overwhelmed by my powers, without a second thought, knowing I'd believe.

Anger, and deep, stomach-churning sadness mingle together, spinning a knot I can't untangle in the confusion of everything Diver's memory implies about me, my powers, and the half-truths and outright falsehoods Dr. Ormandi led me to believe.

"What do I do now?" I flop onto the Luminaut's chair, worn smooth by so many who came before me, including the Luminaut whose Seer I just watched die. "Should I give up and go home? Why bother hunting Light Cores if Light is dangerous — if it can do horrible, evil things, like those Luminauts did in your memory?" I bury my face in my hands, too tired to cry, too heartsick to move. "Was everything I did, and all I put my family through, for nothing?"

Luminaut, the Collective was not Light.

That doesn't make sense. "How can you say they aren't Light when they used it to kill a whole bunch of people? You saw them do it, Diver. It's in your memories."

Come, Luminaut. We will show you.

Light pulses in the Prism again, softer this time. I rise, taking a hesitant step. "No more murder visions?"

No, Luminaut. An old friend.

Old friend? I don't know who that could be, but it's better than killer Luminauts on a power trip.

I reach for the Prism once more, and when my palm connects, warmth washes over me. Comfort, peace, serenity. The waves of nausea cease, and in their place, Mariasol's glowing face fills my mind and heart. The long, wavy hair from her photo is gone, and short peach fuzz under a colorful scarf takes its place — probably just growing back after she lost it to chemo. But her eyes sparkle bright, the amber like burnished gold in her gorgeous Light. She's alone, save for the journal in her lap: one of the journals Dr. Ormandi gave me.

"There is so much I wish to say, my stars." Her voice feels like coming in after a snowstorm to find a crackling fire waiting in the hearth — homey, a little deeper than I expected, but so very gentle. *"These books can't contain everything I want to tell you, because there aren't words to say everything that should be said. Sometimes we have to trust that something is true, even if we can't see it."* She smiles, the expression stretching into her dimples, and she reaches for the Prism on her end of the vision, as though she's caressing my cheek. *"You'll learn so much on your journey with Light, and the*

Luminaut you become will be wise, good, and true. But you'll also find out that not everything about your power is of benefit. Light itself is simply an energy, flowing through the multiverse: it has the capacity for great good, but can also be used to cause harm. I should tell you now there was once far too much evil done in Light's name, and when you learn the truth, it may anger you, sadden you, and make you wish you could forget everything you learned about yourself, and your power."

Wow, way to carve my soul from my body and lay it bare on the Crow's Nest floor. My eyes sting, a lump thick in my throat, and I want to reach out and touch her, to take hold of her beautiful Light and hold it close. To hug her and cry on her shoulder while she strokes my hair, assuring me everything will be okay.

"Help me understand what I'm supposed to do," I whisper. "I need another Luminaut. I can't do this alone."

"There are times you'll think the road is too long, and too lonely to bear," she answers me across decades, defying death. *"And the reality of our past as Luminauts may tempt you to give up, or turn your back on Light. I can't tell you why Light was used the way it was. But people are fallible, and make grave misjudgments and mistakes. Even me."* Her eyes reach all the way to my soul, and I don't register that I'm crying until I become aware my face is wet. *"The one thing I want you to always remember is this: power without love is no power at all. Love is what makes things worth saving, the reason we fight for Light even when we're lost in the dark. Never forget, love is the most powerful force in the multiverse — more powerful, even, than Light. Everything I have done, every decision, was made in love."*

I wonder who this message is intended for: future Luminauts, like me, or herself?

"Whatever you do, do it in love and Light," she says. *"If you hold fast to that truth, you will reach the moon and stars, and defy the night itself. I love you, my dearest. But you already know that."*

The memory fades, and I'm left with her love, a cleansing river trickling through the hurts, a balm to the wounds ripping apart my fragile Light: the way Toran tried to sting me with his words, the way the Light Collective and my own power's destructiveness opened the floodgates of doubt, the way Dr. Ormandi's omission filled me with bitterness... and the way Nate broke my heart. None of the wounds are gone. But they ache a bit less.

Opening my eyes, back in my own reality on the Hem, I notice the Mist doesn't look so thick, and I feel—for once—I'm not quite as alone as I thought.

Except, I am most definitely alone, because Toran and Heike are out there somewhere, wandering around with no map, no supplies, and no shelter, all because Toran was a jerk who made a jerk decision.

But even jerk decisions can be made out of love—and yet, it doesn't mean people are free from the consequences of those decisions.

All my happy feelings fade, and I realize what I probably— really should—do.

"Diver, do you ever get a feeling that something's going to suck, and you want to avoid doing it, but you can't, because people's lives are at stake? Even though you know they'd never do the same for you, if they were in your shoes?"

Doing the right thing does not always feel pleasant, Luminaut, nor does it require reciprocity.

As inconvenient a truth bomb as ever there was.

I sigh, taking my place in the Luminaut's chair as Nemo crawls into my lap, Light building in my hands to scatter the Mist. "Okay, Diver, let's go back to that outpost and Light the dome, and then go find Toran before he kills himself and Heike."

CHAPTER 19
TORAN

"WOULD YOU SLOW DOWN? We need to talk."

Heike pants the words, her lantern swaying in her fist as she runs to keep up with my strides. My chest feels tight, like I've pushed myself and my magic too hard for such a short burst, but it's all for our safety that we get as far away from Callie James as possible.

The sight of her suspended in skyfire, brutally using her magic against the Uldru, brought my wavering decision to a state of finality. Uldru might be dangerous, but ancient, legendary predators like the walking forest deserve not to have their limbs blasted off in a terrifying flash of uncontrolled magic.

And the secret she kept about "Nate"? The monster at the center of her "time crunch," or whatever stupid phrase she says that makes no sense—the one who turns people to ash, and is pursuing her as we speak? It was long past time to strike out on our own. We should have done so in the first place. I knew the second I saw her World Diver that night in Gravenskov: no good would come of our association with a skyfire sorceress. And I was right.

"When we reach the edge of the forest, we'll talk." I can't slow down, despite my sister's red cheeks and damp hair. "We can travel a lot faster on foot than we can in that monstrous, slow-moving, broken-down—"

"You don't like Diver, I understand." Heike cuts me off around a heavy breath. "You've never hidden your dislike of anything about Callie, especially her mechs."

"Aren't you glad to be rid of her?" I stop my forward momentum, just briefly. Mist gathers all around, trying to swallow us, but I hold my hands to my side, palms open, and the Mist moves into the shape I will, creating a protective bubble around myself and Heike. "She was a disaster. We'd have wound up dead if we hadn't—"

"Ditched her." Heike rolls her eyes. "Yeah, I know."

Ditched? Yeah? She's using the same type of nonsensical slang Callie tosses about left and right, as though I ought to know what she's talking about at any given moment without considering Heike and I don't hail from her foreign village. Courtesy has always been lost on her—but Heike is different. Heike was taught better.

"It's good I got you away from her," I say with a nod, affirming my rightness in leaving. "You're starting to sound too much like that sorceress."

"The sorceress who saved my life? And yours? Multiple times?" Heike sets her lantern at her feet, glowing with Callie's skyfire despite the crack along the side. "You ran off rashly, and now, we're lost on the Hem without supplies, and the map we need to find our way back to the forest is still inside Diver. So explain to me, Toran, how we are safer right now than we were with Callie." She pauses, hands on her hips. I've never seen my sister simmer with so much fury. "I'm waiting."

Ice crackles inside my limbs, and I grow cold in the face of Heike's anger. Why can't she understand that I did this for her? To keep her safe?

"You saw what she did. All the broken Uldru limbs scattered across the ground in the wake of her attack. If she could do that to creatures as large as Uldru, what could she do to us?" I shouldn't have to explain anything to Heike, who has eyes for herself. Impatience makes the frozen shards prick my skin from the inside out. "She might have used her magic to assist in certain circumstances, but I have magic, too, and I know far more than Callie about how to control it, and the harm I could do if I don't. She knows nothing, and is unwilling to see reason."

"You also said you'd help her understand how to control her powers," Heike argues, her face stony. "But all you did was insult her and treat her like she's something less than human. She's going to get lost trying to find the Beacons, and you were the one person who could help her."

"I don't care if she gets lost." Every second we waste on the Hem, the more likely we are to be attacked by a predator before reaching the forest. "Going to the Beacons was always a death trap. Better to forget this unfortunate detour ever happened than to dwell on it." I part the Mist with a sweep of my hand, revealing a path forward. "Let's go. I want to be within the tree line before nightfall."

"You really have no regrets about what you did to Callie?" Heike backs away from me, Mist gathering around her ankles and hair when she shakes her head. "She's our friend, and she needs —"

"She was *your* friend," I correct my sister. The last thing I would ever call Callie James is a friend. A menace, a sorceress, a bit of bad luck I happened to stumble upon in the forest, but never a friend. I could more easily be friends with a ravenous dramora. "The only thing I regret is the fact I left my books in her World Diver's head. Some of those were my favorites. Now, come."

Heike stands, rooted in place. Instead of following me, my sister stares, her expression falling around a look of disappointment. "Books are not the same as people."

But they're safer. The thought creeps into my mind unbidden, and even more ice freezes around my heart, forming a protective casing. "I'm not having this discussion with you right now."

"Why?" Heike takes a step when I turn to go, grabbing my arm before I can make much progress. "Why do you have to be so rude and condescending to everyone? I know you're scared of your magic, and I know you feel like everything that's happened to you since your selection is out of your control, but—"

"I am not scared. I am not out of control." Icy spines erupt along my arms, threatening to pop through my wool shirt. If I could encase myself inside the chill to drown out Heike's asinine argument, I would let ice engulf me in its silence.

How can she say I'm out of control? Everything I have done— breaking the rules to sneak into the forbidden section of the Archive so I could learn about my magic, and breaking them again so I could go into the forest in the early morning hours to practice, until the powerful urge to connect to the Mist and fly through the windows in the sky was gone—has been to maintain control. And it works. At least, the magic is quieter. Dormant. I can breathe without water choking me, if only for a short time.

But the words my sister says, and the surge of magic that somehow surfaces in Callie's presence, all of it is too much. Too out of my hands. It reminds me of losing my future when I was selected as Guide without any warning, and told my dreams meant nothing to my village—because the Council needed an easy sacrifice to the forest. Magic manifesting shortly thereafter was one more thing I couldn't have any say in, marking me as a danger even to myself.

Ever since, I have made my own choices, and carved my future from the shards of the past. My magic does not control me. I control it. Soon, with research and practice, I'll learn to control it so well it will be as though I never had magic at all. And I will remind myself of this truth, over and over, until it becomes real.

"You'll feel more like yourself once we get settled in a new village." Yes, this defiance is all Callie's influence on my sister. I grasp her shoulder and grin. "This detour didn't set you back too far in your studies. You can still take the Aptitude Exam once we arrive."

Heike slips out from under my touch. "Stop lying to yourself." More ice, more anger builds inside as Heike continues to press me. "You think things will get better by hiding in another village the rest of our lives? Your magic isn't going to go away. You can't use books to study it out of your life. So you might as well accept it. Callie has a friend that's a Seer, she said she could —"

"I don't want to know what Callie told you." Why won't Heike let this go? "For all we know, she lied about everything."

"You only say that because you want her to have lied." Heike's words lash me, threatening to crack the ice in which I've encased myself. "If she lied, it makes it easier for you to justify what you're doing and how you treated her."

"How did I treat her?" Ice reaches the skin of my neck, and my eyes burn with the blue glow of my magic, but Heike has never been afraid. "I am not the type that gets along easily with others. You didn't seem to mind, until you met Callie." More chill, more ice, needles of it sprouting along my hairline. "Should I have fallen down and worshiped the ground she walked on because she helped evade your execution? Or should I acknowledge that she's reckless, and I don't like her mechs, and I think she's leading us into danger by insisting we accompany her to the Tageveld Beacons to unearth some ancient, long-buried Beacon flare without knowing a single consequence of our actions?"

"But you never cared *why* she was trying to find Beacon flare in the first place," Heike says. "All you did was treat her like an idiot, and run away when you felt like her magic was too dangerous. Better to face a new Village Council and all of their rules that you can learn to manipulate and analyze than to deal with magic, right? Which, by the way, you have, too." She raises an eyebrow. "Am I wrong?"

"Of course you're wrong." I can hardly comprehend this transformation in my risky-but-goodhearted sister. Callie has entranced her into a deluded sycophant, playing the friendly, adventurous older girl Heike could aspire to be, whose life of travel and freedom is all Heike ever wanted. I understand Callie's appeal to my sister, but the fact she turned on me so quickly is a blow I didn't see coming. It makes my insides twist around an imaginary fist pressed deep, and my ice thickens in response, each pin on my skin a miniature knife. "Yes, I'd rather find a new village than accompany Callie to the Beacons, and why not? We know each Council is as awful as the next, but Callie is pure chaos. Every sacrifice I've made is all for you. For your safety."

"For me?" Heike scoffs. "I never asked you to keep me safe. And if it were me who'd been captured by Uldru instead of Diver, you'd have done what she did to free me, or worse. No, this is all about you."

The Mist around me crystalizes, forming ice shards in the air, falling from the sky toward the ground. She's wrong. This is not about me. It never was. She doesn't know what's best for her, what I would or wouldn't have done. She wants to strike out on her own, and make dangerous decisions with little thought. I reign her in. I protect her. I will not yield. I am—

Click-click-click-hissss.

I am about to become a skuddima's supper.

"Ah!" Heike shrieks, ducking out of the way before a skuddima can connect its gaping, sucking mouth with hers. She takes the lantern with Callie's skyfire, holding it high above her head, and the approaching skuddima flies away, but not before a second emerges from the Mist to take its place.

One, four, seven, ten… more than a dozen, and still, they come. An endless onslaught of life-sucking predators, their collective sights set on Heike and me.

"It's a nest," Heike announces the obvious severity of our predicament. "We walked right into a nest."

If I'd had my map, I could have rerouted around the infested area, but alas. I need to figure out some way to make this not my doing, or else she'll never let me live it down. Right before the swirling skuddima decide to move in for the kill, of course.

"If you wouldn't have started arguing with me, none of this would have happened." I form two ice pikes—*not* swords, but Callie isn't here to call them that—with the Mist. I know they're ineffective at killing the skuddima, but a deterrent is better than nothing.

"Sure, blame me." Heike swings the lantern around herself, the skyfire deflecting skuddima far more efficiently than my ice pikes. "You're the one who left the person with the only means to kill these things back at the outpost."

"We just need a distraction." I swing wildly, trying not to hit Heike, who would be far more injured by wayward pikes than these skuddima. "I have read that sometimes—"

"Books and self-control aren't going to help us survive right now." Heike ducks out of the way of another skuddima materializing from a thick patch of Mist, barely escaping.

I wish she weren't so unfortunately correct.

But the thing I wish most is that somehow, someway, my magic would work to slay these creatures so we could escape, and live. I didn't leave one deadly situation so that I could stumble into an even deadlier one in the space of a heartbeat, but fate has a horrible sense of humor, and I was never one for such amusements, anyway. It's only a matter of time—and not much time, at that—before Heike and I stumble, grow tired, let down our guard. There's no way out of this situation except for death.

"If we don't figure out how to get these things off our backs, we're done for." Heike almost drops her skyfire lantern after a particularly violent swing at an oncoming skuddima. Our one means of defense already has a crack—it cannot be shattered.

"Do you have any ideas?" I jab with my pikes, but they pass through the skuddima's ephemeral form. "Since you've informed me books, self-control, and, apparently, ice do not work to our advantage."

Heike grips her lantern in a pale fist, whirling a circle around us both as the skuddima close in, their sucking mouths reaching for the tips of my hair as a chorus of ecstatic clicks and menacing hisses ring in my ears. All my slashing is for nought in the face of this many hungry skuddima at once. I want to tell Heike this is exactly why self-control is needed: because I made one impulsive decision, and look where we've ended up. But pointing it out helps nothing, and I'd rather my sister's last memory of me wasn't my insistence on being correct before the stale breath of a ravenous skuddima took her life.

I'd rather this wasn't her last memory in general.

Aaaaaiiiiieeeeee!

From the Mist, a flare of skyfire, shining like a candle in a far-off window, calling us home. The skuddima scatter, the hated light distracting them from devouring us, and booming footsteps rattle the earth. The outline of the World Diver appears on the horizon, rumbling toward us, and on his shoulder, Callie. Skyfire blasts—her Light orbs—fly through the air toward the skuddima, and even more flee.

But not all.

"You storm off all pissy, and five minutes later, wander into a pack of skuddima?" Callie calls from Diver's shoulder, and the mech sets her at his feet. She rushes toward me, twin orbs glowing in her hands, and the approaching skuddima cry out in fear.

"Don't test me," I snap. She grins, skyfire making the strange little dots on her face glow gold.

"I'm so glad you missed me, Toran." She has to be sarcastic. I did not miss her. But I am, oddly, glad to see her skyfire, because the skuddima that were about to kill me and Heike are terrified of it.

"I missed you." Heike smiles, relief washing over her face. Color returns to her pale cheeks, and determination to survive replaces fearful defeat.

"One out of two isn't bad." Callie turns to me. "Let me see your swords."

I *knew* she would call them swords. "They're pikes."

"I don't give a crap what they are." Callie grasps the ice in my hand, but instead of immediately shattering it with her skyfire, a look of concentration clouds her eyes, and my pikes begin to glow with her magic—imbued with it, but not unstable. "Now they're Light ice. See how the monsters like it."

The skuddima do *not* like the Light ice—a phrase I am only using in this moment of duress. They fly away from me before my pikes can touch them, and the three or four that were brave enough to linger find themselves sliced in half by the weapons, wisps of gauzy remains falling to the ground.

"That's amazing!" Heike is certainly impressed by the maneuver. Callie slings several orbs at the fleeing skuddima before catching my eye.

"Can you make it rain ice?"

"Rain?" I swing the pikes again, taking out another skuddima. No matter how many individual skuddima I slay, more materialize to take their place.

"Yeah, like, make ice fall from the sky." Callie works with Heike to increase the skyfire in her lantern before launching some of her magic at two skuddima attempting an ambush.

"Why would I do that?" Pikes are more effective—well, alright, not as effective as I'd like, since I can't kill more than two skuddima at a time.

"If we can combine our powers to make it rain Light ice, we can kill all these face-suckers at once."

I do not like to admit it, but that's a very good idea. "I can do what you ask."

"Sweet." Callie grins. "On my count, ready? One, two, go!"

I drop one of my Light pikes—skyfire pikes, I mean—and turn my attention to the Mist overhead, my magic easily coalescing it into shards of ice that fall toward the ground. Callie sends a thousand tiny drops of skyfire into the ice, turning each one into a skuddima slaughtering mini-dagger. The melee of screams and falling gauze as the skuddima retreat or die is over as fast as the attack began. The only evidence it happened are the tiny, glowing ice pieces scattered across the ground.

"I'm so glad to see you!" Heike leaps for Callie, embracing her roughly, but Callie is equally happy to see my sister. "Thank you for coming back for us."

"I wasn't going to let the one time your brother made an illogical decision be the last decision he made." She sets Heike to her feet and faces me, taking a deep breath. "Before you say anything, there's a lot I'm going to come clean about. So just listen, okay?"

My first instinct is to insult her, to demean her concealment and point to it as proof that I should not do the thing she asked. But she did just save my life, and Heike's, and came after us when we needed help. And so I nod. "Proceed."

"The biggest thing you need to know is that I'm not from

Tremurheim, I'm from California." She pauses, letting the information I don't understand and yet perfectly comprehend sink in. "It's on another world in the multiverse called Earth, although your myths and stories might call it something different. The things you See — the floating pictures in the sky and Mist — those are called gateways, and on the other side are worlds like mine. Diver and I got here by opening a gateway in California with my Light Core, which is a source of massive energy that can rip the fabric of space and reality. It's in my backpack for safekeeping."

"For safekeeping?" As if a knapsack can protect her from something so dangerous.

"What you call Beacon flare is another Light Core," Callie ignores my concern, as per usual, "and I have to find it before Nate, the Shadowmancer that's trailing me, finds it first. That's the whole reason I'm in Tremurheim. And I need a Seer, like you, to help me not only find the Light Core, but to open a gateway off of this world to another one so I can find even more Light Cores. I have to get to a world called Ensolorada and find a woman named Serai Eradah, so I can learn how to use my Light Cores to save the multiverse from Darkness." Another pause. "Are you still with me? We're good?"

"We are not good, but I'm following," is my reply.

"Fair enough." She averts her eyes, staring at her boots. "I realize it isn't fair to ask you to accompany me to the Beacons, or even to another world, to help me hunt Light Cores. And I know the reason you ran off when I attacked the Uldru was to make sure I couldn't hurt something you love." A brief glance at Heike, and then Callie goes on. "So I'll give you a choice before I get out of your life for good. You can choose to come with me and be my Seer, and we'll help each other learn how to use our powers together — mutual respect, no power plays. Or I can take you back to the forest in Diver and help you get settled in a new village before I head off and find the Beacons on my own. I just ask that you let me keep the map, and maybe tell me how to read it. Is that a good compromise?"

A compromise… something I have never offered her. Why is she offering me one? Why the benevolence? Does she have something to gain? It would seem that she has everything to lose — especially if I'm the one person who can open the windows in the sky so she can continue on her journey. Because as addled as all her talk of the multiverse and other worlds ought to sound, I somehow believe her. That the windows in the sky are more than just visions, but other worlds across an expanse of reality and space, becomes as true as I am standing with my sister and a skyfire sorceress, being offered a choice between something unknown and yet known, and something more familiar.

A strange pull tugs on my chest, drawing me to one conclusion over the other, and I shake my head, trying to dislodge the sticky source. "I don't — I mean, I just think — "

"I'm going with you, Callie." Heike moves to stand by her friend's side. "You saved my life two times now. If I can help you, in any way, I'm going to. No matter the risk, or how strange all of this multiverse talk sounds."

"You would separate us?" The pull inside becomes stronger, a tide carrying me out to sea, and I don't know what a tide is, or a sea of anything besides Mist, but I do know those words somehow, and that feeling. Something out of a dream.

"No one is making you go back to a village, or come with us." Callie drapes her arm around Heike in a way that is natural and sisterly, and I know why Heike wants to stay, but can't deny it hurts. "Heike can make her own decision, and so can you. I wish you'd come with us, but I'm over the blackmail stuff. It's not fair to anyone."

I cannot imagine accompanying her on this Light Core hunt, learning to use my magic openly and forcefully instead of controlling and concealing, and being confronted by the dangers of the Darkness she is tasked to destroy. But even worse, I cannot imagine being separated from my sister forever. To lose her would be the most unbearable thing of all. And so there's no choice, really. As much as I hate it, I will learn to live with it.

After all, Callie *did* come back...

"I shall come."

"Oh, Toran, I knew you'd see this was better than locking yourself up in an Archive!" Heike embraces me now, and when I wrap my arms around her, embracing her too, the ice around my heart thaws.

"It is not better than locking myself up in an Archive," I say, "but it might also not be so bad."

"Did you just — I'm sorry, but did you just say a trip across the Hem to find a Light Core and Dive through the multiverse with my mechs was 'not so bad?'" Callie's hand flies to her forehead, and her eyes pop around an audible gasp. "I'm shocked, Toran. Seriously, am I dead right now?"

She is joking. I know that well enough by now. I roll my eyes and snort.

"Don't take this as a sign we're friends," I assure her, "or that I'm going to enjoy myself."

"I don't think you could ever enjoy yourself," Callie replies, smiling. She pats my shoulder, her skyfire reaching through me, connecting with my magic in the strangest way. "Unless books or making plans are involved. Then you'd *really* enjoy yourself. But who am I to judge, right? I kissed an undead monster, so whatever floats your boat."

Heike giggles. I scowl. I have a feeling this is going to be normal from now on.

"Hmph." I jerk my chin toward her World Diver. "Come, we have several more outposts to find along the path to the Beacons."

"They should be easier to find now that I lit the first one." Callie points to the distant skyfire, shining clear in all directions. "You read the map, I Light the domes, and Heike can pick the music. We'll be there in no time."

"Oh, yes, I can do that." My sister's enthusiasm is not catching. Not for me, anyway. "And I want to hear about the monster you kissed."

"We will all be worse for hearing such an asinine story," I announce. "We're traveling with a purpose, not wasting time discussing Callie James' abysmal taste in courtship partners."

"I wouldn't call it abysmal, I mean, he's the gold standard for hotness despite being a—" she catches herself, cheeks going a little pink, and claps her hands together. "Right, travel. Light Cores don't find themselves, huh? Let's get moving."

"Moving indeed." I turn my gaze to Heike. "And no music. It will give me a headache."

"Callie already said I'm in charge." She skips ahead of me to Diver's foot, hopping on top, and Callie joins her. My last opportunity to go back to the Tremurheim I know fades forever when I mount the mech's foot, and then his palm, riding up to face the scattered disarray of the Crow's Nest and the unknown dangers of the Hem.

I have always considered adventurous types nonsensical, but in the space of a moment, I've become one. And I know, as sure as there is magic in my blood, that there's no going back.

Let's just hope the Tageveld is not as horrifying as the myths make it out to be. Because if it's anything like the stories I have read, we've just doomed ourselves to a protracted, painful, lonely death at the end of this world.

And that is *not* me being morbid.

CHAPTER 20
NATE

"ANOTHER DEAD PIPILO. That's a bad sign."

El and I inspect the tiny, lifeless creature laying beside a rock, the light of El's headlamp illuminating the kitten-like face and ears in its pale glow, one growing paler by the hour the deeper we descend.

"It must have just died," I observe. "It looks like it's sleeping." A quick poke of the wings and spine confirms the flesh is still soft, faintly warm. It's like the creature laid down for a nap, and never woke up. "Why are dead pipilos a bad sign? Does that mean more gigantic wyrms are close by?"

"No." Light bobs along the pipilo's body when El shakes his head. "It means the air is getting too thin to breathe. Or, there are poisonous vents somewhere close. Could be either."

"Great." A pause. "And by great, I mean—"

"I knew you weren't serious." El breathes deep, as though he has to gulp as much air as possible into his lungs to feel like he's taken a full breath. Confirms my suspicion that poisonous vents aren't the problem so much as lack of oxygen.

"Are you doing okay?" I ask. "We can turn around and try scouting another part of the mine shaft. One with better oxygen saturation."

El wordlessly scoops a pile of pebbles over the little pipilo, a makeshift burial, and stands, leaning against the rough-hewn rock wall. "Is that weird call in your gut still telling you to go this way?"

It's not *telling* me to go further into the bowels of the earth: right at this second, it's practically *screaming* at me to go on, angry I stopped to investigate a dead animal. Everything in me says 'don't turn back,' because something somewhere is begging me to find it.

On top of it all, Queen could pop in for a report whenever she feels like it, and any hint I've given up on my Light Core hunt, even if it means saving El's life, will get me ashed. If that happens, El has no hope of survival at all.

My life is cliché, I know. Or, my undead existence is cliché. Which is a cliché unto itself.

But regardless of those two competing desires, festering and fighting for control, I know El's not going to last long if he can hardly breathe. Humans and breathing kind of go hand in hand.

"My gut's still saying go this way, but you won't last much longer." No use lying about it. El takes a few more deep breaths, trying to pull it together, and trudges along, his footsteps dragging.

"I'll be okay, I just might need more breaks." He glances up at me. "It's lucky you don't have to breathe, isn't it? At least one of us won't mind."

My undead monster status isn't exactly something humans should admire. "Tell me when you want to rest."

El heaves a breath around a faint smile. "I will."

I have a sinking feeling the dead pipilo is a worse warning than El thinks.

"I need a rest."

El's last rest was ten minutes ago—what I think was ten minutes ago. It could have been quicker than that. I cease forward momentum, pausing to glance back through the claustrophobic lack of light. He's probably ten yards behind me, bent over with hands on his knees, shoulders and chest heaving around gasps, just like they have since he woke up for the "day."

Who knows if it's day or night? The only things surrounding us are darkness and rocks.

"How long have you been panting back there?" I correct my course, meeting El where he (barely) stands. "You should have said something earlier."

"I thought I could go farther, but I can't." Shallow rasps punctuate El's words.

"Don't talk. Just sit." I steer him into a little alcove made by two boulders and settle him into a position that will help get as much air into his lungs as possible. I did the same thing for Mom, toward the end. "Is that better?"

"Yes." He leans back, more comfortable already. "Thanks."

"You can't keep doing this." I stretch out, grateful for a small break, too. The pull-tug has been moving me at an almost breakneck pace without resting and my legs kinda hurt, especially my calves. "I'm serious—promise or no promise, I'll take you back to the place we fell into this part of the mine shaft. We'll get back to the top of the opening somehow, and you can recover in Aragusti. Being so long without air can mess up your brain, even kill you."

"According to everyone, my brain is already messed up," El half-whispers. "Even if I wanted you to do that, we can't. I forgot to set markers after the ore wyrm attacked us."

"You forgot something? I'm shocked." Probably not the best time to tease, or attempt to make jokes, but El likes to keep the mood light. Just like Mom. She laughed and smiled up until she fell asleep for the last time. "Leave it to you to forget to track our path out of here, dork."

"It's not like you reminded me to do it. Dork." He closes his eyes. "I'm just... so tired..."

"Sleep, then." I switch off his headlamp, the darkness of the shaft swallowing us altogether. Neither of us likes it, but it conserves power in the fading lamp. "I'll wake you up soon."

I can't see El, but I know, even in the tangible dark, he's already asleep. His breaths slow, stretching further and further apart, and his head droops against my shoulder, cheek pressed to my arm. It helps me listen and feel for the dreaded scenario of if — or when — he stops breathing entirely. If that happens, I don't know how I'll revive him.

Stupid El, sacrificing everything for promise. Selfish me, for putting him in this situation in the first place.

What would El say if he knew the whole reason he's passing out five times an hour is that I manipulated him into this mine, all so I could hunt a Light Core for the multiverse's Prime Shadowmancer, because I'm a mopey dweeb with a grudge? That I'm a far worse monster than he knows — one who willingly put his life at risk for my own egotistical desire to destroy, and win?

Telling me I'm the most horrible person who ever existed, and I deserve to get dissolved like a puff of smoke by Queen's Darkness, would just about cover it.

A chill creeps over my skin, raising the hairs on my arms. Capital "D" Darkness is near, and it's not my own. Icy tentacles slip through the Veil toward me, wrapping around my throat and weaving through my hair like a vice closing in.

"*Little one...*"

Bad timing, Queen.

"*Little one, come.*" A different kind of pull-tug manifests at the base of my spine, one that wants to grab me and take me beyond the Veil. Queen's Darkness calling to mine, and mine responding, even as the warm spark that's guided me through the endless earth fights against it. Both forces struggle for control, but in the end, her Darkness is stronger.

Honestly, I've been expecting Queen to call me back and give my report. It's been a while since she tore up my face after I botched the last one. As much as I want to flip her off and tell her to suck eggs, my survival is the key to El's, and disobeying is a surefire way to get us both killed. I ease him away from my shoulder, hoping he's okay by the time I get back, and slip beyond the Veil.

Darkness used to bring me relief: pain gave way to purpose, grief to fury channeled on a target I could make plans to destroy. But now, the Veil feels like a jaw full of gnawing teeth trying to chew me up and spit me out—a mechanism to cause more pain, more grief, more harm.

"Little one." Queen glides through the Darkness toward me, the boundaries of her prison less solidly marked. I can always tell where they end and begin, because it feels like an invisible wall, holding both of us in place. Now, it's almost like they've evaporated, turned transparent instead of opaque.

She's also in a startlingly good mood. The last few times she's called me to the Shadow Plain, she's been furious enough to slay me where I stand, but I'd almost say she's smiling.

Wonder why? But I keep my lips zipped. Questioning means I'm wasting time here instead of getting back to El.

"Have you made progress in your search, little one?" Queen cuts right to the chase.

How much of the truth to reveal? Does it even matter? She's going to hate my answer regardless of how I spin it. "I'm searching, but the Light Core remains elusive."

She sways her chin back and forth, her eyes flitting across the deep scars she left on my forehead and cheek, but she doesn't suspect I'm lying, so she backs off. "That's unfortunate. Do you continue to hunt the Light, even though you've not yet discovered its location?"

"Yes, my Queen." El might die because of my "hunting," but Queen's got me in a bind.

And I'm starting to really hate it.

"The Light Cores were hidden in such a way that only the most persistent and tenacious Luminaut would be able to find them," Queen says. "It was a stipulation of my imprisonment to hide them so well they couldn't be found by just anyone. Light will call only to the worthy."

Implying, of course, that Mom wasn't worthy. Not scoring any points with me today, Queen. But I'm too scared for El to let my face show anything but neutral, expressionless cool. If I get ashed, El's not going to make it out of this mine alive. That's my priority. It's not like Mom would have cared what some Shadowmancer thought about her. She'd have known better.

"I'm not a worthy Luminaut," I say, tone completely flat.

"You are more valuable than you understand, little one." Queen's pale face contorts with sadistic glee. "Everything is unfolding just as it should. I am pleased with the Luminaut's progress in her own hunt for the Light, and soon you will reach the Light as well. Never fear, my Darkness shall soon triumph."

Metaphorical gulp. I don't really want to think about what Queen would do to Callie in order to assure her "triumph." I know for a fact flirting and making out would *not* be involved, and I can only imagine the type of suffering Queen would inflict — something insidious. She won't keep her plans for "triumph" over Light a secret for long, not if she's been busy concocting them while I was distracted elsewhere.

You'd almost assume Queen planned it this way, purposely sending me on a foolhardy Light Core hunt she knows I can't win so I have no opportunity to give in to my "human weakness" for Callie. Like she concocted this deception from the start, so Callie would willingly expose herself to danger in defiance of my betrayal.

Actually, that's *exactly* the kind of long con Queen would pull off.

"I have no doubt the Luminaut will find the Light Core, wherever she is hunting." My dispassionate statement can be read however Queen likes, but to me, it's nothing like a statement of victory. It's a horrific prophecy.

"My servant is loyal." Queen's hair floats about her face, and she places a light hand on my shoulder. Memories of the pain she inflicted the last time she touched me run deep — it's a miracle I don't wince or pull away. But doing so would seal my fate. "I know my little one will prevail in his search."

Hearing myself referred to as "servant" and "little one" again after El's been calling me "Nate" all this time makes my skin crawl. I repress the shudder that'll land me on the naughty list in a heartbeat. I've got to survive this round if I want to get back to El. "I will do my best, my Queen."

She's pleased with my compliance, my lack of emotion. No subversive questions means no threat to her authority, right?

"I've made things difficult, and tested you many times," Queen goes on. Her eyes blaze with sickening fire — the kind that means somebody is going to get murdered soon — in her porcelain face. "I will show you what the others dreamed of seeing before they fell prey to their weakness." Meaning before she killed five other Shadowmancers in front of my eyes. "I will show you the true beauty of Darkness, my purpose and plan for the multiverse. The reason we have done everything we've done, sacrificed our human lives and desires, and toiled here in the Shadow with little but a glimpse of what could be."

If the Shadow Plain is a glimpse of what could be...

"Go, my little one." Queen glides away, but doesn't disappear into her prison. Instead, she stays, watching me with those bloody crimson eyes. "Do the work of Darkness."

For the first time since I Turned, I can't leave the Shadow Plain fast enough. I never know exactly how long I've been away from the human world, and El could have succumbed. It's a thought that scares me more than whatever Queen has planned — the "true beauty of Darkness."

"El?" As soon as I cross the Veil, I come to a complete standstill, listening for the sound of breathing, trying to sense the faint flutter of a pulse. I try his name again, louder this time. "El!"

"Mmmph-huh?" My voice woke him, but at least he can rouse himself at the sound of his name. "Nate?"

I could sigh my relief, except my lungs are as undead as the rest of me. Instead, El switches on his headlamp, and I kneel beside him. "Feeling any better? Do you need food? Water?"

"No." El not wanting to eat is troublesome. "Do we have to walk again?"

I look him over in the light, noting the way he seems ready to nod off again, how his pulse flutters like hummingbird wings, his rapid breathing. Even if I wanted to go further, I know he can't. "You need to go back to Aragusti. I'm making an executive decision to — "

Nate... my stars...

"Mom?" I whip my head around, searching for the source of her voice I *know* I heard calling me. The spark that's been guiding my steps, leading me toward the unknown, warms away the terrible cold of the Shadow Plain, quiets the anger that fuels my Darkness.

"Your mom's down here?" El murmurs.

"No, she's dead."

"Maybe we are, too," he muses.

Nate...

A fresh breeze blows my hair from my forehead, cools my cheek, caresses the scars and comforts me as it soothes away the lingering pain and fear. I close my eyes to the feeling, aching with longing for the source.

"What—what is that?" El perks. "Is that air?"

"You felt it, too?" Whatever this is, I didn't imagine it.

"Yes. We have to find it." El tries to stand, but crumbles to his feet, his energy reserves entirely depleted.

"Hang on." I hold up my hand, mind spinning as I try to think of what this could mean. Queen just called me into the Shadow Plain and told me she'd show me the beauty of Darkness. Is this another deception? A part of her plan? The "beauty" she's trying to show me?

...my stars, don't be afraid...

No, this call is something different than Darkness. Something entirely good, whole, and pure. It feels... it feels like...

There's something I remember about what this feeling might be. Something I shoved down and forgot until it became like it never existed at all, but it's still there, and always has been. And now, it's bubbling to the surface.

The surface.... Why is that word holding me back? The surface of what?

Another breeze blows, this one stronger, more urgent. More than a gentle call, but a stern command to come, seek, and find.

"Okay, here's the deal." I bend down, grabbing El's arms, then pull him up and swing him around onto my back. "Hold on the best you can. I'll carry you until we find where this airflow is coming from. Then you can rest and get your strength back before we decide what to do next."

"What about my food?"

That's the El I know. I snatch the knapsack and secure the straps to my chest. "The food's safe. And because I'm an undead icicle, I'm pretty much a natural refrigerator. Aren't you glad I'm here, saving your skin *and* keeping your ration packs cold? How kind and generous of me. They should give me an award for all this benevolence."

"Except you almost got me killed down here in the first place, scouting the dümfo Cornerstone Key." El tightens his grip around my neck, almost like a hug. "But I'm glad you're my friend anyway."

His friend...

"Stop, El, you're going to make me bawl like a baby and embarrass myself." I start off down the path as the breeze slips through the stale, heavy air around us. Forward, never stopping, my legs moving apart from the rest of my body, the muscles controlled by the source of the breeze more than my conscious movement. I don't know how far I walk. It could be miles. Could be mere yards. All I know is I'm moving, and I don't stop.

There's something just up ahead. Something large, open, brighter than the mine shaft around us. The place my inner spark has been leading me the whole time. The answer to everything.

"What *is* this place?"

All of a sudden, almost without warning, the narrow tunnel we've been traveling opens up into a massive, cave-like cavern, one so large it houses almost an entire subterranean world. Dripping stalactites rain gently into an underground lake far below our feet, bioluminescent plants growing in lush patches along the shore while glowing vines creep up the sloped walls. Every color I can think shines from the vegetation, filling the cavern with glimmering hope. El and I stand on the edge of a cliff, surveying the impossible beauty of something that shouldn't exist.

"I didn't know this was down here," El says. I slip him off my back, letting him rest against the soft creepers along the rock wall, and set his knapsack at his side. "Is this the place you've been trying to go this whole time?"

"Yes." The answer comes unbidden, as if I know it without investigating, without needing to see proof. This is where the spark has been leading me. This beautiful lake below the depths, a place that feels untamed, wild, safe, and secure all at once. Almost like... a home that's been waiting.

From below, a gigantic flash of Light rises toward the highest heights of the cavern, illuminating the plants, the water, the stalactites, the vines along the walls. Everything around me glows, bathed in Light, filling my eyes with the most indescribably gorgeous color I've ever seen, and some colors I've never seen, couldn't comprehend, because I didn't know they existed.

"Wow..." El's breathless proclamation fills my ears, and I can't help but agree.

"It's down there." I don't know why I say it, except the Light formed the words, not my tongue. "I have to go get it."

"Nate?" El tries to stand, making it to his knees. "Where are you going? Not *down* there."

"I have to get the Light." It's blazing through me, begging me to take it. To claim it and unleash it, let it burrow deep inside until it's an inextricable part of me.

"You can't, it's too far." El's protest means nothing, because I know I have to claim this Light, no matter what.

"Stay here," I say. "I'll be back."

Before El can utter another word, I slip beyond the Veil and arrive at the bottom of the cavern. And there, settled inside a bed of brilliantly shimmering flowers and vines, is the Light Core of Ictari.

Floodgates open, a wave of memory crashing through my mind, and I know why I've felt these feelings before, why the spark called me to this place, why I heard Mom's voice manifested in the Light, telling me not to be afraid.

I know, because I found a Light Core once before.

The weather is turning rapidly, dark clouds gathering over my head as the wind whips against the skiff, threatening to send me completely off course. I don't have a lot of time; the first lesson of sailing Mom and Dad drilled into me was to turn around the second the weather gets bad. But I can't leave, not yet. It's there, calling me.

The Light Core shines at the bottom of the sea, about twenty-five feet down. Its Light spirals toward the surface, illuminating the water and the air with brilliant, glimmering gold.

"I found it." Every day for three years I promised myself I'd find this Light Core, and with it, the answers Mom was denied. I spent countless hours sailing up and down the coastline, following breadcrumbs of leads like I was chasing a hunger in my belly that could never be satisfied.

I didn't tell Dad about the onset of my powers. Everything was secret until I knew, for sure, the Light was mine, and I learned the truth.

It's all manifested in this singular moment. Light drew me here with its warmth, its silent call, and now, it's crackling like lightning, breaking the surface of the waves. Mom said it would call the Luminaut meant to find it. But the elusive question remains unanswered, the catalyst for setting off my hunt in the first place: why did the Light call me, and not her?

Maybe I shouldn't take it. Not yet. I should pack it in, get the skiff back to the marina before this storm blows in, and come back tomorrow when I've had a night to sleep on it — to contemplate what it means, and how I really feel. Besides, Dad's waiting for me to watch the Giants game on TV. He'll probably get pizza for dinner. I'm starving, and the thought of pepperoni, jalapeño, and pineapple makes my mouth water.

But if I miss this chance, the Core will drift out to sea again, and with it, the answers I've been desperately searching for.

And so I dive in.

My first attempt, I can't quite reach. My lips bob above the surface of the water, gulping air, but I'm not deterred. I'm a good swimmer, and I've been in and around these waters off Verona Beach my whole life. My second attempt gets me closer, but there's a current just below the surface, one pulling me further into deep water every time I go down. Third and fourth tries are equally fruitless, and I'm tiring out after a long day of maneuvering the skiff through gales and oncoming squalls.

"One more time," I promise myself, rain dripping down my forehead and nose as gathering waves rake over my head. A deep breath, and down I go again, swimming with all my might.

It's so close… I stretch my fingers, inching toward the Light… the Core pulses, glows, begs me to take it. My whole being wants to take it, but the current is stronger. There's something different about the water surrounding me — something darker, and colder.

Something almost like a sign. An answer. A choice.

My lungs burn, my vision blurs. I need air, and fast, or I'll get hypoxic. Straining, with one last push toward the ocean floor, I brush the edge of the Light with my fingertips. Another half inch, and I can just curl my fingers…

As quick as the moment comes, it's gone. The current drags my body into the deep, away from my Light, away from my skiff. I fight against the pull, desperate to get to the surface for air.

My heart and lungs are on fire, my vision rapidly deteriorating around black spots. Arms and legs move, but I can't tell up from down anymore. The surface recedes around a dark, circular hole as I drop down, down, down, losing all sense of time and place.

Where am I? This isn't the ocean, this isn't… anywhere. Am I dead? No, I still have a pulse. But air sticks inside my lungs, and I can't breathe in or out. I'm suspended, trapped, unable to stay or go.

And then, I hear her voice for the first time, calling me away from the Light and reeling me toward my Dark future – the pull-tug at the base of my spine I'd learn to know all too well.

"Come, my little one," she beckons, her eyes materializing inside the Darkness worming through my brain, stopping my pulse cold. "Come with me, and I will teach you the truth about the Light."

The Light... I can still see it in the distance, slipping further and further away.

Didn't it call me? Why couldn't I take it, if it was truly mine? What if it tricked me – if it never really cared, just like it never cared about Mom? What if I'm just another pawn in the same grand betrayal that stole Mom, allowing me to get close, but not to succeed?

And, more importantly, what's the supposed truth this creature in the Darkness knows that I don't? Do I want to risk everything to find out?

One last chance to go back, to choose drowning over Darkness, and give up the truth forever. Or, just maybe, she'll tell me everything I ever wanted to know about Light, and more.

"Little one..."

"Yes. I'll come." I let myself float away, receding into the Shadows until the ocean is no more, the golden glow of Light fading into the depths of Shadow.

I blink, zipped forward through time to the present, and my feet land on solid ground, staring at the Light Core, the infamous Cornerstone Key of legend. The thing that called me into this space just like it called me that day in the ocean; a Light in the dark I was always meant to find, despite my roundabout path to getting here.

The Light Queen wants me to bring her for destruction.

My fingers curl around the Light Core, grasping the thing that's enraged, eluded, and fascinated for as long as I have memory. Light surges through me, fills my veins, occupies the empty spaces in my lungs and heart. Warmth like I've only dreamed of mixes with wildness, goodness, power, and freedom. Once it's in my hands, Light sinks into me, flows all around, and for the first time since I was Turned, I feel like I can breathe.

I don't realize I've actually done it until air leaves my lungs in a glorious exhale. When I open my eyes, I realize my hands are glowing.

Skin shimmering, Light surging, lungs breathing…

I drop the Light Core, terrified of what's happening, what it all means about me and the choices I've made. Jumping away, I stare at my shaking, golden fingers, filled with both awe and horror.

This — this means that I — that *I'm* a — that I've always been —

Crrrrraaaaack!

The walls of the cavern shake, the stalactites overhead crunching, swaying, and knocking into each other before they fall from the ceiling and splash into the lake. An earthquake rumbles, threatening a cave-in, and the entire cavern will soon collapse.

A cavern El and I are still inside, separated by a cliff more than fifty feet high.

"Something's happening!" El's voice, shrill and petrified, reaches me at the bottom.

"Sit tight, I'm coming!" How I'm coming, I don't know, but I have to figure out a way.

Darkness manifests before my eyes, swirling around the flowers and vines, sucking the life out of them before turning them to putrid ash, leaving tentacle-shaped patterns of destruction in its wake. I tremble in the cold, the Shadows threatening to steal the Light from everything it's touched — including me.

This isn't my Darkness. This is Queen's Darkness bleeding

beyond the Veil, her power and rage rattling the cavern. Her demonic laugh rings through my ears, the murderous vengeance it contains palpable, and I know I have to get El out of here, or this cave-in will crush us any second.

Seconds neither of us have.

CHAPTER 21
NATE

THE VEIL. I need the Veil.

But it's gone.

Chunks of the ceiling and massive stalactites crash into the churning water, waves and splashes soaking me through. Thunderous booming shakes the walls all around. El and I have got to get out of here, but without the Veil, we're stuck.

I can never catch a break anymore, can I?

"Come on," I mutter. I pick up the Light Core from where I dropped it, shoving it in my jacket pocket. Light surges through me, drowning out the weakening Darkness, but at this moment, Darkness is what I need—if only to use the Veil to get back up to El.

I reach inward, trying to shove down the Light momentarily and channel the Darkness. It's there, fighting against the power of Light, struggling to surface.

"Let's go. Veil. Now." I focus on the Darkness, letting it rise through the Light until I'm physically ill enough to throw up, and search, dry heaving around a gag, for the Veil.

There. The foggy tendrils materialize before me, Darkness beckoning me away from humanity and Light. With one final push, I slip beyond and reemerge back in the human world on the cliff where El is waiting as even more of the ceiling crashes down on the spot where I'd just stood.

"El!" Where is that kid? I hop-skip out of the way of tumbling rocks, whirling all around. "El, where are you!"

"Over here, dümfo!" El calls me from his hiding spot at the mouth of the airless tunnel. I run toward him, careful to avoid debris. "I hid as soon as the rocks started falling. How did you get back up here so fast?" El asks when I finally join him. The mine shaft surrounding us rumbles, and before long, this spot isn't going to be safe, either.

"Monster stuff," I answer.

"Wow, your hands are glowing! It's like you've got thousands of tiny spark fins now! Did you find the Cornerstone Key?" El eyes the Light Core, blazing in my pocket. "Is that it? Did you cause the cave-in when you touched it?"

"No, that only happens in movies." This isn't Aladdin and the magic lamp, this is Queen unleashing her fury on her home world — which ought to sound even more fantastical than a movie about flying carpets and genies, but here we are, in reality.

Somehow, me taking Ictari's Light Core meant she could break free of the Veil. Or, at least, her Darkness could. I don't know how that's possible, just like I don't know what to think about the Light Core activating and making my hands glow, because it would mean that everything I thought I knew and remembered about the last moments of my human life are now suspect. But soul-searching can wait until El and I escape this cave-in.

"This is amazing!" El takes the Light Core out of my pocket, the glow fading into something gentle and benign in his hands. He turns it over a few times, grinning in awe. "I didn't think the Cornerstone Key was real, and here it is!"

"It's called a Light Core," I correct him. A landslide of rocks accumulating around the mouth of the tunnel reminds me we have to get out of here as soon as possible.

"Why does it make your hands look like spark fins and not mine?" El scowls, a little disappointed.

"Don't worry about that. You just gave me an idea." If the Light Core does nothing in El's presence, but sparkles like a firework in mine... Is it possible to trick the Veil? "Here's what we're doing," I say, and yet another barrage of rocks cascades around us, reiterating the need for urgency. "You're going to put that thing in your knapsack, and then, I'm going to take you beyond the Veil and get us out of here."

And hope that even seconds in the Shadow Plain won't kill humans, but I'm not going to mention that unsavory potential consequence. In certain-death versus maybe-death scenarios, I'll go with maybe.

"What's the Veil?" El's expression falls, appropriately leery. "Isn't that monster stuff?"

"Yes." I search his eyes. "Do you trust me?"

More rocks, more rubble, less time to decide. El's gaze darts toward the cave-in, then back to me.

"I trust you." He shoves the Light Core into his pack and nods. "Let's go."

Alright. Let's go.

I grasp his shoulders and pull him close, reaching for the Veil — easier now that I'm not holding a Light Core and the power has retreated inside, nestled against my heart like a glowing ember. In the space of a blink, we're through, and I search for Aragusti as fast as I can.

Darkness moves in for the attack as soon as it senses the presence of a human, and it takes most of my concentration to keep the slithering tentacles of Shadow away from El. He writhes in fear and tries to scream, but no sound comes out, his voice lost and stifled. I keep him as far from the Darkness as I can while I search, desperate for our destination.

Come on, Aragusti, where are you? Why can't I see it? It should be right there, exactly where we left it, but all I can see through the murky gauze is a huge hole in the ground where a city should be.

Darkness descends around us, grasping for El, searching for his inner Light to destroy, and I decide a huge hole in the ground will have to do. I jump beyond the Veil with El, both of us mercifully intact, and skid to a stop face-first in a pile of ash.

"Are you okay?" I ask, crawling to my knees before I lean back on my heels and look around. Wherever we are, it's not Aragusti, but it's also not caving in around us, so already a marked improvement.

"No." El curls into a ball, his face drained of any hint of color it might have once possessed. His limbs shake uncontrollably when he tries to right himself. "What was that place? It was worse than any nightmare I've ever had. I… I didn't know monsters like that existed."

I hate to burst your bubble, El, but you're looking a monster square in the face. I help him sit up, brushing ash off his clothes and face. "That was the Veil. It's how I get around the multiverse."

"What's a multiverse?" El can't seem to decide if he's confused or still terrified.

"I'll explain everything later. Let's get you back to your place so you can rest and eat."

El perks up at the mention of stuffing his face. "I could use some food and a nap. Hopefully Caro and his dümfos are gone for the day." With jellyfish legs, he stands, shouldering his knapsack as he surveys the sinkhole of desolation we landed in. "Where are we? Is Aragusti close?"

"Don't know, but you can breathe and hike again, so let's see if we can find a way out. Or, any clues to point us in Aragusti's general direction."

El finishes bushing the ash off his jumpsuit. "That's a good plan." He checks his palms, made black by the ash, and gives his hair final shake, sending even more particles flying. "It looks like a fire happened."

"I was thinking the same thing." Surveying the massive, burned-out hole gives me a sense of dread, a brick originating in my stomach that drops toward my toes. Something awful happened here, and it makes my skin crawl, like I've stumbled onto the scene of an apocalyptic murder. The screams of the former inhabitants of whatever this place was ring through my ears, a fresh echo of horror. "There aren't even any burned-out buildings, it's all just... ash."

Ash. Piles and piles of it. None of it warm — not a specter of smoke, or the reek of char. Just... destruction.

A realization quakes through me, almost taking me to my knees. I know this type of ash, and it isn't made by a fire.

Ash like this is what happened when I tore a hole in the roof of the VBHS gym with my Darkness, trying to scare the pants off of Callie. A fine, silt-like ash rained down on the polished wooden court, covered the bleachers, coated the league championship banners hanging from the rafters. And ash is what remained of the ore wyrm that attacked me and El in the Cursed Mine — no trace of warmth or life. Just... ash.

This ash is the calling card of a Shadowmancer.

"El," I force words to leave my tongue, the horrifying memories solidifying into an even worse reality. "I... I think this is — was — Aragusti."

El's eyes bulge as he looks all around, the same stark reality slamming into him, too. "No." Another turn this way, then that. "This — this can't be Aragusti. Where are all the people? The houses? The vents and mines and lights? Where's my place? Where's Marini and her garden?"

Creeping chill, like venom tracing a path through veins and arteries, slips around my legs, my arms, culminating around my neck. The same Darkness surrounding me traps El in place, and I feel his fear as clear as my own when he sees what's going on.

"This—this is—it's a—" El stammers.

"It's a Shadowmancer—and it's time we got out of here." I reach for El, motioning for him to join me. He rushes to my side, but the Darkness persists, menacing us with torturous glee.

"Are you doing this?" El trembles at the sight of the slithering tentacles of Shadow. "They look like the things you used to kill the wyrm."

"No, this isn't me." Shadowy poison invades my being, sniffing out the Light buried inside. "But I know who it is."

And now she knows my secret, too.

"Little one."

Everything in me shifts, lurches to a screeching halt. My lungs and heart slam into the wall of my chest, and my brain fizzles to incomprehensible, terrified mush as the Queen Beyond the Stars appears before me. Beyond the Veil. Physically manifest in the human world. Every impossibility she claimed was a stipulation of her sentence, the cruelty of the Luminauts and Seers who imprisoned her in the Shadow Plain, are lies laid bare by the truth of what's in front of me.

"Don't you think my creation is beautiful?" Queen spreads her hands wide, as if to encompass every inch of ash around us. She's tiny, now that I see her in the human world—petite and slender, like most Ictarans I've encountered, with silvery, white-blonde hair down to her waist. But her eyes, those terrible, malevolent eyes, burn as red as ever.

"Where is Aragusti?" I know the answer before she speaks,

but her next proclamation confirms everything.

"It is here." Queen's horrid smile parts her lips, razor teeth gleaming. "I purified it." She stoops, cupping a pile of ash that could have once been a person — part of a person — in her palms, watching the remains slip through her fingers. "Light brings nothing but suffering to humans. All through the multiverse, Light causes emotional pain, turmoil, and strife. Evil permeates all it touches."

"There were tens of thousands of people living here." Every inch of my insides rise into my throat to expel themselves from my sickened body. "Old people, families, little kids…"

"Yes," Queen agrees, "and I've given them rest, and peace. These people would have languished and died slowly because of the Light inside them. Now, they are free."

The runaway train that is Queen's ultimate plan for the multiverse, the "beauty of Darkness" she was so eager to show me, flies off the rails and crashes into me, until I stumble under its unbearable weight.

This has been her plan all along. It was never about destroying Light Cores so Callie couldn't unleash some future untold destruction, because Queen knew the plan for ending Light was "destructive" from the beginning. This was — and always has been — about removing all Light from the multiverse: one human, one city, one world at a time, until nothing but ash and Darkness remain. The whole multiverse transformed into an unending Shadow Plain.

"I never wanted this to happen." I wish I could tear my gaze away from the ashes of the people who lived here, left to sit for all eternity in a blackened-out cavern under the snow, but I can't. No one remains to remember them or love them, because everyone they knew and loved is a pile of ash, too.

"Of course you wanted this," Queen replies. "You wanted the

ultimate truth about the Light. This is the truth. Light is the source of all that is evil and corrupt in the multiverse, and we, the rising Darkness, must purify it."

No, no, no. This isn't happening. This isn't what I gave up my human life for—it can't be. These piles of ash aren't pure. They're tragic, horrible. The work of a monster.

But it *is* what I sacrificed everything for, and always has been.

A part of me feared it, festering like a nagging pinprick in the back of my mind. Queen spoon-fed her hateful stories about Light and Luminauts, warping my memories, and played my anger and grief to her favor until I accepted her lies as truth. It didn't matter what awful things Queen asked me to do in her stead, Mom had already suffered worse because of Light. And I played along, a willing participant in her chaos if it meant avenging the one person I loved most. My endgame was still my own, wasn't it?

No. It never was. It was always Queen's, and I was her *servant* that enabled this. I've done nothing but cause pain and fear since the moment I became a Shadowmancer—and all for *this*.

The "beauty" of Darkness is death.

But...

But if Darkness is death and Light is in me...

Something shifts, an upheaval of my understanding, my thoughts, my desires. The spark of Light that guided me to the subterranean cave glows bright under my heart, reaching for my mind, filling me with a truth I never could have arrived at on my own. A truth Queen tried her best to keep blunted and out of sight.

Darkness is death, but Light is in me... I forgot what I am, what I've always been...

But I won't forget again.

"I believe," Queen speaks, breaking the barrier of shattered beliefs and resurrected truths, "the boy has something that belongs to me."

El stiffens at my side, and cries out in horror when Queen's Darkness flies toward him, seconds away from leaving him and the Light Core in his pack a pile of ash, too.

"No!" I leap in front of El to block him from Darkness, throwing my hands out in front of me. I don't care if it hurts, or if I have to fight a throwdown there's no way I can win. Queen is *not* going to hurt El, or destroy my Light Core.

She's not going to take anything else from me. Not if I can stop it.

Light, a vision as brilliant and blinding as the sun, flares through the cavern, burns through my mind, and fills me with a sensation like floating and falling all at the same time. I don't know if I'm up or down, if the Light is real or all in my head. The bright flash of an exploding star fills the space around me, and I can't see Queen, can't see El, can't see the ashes and destruction, or any trace of Darkness. All I can see, sense, or know in this moment is Light.

And then, it's gone, and I fall, head hitting the ground with a thud before it all goes black.

"Nate, get up!"

El is shaking me awake. Awake? I don't sleep. What just happened?

"She's gone, come on, let's go!" El shakes harder before he punches my arm.

"Ow!" Okay, now I'm awake. I sit up and smack him back. "That hurts, dingus!"

"Don't hit me, I'm not the one who made fire with his hands and passed out. I thought you were dead." El hits me again, his bony hand jabbing into my skin, and I'm glad I can't bruise, because I'd have four circular spots the exact shape of each knuckle in his curved fist.

"I didn't make fire with my hands." Dad's a Fire Manipulator, not me.

"Yes, you did," El argues. "You made a gigantic light, sort of like a fire. Except, it was brighter, prettier … I can't really describe it. But it filled the whole cavern without burning anything. The monster woman got this really scared look on her face and disappeared. Then you passed out." Another jab to my shoulder for good measure. "I know what I saw."

I kinda miss lack-of-oxygen El. He talked less. Didn't hit me as much.

"Whatever. Not worth arguing about." I stand, brushing ash off my pants. Queen's long gone, just like El said. Or she's hiding in the Shadows until she can strike again. Either way, El and I are alive, but sticking around could easily get us killed. "I need to figure out what to do."

Namely, where to go next.

"She didn't get the Cornerstone Key," El assures me. "It's still in my backpack. It kind of hums, did you know that? It's making my butt numb."

"The last thing I want to know is the current state of your butt, El." But the fact he's still got the Light Core reminds me Callie has no clue about Queen's plans, and whether she found another Light Core or she's still hunting, she's walking straight into a trap.

Would she believe me if I warned her about the danger? Or would she Light blast my head off? Something tells me the latter is more likely than the former. Regardless, I have to warn her what's coming before Queen gets to her first. Whether or not she listens, that's on her. And also on me, for twisting my words, making threats, being an untrustworthy sleaze, starting actual fires, telling lies—

Okay, yeah, I guess I'm at fault if she walks right into a trap. Still, I have to try. But in order to find Callie, I'd have to use the Veil.

"Do you trust me for one last nightmare?" I glance at El. He tenses.

"The Veil?" When I nod, his jaw hardens and his face pales. "Why?"

"Because there's this girl..."

El makes an "oh" shape with his mouth before a slow smile spreads across his face. "A girl, huh?" I swear, if he hits me one more time—too late, he did. "Do you like her?"

I rub my smarting arm. "She's in trouble. Liking is irrelevant."

"So, you like her. Is she pretty?"

"Also not relevant."

"That means she's pretty."

"Stop getting distracted by things that aren't important." I square my shoulders. "Look, there's this girl I know, she's hunting a Light Core, too, and the monster that attacked us is going to attack her next, so I need to warn her. Got it?"

"Are you sure the fact she's pretty isn't important? Because your cheeks are kinda red."

"It's impossible for me to blush, my circulatory system isn't functional," I retort. "Now hang on so I can get us in and out of the Veil as fast as possible. Unless you want Queen to come back and ash you, in which case I'll just leave you here."

"No, not interested in that," El replies. He steels himself, gripping his knapsack straps with white knuckles. "How long will this take?"

"I'll go as fast as I can." It's not like I want to go beyond the

Veil, either. Especially not if Queen can use it now, and sense movement along the Shadow Plain's borders. "Just close your eyes."

El squeezes his eyes shut, and I let the Veil swallow us one last time.

Except as soon as I do, the Darkness wants to spit me out. Light shines around me, trying to protect me from the Darkness, but soon it's going to be swallowed up, and the Shadows raining down like a hurricane will devour El and me without a second thought.

Callie James, where in the multiverse are you?

For all I know, she could have gone back to California. But something tells me that's not the case. That she's lost and alone, struggling with the same questions and hardships I've been dealing with.

Light warms me, calls out into the distance, and from across the stars, through the furthest reaches of space and time, somebody answers. I push forward through the Veil, getting closer to my destination, and brightness overtakes my sight until the Veil ejects me and El onto solid ground somewhere entirely different than where we were before.

"Am I alive?" El lays on the ground, hands over his eyes.

"No, dork, you're dead as a doornail," I deadpan, then grasp his elbow and pull him to his feet. "You're fine. Open your eyes."

While El's busy inspecting everything faster than he can make sense of surroundings, I figure I might as well survey the landscape, too.

Fog. That's about all I can see. Fog like soupy, sticky swirls, the texture of it halfway between marine layer and cobwebs, encompassing the entirety of a plain that reeks of damp and ancient rot. A tomb-like smell, reminiscent of a funeral in the rain. Decayed toothpick trees peek through the quagmire, ghostly sentinels rising from the earth to warn whoever's been stupid enough to stumble upon this wasteland to turn back while they have a chance.

"What is this stuff?" El brushes the fog away from his arms. "It won't leave me alone."

"I don't know, but it's friendly." I brush the fog off of my arms, too.

"Is the girl you like somewhere out there?" El peers into the distance. "I don't think people live here."

"I have no clue where she is, if we made it to wherever she's at, or if—"

Boom… boom… boom…

The ground under my feet rattles with heavy footfalls coming from somewhere far away, getting closer and louder with every subsequent step.

"What's making that noise?" El asks, trying to find the source in the fog.

Boom… boom…

I don't have to look, because I know without seeing it exactly the kind of being large enough to take such quaking steps. Sure enough, he appears in all his bronze, cog-and-gear glory a moment later, the humanoid shape of his massive frame emerging on the murky horizon. A mech I've known since before my first memory formed, as much a part of my family as Mom and Dad.

We didn't part ways on the best of terms. Wonder if he'll remember how much devastation I caused that night in Verona Beach. Are mechs inherently more forgiving than brokenhearted Luminauts and deceived dads?

Guess I'm about to find out.

Boom… boom…

"That," I tell El, "is a World Diver."

CHAPTER 22
CALLIE

LIGHT CALLS TO ME as if in a dream, piercing the dark veil of sleep.

Across the expanse of the multiverse, I feel it, distantly at first, and then closer. This Light is not mine, or Diver's, or an echo of Mariasol's, or the inner Light of a typical human. This is another Luminaut—a fragile Light, and uncertain—but one desperate to connect. Warmth surrounds my heart; a longing, a pull.

Where are you? My mind mumbles through a haze of drowsy slumber. But I hear no reply. What I do hear is—

"Callie! Get over here!"

Why does Toran's insistence on barking orders instantly set my teeth on edge? Oh, that's right. Because it's Toran. Barking orders.

"I was having a nice, long sleep after I kept watch last night," I counter from my bed on the couch. "Scaring skuddima away with my Light so you could get your full eight hours is exhausting."

Was my dream of Light simply that—a dream? I know I'm overtired, and I wasn't joking when I said I was awake all night. We passed the last outpost on Toran's map two days ago, and skuddima nests have become a prevalent fixture this deep in the

Hem. The nasty pests like to toss themselves at Diver's head and scream in the middle of the night. Because skuddima suck in every sense of the word.

"You need to see this," Toran persists. "There are two people down there."

Stop trying to be funny, Toran. The sourpuss thing is your vibe, own it. I close my eyes and pull my blanket under my chin, body sinking comfortably into the couch cushions and throw pillows. "It's probably one of those gator-angler-fish again. Diver knows better than to fall for that. Now, let me sleep."

"It's not a predator," Heike corroborates her brother's tale. "It's two boys. Human boys. One of them looks young, maybe ten or eleven, and the other is Toran's age."

This is ridiculous. They're seeing ghosts, or the skuddima have figured out how to walk around in the husks of their victims. Either way, I don't want anything to do with it. But since they're both standing there, noses pressed to the window glass like befuddled Tremurheimian puppies, I guess I'll investigate.

"This better not be some awful attempt at a prank," I threaten, approaching their lookout, "because I'm tired, and cranky, and also, I'm—"

Holy freaking crap. It can't be who I think it is. I lean closer to the glass, and even from this distance, our eyes meet.

My whole world crumbles in a single instant, memories of betrayal, heartache, and every other trauma I faced that horrible night in Verona Beach—the night I Dove away—bubbling to the surface, a building tidal wave of sorrow and rage ready to smash into the unsuspecting shore.

"Son of a lying jerk-face." Light flares into my hands, and I march toward the hatch door, my skin humming with anger, fear, and the deep, primal agony of an animal whose heart was torn to pieces by somebody she thought she could trust. "Diver, stop."

Yes, Luminaut. The son is—

"I know who it is," I snap, pulling on my boots and jacket.

"You do?" I almost forgot Heike and Toran are trailing after me, and they have no idea why I'm flying through the door like a bat out of hell with furious Light blazing in my palms, ready to strike down an army if that's what it takes to protect myself, Diver, and my Light.

"Yeah." I saunter across Diver's shoulder to his palm, waiting to lower me to the ground. "I do."

"Aren't you going to explain yourself?" Toran hops onto Diver's palm, too, and catches Heike when she leaps.

"I've never been obligated to explain anything to you." Honestly, if Toran could not be Toran for, like, ten minutes, it would make this easier for everyone. "But just so you're not shocked when he turns into a literal nightmare, that's Nate Ormandi."

Heike's blue-gray eyes bulge. "The monster you kissed? The one that turns people to ash like the Witch of Arjendenstag?"

"Nailed it."

"Why are you practically sprinting to greet your enemy who's trailed you and your Light Core across the multiverse?" Toran, please. Just don't.

"Remember how I said I wasn't obligated to explain things right now?" The thing I just said two seconds ago when you demanded I explain myself? Toran might have reluctantly decided to come along to the Beacons, but his angry-badger attitude has not improved an iota.

"Since I'm the Seer in this scenario, I believe I deserve to know what kind of monster is about to put us in grave danger," Toran says, in a tone that can only be described as the epitome of Toran-esque.

"That particular monster over there, with the rando kid."

Speaking of being a Seer, he should learn to use his eyes for something other than controlling Mist, when he isn't narrowing them on me.

"You never said he was so handsome." Heike stares like a gape-jawed goldfish.

Yeah, Nate's hot. Which is too bad, because the sight of him makes my heart leap into my throat in spite of myself.

"Don't let the face fool you." I jump off my mech's palm onto sturdy ground, leaving a trail of fiery Light in my wake as I approach Nate and the younger boy with him. Turning, I call over my shoulder to Toran and his sister. "Stay back, and get an ice sword ready!"

"It's a pike!"

Sigh.

Heike and Toran take cover beside Diver's feet as I cross the space separating me and Nate. Heike was right, the boy at Nate's side is young — eleven, tops, and that's only if he's particularly short. White-blond hair the color of silvery snow falls in messy curls, framing his round, pale face. Dark brown eyes, large and almond-shaped, peer at me warily from under a busted headlamp strapped to his forehead.

But the kid is a blip in my periphery compared to Nate encompassing my entire field of vision. He's in human form, the illusion fitting his frame with surprising ease compared to the sharp edges that always peeked through in California. He's still wearing black clothes that fit his hotness — I mean, um, his athletic build — like a glove, still the same wavy, brown-black hair a little more messed up than normal, still that same pouty bottom lip that screams "kiss me, I'm unfairly gorgeous."

All of that pales in comparison to the horrific scars running down his face: two ghastly black lines originating on his forehead, slicing the corner of his eyebrow, before finally fading halfway down his cheek, opening the skin around spidery veins.

"What happened to your face, Nate?" My voice loses its distinctive Callie quality inside the intense Light surge. "Decided to make the outside match the inner hideousness?"

A nervous half-smile quirks his lips. Nervous I'll blow his head off, probably, and rightfully so. "Hey, Callie. 'Sup?"

That voice — all I can hear is him confessing his supposed feelings, his kiss driving a spike into the heart of the lie. He manipulated me, and I let him, like a heartsick fool who can't think for herself.

"Don't stand there and pretend like we were friends," I snap back. "Why are you here? How did you find me? And why is there an actual child with you?"

He doesn't answer, just watches me with a look in his eyes I can't read. All I know is I've never seen it before.

"I need to talk to you." When he speaks at last, his words shake. His acting got a lot better, because he almost convinced me he's genuinely afraid of something. Or, someone.

"No. Now get out of here, before I finish what I started last time and Light blast you into oblivion, just like you ashed my family."

"I didn't hurt your family." Nate's eyes say it's the truth, but I know better than to trust him. He's lied too easily to take his word, no matter how much I want to.

"You're lying." *But he didn't lie about your powers...*

"I'm not lying. They're safe." He looks at me deeply, his gaze worming through my doubt. "I never intended to hurt them. I promise, they're alright."

I shake my head, Light growing brighter, more fierce in my hands. "I don't believe you."

"I figured you'd say that," Nate murmurs.

He *figured*? I make two gigantic orbs, nuclear fireballs of Light, and launch both at his face—one for the lies of the past, and one for the lies he's telling now. He and the kid duck just in time, but he doesn't pull the disappearing act he did in California.

Strange.

"I don't think she likes you very much," the kid says. Nate's brow pinches in the center.

"Yeah, kind of an understatement." Nate makes his comment to the kid, who smirks.

"What's your name?" I ask the boy. He darts a glance at Nate, like he doesn't want to answer and it wasn't part of the deal he'd have to talk to me, but Nate nods a vague permission.

"I'm Elion," the kid replies at last.

"Elion... what?"

Elion blinks hard, then shakes his head. "Elion. I already told you that."

"El doesn't have a surname, they don't use those where he's from," Nate offers an explanation.

"I didn't ask you." I aim another Light orb at his head. This time, Nate takes a bold step forward, coming too close to my sphere for safety. "You're on thin ice," I remind him. "Back off."

"I'm not here to cause harm." Nate holds his hands high. "I just want to talk."

"And I already told you no." I face the kid, Elion. "Did he hurt you? Manipulate you? Are you okay? What did he do to you?"

Elion couldn't be less impressed with me. The disdain curling his upper lip mirrors the mistrust in his dark eyes. "Nate is my friend. He didn't manipulate me, or hurt me."

"Whatever he promised, it comes with a catch." I lower my Light, beckoning the kid to my side. "Come with me, I can keep you safe."

"You don't look very safe," Elion retorts, crossing his arms defensively. "You look like more of a monster than Nate is."

What does that mean? He knows Nate's a Shadowmancer, and he's still hanging around?

"Nate saved my life three times," Elion adds. "All you've done is try to kill us with your fire hands. Why would I go with you?"

Nate did *what?*

"El's from Ictari, another world in the multiverse," Nate explains. "It's where I've been hunting a Light Core."

All sensation grinds to a halt—heartbeat, thought, breath, feeling. The only thing registering in my brain is panic. "*You* hunted a Light Core?"

Please, let him not have found it. Because if he did, that means a Light Core I desperately needed is no more. My whole reason for Diving away from Verona Beach, and everything I've gone through in between, has been for nothing.

"Yes, I did." Nate searches me, his eyes so unlike they were before. Instead of sharp and coal black, they're soft brown with flecks of amber. If I had to name the emotion flooding them, it would be desperate. "Please, Callie. Can you—"

"Don't 'please, Callie' me. Do I need to remind you how I begged 'please, Nate?'" I spin a Light orb for each promise he broke. "'I'll protect you, Callie.'" One. "How about, 'you're the only one who gets it.'" Two. "Remember 'I'm completely infatuated with you?'" Three. "Or maybe you only recall the threats? Ashing my high school, threatening my family and your dad, it was a hilarious joke, wasn't it? Even if you didn't hurt them, you let me believe you would, all so you could steal my Light Core." Three more, equalling six total, all of them spinning around Nate's head, ready to blast him at my command. But he remains standing, undeterred.

"You really did all that?" Elion shoots Nate a raised-eyebrows kind of look.

"I thought I mentioned once or twice I'm a monster," Nate

replies.

"Dümfo," Elion mutters. I don't know the meaning of that word, but based on his tone, it's clearly meant to insult. Instead of obliterating the kid, Nate rolls his eyes, and nothing more.

What is *wrong* with him? Is this the world's biggest long con, and I'm just not connecting the dots?

"I know you don't trust me," Nate begins, his eyes resting on mine. I shouldn't have such a hard time breathing under his gaze. "All I ask is that you listen to what I have to say, then decide for yourself if I'm telling the truth. And to prove I'm serious about a truce, I have a peace offering." He turns to Elion. "You can give it to her now."

Elion makes a wary face. "Are you sure?"

"Yeah. Go ahead."

"Give me what?" I ask.

Elion whips his backpack over his shoulder and unbuckles the straps, reaching deep inside. From the depths, he pulls the one thing I never expected to see in Nate's presence: a Light Core.

"Here." Elion carelessly lobs the Light Core my way, like he's tossing a baseball. Once it's in my hands, the Core activates, glowing brilliantly golden as the Light in the Core connects to the Light in me.

"Hey," Elion turns to Nate with a grin, "it makes her hands look like spark fins, just like yours did!"

Like *Nate's* did? How would Nate's hands have glowed with Light? He's a Shadowmancer. Something isn't adding up, because somebody isn't telling me something important.

I assess Nate one more time, trying to come up with a reason I shouldn't hear him out. But I have too many questions about this Light Core, why he was hunting it, how he managed to find it, and what that possibly means. The ball is in my court, and he knows it. But I'm not cutting him an inch of slack.

"We talk in Diver, on my turf." I shove the Light Core in my hoodie pocket before I inadvertently open any gateways nearby. "You have exactly one hour. And *no* Darkness, not even a shadow. Got it?"

"I understand. Thank you, Callie." Nate's dimpled smile stretches wide across his face, the sincerity in it fluttering through my stomach. His voice is too gentle to be the Shadowmancer I know. I squash the butterflies.

"Don't thank me yet." I channel my mech's consciousness. "Diver?"

His anxious energy is palpable. *We are here, Luminaut. Is Luminaut safe?*

"I'm fine, buddy," I reassure him. "If the lying sleaze tries anything funny while my back is turned, squish him like a bug. Got it?"

Yes, Luminaut. More than a little glee colors Diver's reply.

Good.

"She *really* doesn't like you, does she?" I hear the boy, Elion, mutter behind my back as I walk toward Diver, Toran, and Heike.

"No," Nate replies, and I'd almost say he sounds regretful. "She doesn't like me at all."

At least he knows where we stand.

"What's going on?" Toran demands as soon as I'm in earshot. "Why is he following you?"

"We're going to talk, that's all," I reply, hopping onto Diver's waiting palm. "Come on, we need to get up before he does."

"Talk?!" Toran's eyes harden into solid chunks of ice as he and Heike scramble onto Diver's palm. "If you put my sister in danger, exposing her to a monster, so help me, Callie, I'll—"

"If he tries anything, I'll Light blast his face off, so chill," I interrupt. "I'm kind of dealing with a lot right now. If you wouldn't mind keeping your many opinions to yourself, I'd appreciate it."

"Did he always have the marks on his face?" Heike asks. "They look painful."

"No," I answer. "That's something he's going to explain."

Along with a thousand other things.

"Hey, you kept the couch!" Once we've all gathered in the Crow's Nest, Nate grins like a child at the sight of the threadbare piece of furniture that's functioned as my bunk, flopping down and stretching his arms across the back. His wingspan goes almost end to end, fingertips curling over the cushions. "I used to take naps here while Mom worked on installing the electrical wiring." His eager gaze comes to rest on his old record player and the milk crate of vinyl. He tilts his chin. "You stole my albums?"

"I didn't steal them. I borrowed them indefinitely," I retort.

"Half are Mom's, technically. You didn't scratch them, did you?" Nate swipes his way through the crate. "Some of these were mint."

"What's this?" Elion bounds up to the Prism, circling it with a wide-eyed look of awe, before he loses interest and finds something else to inspect. The Luminaut and Seer's chairs capture his attention. "These are nice chairs. I like them. Do you have anything to repair my headlamp? It broke when the monster woman attacked us."

Monster woman? What's he talking about?

"You switch gears fast." I can't hold back my smile. "I have a screwdriver somewhere, let me see—"

"What's this? I love it!" Elion has spotted Nemo, Nemo has spotted Elion, and if mechs are capable of love at first sight, Nemo is head over heels. He whizzes up to Elion and demands to be picked up, something Elion is all too happy to do.

"That's Nemo," I reply. "He's my mech. What do you mean when you said the monster woman attacked you?"

Before El answers, music blares from the record player — *Debaser*, by Pixies. Nate starts bobbing his head along with the rhythm. "This one's my favorite," he raises his voice over the ringing guitars and pounding bass.

"For somebody who's only got an hour to answer a crap-ton of questions," I say, turning off the music, "you're certainly making yourself at home."

"I want to know the answers to all these questions, too."

Oh, my gosh, Toran, just… no. Be quiet right now.

"Why can't I understand what the boy is saying?" Heike asks with a glance at Elion. He's so enraptured with Nemo, showing off his Gravenskov prison keys, he seems to have forgotten all about his broken headlamp.

"Because he doesn't have magic or powers like Toran and me," I say.

"And me!" Nate leaps from the couch, approaching Toran with a half-smirk, and the thing I really wanted to avoid happening is about to go down. "Who are you? Since you like to go around inserting yourself into conversations that don't involve you."

Toran puffs out his chest aggressively, his angular jaw hard as stone. Nate's eyebrows rocket up his forehead. This isn't going to end well — for Toran, anyway. "I'm Toran Rykjiersen, Guide of Gravenskov. My sister is Heike. If you cause her any harm while you're here, forest spare you, I'll — "

"He's a Seer," I cut Toran off. "He's helping me find Tremurheim's Light Core in exchange for getting him and his sister away from their murder-happy village."

"A Seer? Really?" Nate faces Toran. "What's your elemental Manipulation, sucking the fun out of a party?"

Darn, I'm disappointed I didn't come up with that one. I pretend to cough to cover a laugh.

"I'm serious, Callie, where did you *find* this rare specimen of grumpitude?" Nate tilts his head, inspecting Toran like a museum patron dissects the finer points of a statue. "Look at the scowl! It's so surly, downright belligerent. Hey, Toran, my man, you gotta tell me—does your brain scowl, too? Like, your thoughts just appear to you as various types of scowls that migrate down your face to communicate your impressive scowlery?" Another once over. "This is a rad outfit. Leather, buckles, wooly fur. You're the thing that would spawn if a Boy Scout and a Viking decided to have a baby. A really big, scowling baby."

Honestly, that's the most spot-on assessment of Toran I've ever heard. A laugh flies from my lips, and Nate catches my eye, smiling. Okay, so he's funny. Doesn't mean anything.

"Get away from my face," Toran barks, raising a fist at Nate like he's about to throw a punch. Nate backs off just in time.

"Don't worry, Boy Scout," Nate says, smirking the way I remember. "I'm not interested in a testosterone-rage pissing match."

"What you should be interested in is explaining your presence, and how you found that Light Core you offered," I cut in. "Tick-tock."

"So kind of you to remind me I'm wasting time while I was busy admiring your Seer's impressive ability to emote via scowls." Nate sinks onto the Luminaut's chair, and Toran grumpily crosses his arms off to the side. "Interrogate away."

"How did you find this Light Core?" I pull the "peace offering" Nate proposed out of my hoodie pocket. He squints in the face of its brilliance.

"First of all, can you put it away? When a Luminaut holds it…"

"Oh." I shove it in my backpack with the other Light Core, stifling the blinding glow. "There. Now, answer the question."

"I was tasked with finding the Light Core on Ictari by the Queen Beyond the Stars." Nate relates this world-shattering piece of intel with indifference, same as he might answer a question on *Jeopardy!*. "After I screwed up in California and failed to secure Earth's Light Core for her destruction, she sent me to hunt Ictari's before you had a chance. At least, that's how she presented it. I'm pretty sure she had some ulterior motives."

"The Queen Beyond the Stars." I repeat the name I've heard only once before. Once was enough to terrify me. "She was the Prime Shadowmancer."

"Bingo." Nate rests his arms behind his head.

"She's gone." I can't believe what Nate is saying might be true. "Your dad told me she was defeated."

Then again… given everything Dr. Ormandi neglected to tell me…

"Defeated doesn't mean dead," Nate corrects my assumptions. "She's been imprisoned in the Shadow Plain for millennia." He shrugs a little. "To be fair to Dad, he didn't know she's still alive. Mom's cancer was always a more immediate threat."

"And she's your boss," I surmise with an audible gulp. "The Queen is calling the shots?"

"Right again. She's the one who Turned me to Darkness," Nate says. His eyes lose their clear focus, blurring while he speaks. "She's the one who sent me after you and your Light Core in California. She gave me these." He traces the terrible scars running down his face. "She tried to ash me and El out of existence. And she killed every single person in a cavern-city of nearly thirty thousand. 'Purified them of Light,' she said."

My hand flies to my mouth. I can't comprehend such a massive loss of life, all at the hands of one single being: a Shadowmancer bent on destruction.

"She's coming for you next." Nate's ominous words sound more prophecy than statement.

"What's the Shadow Plain?" I switch gears, because the existence of a Shadowmancer with the capability to commit that level of mass homicide is too much to consider right now.

"It's where Shadowmancers exist when we aren't in human form beyond the Veil," Nate explains. "The Shadow Plain lies outside time and space; it's a whole separate reality. Nothing but Darkness, and Queen's shadowy prison. The Veil is the border of the Shadows, it edges the human world. It's how Shadowmancers spy on targets before we make a move."

"And that's how you spied on me in California. From the Veil." I lean my elbows on the back of the Seer's chair, a frown twisting my lips. "You didn't, like, spy on me all the time, did you? Not while I was showering or anything—"

"No way." Nate's face contorts into something equal parts offended and disgusted. "I didn't come sit in your room to watch you sleep, like a stalker creep. I have boundaries, okay?"

"So invading my bedroom and car's passenger seat were great, healthy boundaries," I deadpan. "You conveniently chose to 'haunt' me when I was most vulnerable."

Nate's jaw tightens. "I'm sorry."

"Excuse me?" Did he really just say what I think he said?

"I'm sorry." Nate dares to raise his gaze. "I did a lot of things that were—"

"Nate!" Elion's voice distracts us, and we both turn. He's playing with Nemo and Heike, shoving the contents of a Tremurheim ration box in his face, and points at Toran's sister with a broad grin. "Her name is Heike. She gave me food. She's nice."

"Cool, El." Nate gives the kid a double thumbs up, and Heike giggles.

"Did he say something about me?" she asks. "I still can't understand..."

"He thinks you're very nice," I translate. When Heike smiles, El's cheeks flare pink.

"Precious middle schoolers, right?" Nate feigns a swooning sigh. It's a weird sound to hear from him, since he's never breathed in my presence—even weirder than his apology. "Anyway, where were we?"

"The Shadow Plain, the Veil, the Queen Beyond the Stars, my imminent doom and destruction," I tick off the list on my fingers. "You being a gigantic slime-ball who took advantage of me in weak moments."

"Right." Nate doesn't confirm or deny the slime-ball accusation. Instead, he shifts in his seat and clears his throat. "So, what I didn't realize—one of the many things kept from me—was that Queen has been keeping tabs on your Light Core hunt. She told me it was impossible for her to interact with humans, but she lied, or omitted crucial details. Have you ever seen her? Sensed her Darkness?"

The Darkness I felt in the outpost, the way it crept like poison through my veins but stayed well out of sight, teasing me in a way Nate never did... I thought he was playing games with a new set of tactics. But what if it was never him to begin with?

"I—it's hard to know what could have been her, and what was you," I reply. "I used to think every time I was pulled into the shadowy realm, it was you calling the shots, but—"

"You were in the Shadow Plain?" Nate looks afraid. "How? You're not a Shadowmancer. I took El beyond the Veil twice to escape Queen on Ictari, and he barely survived."

"I was sure I was going to die," El adds, adjusting a few of the casings on his headlamp with my screwdriver he managed to find. Nemo looks on with interest, like the headlamp might be a new mech friend.

"So you're saying when I was pulled into the Shadow Plain in Verona Beach, at the cemetery, and the pier, that wasn't you?" I recall each nightmarish memory, what I saw, felt, and heard. "I sensed Darkness here, in Tremurheim, not too long ago... I thought it must have been you."

"Negative." Nate shakes his head. "At that point in the timeline, I was figuring out how my useless lungs were going to perform CPR on El if and when he passed out from lack of oxygen. I had no clue where in the multiverse you were."

Two Shadowmancers. I joked around with Dr. Ormandi about twins, but never imagined I'd be right. Was this what Nate meant when he said there were evils bigger than I could imagine lurking in the dark? Was he really and truly warning me about the Queen? There were times when the Darkness stalking me felt different: colder, venomous, more deadly and sinister. The Shadowmancer in the dark always called me Calliope, not Callie.

Time for one final test. "What's my name?"

"Um... Callie." Nate makes a face, confused by my seemingly random line of questioning.

"No, my whole name," I press.

"Callie James." Nate shrugs. "I don't know your middle name. Why are you asking me this?"

"Because the Shadowmancer in the dark realm knew my full name—Calliope." Judging by the genuine surprise on Nate's face, he didn't know that information prior. "They had long, white hair that looked like a spider web, and sounded female, whereas you always sounded like—well, like you. I thought you were changing your appearance and voice somehow, but..."

"I can go between human form and the Shadowmancer, but they look relatively the same." Nate's answer confirms my fear. "Queen's got white-blonde hair like that. It moves like she's underwater, even when she's not." He pauses, grinning. "Cool name, by the way."

"It's true, about the hair," El corroborates Nate's description of the Prime Shadowmancer. "She's scary."

"How is she — the Queen — doing this? Spying on me? Pulling me into the Shadow Plain?" Somehow, questions penetrate the wild storm of thought.

"It has to do with Light Cores." Nate's eyebrows knit together. "Every time one is found, she gets stronger. You found the first one in California, and suddenly, she can pull humans like you beyond the Veil, her Darkness manifesting like fog. When I found the second one on Ictari, she could leave the Veil and appear outside her prison in the human world, and kill thousands of people. It's like they're keys holding her power in check, but whenever one gets found, she gets closer and closer to breaking free completely."

"What will happen when I find the Light Core on Tremurheim?" Because if finding Light Core number two meant she could kill a whole city full of people...

"I don't know." Nate's downturned expression is as futile as I feel. "All I know is it can't be good."

I take a moment to search him for any crack in the façade, any sign of a lie. He's neutral, but that doesn't mean he isn't feeding me a thousand different well-rehearsed lines, all of them engineered to prick my sympathy and regain my trust.

On second thought, that's *exactly* what's going on here. Two dangerous Shadowmancers working in tandem, giving me the answers I want most so I'll be properly buttered up when they strike their fatal blow.

"Let me guess," I scoff at my stupidity, "she sent you to tell me all this, right? To relay her message and force me to turn back, just like you tried to stop me before?" I shake my head, sneering at myself. "Of course, this all makes sense now. I can't believe I almost fell for it again." I stand, my glare as frosty as Toran's favorite ice swords. "I should have known better than to listen to your lies again. Your hour is up."

"Callie, I'm not lying," Nate stands, too, and when he takes a step toward me, Light flares into my hands. I hold two orbs at neck height.

"Back. Off. Unless you want those gashes to extend down your throat."

"You don't believe me." When he doesn't stand down, my Light blazes even more fiercely. Toran uses the lingering Mist in the Crow's Nest to form icy daggers in his hands, instinctively moving to guard Heike, and Elion leaps to his feet.

"Nate, we need to get out of here." The boy casts a fearful look at my Light, at Toran's Seer's Eye and his ice. "They're going to hurt us."

"Would it make a difference if I told you I had no idea what Queen was planning any more than you?" Nate ignores everyone in the Crow's Nest except me. "Everything she told me was meant to keep me hateful—and compliant. She told me Luminauts and Seers were the villains. That the only way to avenge Mom was to destroy the Light that let her die. She turned me against Dad, against you, she twisted my memory of what actually happened the day I was Turned—your hair is in your face, did you know?"

He stops short of a confession, reaching for me with trembling fingers. Softly, he brushes my hair away from my cheek, and my heart lurches toward him.

"What happened the day you were Turned?" I want the truth so desperately, just like I ache for him to touch me again, his hands telling me everything his words can't.

"It doesn't matter now. All that matters is she fueled my doubt until anger was all I knew." Nate's hands fall to his side, and he takes a step back. "She convinced me that Darkness was the only way to get what I wanted. You know what it's like to have somebody you trust force your hand. I know you do."

Oh, do I ever. There's no truth with Nate. I learned it all too well. Just deception, and hollow words. He nearly fooled me twice. But never again. I cross my arms, backing away from him.

"And now you're having second thoughts, is that it?" I sneer. "How convenient you changed your mind about Darkness and the Queen Beyond The Stars the second you showed up in Tremurheim."

"What part of 'she tried to kill me' isn't computing for you?" Desperation flashes in Nate's eyes. "I disobeyed direct orders so many times I'm lucky I'm not an ashtray right now. You think I didn't take a massive risk coming to you?"

"I think you'll say whatever she told you to say, just like last time." I turn to Toran and nod. "Keep your knives on him, and I'll tie him up."

"Excuse me?" Nate glances between my Light and Toran's approaching ice daggers. Elion leaps to his feet, and so does Heike.

"Nate! Let's go! Now!" Elion cries.

"Toran, stop!" Heike demands.

"Until you can prove, without a doubt, you aren't lying, you're my prisoner," I say. "I can't have you running back beyond the Veil to report everything to your boss, can I?"

The rush of feeling in Nate's eyes is like nothing I've ever seen bleeding from their depths: sadness, betrayal, and heartache coalesce, and I get the uncomfortable feeling of being shown a mirror of my own face at the VBHS gym when he first revealed he was a Shadowmancer. The night he broke my heart, and my trust.

"The heavy weaponry isn't necessary, Boy Scout." Nate holds up his hand, halting Toran short of brandishing the ice daggers at his neck. Instead, he sits in the Luminaut's chair, twisting and crisscrossing the leather straps in intricate patterns until he snaps the buckles, tightening them against his chest. El and Heike look confused, and Toran, too. All of them turn to me for an explanation.

"What are you doing?"

"I'm your prisoner, aren't I? Prisoners get tied up," Nate answers. He clasps the last strap into place, and raises his eyes onto mine. "If this is what it takes for you to believe I'm not lying, so be it. In the meantime, it would be in your best interest to start thinking about how you're going to defeat Queen when you find Tremurheim's Light Core."

Wow, he's really trying to piss me off, isn't he?

"Don't tell me what to do, especially after you tied yourself up in *my* chair." I channel Diver in the midst of every other tense emotion racing through the room. "You there, buddy?"

Yes, Luminaut.

"Toran knows the route to the Beacons. If he gives you a command to alter our course, follow it. I don't want to take any more breaks. Keep going until I tell you to stop."

We understand, Luminaut.

Diver walks, then jogs, then runs, his movements jarring the Crow's Nest with every heavy footfall. I stare down Nate, daring him to bat his pretty dark eyes. The Light in my fists coils like live wires at my side.

"If you've been scheming some ambush with the Prime Shadowmancer to steal my Light," I speak a promise truer than the sunrise, "I will become the worst enemy you can possibly imagine."

"There's no doubt in my mind she's planning an assault." Nate grows serious as he regards me. "But I won't be the one who caused it. Be smart, Callie. Don't let your anger get the best of you."

"Is that a threat?" I hold a Light orb close to his face. He doesn't betray an ounce of fear.

"No, it's not a threat," Nate answers. "It's fair warning. Start formulating a plan."

CHAPTER 23
NATE

I PROBABLY SHOULDN'T HAVE strapped myself into this chair quite so tight, because the buckles and straps digging into my skin have really started to hurt. Good thing I can't cut off my own circulation. And I didn't get Light bombed, either, despite multiple threats to do so.

Although if Callie thinks Queen's attack when she finds Light Core number three was a carefully coordinated counterstrategy, a joint effort between Queen and myself, Light bombed is one of the least unpleasant things I'll be. I know all too well what Queen's Darkness can do, the pain it can cause. Excruciating agony, a kind that sears permanently into your mind and never leaves. I'm screwed if I stay here, cozying up to Queen's enemy, and screwed if I try to figure out some way for El and me to escape—the final nail in Callie's "Nate's a sleaze" coffin.

I hate Queen for putting me in this position with Callie. If only I could—

Stop it, Nate. Get over yourself. If anyone's at fault for broken trust, it's me. It's time I owned my screw ups, and quit blaming everything and everyone else. I saved El from getting ashed by Queen on Ictari, and no matter what happens to me—revenge at Callie's hand, or indifferent murder at Queen's—that's one thing

I can say I did right, even if I did every other thing horrifically wrong.

Aaaaiiiieeee!

"Gah!" Callie rushes toward the window, where a ghostlike phantom, something she calls skuddima, attaches itself to the glass in the dark, screeching and sucking like a vampiric lamprey trying to eat us from the inside out.

They'd be right at home in the Shadow Plain, skuddima.

"What was that?" Heike bolts awake, but El and Toran, Flotilla Of Frowns, slumber peacefully on.

Callie flares her Light, scaring the monster away before smiling reassuringly. "False alarm. I took care of it."

Heike settles onto her bedroll, and a moment later, she's asleep. At least, she looks asleep. Her breathing gets slow and steady, like El's does when he's on his twelfth nap. Callie turns back to the windows, keeping a small amount of Light in her hand while she keeps watch. It illuminates her face, makes her freckles glow like flecks of gold, and the highlights in her hair are beams of sunshine in the drawing dark.

I shouldn't stare at her face. But man, I'm doing Mrs. Kim proud with my descriptive language today. Although she'd knock off points for overuse of similes and metaphors.

"Are those things a common occurrence?" I try to make conversation.

"The skuddima?" Callie keeps her eyes on the Misty night outside Diver's head, the nothingness giving way to the occasional toothpick tree. "Yeah, they're common. Especially out here on the Hem."

"Are they ghosts, or what?" She isn't *not* answering questions. Small talk is positive. First step, small talk, next step, letting me out of this chair, and trusting me to help make a plan to evade Queen.

I'm probably aiming too high. Shoot for the moon and you'll land among the stars, as they say.

Callie turns, smirking in a way that means I'm about to get hit with a zinger. "You know more about ghosts than me. Or, at least, pretending to be one." *Zing.* Ouch. Called it. So much for landing among the stars. "Stop talking to me. Everyone's trying to sleep."

"But not you," I point out. Callie glares over her shoulder, her gold-spun hair fading to brown when she turns away from the Light.

"What part of 'stop talking to me' was unclear?" She points her Light at my face, menacing an orb like a torch inches from my neck. Light reaches her eyes, filling their depths, and this moment feels like staring an untamed wildfire in the face: beautiful, terrifying, and deadly.

Where's Mrs. Kim and her notoriously difficult grade book when I need it?

"No part was unclear," I reply, and fall silent. I avert my eyes too, for good measure.

Callie backs off, turns her attention to the landscape below, and looks out for skuddima. Her shoulders tense under her oversized sweatshirt, like her attention is split between two separate threats — me being one of those threats.

I've got to convince her somehow I'm nothing like those skuddima — I mean, even with the scars I'm better looking, but she's not into that angle anymore. But if I don't find some way to earn her trust, she won't be prepared when an even bigger, nastier threat attacks.

What should I say? She doesn't want me to talk, but I can't make any headway if I don't talk, so maybe I ought to —

"Is Mrs. Kim still at VBHS?" my tongue blurts before I can press a cautionary pause. *Mrs. Kim?* What's *wrong* with you, Nate? Talk about a bad opening line.

"Oh, my gosh, you're talking? Seriously?" Callie whips around, Light flaring fiercely.

"Sorry!" I lift my hands as high as they'll go with the straps holding me in place. "I talk a lot when I'm anxious. Bad habit."

"Why are you anxious?" Callie would sooner believe the grass is purple than trust I'm actually anxious. "Worried your scheme with your boss is going to fail?"

"She's not my boss anymore," I counter. "Remember how she tried to kill El, gave me these tiger stripes, murdered approximately thirty thousand people because of their inner Light? I went rogue; it's just me and El now. But I'm imprisoned in this chair, charging through the Mist toward a Light Core with no strategy to defeat her, and if you think that doesn't make me anxious, well..."

I pause for emphasis, trying to see if Callie believes me. She doesn't—her eyes are hard, guarded, and cold. Further confirmation that overcoming my mistakes with her and earning her trust will be harder than I thought. Regret isn't a new emotion for me, especially not lately, but it pricks sharper in the face of Callie's chill. She was always so warm before.

"Despite what you think I'm plotting behind your back— which I'm not—I like talking to you. I always did." My admission is quiet, uncharacteristically shy. Uncharacteristic for what I led her to believe about me, anyway. "But if you want me to shut up, I will."

"I want you to shut up." Callie turns her back on me, and a long silence passes between us. Then she lowers her Light, letting it fade until it's nothing but a faint glow in her palm. She speaks around a drawn out exhale. "Mrs. Kim? Senior English?" She glances over her shoulder, catching my eye. "She's still there."

"Is getting an 'A' with her still next to impossible?" I try another question, because hey, Callie spoke to me! Of her own volition!

Her lips turn; half a grin. "Yeah, she's tough," Callie says. "She's head of the English department."

"Did you have her?" I guess Callie thinks VBHS teachers are a safe enough topic of conversation, one I can't possibly use against her, because she faces me fully, leaning against the glass before crossing her ankles over each other. A faint flip-flop suntan on the tops of her feet remains visible.

Geez, Nate. Staring at her *feet*? Pump the brakes. Eyes on face.

"No, I didn't." Callie shakes her head. "I was taking junior English. I had Evans."

"Evans, King of Themes?"

"I know, right?" she agrees with a laugh. "He's theme-obsessed. Like, a whole year on 'following your dreams,' or something."

Score, I actually made her laugh! "We did 'past meets present.' Crossover between contemporary lit and classics."

When she tilts her chin, a few stray hairs fall across her cheek. "You had him, too?"

"Small world, right?" I flash a smile, and she doesn't seem offended. In fact, she almost smiles back before her mouth turns down at the corners.

"I heard he's retiring after this year," Callie says. "Same with Mrs. Kim."

"Oh." Well, this got awkward, didn't it? Thanks for the reminder the world moved on—a lot—after I Turned.

"I thought you didn't have many memories of high school." Callie tucks the strands grazing her cheek behind her ear. She misses a few, and the thought that I wish it were my fingers doing the tucking spirals around my brain before I can check myself. "'Remembering through a fog.' That's what you said."

"I remember some parts really well, despite the brain fog."

The parts I managed to retain before Darkness blunted as much of my humanity as it could. "I forgot every single person on every baseball team I ever played for. Couldn't tell you anything about what kind of car I drove." I can't swallow, but I wish I could, because some memories are too hard to bear with no emotional release. "I remember Mom and Dad. And I remember her being sick."

The Second Worst Time — it remains my one vivid human memory, the one Darkness let me wallow in until rage and grief became everything I knew. How many happy memories did it steal while my back was turned? Not just of school, but of Mom, too?

"You drove a Subaru Outback. Early 90s, I think." When I give Callie a quizzical look, she shrugs. "I stole it for a couple hours. Two, as a matter of fact."

"Oh, yeah. Two hours. Guess you'd have needed it." Would it help to say that was a completely arbitrary number, and I lurked around the pier like a dweeb until I spotted Diver on the beach, because I'm crap with timekeeping since I was Turned? Probably not. "So, um, Mr. Evans, huh?" I switch into neutral gear rapidly (car pun!). "I forgot you're a year younger than me."

Callie snorts wryly. "A year younger? Dude, you've been dead since—"

"Undead, technically," I interrupt. "It's a gray area subject to loose interpretation. And you're right. I was gone for a long time." It feels less uncomfortable than I thought it might, being vulnerable with her. "Time doesn't exist in the Shadows. It was a blur for me, like no time passed at all. I stayed seventeen and pissed off, but everyone else got old, and forgot me." Speaking of forgetting... something she said earlier comes to the front of my mind, a throwaway line that's stood out as heavy, significant. "Did you say Queen pulled you into the Shadow Plain the first time at the cemetery?"

"Yes..." Her eyes turn wary, and the Light grows stronger, crackling with menace. I'm treading on dangerous ground, but I want to know. A part of me feels like it *has* to know.

"Why were you at the cemetery?"

"None of your business." She's withdrawing, and I'm losing any tentative footing I may have gained. Backpedal, backpedal.

"It just—I wanted to know if I—do you know—" How to phrase this without being morbid? On second thought, it's too late for that. "Do I have a marker, or anything? A headstone?"

Callie doesn't seem to expect my question, because she startles as if I'd been another skuddima, screaming at her from outside the glass. "Uh, yeah. You do. Why?"

Hello, guilt and pain, my old friends. My shoulders droop, the straps cutting into even more uncomfortable spots. "Queen always said Dad wouldn't remember me after I Turned. That he'd forget, just like he tried to forget Mom. There would be no headstone, no pictures. Nothing. Made it easier to stay away, even though I could have gone back in human form, or watched him from the Veil. She must have known if I saw him missing me, I'd have second thoughts." I suck in a breath to blow a raspberry. "I don't know why I believed her. Why did I believe anything, right?"

Callie remains silent, her eyes focused on the Light in her hands, the way it shimmers like a thousand tiny prisms. A feeling stirs deep inside, a call to reach out to her Light, to let something rise and spill to the surface. To join her Light in a dance.

"I don't know how Dr. Ormandi acted after Mariasol died," Callie's voice goes soft, "but he didn't forget you. He has pictures of you everywhere. He talked about you all the time. He really loves you."

"I know. I saw it in his eyes that night." The night everything went so horribly wrong. The night I wish I could take back — just not for the reasons I wished before. "I saw it in your eyes, too."

It's a line that could get me zapped back to square one or worse, but out it comes anyway, crossing my lips, lingering in midair somewhere between us. Her gaze lifts, meeting mine. There's something unspoken going on, something I don't know how to explain. All I know is if these straps weren't holding me in place, it would take so much effort to not to go to her, to stand and drink in her Light, letting it melt into mine. Together, we'd be so bright...

"What happened when you found the Light Core on Ictari? Why didn't you destroy it?" Light glows through the strands of hair surrounding her face, bouncing off her earrings — coral-colored studs shaped like mermaid tails.

Was she wearing them that night on the beach? Why didn't I notice?

"The second I touched it, I remembered things." Things Callie wouldn't believe.

"Like... what?" She waits for me to explain.

"I remembered everything that happened the day I was Turned. Not what Darkness and Queen spoon-fed me, but the actual truth." Time to test this 'not believing a word I say' theory. "I, uh — I found your Light Core. The one on Earth. In Verona Beach."

"You what?" Callie's face drains of color, and she starts to shake. I wish I could get out of this chair to assure her it's okay, that I didn't have any claim on it and never did, but I've literally put myself in a bind.

"I didn't take it," I promise. "It's yours. It's always been yours. You were meant to find it, not me. Besides, Queen got to me first, and — "

"How could you have found Earth's Light Core as a human?"

Callie rakes her hands through her hair, turmoil manifesting plainly on her face. "You found two. That's more than I've found."

"Well, it's not a race or anything." Nonchalant shrug. "There's no Light Core Olympics, and even if there was, nothing's wrong with a silver medal."

"El said your hands glowed like mine," Callie ignores my joke. I thought it deserved at least a pity-laugh, but okay. "How is that possible?"

"I'm still working through the answer."

Her eyes search me in her confusion, her fear. She's looked at me like this before, but open, vulnerable, trusting in a way she isn't now. "Why did you come back to me? I thought I knew what you were, what I was, and even though Light might have been used in crappy ways in the past, and you weren't completely wrong about the fact it can cause harm, I knew where I stood with it. I was going to figure out the hard answers. But now… you just reminded me I don't know anything at all, and answers are further away than they've ever been."

Callie closes her eyes and turns away, but not before I catch sight of how torn up she is inside, her screwed-up face betraying everything she doesn't want me to see — the uncertainty about her powers, and the overwhelming decision of what choice to make next, because all her choices in the past might have been wrong.

It's everything I feel, too.

"Callie." When I say her name, a soft ache blooms in my chest, one more pleasant than painful. "I don't know what's happening any more than you. I don't know what to think about Light, or Luminauts, or the things I remembered when I found Ictari's Light Core. I don't know if Light is something good, bad, or indifferent. All I know is Queen is going to continue murdering people to destroy their inner Light until the whole multiverse is one giant Shadow Plain, and I refuse to be a part of it—not if I can help stop it."

And here it is: the heart of the matter. The culmination of all the ways I was wrong about her, crossing my lips like an oath.

"I told you once that you were going to destroy everything with your Light, but the only person I was fooling was myself." Please, Callie, believe my words are true. "You care too much about people to hurt anyone, even if you're more than justified in doing so. You'd risk sparing a monster like me instead of killing me, because you'd never use your Light like that. The reason I came back and gave you that Light Core is because I don't deserve to have that power, but you do. If anybody I know could use Light to help people and not cause harm, it's you."

"Power without love…" she murmurs, and opens her eyes at last. The look in them is a lyric to a song I've never heard, but know by heart, and I remember the second part of the verse. *Power without love…*

"Is no power at all."

Callie stands still, and quiet. I can't hear anything except the breathing of her companions in the background, and the strange noises on the Hem that aren't quite wind, not quite the rocking of waves. If my heart still beat, it would drown out any other noise with its pounding.

"How did you know what I was going to say?" Suspicion gives way to curiosity, and something in her shifts as she regards me anew, like a picture that was obscured is coming into focus, developing before her eyes.

"I remembered it all of a sudden." I feel it now, stronger than ever as she stands over me, the Light in her reaching out for the Light in me.

"Something happened to you in Ictari." She approaches me, coming so close her thighs graze my knees. Her touch is bottled lightning, electrifying me back to life. "Where's smooth, flirty Nate with all the bad puns?"

"I promise I'm still punny." My response is too rough, too raw for that kind of question.

"Everything you told me could be nothing but more lies and tricks." When she peers down, her golden-brown eyes resting on my face, the softness inside them catches thick in my throat—sparking a feeling that's never been there before, not even when I was human. "I'll give you this, you've gotten a lot more convincing."

Aaaaaiiiieeee!

Callie leaps, and when I startle, these stupid straps and buckles tear into me yet again, blocking forward momentum until I give myself whiplash. A skuddima shrieks, waking just about everyone, and Callie dashes off to scare it away before calming El and Toran's sister, while he gripes about this trip needing to be over as soon as possible.

There's no way Callie will hear me over the noise this particularly aggressive skuddima is making, or the shouts of her even more aggressive Seer, but that's for the best. I can admit it to myself, and know it's true regardless of what she might think.

"I didn't lie." Not even close.

But unless she believes it, too, my truth doesn't matter. We're barreling toward a trick play at the bottom of the ninth, and Queen's going to play hardball.

And if I know one thing about Queen, she'll play dirty—make no mistake.

CHAPTER 24
TORAN

THE BEACONS ARE REAL. Lands Beyond, they're actually real.

I stare at them through the Crow's Nest window, the four cylindrical buildings rising into the Mist, broken, crumbling relics of Tremurheim's past lost to time and memory. They have the odd appearance of upside down funnel shapes made of rough-hewn stone, with shattered glass domes similar to the Diver's head atop each one. All the while, Callie hops around, shouting all the "I-told-you-so's" she knows how to say. It's one of her most irritating and frequent habits, pointing out when I'm wrong.

But if the Beacons are real, and a Light Core is hidden inside of one, that means I am about to be away from Callie and her "snark" for good, which is the best news I've had in a long time.

"Aren't they massive, Toran?" Heike stares at the Beacons in awe while I use my power to hold back the Mist threatening to swallow them. "They're as tall as two of Diver!"

"Hmm. Yes." I assess Heike's statement, looking over the buildings in question with a discerning eye. They're certainly tall, especially from a short distance away. What I'm more concerned about is what lies just beyond: the churning storm of Mist, with hills and valleys of gray rising so high they practically touch the sky.

The Tageveld.

"Isn't the Vredis said to live in the Tageveld?" Heike scans the horizon fearfully, as if trying to spot the nightmare of so many childhoods.

"The Vredis isn't real." Why do people keep insisting not-real things are real?

"A lot of things you didn't think were real have turned out to be real," Heike reminds me.

"I'll grant you that, but the Vredis is different." Honestly, there are swaths of legends about the Beacons, but the Vredis is a children's story.

Heike glances up at my burning blue eyes, then turns her gaze beyond the safety of our lookout. "It's so frightening, like the Mist wants to swallow us whole," she says, and I can't disagree. "Do you see any gateways to other worlds out there?"

"Yes." I don't know how I know gateways are called gateways, but instinctively, like something ingrained in my reflexes before I was born, I See windows in the Mist and sky leading to every type of city or landscape I couldn't imagine. Mist shimmers around them, tinkling with a hundred tiny bells only I can hear, calling out to my magic as if to greet an old friend — some songs bright, some low, all with different meanings and stories, leading to infinite possibility. I can't turn away and ignore them, or refuse their call. There are simply too many.

"Do you see one to Ensolorada? The place Callie says we're going?" Heike looks out at the Tageveld with more hope than I'd allot a dangerous plain of storms and Mist. If I know my sister, she's painting a picture of our destination in her mind's eye.

"I don't know what Ensolorada is supposed to look like," I reply.

"Orange-yellow sky, brown hills of dunes as far as you can see, and then rising from the sand, oasis cities made of crystal and glass, surrounded by flowers and palms and walls of cascading water," Nate, the monster, interjects. He grins from the chair he's bound himself to, and the hideous scars butchering half his face draw one side of his smile off-kilter and crooked. "My mom was Ensoloradan. It's a gigantic desert. Futuristic tech. Largely nocturnal population." His grin morphs into an expression caught between a sneer and a smile. "Gonna be a bit of a culture shock for you, Boy Scout."

"Don't call me that," I snap.

"Are you ready to get Tremurheim's Light Core?" Callie bounds up and stands between us, rubbing her hands excitedly. She's wearing the stupid hat with the fuzzy nargush egg, her colorful pack slung across her shoulders. "I have a good feeling about Beacon Two. I think we should start there."

"I'm going to take this moment to remind you that after we find the Light Core and Dive through the gateway, my part of our bargain is done." I hope she can see how serious I am, because Callie is not the least bit serious herself. "I have no interest in being a Luminaut's Seer. Once we've arrived in Ensolorada, Heike and I will go our separate way."

"Trust me, Toran, we'd kill each other as a working Luminaut and Seer pair." In a rare moment of reason, Callie agrees with me. "I'll happily release you from any and all obligations, so long as we get through our gateway without a hitch." Her smile betrays a slyness I see rarely, but when I do, I end up on the wrong side of a scheme. "But you've got to See that gateway for us so we can Dive in the first place. Don't forget, you haven't done your part yet. Mmkay, Seer?"

Meaning, she will use my powers however she sees fit for as long as she can, because she can, and I gave up my one and only chance to back out of her plan. I pull on my coat, and the way Callie grins like she's laughing, I know I'm scowling again.

"There's another matter I wish to discuss," I say.

"*'There's another matter I wish to discuss,'*" Nate mimics the exact lilt of my words, perfectly replicates my tone. The boy, Elion, laughs hysterically, Nemo whir-chuckles in Elion's arms, and even Callie snorts back a chortle. "Seriously, Callie," Nate adds, "where did you *find* this guy?"

Joke at my expense all you'd like, Nate, because the matter at hand that requires clarification is you. Specifically, whether or not we're going to throw him into the Tageveld, abandon him on the Hem, or lock him up in a Beacon until he rots.

"Callie!" I'm being rough, but I don't care. Her feelings are the least of my concern. Sure enough, she rolls her eyes and follows me behind the Prism near the door, waiting expectantly.

"What's the problem now, Toran?" she asks with a sigh.

"What are you planning to do with the disfigured prisoner after we find the Light Core?" I don't care if it's blunt. Better to be honest and leave no doubt.

"I heard that!" Nate calls from his chair.

"I, um…" Callie trails off, and just as I suspected, she has no apparent plan. "I hadn't gotten that far yet."

"Is he coming with us to Ensolorada? Are you abandoning him here? How long do you intend to keep him imprisoned?" She squirms at my words, but one of us has to figure out what to do with an actual monster in our midst. "You've been soft on him. I don't know why, but you have."

"Because, she's still in lo—"

"Heike!" Callie's face burns red, and my sister claps her hand over her mouth, a fierce blush blooming across her cheeks, too.

"Sorry! I forgot he can understand me."

"Understand what?" Nate interjects.

"You should have killed him when he gave you the Light Core, and been done with it," I say.

"I heard that, too," Nate calls over his shoulder, and Elion and Nemo growl.

"See, Nate?" The boy speaks up. "I told you the big, angry one was no good."

Big, angry one? No good? I ought to wring his neck, that mewling little dramora spawn. I'm not the one who's the monster here. His "friend" Nate is.

Callie looks shocked, then deeply disappointed in my suggestion. "I'm not going to kill anyone," she replies, shaking her head. "It's wrong no matter how you spin it."

"Even if the person deserves to die for what they did?" I can't believe she'd be so stupid.

"Yes, even if they deserve to die," Callie persists. Her eyes go flinty and cold when she regards me, despite their perpetual warmth. "It's called *mercy*, Toran. That's the whole point."

"Can both of you stop speaking about me in third person?" Nate asks. "I'm right here; I can hear everything you're saying."

As if I care that an enemy knows I think he should have been long dead by now.

"We're wasting time." Callie shifts her knapsack into a comfortable position and zips up her coat. "Nate, stay where you are, we'll be back in a bit."

"Watch out for murderous Shadowmancers!" He's far too blithe for the topic at hand, and it sets my teeth on edge.

"Shadowmancers like you?" I snarl. Nate turns and catches my eye, his own flashing dark.

"I haven't murdered anyone, thanks," he retorts. "I'm also not the one who was suggesting it without a second thought."

"You did murder an ore wyrm," Elion says, tossing a miniature paper creature he's folded for Nemo to fetch. The one positive outcome of their presence is Nemo hasn't pestered or pinched me since Elion arrived.

"I don't think killing a man-eating, predatory wyrm in self-defense counts as murder, El."

Wasting valuable time, both of them. Useless, idiotic banter for no reason at all.

"Elion, you're coming, too," Callie announces, and every eye in the Crow's nest looks to her all at once.

"No," El objects.

"What? Why?" Nate's face tightens, betraying panic.

"Why him?" Heike asks.

"Yes, why does the child need to come?" I concur with Heike's confusion.

"I'm not a child!" El bares his teeth at me.

"Shut up," I growl.

"Watch it, Boy Scout," Nate threatens, a chill slithering through the air as his eyes turn even blacker.

"I thought you weren't interested in testosterone rage pissing matches?" Callie raises her eyebrows at Nate. "Just in case you get any funny ideas about sneaking away while we're down there, Elion's collateral."

"I'm not going to—" Nate catches himself, and his mouth disappears into a frustrated frown. "Fine, take El."

"I'm not going with her." The boy leers at Callie, hackles raised. "She'll burn me with her fire hands. She's not safe."

"Callie's okay," Nate replies. "I promise, she's not going to hurt you."

"But she hates you," Elion objects again. Nate nods in agreement, his expression almost a wince, and I can't be sure, but Callie might wince, too.

Don't like people pointing out your obvious dislikes to your face, Callie? Why should she care if Nate knows she considers him a threat? Better to know where you stand with those trying to defeat you and take away your agency, that's what I say.

"She hates me because I'm a monster," Nate says.

"A good monster," Elion corrects his friend.

"A monster is still a monster."

"Enough discussion of monsters." I'm getting tired of sidetracks and useless conversations that get nobody anywhere. "Heike, you're coming, too. Now, let's go get the Light Core from the Beacons."

"Why am I coming?" Heike's contrary tone has become far too much like Callie's for my taste. "Those Beacons could be infested with skuddima and predators."

"She has a point," Callie agrees.

"You're willingly exposing El to skuddima?" Nate glares at me and Callie. "Thanks, appreciate it. I'll just sit here, strapped to this chair, worried he's going to get attacked not only by Queen, but face-sucking phantoms. Should be a fun-filled hour and a half."

"Stop interrupting, or I'll slit your throat." Ice shards crystalize in my hands, because I've had more than enough of Nate and his backtalk. Isn't he our prisoner? Who does he think he is, speaking that way? I whirl on Callie, one ice shard pointed at her, the other at Nate. "I'm not leaving my sister up here alone with your sworn enemy, and you'd be wise not to pursue the topic further. Is that perfectly understood? Or should I make my point more clearly?"

She bleeds fury from every inch of her lanky frame, gets in my face, and leans on her tiptoes to hiss, "You're an insufferable scumbag, Toran."

I don't know what "scumbag" means, but if it means I'm rational and competent when she's overemotional, erratic, and refuses to make logical decisions, then thank you. I take it as a compliment.

"Bye, everyone! Have fun on your field trip! Don't forget sack lunches and Light bombs for the Darkness deathtrap!" Nate calls over his shoulder as we file out the hatch door and Diver lowers us to the ground.

I part the Mist, allowing Callie to lead, El behind her, while Heike and I bring up the rear. My sister remains tense from the multi-way confrontation back in the Crow's Nest, her arms tight around her middle and shoulders grazing her ears. Her knapsack and Light lantern are the only things not boiling over with palpable anger.

"You want to say something," I speak first, breaking the silence.

"Why are you acting like such a dramora spawn, turning an ice weapon on Callie like that?" Heike unleashes on me. "I thought you were going to be nicer after she came back for us, but you're worse."

"Don't say 'dramora spawn,' that's cursing," I chastise her. "And I never promised to be anything other than what I am. I said I'd get us to the Beacons and through a gateway, and I've performed half of my end of the deal."

"You say 'dramora spawn' all the time." Heike holds her Light lantern high, allowing me to back off a bit with my Seer powers. It's somewhat a relief not to have to concentrate so hard, and makes conversation easier. "And it's not a badge of pride that everyone thinks you're one," she adds.

"I don't care what people think of me, I'm here to keep you safe, and find us a new home where we won't be persecuted for my magic," I remind her of our purpose.

"And to go our separate way from Callie. I know." Heike's chilly demeanor is nothing like my little sister. "You can't stop me from being friends with her if I choose."

"Heike—"

"When we get to Ensolorada, I'm making my own choices."

Heike's decisiveness in this moment startles me—almost scares me. "You might have had to stand in for Mama and Papa when I was little, and I appreciate all you did for us, but I'm thirteen now. I'll make my own decisions and suffer whatever consequences—with, or without magic." She smirks. "Is that perfectly understood? Or should I make my point more clearly?"

If she's trying to be funny, using the same turn of phrase I did earlier, it isn't humorous.

"Callie is hardly a good friend for you." I argue. "She did a kind thing, coming back when we were attacked on the Hem, and perhaps I trusted her judgment at that moment. But everything she's done since Nate arrived is nothing but impulsive, emotional idiocy at its finest."

"Why? Because she didn't kill him?" Heike glares around her lantern. "She's right, you know. Murdering people is wrong."

"He's not even a person, he's—"

"Hey!" Callie glances over her shoulder at me and Heike, Mist swirling around her hair. Elion has Mist accumulating in his hair and clothes, too. He swats it away, agitated. "Did you forget you have Water Manipulation, or what?"

It would be easier to forget how to put one foot in front of the other. With a swish of my hands, the Mist flies away, leaving everyone alone. Serves her right for questioning my powers. Once we're away from her divisive influence, Heike's spirit will calm and she'll become the sister I know, not the one Callie has poisoned to question my every action.

"Okay, any idea how to get inside?" Callie comes to a halt in the face of the Beacon, the massive structure towering over us like a giant watchman on the very edge of the world. Which, I suppose, is what it is. There's no door I can see. Just a rounded building, sides sloping upwards, but no apparent point of entry. Not even a window or climbing holds.

"I'll figure it out." Elion puts his hands flat against the walls of the Beacon, slowly walking a circle around the perimeter. He presses the stones beneath his touch, lips pursed, eyes narrowed in concentration. "When I was little and lived in the mountains, we had to open cave doors like this. They were hidden so cavern scouts couldn't find them."

"I'd prefer you didn't talk about what you're doing, and just did it," I inform him. Elion gives me a nasty look I'm sure Nate taught him.

"And I'd prefer you shut your dümfo mouth."

"Yeah, Toran, rude," Callie agrees.

Why don't we all snap at Toran for pointing out that the boy shouldn't be talking if he's hunting down a hidden door? Any other flaws everybody wants to discuss? Since I'm nothing but a target for insults today, let's continue. It's not like Callie would ever acknowledge she needs me to clear the Mist away from this building so Elion can conduct his search in the first place, or keep the Tageveld from swallowing us whole. See how everyone gets on without a Water Manipulator. I guarantee they'd miss me.

About halfway around the Beacon, on the side facing the Tageveld, Elion stops, his eyes widening. He gives one of the stones a press, pushing it inward, and then another two rows over and up. His hands fly about, searching for more stones, and he finds two additional ones near the ground. With all four pressed, the surrounding stones push inward, then part down the center, revealing a door inside.

"Good job, Elion!" Callie throws her arm around the boy's slender shoulders. "That was awesome! I never would have checked for a secret lock mechanism, that's really smart thinking."

"Thanks," he replies, grinning. "You can call me El, if you want."

How lovely, they're finally bonding—makes me want to

retch.

"If you're going to stand around complimenting one another, wasting my time, I'll go inside to look for a Light Core. Which, by the way, is why we came here in the first place." I stride past Callie and Elion into the Beacon.

"Watch out for snakes, I'd hate for you to get eaten alive before you get me through my gateway, jerk." A sarcastic reply from Callie—hardly a surprise. She follows after me into the Beacons, joined a moment later by Elion and Heike.

As soon as we're inside, I know something important has been hidden in this room. The sensation of my eyes glowing, a slight tingle under the lids as gentle warmth of the magic fills my vision, responds to Callie's Light glowing bright. It illuminates the circular Beacon, a wide room with soaring ceiling and no furniture—only crumbling rafters overhead. If there was any type of living space here, it's long gone, because the floor is coated in a blanket of dust older than time.

"Isn't this incredible?" Heike murmurs, drinking in every detail. "We're the first people to set foot here in thousands of Seasons."

"The last people that were here didn't make it out alive." Callie's proclamation darkens Heike's awe with a sense of foreboding. "I know there's a Light Core here, I sense it calling." She turns to me. "You sense it, too, don't you?"

"Obviously." Can't she see the glowing eyes? I look around the empty room. "The only question is, where is it?"

"The Light Core Nate found hums a lot. It made my butt numb in my knapsack." We all turn to stare, and I can't read minds, but I'm sure Callie and Heike are wondering what Elion's point about his numb butt is, too. "Well, anyway," Elion turns a little pink, "there's something humming under my feet."

Callie bends, scattering dust, and a small door in the floor appears, with a circular pull almost entirely corroded by age and rust. Light flares through the cracks, reaching out to Callie, shaking the slatted door in its desire to be freed. With a tug, the pull falls off, but not before Callie manages to get the door open. Light floods the room, responding to Callie's power, calling out to me. The opening is just big enough for Callie to reach inside and grasp the Light Core. In her hands, it becomes a sparkling burst of gold and glistening color, a thing of true beauty.

"Yes!" Callie leaps to her feet with the Core. Heike and Elion shield their eyes, but mine feel just fine, as though I can See something in the Core the others can't.

A sense of purpose fills me, and peace. Something calm and good, a quiet place I have always sought, but never found. Inside the Light is freedom from Tremurheim politics and predators, all the monsters that seek to destroy me and everything I care for. In a matter of minutes, I'll be on the other side of a multiversal gateway, no longer bound to this place of my birth that brings nothing but death. I'll have a chance to truly live.

But all good feelings fade in an instant, just as the walls of the Beacon crumble at our feet. The ground rumbles and sways, as though Diver's frame is climbing the cliffs from the depths of the Tageveld, yet he remains stationary, unmoved. The gray sky that appears suddenly over our heads fills with black, twisting tentacles, latching themselves to the other Beacons as, one by one, they fall, disintegrating into piles of ash.

"What's happening?" Heike screams, surveying the scene with horror.

No one responds, although we all know what it is. The evil power Nate promised would come for us — Darkness.

Over the edge of the cliffs, one clawed paw the size of a boulder appears, rotten and half-bone, and then another: a creature long dead brought back to terrifying life. With a roar, a head appears, mangled fur and bits of bone exposed around decayed flesh: the face of bjorir, but larger, more dangerous and hungry.

And so it would seem the Vredis is also real.

"Toran," Heike can hardly speak around her trembling. "T-that's the—"

The eyes of the Vredis glow red and black, mirroring the eyes of the person riding atop its unearthly head. A woman with white hair flowing long across her back. The violence bleeding from her distant leer strikes fear into my heart despite the fact I never wanted to betray such a weakness.

This is the monster Nate spoke of, the Queen Beyond the Stars.

"Hello, Calliope," the Shadowmancer says. "How delightful to meet you in the human world at last. Shall we begin?"

CHAPTER 25
NATE

WELP, QUEEN SHOWED UP. Called it.

And of course, Callie has zero plan of action, given the way she and everyone else dash toward Diver like they're going for a world record in sprinting. Horrified looks plaster themselves to their faces while they fumble around, trying to avoid the Darkness swirling beside the cliffs and Queen riding a gigantic zombie-wolf-corpse.

Called that, too. Although, the Darkness-possessed zombie-wolf-corpse is an unexpected plot twist I didn't see coming. Regardless, I've got to get down there and save an unprepared Luminaut and her pals from imminent destruction.

This is what I get for trying to warn people, you know?

"Come on, stupid straps." I really should have thought this through when I was imprisoning myself in the Luminaut's chair. Why did I have to tie everything up in these complicated knots from which I can't easily extricate myself? Is this one big, obvious metaphor for my own complicated feelings regarding Luminauts (one in particular), my actions as a Shadowmancer, and my repressed memories of my Light powers? Is there any cliché left for me to hit?

Who knows, and who cares about metaphors right now? I

force myself to concentrate on the buckles and straps I've tied in knots, working them through until, at last, I'm able to escape.

"Finally!" I leap from the Luminaut chair and race for the door, but Diver activates the lock mechanism, trapping me inside. "Really, big guy?" I try to open the hatch, but it won't budge. "Please? This is urgent. Meaning, Callie will die, and you'll be stranded here to rust at the edge of Tremurheim with Boy Scout as your scowling company. Is that the fate you want?"

Another try, but it's useless. The door to the Crow's Nest is locked from the outside, and with Diver making sure it stays shut, I'm screwed.

"I know you don't trust me," I say, hoping he can hear me, knowing he probably can't. "And I don't blame you. Between you and Callie, you each have a thousand reasons not to trust me." It's only a few steps to the Prism, and I rest my hand and forehead on it, because if anything in here can send my telepathic plea to Diver, maybe it's this. "I know an apology is far too late and even longer overdue, but I'm sorry, and I don't want Callie to get hurt down there. I need you to believe that."

Out of the internal quiet comes a small voice, like a flickering candle in my mind.

We believe.

The hatch door unlocks with a click, and I run to open it, letting in Mist. "Thank you, big guy!" When I get to the edge of Diver's shoulder, I stop short. It's a long jump, and I'm not about to use the Veil, not with Queen this close controlling what looks like all the Darkness in the Shadow Plain. "Could you, uh, put me down?"

Yes.

Diver's hand flies up and lowers me to the ground quick as a flash, and I'm surrounded by Queen's Darkness, Callie's Light, and Boy Scout's ice storm in a literal hurricane of superpowers.

It's a deadly mess down here, with Queen's Darkness phantoms coming in wave after wave of twisting evil while she controls the entire battle from atop the zombie-wolf-corpse. I spot El and Heike behind the giant mech's ankle, taking cover.

"Are you guys okay?" I shout their way. El looks so relieved to see me I'm worried he's going to jump up and hug me, exposing himself to Darkness.

"We're okay," El replies, thankfully keeping low. Heike doesn't look quite as okay; she's pretty scared if her eyes are any indication, but she's holding up, swinging her Light lantern at any Darkness that comes too close. Boy Scout's ice walls and hail blasts are at least a temporary deterrent, and between him and Callie, they're holding the onslaught at bay. For now.

"Any idea what that monster is called, Boy Scout?" I nod toward the zombie-wolf-corpse. Another ice wall appears to block Darkness from El and Heike's hiding spot before he answers my question.

"The Vredis."

The whatchamacallit? "Gesundheit. Can you handle keeping those things off the kids, or do you need backup?"

"I've got it covered, but not for much longer," Toran answers, making two ice daggers like the ones he threatened me with earlier to slash two approaching phantoms. It's too bad that we need him to get off this rock, or else I'd let Darkness have him. "Go find Callie and tell her to end this. Fast."

Wow, he really likes being in charge and giving orders, huh? I bet that goes over with Callie like a lead balloon. But finding her and making sure Darkness doesn't take her out remains my main objective at the moment, because she's an equally important part of the "getting off this rock" equation.

"Sure thing, Boy Scout." I give him a clap on the shoulder that's more like a slap, because if he thinks I forgot the way he called me disfigured and threatened to slit my throat, he's got another thing coming. Running off, I fight my way through Darkness toward the spot the Light blasts are originating.

"Callie!" I call for her, peering through the chaos for her Light.

"Nate?" Callie appears at my side, Light bombing a gang of Darkness phantoms before they can slip past her and attack me. "How did you get down here?"

"Diver put me down," I answer.

"He did what?" Callie blasts another slithering tentacle.

"I asked him to put me down so I could help save your collective necks, and he did," I reiterate.

"How could you tell him what to do?" She frowns. "Only Luminauts can give him commands. Marginally, Seers."

"I warned him he'd be stuck with Boy Scout as his sole life companion if you died, and he was pretty helpful after that." I duck and dodge both her Light and a fresh wave of Queen's Darkness. "Your aim got a lot better, by the way."

"Thanks, I've been practicing," she says, taking out even more Darkness. "I always pretended I was aiming at you, but now..."

"I know. Irony." I keep to her side while she works on the Darkness, aglow in the power of Light, all at once gorgeous and fearsome. I never saw Mom use Light this way, never knew what the full power of a Luminaut looked like. All I know is if Queen didn't think Callie was a worthy opponent, she's dead wrong.

"So, what's your plan?" I ask. "Did you make one?"

"I'm not exactly a making-plans type of Luminaut." More Light blasts, taking out Darkness threatening to sneak around Toran's backside. I doubt he'll thank her. "I'm more of a boho, go-with-the-flow Luminaut."

Clearly. She's doing okay, but without a strategy, she's going to find herself overwhelmed. "Lucky for you, I'm a making-plans guy."

"So what's your plan?" Callie asks, pausing for breath. Sweat lines her brow, and ash from the dearly departed remains of the ancient Beacons smears her cheek.

"Does this mean I'm no longer your prisoner?" Darkness appears over her shoulder. "Coming up fast on your three."

Callie whips around and Light bombs the approaching phantom into oblivion. "Thanks. And I've decided you make a better ally than an enemy at the moment, considering you at least marginally understand how she works."

"I agree." I hold out my hand for her to shake. "Truce? For real this time?"

She takes my hand. "Truce."

Her Light reaches for me, and the ember glow under my heart blazes bright, rising up to meet her. Light holds us tight in a kindred embrace, as if Light is calling our souls together, forming a continuous flow between me and her. She stares at our hands, still stitched together, her jaw going slack. Not even Darkness can touch us. We've left the melee far behind, standing on our own in a more peaceful plain.

"You have Light, too." Callie sees something in me that makes her eyes go wide, manifesting surprise and hope. "Not like regular people have Light, but like me."

"It's a new development." A new old development? Doesn't matter. It's also a bad time for pithy remarks, but that's not stopping me from making them.

"We both feel it, don't we?" She holds my hand tighter, fingertips pressing into my skin as Light flows all around, and I don't know if this is all her, all me, or both of us together. "You're a…"

For some reason, neither of us can say it aloud. Saying it makes it too real, simplifies something that feels so complicated.

Except, maybe, it's not complicated at all.

"Are you going to make me finish all your sentences?" I make another pithy remark instead, a recollection of a moment we've shared before, when we were opposing forces in a fight, and both thought we knew how this would end.

But now, the tables have turned in a way nobody ever predicted. Not her, not me. I don't even think Queen knew it would come down to this moment—me and her, standing together in Light at the edge of the world.

"Hello, little one." Aaand Queen's talking to me. Not good. "Did you think I wouldn't know you'd betrayed me?"

"No, I mistook you for somebody with half a brain cell," I deadpan, facing my former boss. Is it truly a boss-type relationship if you're abused, tortured, and never get paid? I feel like I'm owed serious overtime. "Realized I wasn't copacetic with your plans anymore, huh? Aren't you supposed to be ancient and all-knowing? Or is that another lie you fed me?"

"What in Lands Beyond are you doing?" Toran growls, ice armoring his arms and chest while he fights off Darkness with two long icicle-like sabers. "Are you *asking* her to attack?"

"I hate to side with Toran on anything, but I'm kinda with him on this." Callie blasts more Darkness, but Queen's almost forgotten about her and Toran, her hatred for me the most tangible thing in the multiverse.

"I'll admit, you put on an impressive display of your old powers to save your little friend," Queen goes on, staring at me with so much intense rage it's like she wants to drill a hole through my skull. "It seems you weren't able to overcome your greatest weakness after all."

"Nope! Surprise!" I spread my hands wide and smile. "Are you shocked?"

"Okay, now *that's* dramatic irony," Callie points out.

"I thought it was particularly ironic timing, too," I say.

"Flawless." We share a fist bump.

"Stop bantering and attack her!" Toran yells. "What *is* it with everyone and banter?!"

Boy Scout. Can you not lose your cool at this precise moment? Count to five. Breathe.

"The Seer is correct," Queen menaces from atop her zombie-wolf-corpse, maneuvering her Darkness and mummified ride into attack position, ready to swoop in and snap us up in heaving jaws. "It's past time to eliminate the unnecessary annoyances."

Looks like I've got about half a second to strategize a legitimate escape plan. I turn to Callie, who's still deflecting Darkness. "Here's my plan. I'm going to start a Shadowmancer cage fight to distract her. Following?"

"Easy enough." Callie blasts some phantoms. "After that?"

"You're going to sneak around and Light blast her with everything you've got. Queen's a little shortsighted, and too overconfident to expect somebody would ambush her from behind."

"Sweet, I like the idea of smoking her in the backside." Callie's Light swirls all around, beating back the creeping Shadow with grace and precision, and I don't think I've ever been more impressed by anyone, because she's really, *really* good at this. If I'm not careful, I might fall in love with her.

I mean, uh, I have a healthy amount of respect for her, and her Luminaut prowess.

"Boy Scout can help get El and Heike inside Diver while we're working on taking Queen out, and theoretically, that'll give us enough time to escape with everyone to safety. I think."

"Why use Darkness?" Callie Light blasts some of the Shadow tentacles in question. "You can use your Light against her, too."

"I can't control it yet, not like you can." Although, I wish I could, especially since Queen's spewing a never-ending supply of phantoms from her fingertips. The zombie-wolf paws the ground, prepping to charge, as a wall of looming Darkness builds behind them. "It's too erratic, too big for me to handle. I blasted her so hard on Ictari I passed out. I'm no good to you if I go into a coma."

"Yeah, okay. Makes sense." Callie's gaze shifts toward Queen and her terrifying, pregame warm-up. "Will you be able to fight something like that?"

"I don't know." I face Queen, steeling myself for the attack. Which will hurt. "Guess we're about to find out."

"Nate." Callie grasps my arm, fingers tightening as she pulls me back, looks in my eyes and comes close. "Be careful."

"You, too." I reach for her, wiping a smudge of ash on her cheek with the pad of my thumb. I have just enough time to memorize the pattern of her freckles, golden in the glow of her Light, before I turn away. "Get the kids inside the Crow's Nest as soon as you can, Boy Scout."

"Where do you think you're going?" Toran demands.

"Nate?" El's voice, panicked and shrill, calls for me. I can't explain, I don't have time. I just have to trust that he'll make it out okay — that he'll be alright in the end.

Because I'm more than a little worried I won't.

"Hey! Your Majesty!" I approach Queen, shedding my human form to become the Shadowmancer one more time. It takes effort now, the Light screaming against the Darkness, but it's still there, bubbling over to a boiling rage as I face down Queen and all the ways she deceived me. I focus on that, let anger at her morph me into the monster, feel myself grow cold and sinister, channeling all of it at once. "Why don't you leave the humans alone? Fight an equal, on equal ground."

"You were never my equal." Queen bares her razor teeth, sending a cascade of gnawing Darkness my way. I beat it back with mine, but just barely. "Do you truly think I've lied to you?"

Another Darkness assault, this one stronger than the last. Her zombie-wolf takes a few booming steps, glowing red eyes fixed on me. "I told you the Luminaut would be your downfall." More Darkness, and the wolf picks up speed, charging head on. "I just didn't specify which one. Your annihilation has proven to be of one your own making."

"My own making?" Anger like I've never felt festers inside, takes over every sense, every thought, building like a forest fire in the depths of my gut until Darkness I didn't know I had culminates around me in a wave of Shadows as massive as Queen's. "You're the one who lied about my mom, and twisted my memories, and suppressed my Light powers. My only downfall is being stupid enough to believe a word you ever said."

My Darkness rises to meet Queen's, and in a last ditch effort, I hit her hard with everything I have as the zombie-wolf-corpse barrels into me. The Shadows keep the monster static, a push-pull of Darkness between me and Queen, but this dance is going to end sooner or later, and only one Shadowmancer will be left standing.

"You aren't strong enough to defeat me, little one." Queen's zombie-wolf gets right in my face, its reeking, rotted teeth pressed to my nose, ready to snap my head off. Out of the corner of my eye, I see a flash of Light—one Queen is too angry with me to notice.

Flawless timing, Callie.

"No, I'm not strong enough." I shrug. "But she is."

Callie's Light slams into Queen, rocking her completely off guard. Queen rallies her Darkness, switching her focus from me to Callie, but she's not fast enough, and Callie hits her again. Queen disappears beyond the Veil in retreat, and I turn, running from the zombie-wolf as it falls to the ground, a useless carcass without Queen's powers controlling it.

Callie — 1. Queen — 0. The James-Ormandi brain trust comes through in the clutch.

Not gonna lie, I like this whole working together thing. I like it a lot.

"Hurry!" Callie rushes to join me at my side. "We have to get inside Diver."

"Tell Toran to make sure El and Heike get up first," I say, meeting her halfway. "If you want to make it out alive, you're going to have to work fast." It takes a second for me to realize I'm still the Shadowmancer, and she isn't looking at me with hate or disgust. In fact, she reaches for my hand.

"You, too," Callie insists. "We're not leaving you behind."

I reach for her, to take her hand, to finally shed this monster skin. Light resurfaces, fighting back my Darkness until I'm something halfway like whole as our fingertips meet. This time, when I smile, she does, too.

All of a sudden, tendrils of venomous cold wrap tight around my neck, a sharp pull-tug at the base of my spine dragging me away from the human world. Callie screams my name, barely audible over Queen's insidious laughter filling my ears.

The last thing I see before the Shadows swallow me are the golden pattern of Callie's freckles, the Light in them fading as I drown all over again in the suffocating Darkness.

CHAPTER 26
CALLIE

NATE IS GONE.

He was standing there, our hands almost touching, the Shadowmancer fading from his eyes. I saw the Light in him, felt it as clear as my own.

It was the most beautiful thing I've ever seen.

His smile when I said we weren't leaving him burns into my memory, a tattoo on my heart of a moment I can't comprehend ending the way it just did. We were triumphant, getting ready to Dive. Maybe we didn't win entirely, but we'd kept three Light Cores safe, and bought ourselves time to get to Ensolorada and make a better plan. I was going to teach him how to use his Light. To make orbs and blasts, and get mad at him when he inevitably proved to be a natural. We'd figure out the Shadowmancer thing, deal with the undead complication, work through past hurts, and learn who the other was on equal ground.

But more than anything else, I could rest easy knowing I wouldn't be alone in the multiverse as the last living Luminaut—and neither would he.

And then, something happened. Darkness and the Queen Beyond the Stars reappeared, fear filled his eyes, and before I could blink, he disappeared.

El rushes headlong into the Darkness, toward the piles of ash scattered around the cliff, screaming incomprehensibly for Nate.

But Nate's not there to hear.

"Elion, come back!" Heike cries, bolting after El.

"Heike! Stop!" Toran takes off after Heike, and before I know it, all of us are barreling into an oncoming tidal wave of Darkness led by a huge, mummified bjorir zombie, controlled by the multi-verse-breaking, Lightbridge-destroying Prime Shadowmancer.

This is going to end in Light and murder, just like Diver's memory of the Beacons and the Tageveld. I'm about to make him relive the pain and suffering of losing everyone he cares about in the exact same way.

I'm so sorry, buddy.

"Callie, what are you doing?" Toran's ferocious shouting breaks through my wall of stunned shock. "Use your Light! Heike is about to be attacked by those things!"

Right. My Light. Because we're in clear and present danger, and if I can somehow use it the way Mariasol said—with enough love to conjure a miracle—we might be able to get through the gateway to Ensolorada after all.

I blast the phantoms descending on Heike, and they vaporize like puffs of smoke. Heike pulls herself to her feet, her only line of defense a Light lantern in her shaking hands.

"Get back to the Diver," Toran shouts at his sister. "I'll meet you there."

Heike catches Toran's eye, then looks at me. I blast some more Darkness, and nod.

"Go on, Heike, we'll find El."

Spinning away from the phantoms at her back, Heike runs as fast as she can toward the safety of Diver and his relatively shielded ankles and feet. Now to find El, so we can Dive.

"Come, Callie, let's go." Toran makes a dash for Diver, but

stops short when he realizes I'm not following. "We must leave. Now."

I shake my head. "Not without El."

Rushing into the Darkness closing in around us, heading straight for the zombie-bjorir and Queen, I find El, running around frantically. I Light blast a whole pack of phantoms aiming to swoop in on him, ones he's too agitated to notice.

"El, we gotta go!" I shout.

"No, I have to find Nate." El's eyes show evidence of tears, red-rimmed and swollen, but none fall down his face, like he's too sad to weep. All he can do is dash about, screaming Nate's name, until time reverses and changes what happened. I'm heartsick to see him this way.

"He's gone, El." Taking the kid by the shoulders, I halt his frantic movement. "She took him. He's gone."

"He'll come back, he always does." El's voice trembles. "She's taken him before and he always comes back. We can't go yet. He's coming."

I wish I could tell El otherwise, but this time, I don't know if Nate's going to reappear, and a sinking feeling in my gut tells me something truly awful might have happened. "I wish he was, El, but..."

"Going somewhere?" Queen turns the zombie-bjorir and her Darkness onto me and El, her demonic smile piercing my heart. "Oh, Calliope, you can never run from me for long."

Darkness swirls all around, threatening to envelop us completely. The gray sky overhead blacks out, and tentacle mouths reach for us, sucking and grasping. I call for my Light, vaporizing the Darkness out of our way, and pull El along in a run. But wherever I've destroyed Darkness, more materializes to take its place.

"How long are we going to play this game, Luminaut?"

Queen's icy half-whisper in my ears comes from close by, as if she's right behind me. I whirl, only to find Darkness in place of her face. "An hour? A day? Year after year?"

"What do you want?" I scream, blasting more Darkness, dragging El by his elbow toward Diver. So much distance lies between me and the safety of my mech, it might as well be a thousand miles. "You want my Light Cores?" Light meets Darkness, and I fight it back, only for Darkness to surge again. "You want to kill me and everyone I ever cared about?" More Light, more Shadow, more chaotic back-and-forth as neither side gains a foothold. "Why do you hate me? I don't even know you!"

"Hate you?" Queen tilts her head, the zombified-bjorir Vredis roaring a mournful howl, a haunting sound straight from my darkest nightmare. "I don't hate you, Luminaut. You and your Light Cores are the keys to everything I plan to accomplish in the multiverse. You may keep them, for now. They'll be mine soon enough."

"Then why are you hurting me?" A pause in the Light and Darkness war, each of us regarding the other. Me, a seventeen-year-old, self-trained Luminaut desperate to escape with my life, and her, a millennia-old creature of pure Darkness and rage, who almost destroyed the multiverse once and plans to finish what she started now that she's been freed.

"Lovely Calliope, I want to know if you're worthy of being my adversary. A fight is no fun when it's one-sided, don't you agree?" Queen simpers, her smile chilling me to the bone as razor-sharp teeth glint under thin lips. "The best way to determine how strong you are is to measure what it takes to break you."

Darkness attacks, and I'm prepared to meet it, Light flaring from my palms as the two disparate powers meet in midair, neither gaining ground, neither backing down.

Diver, please, I reach out to my mech. *I need you.*

We are here, Luminaut. We are coming.

Diver's footfalls boom like a thunderous godsend. And yet, somewhere beyond the howls of the zombie-bjorir, the groaning rumble of Diver, and the electrifying crash of Light and Darkness, a bloodcurdling cry like the one in Diver's memories tears through my ears.

"What was that?" El looks all around. I blast some Darkness away from him.

"Don't know, but our ride is almost here." Searching the melee as best I can, I hunt for any sign of the other two people who need saving. "Where are Toran and Heike?"

As if taking a cue, Toran sprints toward us, his whole fist coated in ice around a pointed shard long enough to run a person clean through. His eyes blaze, but not with his bright blue Seer's Eye. He's scared, and not bothering to hide it. "Where is Heike? Do you see her?"

Didn't he notice I'm battling an onslaught of Darkness trying to keep El and myself alive? Toran is nothing if not consistently myopic. "No, I thought she was with Diver."

"I've been trying to get to the stupid mech, using my powers to keep the creatures away." Toran demonstrates his ineffectual ice-wall skills against the Darkness coming up on our right. I have to bomb the phantom Shadows away when they easily scale his obstacle, sending ice crystals flying everywhere, too.

"Here's Diver," I announce as my mech comes to a halt before me. "I bet she's riding his ankle, or his shoulder."

But Heike isn't with Diver. She's nowhere in sight.

"My sister didn't make it?" Toran's face turns ghost-white, and the scream I heard earlier comes back to me with prophetic chill. Queen launches a full-on counterattack of Darkness right at Diver, her zombie-bjorir charging with fangs on lock.

"I don't see her." I try to look for Heike in between all my other tasks whilst Toran stands there, ice sword in hand, slack-jawed. "Go find her, and come back to Diver as fast as you can. I can't hold Queen back much longer."

"Weakening already, Luminaut?" Queen taunts. "Such a shame. I expected you to last longer." Something sparks her interest just beyond my vision, something further out on the Hem, and her smile turns homicidal. "Ah! There's the little girl now."

"Hey! Over here, you ugly dramora spawn!" Heike's lithe frame quakes with terror, but she bravely stands her ground, holding her Light lantern high in the face of Queen's perpetual Darkness. "Leave my friends alone!"

Oh, no. Heike. We needed a diversion to escape, but not like this.

"Go on! Get out of here!" Heike calls to us as Darkness descends all around. She swings her lantern wildly, like a flashing firework of Light, battering Queen's phantoms as they draw in closer with every passing second. She's terrified—but she's determined. And she's not about to back down if it can save our lives.

If I can help you, in any way, I'm going to. No matter the risk. She picked a truly awful time to make good on her promise.

"Heike!" Toran takes off at a run for his sister, but Darkness erupts before him, halting him. I send a Light burst Heike's way, eliminating some of the Darkness Queen launched, but even more comes.

"We have to save her!" Toran takes on the wild look of a rabid animal, unable to control his powers. Ice spikes appear everywhere along his arms and legs, and ice like jagged mountains rises from the ground, stabbing Darkness and the paws of the zombie Vredis where it stands, roaring. So much noise, so much confusion. I can hardly focus.

"Heike!" I call, trying to go after her with El, but Darkness blocks me in every direction, and I can't get past it fast enough.

I clear away the phantoms of Shadow, every ounce of energy focused on saving my friend from the worst fate I can imagine. Light like an inferno pours forth, shattering the wave of Darkness, but Queen isn't backing down, sending an ocean of Shadow straight for Heike. One more Light blast, all my strength concentrated into striking a fatal blow. I scream against the power, the fear inside it, as well as the fury. No time for using power in love. Just desperation, mounting to a break. I'm about to drown in the Light, hanging on by a single thread before I lose control. *This has to be enough to save her. It has to be.*

But it's not.

My Light fades just in time to see Heike and her whizzing lantern swallowed by the Darkness. I stand, holding El, both of us statues of disbelief that this could be happening. I can't cry her name, can't force my tongue to work, or my legs to move. And when the phantoms finally fly away like smoke on a breeze, she's gone.

No ash, no remains. Just nothing.

Toran howls louder than the zombie-bjorir, falling to his knees as ice crystalizes into deadly spines around him, a gigantic, glacial sea urchin of horror and suffering. He breaks through his own encasement and tries to run toward the spot Heike just stood, and we use our powers combined to break through the Darkness. But Queen has figured out what we're trying to do, and stops us at every turn.

"So sad for the little girl, dying out in the wasteland," she purrs, not the least bit sympathetic to Heike's fate.

Luminaut, there is no time. We must go. Diver's urgency punches a hole in my heart.

"I know, buddy." I grasp Toran's arm, sending a Light bomb at Queen. It's blocked. "Toran, we have to Dive."

"No." Toran shakes this head.

"I'm sorry, Toran." I pull him toward Diver, but he refuses to budge. "She's gone. It's terrible, and I wish it wasn't true, but she did what she did so we could have this chance. We have to take it."

"She didn't want to die," Toran snarls, yanking his arm out of my grasp. "I don't care what you say, I will slay that monster who took my sister, or perish trying."

"The Darkness will definitely kill you." To reiterate my point, I blast some phantoms trying to take him out from behind.

"Let it kill me."

"And what good was her sacrifice if you die, too?" More Light vaporizing Darkness. Queen can play this game all day, but I'm shot, and I'm not going to be able to defend El and Toran much longer. "We have to go."

"No, I won't let it end this way. Not my Heike…" Toran tries once more to run face-first into the Darkness halting his path, ice-fighting with every weapon and trick he can recall, but it's useless. Soon, he'll trip up, and become a pile of icy ash. I wish I didn't have to do this, to take us all so abruptly from the spot we just lost our friends with no time to say goodbye. But if I don't act, one by one we'll suffer the same fate.

"Diver." The heaviness in my heart weighs on my command. "Get us up. All of us."

Yes, Luminaut.

Diver scoops El and me in one hand, and curls his fist around Toran in the other. Without even stopping at his shoulder, he shoves kicking and screaming Toran through the hatch into the Crow's Nest, and El and I rush after him, fighting off Darkness the whole way. Only when the door closes and locks tight do I get any relief.

Nemo whizzes up, looking between the three of us with

strangely well-placed worry when he realizes two of us are missing. I guess Nemo is more perceptive than I give him credit for.

"Okay, Toran, I know you're not emotionally prepared to See us through a gateway, but I need you to pull it together." Darkness swirls around my mech, the Vredis howling with Queen's fury. I take Tremurheim's Light Core from the inside pocket of my coat—by some miracle, it didn't fall out during the battle—and place it in the Prism. Light pierces the Tageveld through the oncoming Shadows, calming the Mist sea into placidity beneath hundreds of gateways lit up like softly glowing windows, each a sparkling star in an infinite heaven. "Which one is it?"

The Seer on the floor doesn't respond. He lays there, practically flatlined.

"Toran, please." He doesn't care about begging. Or, apparently, dying. "Toran!"

Nothing.

The zombie-bjorir charges Diver, Darkness twisting all around my mech. It roars a challenge, and Queen smiles like a snake above it all.

"Diver, take care of that yappy dog," I command. "I can't deal with distracting critters right now."

Diver is too happy to oblige. *Our pleasure, Luminaut.*

My mech grabs the Vredis by its lower jaw, throwing it so hard by the rotted mandible the entire bone falls off in Diver's hand. The Vredis flies through the air, landing in a heap on the opposite end of the cliff.

"Thanks, buddy." In the meantime, I grab Toran's arm, trying to heave him up, and meet El's gaze. "Find something to grab onto, and hang on tight."

El doesn't argue. Tears pour down his cheeks when it becomes clear, with stunning finality, that Nate isn't going to reappear from beyond the Veil. He grasps the leg of the bolted-down couch, wiping his face without a word. Nemo climbs in his lap, patting his hand, but nothing my mech does comforts El.

I wish I could sit there and sob right along with him. To lose both Nate and Heike the way we did... But the gateways are fading with no Seer to concentrate the Mist around them. Toran and I are running out of time.

"Come on, dude, let's go!" Using all my strength, I force Toran to stand. It would be easier if he wasn't a bony, six and a half foot tall lump of grief right now. "Which gateway goes to Ensolorada?"

Toran glances out Diver's windows, as much a zombie as the Vredis. "There." He points to a nondescript gateway on the horizon.

"Can you concentrate the Mist so I can Dive?"

"No."

"*Toran!*"

He flops into the Seer's chair with a resigned sigh and holds his hand in front of his face, palm facing the starry gateways. One in particular begins to take shape, becoming more distinct and clear until a landscape of brown sand dunes and orange-yellow sky appears before me. Just like Nate described.

Ensolorada. Finally! Serai Eradah, here we come. Hopefully, she has the answers for exactly how to take down this Queen bee for good, and avenge the two people I just lost forever. I buckle into the Luminaut's chair. "Hold that pose, Toran, it'll be over before you know it."

Except, it won't. As soon as the gateway appears, everything goes black.

Darkness curls tight around Diver, blocking my vision, and in its midst, terror, rage, and hate manifesting in my heart as Queen appears before me. She hangs in midair, suspended by her Darkness just like Nate that awful night in Verona Beach, the one that feels like yesterday and a million years ago all at once.

Nate had been full of despair; fear tinged by regret and sadness. I saw it when I looked into his eyes. Queen feels none of those emotions that indicate even a temporary defeat. In fact, she seems happy. Her smile, beaming with something like sick and twisted pride, makes the blood freeze to a crawl in my veins.

"This was fun, Calliope," Queen says, so sadistic I could scream. "I have so enjoyed our games today."

"Games?" I spit the word. "Are your 'games' the reason you took Nate and Heike? Games are the reason they're gone?" Her smile grows along with my anger, my anguish. "Answer me!"

But Queen won't be commanded. She'll answer on her own terms. "The multiverse *will* be purified," she says instead. "I will finish what I started. This, I promise. What the Light Collective began will end. Forever."

"What does that mean? What are you planning to do?" I'm so afraid I don't know how my tongue forms the words. Instinct, I guess, or some overwhelming need for truth.

Queen doesn't reply. Instead, she puts her hand to the glass dome of Diver's head, like she's stroking my face, my hair. The kind of affection somebody would give a dog they're about to put to sleep. "I'll see you soon, Luminaut."

"Diver, go!" I cry, and my mech barrels through Queen's Darkness toward our gateway. An unsteady leap off the cliff face leaves us suspended in the air for a terrifying moment before the Light in the Prism catches the gateway and draws us through, leaving all of Tremurheim behind.

Falling through orange sky.

Sand dunes drawing closer and closer.

Screams as everything in the Crow's Nest flies forward,

toward Diver's curved glass dome, the ground beneath us materializing rapidly.

A sickening crunch when we crash, skid down a dune, and come to a landing in a thick mound of sand even finer than the sugary grains that make Verona Beach so famous. Once the sand cloud clears, settling into a mini-dune around Diver's head, I look around, assessing the situation. We landed sideways again, and the one strap I managed to buckle before we Dove is trying to throttle me, but other than the desert heat and the sand accumulating around Diver's domed window, we seem to have made it in one piece.

"Is everyone okay?" I ask, unstrapping myself. I can stand, breathe, and think—which means miraculously, I'm not broken. Neither are Toran and El, by the looks of it. No limbs are out of place, and their heads are still attached to their shoulders. Nemo whizzes up to me, whir-screeching his unhappiness with my lack of Diving skill while he shakes his fists at my ankles, but his robot-rage means he isn't broken, either.

I take Tremurheim's Light Core from the Prism and add it to my backpack collection. "How about you, Diver?" I ask the only being whose wholeness I haven't assessed. No response. "Diver?"

Luminaut, we are fading.

The Light I've always sensed in my mech grows dim, the faint pulse of a dying heartbeat thrumming through the Crow's Nest. With sick realization, I look at the Prism again, and almost throw up.

Diver's domed head has been split down the middle where he handed, the Prism cracked in two. The break is near the top—I didn't notice it before—but now that I see it, I know Diver doesn't have long.

"Hang on, buddy." I rack my robotics brain, trying to come

up with a way to triage the damage, to keep Diver afloat until we can find a city or town where I can repair him properly. *If* I can repair this kind of damage. "We can fix this, okay?"

Luminaut...

I don't care what happens to Toran and El at this point, both of them complaining in the background as they pick themselves up and check their bodies for harm. I don't even care what happens to myself. I can't lose my World Diver. Without him, I'm more than lost. I'm not even a Luminaut.

"Please, hang on," I whisper, panic smoldering in my chest. "Please..."

"I know an apology is far too late and even longer overdue, but I'm sorry..." Nate's voice fills my ears, and I see in my mind's eye a vision of his face pressed to the Prism, his remorse so deep it bleeds into my heart and aches like my insides have been ripped in two.

A memory. One Nate created and gave to Diver to tell me he was sorry. No lies, no pretense. Just honesty. Truth. All the things I swore he was incapable of, they're here in this memory, created in a moment when he knew I wouldn't believe him, but he spoke his piece regardless. And now, it's too late to accept, even though I wish with my very soul that I could.

This is the last time I'll ever speak to either of them, if I don't figure a way out of my latest mess.

"Diver, please don't go... I need you, buddy." A pause. Nothing. "Diver?"

But Diver doesn't respond. Nate's soft, husky voice says nothing more, and never will again. Both of them are gone, and it's my fault.

CHAPTER 27
NATE

MY EYES ADJUST THEMSELVES to Darkness, the void of the Shadow Plain manifesting all around. Shadows twisting into the form of gaping phantoms, nothing but solidified hate, rage, despair, devastation. Light feels as far from me as the most distant dying star from the center of the sun.

Back where I started. Only this time, I'm unable to move.

Invisible shackles bind my wrists and ankles, keeping me firmly in place.

"What the actual—" All the worst words I know stitch themselves into the Darkness above me, but protest is useless. I'm trapped.

And somewhere far away, someone is crying.

"Hello, Nathaniel." Queen doesn't call me "servant" when she approaches, or "little one." She uses my full name instead. She calls Callie "Calliope," I guess she's into full names. But I know her using my actual name—my human name—is anything but a comfort.

"What did you do to me? What happened to Callie and El?" If I could rip myself out of these invisible chains, I'd send every last ounce of power in my body flying at her smirking face.

All the while, the crying gets louder, more desperate. But I can't make out the source.

"You're remarkably hard to extinguish." Should've known Queen would monologue instead of answering my questions. "Your Light refused to die, no matter what I tried." She floats over me, throwing her ability to move around in my face as I fight against the clamps holding me back. "The best I could do was put a block on it. Hide it from you until such time as I decided it was necessary to remind you what you were."

"Oh, so now I get to hear the big villain speech where you reveal your secret, evil plan." This is such predictable Queen behavior. "That's why you sent me to find the Light Core, isn't it? To reactivate my Light powers. All that talk of eliminating weaknesses and second chances was a bunch of mind-poison, just like everything else."

"The current Luminaut remains frustratingly independent of any particular path I might have anticipated she would take." A sneering grin appears on her face, the one she gives the Shadowmancers she's about to ash — except this time, she doesn't lift a finger. "And so I decided having a second option to finish the work of releasing Light would be beneficial. One slightly more… malleable."

"I'm not malleable to anything you say," I promise. "I never was. You were a means to an end, and now that I know the truth, the only thing I'm going to do is destroy you. You made a big mistake, reminding me of my Light powers, because trust me, I am *not* an enemy you want to have."

"Oh?" Queen lets her Darkness loose to tickle my scars, pain scorching through them all the way to the bone and beyond. "I think, perhaps, you're more easily bent to my will than you think. After all, you know the torture pain can inflict, the intense weight of grief. What would you do to save Calliope from torture and death? To save the little boy?" She chuckles, low and menacing.

"Yes, Nathaniel, I think you'll be very malleable to my plans indeed."

More crying, coming closer and closer. It's a girl, I realize.

A girl...

Fear rips my heart clean in two. I can imagine some heinous torture, but whatever my mind can conjure, I know Queen will do worse. Is Callie here, in the Shadow Plain? Is she the one crying? "What are you going to do to her?"

"Nothing. For now. I'll be watching. Waiting." Her smile chills me to the core. "Calliope and the boy remain safe, but you'll know when they aren't." She tilts her head, eyes flashing in a way I've never seen before. "Do you know what happens when a Luminaut dies, Nathaniel? The Light inside them fades, returning to the ancient source that gave it birth, and all other Luminauts can feel their anguish, their terror as the Light they carried leaves their body cold, abandons them to the downfall of mortality. Every part of their soul tries to hang on to the Light, and the final moments are ones of intense pain and horror as they realize the Light has abandoned them for good. When Calliope finally meets her end, you will know, and you'll suffer along with her."

Implying I'll be locked away down here, useless to stop it from happening.

But if Callie isn't the girl crying, who is?

"In the meantime, I want to thank you for helping me realize another truth," Queen says.

"What are you talking about?" My voice cracks. Any truth Queen has realized usually means a lot of people are going to die.

Queen sweeps her hand wide. "You'll see."

All around her, Darkness manifests, but something about it is different. These aren't the slithering phantoms, the faceless, sucking mouths of tentacles we control ourselves, manifesting our emotions physically. This Darkness is humanoid, sentient. A body and mind capable of thinking for itself, and bent on annihilation.

What has she *done*?

"The problem with creating Shadowmancer servants from humans is that humanity remains somewhat intact," Queen says, caressing one of her hideous creations. The Shadowmancer hisses, its glowing red eyes burning bright at Queen's touch, awaiting her command with chilling obedience. "The humanity questions. Thinks. Feels things Darkness can't completely overcome. Even my most committed little ones fell, one by one, because they couldn't deny their humanity. I thought perhaps turning a Luminaut against Light — much like myself — would result in true loyalty, yet you were even harder to control than the others." She pats another Shadowmancer's head, and it opens its eyes, burning like an inferno in the Dark as it awaits her words, her will. "But when Darkness itself is taught to think, now, that's the solution. No weakness exists. Simply perfection."

Shadowmancers created from Darkness itself. The most evil thing I've ever seen, standing before my eyes, and Callie has no idea what's coming for her. Even worse, there's no way I can warn her. Not this time.

"Also, we have a special guest." The crying takes the form of screams, and from their sinister ranks, two of Queen's Darkness demons push their way through the rest, holding a person — a living human — by the arms.

It's Boy Scout's sister, Heike.

"Nate!" Heike shrieks when she sees me. "Help me, please, get me out of here!"

"What are you doing to her!" I rage against the restraints holding me back, almost popping my shoulders out of socket. "She's going to die!"

"Exactly." Queen floats to Heike, stroking her terrified, ghost-white cheek. One of Heike's tears catches Queen's fingernail, and she holds it to her eyes, inspecting it with genuine curiosity. "She won't last long in the Shadows, and neither will you, to be honest. But if you manage to free yourselves — and I'm certain you will try very hard — you'll run back to Calliope and her Seer." Queen moves for me, smiling like a vampire moving in for the kill. "The second you cross beyond the Veil, I'll know, and my new servants will be waiting to follow you, to capture the Luminaut and her companions. Then a new Luminaut, one working for my benefit and willing to do anything to save his friends from torture and death, will take her place. Can you imagine who that will be?"

A pat on my scars sends pain rocketing through me, temporarily stealing my sight. When my vision clears, Queen leans back, fading into the Dark as her hideous creations follow, leaving me in chains and Heike weeping, her fragile inner Light fading by the second.

"I'll let you know when you're needed. Farewell for now — Luminaut."

CHAPTER 28
CALLIE

"I'M DYING."

El's faded whisper would set my skin cold with fear he might be right, if it wasn't so unbearably hot. And when I say hot, I mean, like the surface of Mercury hot. Inside of a raging volcano hot. The sun feels closer than it does on Earth, and burns our skin with unrelenting intensity. Not a single cloud overhead provides shade, no relief in the form of a desert spring. Just dunes, the sky, and deadly heat we can't escape.

"You aren't dying," I force an upbeat reply. "We're just lost, and dehydrated." I slip and slide up and down yet another rough, unforgiving sand dune, one of many in this sea of miles and miles of endless dunes. "We're getting close to a town where we can get some water, I feel it."

Another lie. There's no civilization in sight. Just a white hot sun, golden-orange sky lit up like wildfire, and sand, but I'll say whatever I have to if it keeps El going. I couldn't save Nate, couldn't save Heike, and I don't know if I can save Diver—I have to try to save Toran and El.

If I don't try, Darkness wins.

Temporarily abandoning my mech, like a broken-down car on the side of the road, left to corrode in the heat, broke my heart.

And even though I know it won't make what happened on Tremurheim hurt less, I'm resolved to at least try to find a way to fix him, to repair the damage I did in my folly. Because any more permanent loss would break me irreparably.

"Nate... I see Nate." El's scorched face swishes and lobs around on his neck like a bobble, his cracked forehead marking my shoulder with blood. "He's over there. We have to go to him."

Nate's not there. I know he's not, because nothing is "over there." To my left and right, only the desert surrounds us. No life. No water. No signs of humanity. Just the sand and orange sky, stretching on forever.

This can't be all there is. There has to be an outpost. An oasis. Something life-sustaining. And we're going to find it. I have to keep going until I find it.

Nemo moves back and forth between my shoulder and El's sagging frame, checking each of us to make sure we're alright. He taps El's head, and the blood from third-degree sunburns on El's scalp marks my mech's claw-hands with streaks of red. When El doesn't respond, Nemo catches my eye and shakes his head.

Not a good prognosis.

"You'll make it, El," I assure my young friend around panting breaths, starting my climb up another dune. "We just have to get to the top."

"What's at the top of this dune? Water? Food? Everything we need for survival?" Toran whirls around, giving me a look that could absolutely kill, and I have no doubt that if there was water in the air for him to form any kind of ice-weapon, he'd stab me through the heart and not think twice.

"Not the best time to start an argument," I mutter.

"There's no argument to be had. Your incompetence was never up for debate." Toran spins on his heel, his back blistered by the sun and peeling into strips of charred flesh. Only his forehead, wrapped in his henley shirt, is untouched.

We all removed as much of our outer clothing as we could a while back, our limbs and hair soaked straight through after sweating out every last drop of water in our systems. Now, I've realized how horrible that idea was, because exposed skin burns easier and faster. My arms outside my tank top are completely fried, and El has burned to a crisp in his patchy long underwear without his jumpsuit.

But turning around for our winter clothes and jackets would take too long, and nobody has the energy. It's taking more than enough energy to survive.

No matter what, we have to survive. I have to save Diver. I have to fix this.

"I—I think I see—Nate—we're over here..." El falls to his knees. His eyes roll toward the back of his head, blood-matted curls collecting fine desert sand when he passes out, his limp body sliding halfway down the dune we just climbed.

"El!" I rush toward him, turning him onto his back. His pulse is weak, so faint I barely feel the flutter of it under his wrist. "Toran, help me!"

"Help you what?" Toran halts his laborious ascent. He can't catch his breath.

"El doesn't have much longer," I reply, heaving El's arm over my shoulder. "Help me carry him until we find civilization."

"Leave him," Toran replies. "He's as good as dead. We all are."

"I'm not giving up on him... I can't." A lump fills my throat, but I have no tears to cry. My eyes are too dry. *Hang on, El. Hang on, Diver.*

"Amazing how you won't give up on El, but you were more than willing to let Darkness kill Heike." Toran's hatred scorches me worse than the Ensoloradan sun.

"She sacrificed herself so we could get away," I say, trying to lift El with what little strength I have left. "There was nothing I could do."

"Say what you want to convince yourself you aren't guilty, but you murdered her." Toran spits his words. "You're the one who took in that monster, Nate, and we walked right into a trap he likely helped set. You're the one who dragged us to the Beacons, who convinced her she could be brave, and take risks. She wanted to be just like you, did you know that? But now, you're alive, and she's dead."

"Heike was my friend, Toran, I never meant—"

"I don't want to hear your excuses," he interrupts. "The only person I ever loved is gone because of you, and your idiotic decisions are about to kill me and Elion, too." He shakes his head, staring at me like I'm something completely inhuman, something only worthy of revulsion and disdain. "You are the worst Luminaut that has ever existed. Everything you touch, you destroy, and I would rather have been eaten alive by dramora, devoured by nargush, had my soul sucked out of my body by skuddima, or any other death a Guide might suffer than have *ever* trusted you."

He resumes his climb to the top of the dune, leaving me wounded worse than a bullet to the heart in the wake of his hateful speech. There's no way to convince him we should keep going, that hope is close, we just have to endure a few more dunes—I know no matter what I say, he won't listen. All I can do is wordlessly follow, dragging El through the sand.

Even if Toran gives up, I won't. I'll save us, he'll see. We'll survive. Darkness won't win. Our losses won't be for nothing.

"One more step, one more step..." Each one heavier than the last, but more urgent and necessary. We have to keep going, we have to make it.

Toran reaches the top of the dune first. He looks around, then falls to his knees, his angular shoulders dripping with blood as his skin cracks and frays under the blazing sun.

"I give up." Toran's final pronouncement of his fate. "I will go to the Lands Beyond and meet my ancestors." With those words, he falls, skidding down the face of the dune.

"Toran!" I rush—as fast as I can with El's dead weight on my shoulder—toward the top of the dune. My lungs can't take the heat of gasping this air; it burns worse than fire. Despite buckling legs and a blazing heart, I push through, dragging El, praying that on the other side there's a sign. A sliver of hope is all I need.

I crest the top, looking across the expanse of the vast desert before me. Nothing but dunes and sand as far as I can see. No sign of life, or people. Just endless heat and sun.

"What am I going to do, Nemo?" I close my eyes to the reality before me, the sinking dread that we won't survive this. We're all going to die here, whether it takes minutes or mere seconds. Darkness will defeat Light, and I'll lose everything I set out to protect. El gave up. Toran gave up. How long before I give up, too?

Power without love is no power at all.

Mariasol's words in the face of her own death. She didn't give in to despair, because she knew there was something worth fighting for, even at the very end when all seemed lost—because Light is nothing without love. And here, in this hopelessness, this apparent defeat, I have my Light, more than enough for Diver, El, and Toran—even if they can't find it in their hearts to forgive me.

I call Light into my hands, forming an orb of shimmering brilliance. "Please," I whisper to the glowing power in my palm. "Please, work."

Using all of my energy, every last ounce of resolve, I toss my Light into the air, a thousand glimmering droplets hanging there in space, a flare growing and glowing in brilliance to combat even the fierceness of the Ensoloradan sun.

With a sigh, I watch the Light, glimmering above me like fireflies mixed with starshine, and if it's the last thing I ever see, at least it's beautiful, and mine. Darkness couldn't take it from me, even though Queen tried. My Light was mine until the very end.

I stand there, basking in the loveliness of Light until, at last, my legs can't take the strain, and I drop El before falling myself, my entire body crumpling in the sheer enormity of exhaustion and heat.

Power without love… I loved enough to try to save us. To save Diver. It's the best I could do. All I could do. Mariasol would be proud, even if this desert on her home world did end up —

Whhhhhhrrrrr.

A whoosh of air flies across my face from somewhere in the distance, a few strands of hair slipping across my forehead. I'm so weak it takes every last bit of strength to turn my neck and see what could have caused it.

Dark spots on the horizon, barely formed shapes against the backdrop of orange, cloudless sky and white sun.

Airships? Speeders?

Something is flying toward us. People, coming to our rescue. To Diver's rescue. My Light called them, and they answered.

Nemo speeds down the dune, waving his arms, and I flip onto my belly, crying out in pain as my stomach drags across sand that feels like a blanket of a hundred dull knives. I don't care how much pain it causes. I'm going to save us.

A sliver of hope. That's all I need.

"Here!" I wave my hand, weakly tossing as much Light as I can into the air. "Over here!"

My vision fades, the airships blurring and wobbling out of focus. But I can't fade out. Just hang on. Hang on for Diver, for El.

For Toran. Don't let what happened to Nate and Heike be in vain. Their loss can't mean even more death. Darkness can't triumph.

Just hang on…

Black spots, then white. My legs go numb, then my arms. My head bobs on my rubbery neck, heavy as a bowling ball attached to wet spaghetti noodles.

"Help…" My face hits the sand, and I fight to keep my eyes open, to stop the lids from drooping to a close. I won't let go. I can't.

Just hang on.

"Please…"

It would be so easy to slip away. Like falling asleep.

"Hold on. Hold on."

The blackness surrounding my vision closes in on my mind, threatening to overtake me, to snuff my Light. It glows still, faintly, a single candle in the midst of a dark and silent room — a tiny flicker waiting for a hint of a breeze to extinguish it entirely.

Someone, from somewhere, lifts me off the ground, and as I'm floating toward the abyss, into the infinity of stars and endless Light, I think I hear a voice — a human voice — speaking from far away. I don't know if the voice is here, or across the expanse of the multiverse. My mind tries to hold onto it, to latch itself to the dying glow of the tiny flame under my heart… to focus on the voice of my rescuer.

"Cordonanza… healer… desatting rapidly…"

"Help." I don't know if I say it, or somebody who sounds like me that exists outside of my dying body. I'm vaguely aware of hands holding me tight.

"Critical care teams on standby. Two males, one female, stage five sun sickness. Prepare the sickbay." A warm palm presses gently to my forehead. When did my skin become so cold? "We've got you. You're safe now."

"Diver... save Diver..."

Luminaut... I imagine, somehow, he's calling to me.

Hang on, buddy. I'll save you.

I will save him. I have to save him. I'll fix this...

Power without love is no power at all.

It's my last thought before the blackness overtakes me, and the flickering flame fades out.

The adventure concludes in

SHADOW ENDER!

Callie's Light Cores are gone. She's imprisoned in a desert world. Her Seer Toran blames her for the death of his sister. Oh, and the Queen Beyond the Stars is one step closer to destroying the multiverse.

So, things are just great.

Callie must find the remaining Light Cores before the Queen's evil Shadowmancer minions do. But this world's Light Core is hidden at the center of a homicidal death maze that only a Luminaut can conquer. Figures, right?

To make things more fun, formerly evil, mostly undead (and still smoking hot) Nate Ormandi arrives to help Callie and her friends. And he's got Toran's very much alive sister with him. Surprise!

However, as Nate and Callie work to conquer the death maze, Toran keeps leading them into traps. Is Callie's grumpy Seer trying to get them killed, or is someone else pulling the strings?

Time is running out. The Darkness is stronger than ever. As the line between enemy and ally blurs, the last Luminaut will face a terrible choice, one that will change the whole multiverse forever.

ACKNOWLEDGEMENTS

Sequels are oftentimes hard to write, and this one was absolutely no exception. I have nothing but love for this book now, but getting to that (admittedly, quite mean) cliffhanger was a slog. I owe so much to my editors, Amy Williams and Katie Phillips, my critique partner Margaret McGriff, and my intrepid, beta-reading Nerd Squad who helped shape this book from a nebulous concept with far too many subplots into the book you hold in your hands.

Thank you, most of all, to my family, my husband and kids, and friends far and near for your support when *Light Hunter* originally released, and now during its relaunch. Your unflinching love means the world to me, and you have my immense gratitude, now and always.

ABOUT THE AUTHOR

Haylie Hanson is an author, teacher, and disability educator who loves everything geeky. When she isn't dreaming of adventures in a galaxy far, far away, Haylie can be found drinking too much coffee and writing stories about kids with superpowers, a love of STEM, and snarky humor. Haylie lives with her family in Colorado.